All My Love Old Pal,

CAROL KERN

All My Love Old Pal

Copyright © 2016 by Carol Kern

No part of this publication may be reproduced, distributed, or transmitted in any form or by any means, including photocopying, recording, or other electronic or mechanical methods, without the prior written permission of the author, except in the case of brief quotations embodied in critical reviews and certain other non-commercial uses permitted by copyright law.

Tellwell Talent

www.tellwell.ca

ISBN

978-1-77302-294-9 (Paperback)

978-1-77302-293-2 (eBook)

TABLE OF CONTENTS

PROLOGUE..V

JOSEPHINE, HIS MOTHER...1

ANDRE, HIS FATHER..9

ADRIAN JOSEPH TESSIER...15

MADELYN EMMA DUBOIS, THE LOVE OF HIS LIFE......................23

MAY, 1927..29

JUNE, 1930..43

JULY, 1932...55

AUGUST, 1932...77

OCTOBER, 1932...89

MAY, 1934..107

MAY, 1934..121

MAY, 1934..131

OCTOBER, 1934...165

NOVEMBER, 1934..195

NOVEMBER, 1934..213

MAY, 1936..223

NOVEMBER, 1936..255

MARCH, 1937..263

NOVEMBER, 1938..287

JANUARY, 1942 TO JANUARY, 1945..................................297

JANUARY, 1945 TO JUNE, 1950......................................305

JUNE, 1950 TO OCTOBER, 1956.....................................319

ABOUT THE BOOK AND THE AUTHOR................................349

PROLOGUE

There's a widely held belief that there are no accidents, no coincidences in life. My father believed exactly the opposite. He believed that all of life was a coincidence; that he existed, along with everyone else, solely due to the chance meeting of one particular sperm with one particular egg. He believed that choices made for generations before we are born create our circumstances at birth, and we continue creating our coincidental lives according to the choices we make after we enter this world. He believed that even such mundane, random choices as deciding to turn left down a particular street rather than turning right - or going down an entirely different street could alter a life, change everything.

My father couldn't seem to resist turning down those streets. He was an explorer in a city jungle, an entrepreneur at life, a ladies man, a con man, a rogue, and a charmer with an immense heart and a compelling story to tell. But most of all, he was just an ordinary man.

It's been a long time since I promised my father I'd tell his story. I made that promise to him when I was seventeen and my march through time now has me in my late seventies. I gave myself a lot of excuses for waiting nearly sixty years to fulfill my promise, but I always thought of those excuses as legitimate reasons. First I told myself I had to wait until my mother was no longer living, but after she died it seems I could always come up with a reason to wait until someone else died too. Every time my conscience compelled me to open my special keepsake box to look through the notes my father had dictated to me back then, and the stack of letters that had been written long before that, I would find some excuse not to tell the story my father wanted to have told. I had convinced myself that there was always someone still alive who might be hurt, ashamed or embarrassed by the story. The real reason of course was that person might be me. I still don't know if I am ready to divulge some of the things I have been burdened with knowing all these years. All I know for sure is that I can't wait any longer. I'm at an age where I can no longer afford to delay by making excuses, or the next person I will be waiting to die before telling the story will also be – me.

My father died that autumn of my seventeenth year, back in 1956. When he told me his story, and showed me the letters, I don't think he had an inkling he would be dying anytime soon. After all, he was still a young man; just forty-eight and likely feeling invincible. No doubt he would think his dying suddenly when he did, shortly after making me promise to tell his story, was just a coincidence; a fitting end to the series of coincidences that made up his life.

Since he believed that chance and circumstance and the coincidences that would shape his life began long before he was born, that is where I will begin the story of my father Adrian Joseph Tessier. And, the story of his life will end with the coincidence of my having written it – if in fact it is a coincidence at all.

That's for you to decide.

JOSEPHINE, HIS MOTHER

JOSEPHINE NEVER KNEW EXACTLY WHERE OR WHEN HER LAST child was born. Adrian Joseph Tessier came into the world screaming in outrage in the pre-dawn hours of March 30, 1908 in the bottom berth of a sleeper car on a train lumbering through the countryside somewhere between Quebec City, Canada and the U.S. border. Josephine delivered her son herself as the baby's stone deaf father snored loudly in the upper berth, drowning out any groans or gasps of pain that might have escaped her tightly drawn lips.

She knew what she would have to do as soon as she had felt the first contractions, about two hours before she and her second husband, Andre, were due to board the train that would take them back home to Holyoke, Massachusetts. She was determined that this child, like her others, would be born a citizen of the United States; no question about it. Once she made up her mind about something, Jo, as she was familiarly known, would see her plan through to the end. At the age of forty-three, and with the tenacity of a bulldog, she had to be in control of any situation in which she found herself. No child of hers was going to change that merely because it chose to arrive at an inconvenient time. What's more, if this child knew what was good for him, he would not have the temerity to inconvenience her again.

Cradling the infant in the crook of her arm, Jo sighed heavily as she lay with her head propped on the pillow, waiting for the train to pull into a station so she could determine when she was safely inside the U.S. border.

Josephine was the only child of Francine and Gilles Brunet. They had married when in their late thirties then immigrated to Massachusetts two years prior their daughter's birth in hopes of escaping the extreme poverty of rural Quebec. Jo was a precocious child; intelligent, domineering and determined to possess the fortunes of life in America that continually eluded her unfortunate parents. As a toddler she accompanied her mother every day to the hospital laundry where she worked. While Francine wore her hands into rough, raw, blood-red appendages from the washboards and harsh lye soap, little Jo learned to speak English as she listened to the chiding banter of the laundry bosses toward the *'frogs'* in their charge. To her, English was the language of authority, the means of moving up in the world.

Her strict schooling by the Sisters of Charity ended when she was twelve and she was orphaned at sixteen, losing first her mother then her father to tuberculosis. Knowing she faced the next two years as a ward of the state orphanage run by the sisters, Jo sold her parents meager household furnishings, packed up her few remaining belongings, and moved to the other side of town where there were far fewer French speaking people. No one on the other side of town knew anything about her, which, with her mature figure, made it easy to claim she was four years older than she actually was. Whenever she thought back to that day, she thought of it as the day her life began.

Jo, with her impeccable command of the English language and her stern demeanor, wasn't long in securing a position as governess for the vivacious twelve-year-old daughter of a wealthy real estate magnate. The girl had become difficult to handle, and her beleaguered, widower father felt that straight-laced, plain-Jane, authoritative Josephine Brunet was exactly the right person to keep her in check. He also hoped she might be a positive influence on his dilettante son, Charles, and considered her French speaking background an asset rather than the liability it had been on the other side of town.

For the next five years Jo saw to the upbringing of her young charge, Amelia, and became somewhat of a confidant to Charles, helping him out of one scrape after another. Gradually she began taking over the running of the household, making herself virtually indispensable to her employer, Robert Umber. To his great delight, she even took an interest in learning about his real estate holdings, his rental properties in particular, and soon began taking charge of the bookkeeping associated with those properties.

Robert Umber did not often invite people into his home, preferring to socialize at his men's club or in the homes of associates. As a result, Jo found very little opportunity to ingratiate herself to her employer on a personal level. She was frustratingly at a loss as to how to charm Robert into seeing her as an appropriate mate, her objective ever since she had been employed, when fate intervened. Robert Umber simply dropped dead from a heart attack one sunny, fall afternoon while returning from a round of poker at the men's club.

Charles and Amelia were devastated by the loss of their doting father and began relying on Josephine more and more. They knew nothing about their father's business until his attorney revealed at the reading of his will that he had, over the years, gambled away nearly all of his holdings. Jo had known the income from his properties was continually declining, but had been reluctant to bring it up with Robert. She thanked God for making her unattractive to her employer thereby preventing her from making an unfortunate blunder. Marriage to someone who was on the path to losing everything had not been in her plans. But, maintaining what little was left, and obtaining it for herself became her obsession.

Less than a year after Robert Umber's untimely passing, Jo had realized all of her objectives. The manor house in which she had lived with the family for nearly six years had been sold with the proceeds safely hoarded away in the bank. Charles, Amelia and Jo then took up residence in a large first floor apartment of the one remaining building Robert had owned. According to the terms of the will, the huge three-story brownstone building that encompassed an entire city block now belonged to Charles. And after Jo inveigled the hapless young man into a marriage in name only (she had no intention of ever consummating the union with such a foppish fool who obviously preferred the company of other men anyway) the building belonged to her too, along with the funds in the bank. With a steady income from the other twenty-three apartments in the building, Jo, at the age of twenty-two, considered herself set for life.

She was basically content for the next ten years, ridding herself of the burden of Amelia when the useless girl married and moved to Boston. Charles, though useless in Jo's estimation as well, was a good deal more manageable than his younger sister. He was placidly inebriated from the time he rose in the morning until he fell unconsciously into his bed at night, his rare moments of sobriety punctuated by a grinding hangover that robbed him of all ambition. It never occurred to Jo that she was the main reason he chose to anesthetize himself from the world around him.

During one of Charles's bouts of delirium tremens, which had been occurring with increasing frequency, the apartment building's janitor who had been there since before Jo took up residence, just up and quit without notice. An extremely frazzled Jo, plagued with the complaints from tenants that were usually shouldered by the janitor, lost no time in placing an offer of employment in the local newspaper, complete with a basement apartment included in the wages. Expecting there would be several men to interview, she scheduled an entire day for the task. But, at the hour stipulated in the employment notice, there was only one man waiting to be interviewed.

Without speaking, the man handed Jo a piece of paper on which he had printed in large block letters 'I AM DEAF - I CAN READ LIPS - I CAN TALK'. Seeing a look of disdain on her face, he had addressed her pleadingly saying "I am a good worker, I know how to fix things and I am willing to do anything you need done. I am not feeble-minded. I am deaf from too much noise working in the steel mill and I need to have you look at me when you speak so I understand what you are saying. Please", he added.

With an air of resignation, Jo conducted the interview. She found it more than a bit disconcerting the way the burly, handsome young man with the unruly lock of wavy chestnut hair cascading across his forehead had watched her mouth form words. It was almost a relief for Jo to quit talking and listen to what the man had to say. Always in control, she was also aware of a flush staining her cheeks by the time she told the man, haltingly, that the job was his but on a trial basis of course. Later that day Andre Tessier took up residence in the basement apartment of the large tenement building; a building that became his home for the remainder of his life.

That night in her room, Jo assessed herself in the pier glass as she thought through what Andre had disclosed about himself. Loosening her hair, she let it drift into a pale honey brown cloud around her shoulders as she recalled how Andre had also been an only child, caring for his parents until their deaths, just as she had. Leaning in close to study her gray-blue eyes and long aristocratic nose, she once again heard him tell her about his work in the steel mill and how he had lost his hearing. Stepping back for a view of her ample body with its small waist and wide hips, she felt her cheeks redden remembering the way his startlingly green eyes had focused on her lips and the way he tended to talk with his hands, making his muscles ripple under his shirt. Jo became aware of an overall breathless, tingling feeling that was completely unfamiliar to her. Swallowing hard and wondering if she could possibly be coming down with something, she turned away from her reflection to think matters through further. She eventually came to the conclusion that her discomfiture was the result of not feeling quite in control of things; nothing more.

For the next two years Andre took a tremendous burden off Jo's shoulders, tending not only to the non-stop demands of tenants, but to Charles as well on the occasions he had collapsed into a drunken stupor on the front steps of the apartment building. When Charles failed to waken from one of his episodes and instead lapsed into a coma and stopped breathing, Jo felt nothing but relief. As she had all her life, she nightly asked God to help her bear her burdens and set her life on the right course, and her prayers had been answered once again. Not that she ever prayed for anyone to die so that she might be spared, she told herself. After all, who was she to question why God chose to remove her burdens in such a remorselessly final manner.

Three months after Charles's timely departure, Jo approached Andre with an offer of marriage and a step up in the world. She had reached an age when she knew she had to have children soon or risk being childless. Circumstances had afforded her no immediate options other than Andre. Since he was an acceptable and manageable choice, she felt the decision was actually made for her through divine intervention. Andre accepted the proposal more out of a lust for social position and the regularity of sexual favors such a union would afford, rather than for any feelings of love or even affection. Jo knew he felt little more than a respectful regard for her, but considered her undeniable desire for him more than sufficient. After impatiently waiting a customary six months following Charles's death, she wed Andre in a small private church ceremony then lost no time in consummating the marriage. Jo felt certain she had been safely impregnated on her wedding night since she had fervently prayed for that to happen.

One day short of nine months later, following twenty-two hours of exhausting labor, Gilles Andre Tessier made his presence known with a weak sounding wail then promptly fell asleep for six hours. It was the longest stretch of silence Jo was to experience for the next twelve months. Andre of course could never hear his son, day or night, so was never bothered by the continual colicky squalling that robbed his wife of both her sleep and her good will toward him. She spurned his advances so often that he almost stopped making them entirely. As a result, it was a full three years later that a second child, a daughter, was born. Anna Marie Tessier was as placid as her older brother had been cranky. She was as healthy and sweet of nature as Gilles was sickly and morose. She was her father's darling bundle of joy while her brother was her mother's cross to bear.

Five years later, when Jo was nearing her eighth month of an extremely unwelcome third pregnancy, a letter arrived in the mail for Andre which left Jo wondering what else she did not know about her husband. As was her custom, she had opened and read all the mail that arrived before passing anything on to Andre that required his personal attention. That was how she discovered he had been married before and had two half-grown sons being raised by their great aunt Agnes in Quebec following the death of their mother at the birth of the second child. The letter was to advise Andre of the serious illness of his mother's sister, and a request for him to come to Quebec to collect his two sons that she could no longer care for.

With Gilles and Anna Marie left in the care of a long time tenant, Jo and Andre arrived in Quebec only to learn that the two boys could not immediately return with them to Massachusetts because they were born citizens of Canada. It took much longer than expected to get the paperwork started for immigration, and when they learned it could take as long as a year for approval they began a search for a suitable home for the boys in the interim. During the search, the boy's beloved Aunt Agnes died. The two teenaged lads were somewhat consoled when a kind, aging, childless couple who owned a small dairy farm just outside Quebec City offered them a home in exchange for their help. Jo felt that, if she prayed hard enough the boys might be denied entry into the United States and could happily remain on the farm indefinitely. She prayed that the elderly farm couple, having no heirs of their own, would grow to love Andre's boys and want to adopt them. Prayer, she had learned, could make desirable things happen. And it was always fortunate if God's will happened to coincide with hers as it so often did.

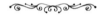

Two hours prior to boarding the train for the return trip home, Jo had something else to occupy her mind as she felt the first stirring of labor that signaled the imminent birth of her third child.

ANDRE, HIS FATHER

ANDRE HAD AWAKENED TO THE SMELL OF BLOOD, HIS NOStrils dilating as he inhaled the coppery stench that was forever emblazoned in his mind. At first he thought he was still a young lad, panic stricken as he tried to hold back the blood gushing from his father's severed arm. With a sharp intake of breath, his eyes had snapped open as he recalled how his father's eyes had clouded over then blinked shut never to open again.

Leaning far over the side of the upper berth in the sleeper car, he saw the stained sheets piled next to the cot, illuminated by the soft glow of a lantern. Then he saw the swathed babe lying in the crook of Jo's encircling arm and understood the odor that had awakened him. *How like her to keep this from me and not seek my help,* he thought as he lay back and pondered the enigma that was his wife, Josephine. She had taken the account of his former marriage and the existence of two nearly grown sons with all the aplomb of a martyr untroubled by an unimaginable fate. All she had requested of him was an explanation after he had assured her he had not lied to her about anything in his past. He had simply not told her everything because she had not asked him to and because it was easier not to.

Pulling the curtain back from the window, Andre could see nothing but blackness. *It is darkest just before dawn,* he thought. He couldn't determine exactly where they were. After their experience in Quebec, he knew for certain why Josephine was keeping the news of the birth to herself, and why he must wait to learn if he had another son or, hopefully, another daughter.

Andre's father, Francis and his mother, Emilee had lied to their families about eloping and being married by a judge when Emilee first realized she was pregnant. They thought the lie would improve their situation, but it didn't. Both just seventeen, their families never let them forget how they had shamed them along with the Catholic Church. They had been castigated physically and verbally then cast out to fend for themselves. The young lovers had managed to flee into Vermont where they were taken in by a fiercely devout Protestant couple who knew nothing about their nefarious background or their lack of nuptials. Francis, a strong muscular lad, spent his days cutting and hauling logs, while slender, frail Emilee performed cooking, housekeeping and laundry chores, with only a brief pause to give birth to a son they named Andre. Although they had always intended to legitimize their union, they saw no way to do so without revealing their lie. And the passage of time made it seem less and less important. They spoke very little English when they arrived in Vermont, but by the time they left ten years later, they and their sturdy young son were fluent in the language.

Longing to see their families again, Francis and Emilee returned to Quebec where they acquired a small parcel of land in the parish where they had been raised. Believing them to be married, they knew their parents finally forgave them outwardly, but were painfully aware they were never fully forgiven in their parents' hearts. To their great sorrow, their beloved son, Andre, conceived in sin in their parents' eyes, found no acceptance beyond a conciliatory tolerance from any family member other than Emilee's older sister, Agnes. Though the boy did not seem aware of the constant slights inflicted by family members, his parents were, and his mother often wept bitter tears over the injustice.

Francis and Emilee both worked long hours in the nearby textile mill that was the source of employment for the majority of their relatives. When Andre was fourteen, he joined his parents at the mill working as a runner. His mother worked at a loom, breathing in particles of lint all day then coughing all night, while his father worked on the cutter. It was the most dangerous job in the mill, but it paid the top wage. Francis, constantly concerned for his frail wife's health, was working toward the day when Emilee would no longer have to work.

The accident that completely severed Francis's right arm from his body was the result of a split second's lack of attention on Francis's part; a split second that would forever alter the lives of his wife and young son as surely as it ended his own. Emilee, out of necessity, kept working at the mill until her lungs finally gave out and she drew her last breath. Andre was sixteen at the time of his father's accident and twenty when his mother had stopped breathing some time during the night. His father's deadly accident had been the source of nightmares for his mother for the four years that followed, robbing her of any rest as she woke screaming and breathless, night after night. Andre, though greatly saddened by the loss of his beloved mother, felt nothing but relief for her when death set her free.

Two years later Andre had married a plain, shy girl who thought the sun rose and set at his command. Her adoration appealed to him immensely, even if she didn't. One year after their marriage he was the less than enthusiastic father of a boy they named Jon Paul, and eighteen months later his wife, Celine, delivered another son they named Jon Marc. Celine never left the bed in which her second child had been born, her lifeblood seeping from her as steadily and surely as it had seeped from Andre's father. Sickened anew from the stench of life-ending blood, Andre could not bear to even look at his newborn son. The day after his wife's burial, he hopped on a flat car on a cargo train heading south, leaving his two sons in the care of his mother's spinster sister, Agnes. He jumped off the rail car in Holyoke, Massachusetts – and decided to go no further.

Andre found work in a steel plant making rails for the booming railroad industry. The heat, physical demands and the constant noise plagued him, but he put in long hours every day in order to send Agnes money for the care of his sons. He was exceptionally strong, and when fellow workers talked him into doing exhibition stunts at the local boxing arena, he saw it as a way to earn enough money so he could cut back on the grueling work at the steel plant. His stunt was to bend over making a level surface of his back while bracing his arms on his bent legs. A large wooden platform was then placed across his back, and members of the audience were invited to climb onto the platform, one at a time. Ten men was usually no problem for him, and the wagers started as that number was exceeded, the audience gauging the weight of the men on the platform. When the weight of the men became too much for him, Andre's legs would begin to buckle, unbalancing the platform and sending the men hurtling to the floor to the tune of uproarious laughter. It was an immensely popular stunt for which he was well paid and that he looked forward to performing three nights a week.

Andre had been aware for years that his hearing was failing. It had begun when he was eight years old following a serious ear infection from swimming in a filthy, contaminated creek. Then, after several more infections and years of noise in the textile mill and the steel plant, he woke one morning to what sounded like snakes hissing inside his head followed by dead silence as he sat upright in bed. He was thirty years old and stone deaf. Since he had been reading lips for years in an attempt to hide his progressive hearing loss, he had little trouble adapting to hearing nothing at all.

The boarding house in which Andre had lived since arriving in Holyoke had become residence to too many unwholesome characters for his liking. He went to the newspaper office to place an advertisement for a new residence, waiting in line behind a woman writing out her advertisement for a janitor / handyman for a tenement building, complete with a basement apartment. When the woman placed her ad and payment in the box on the counter then left, Andre quickly pocketed both the ad and the money then followed the woman back to the building that was the same address as in the ad. It was a handsome, well-kept building in a prosperous neighborhood, and Andre immediately had visions of living and working there, and of moving up in the world.

He had been close to believing in miracles the day he was given the job and had moved into his new apartment, but when, two years later his new employer proposed marriage to him, he was certain that miracles happened. At first he had plans to send for his two sons then thought better of it, thinking it would perhaps be more prudent to take a wait and see attitude. Then, when Josephine presented him with a son that turned out to be a real handful for her, followed by a daughter three years later, he rarely thought about his two older sons and even more rarely remembered to send any money for their keep. It wasn't until that fateful day Josephine had opened his mail and read the missive about collecting his two boys that Andre thought seriously about them again.

Andre figured the younger boy, Jon Marc would be about the same age as he had been when he began work at the textile mill, and his older son, Jon Paul would be the same age he had been when his father was killed. He would be a stranger to both of them, as they would be to him. When he finally saw them again in Quebec he felt nothing. Neither boy would look him in the eye. Neither of the boys could speak English and he could not lip - read the little French he knew. He saw that both boys were slight and frail looking, taking after his mother, Emilee as did his other son by Josephine, Gilles. Only his daughter, Anna Marie was robust and healthy looking, making him hope fervently that the child Josephine was carrying would be another daughter. He felt that he was quite obviously not a good producer of sons based on the evidence of three inferior ones.

Leaning over the side of the upper berth once more, he peered down at the infant in Josephine's arms trying to determine its gender by the appearance of its face. In the dim light he thought perhaps it looked more like Anna Marie than the others had, and that made him hopeful of another daughter. Sighing, he scrunched the pillow so it elevated his head, folded his hands over his belly, and waited for his wife to stir.

ADRIAN JOSEPH TESSIER

JOEY'S EARLIEST MEMORY WAS SITTING IN HIS WOODEN HIGHchair fearfully looking down on his adored big sister having the seat of her white bloomers paddled with a wooden spoon. He remembered wailing along with her, pained by her ordeal, and his mother asking him if he would like to have something to cry about too. What he didn't know was the reason why that particular memory stayed with him, or how that brief incident had affected and colored his relationship with his mother for all time. What he did know for sure was that his mother was the no nonsense disciplinarian in the house while his father was the playful and loving soft touch.

His father had called him Joey the first time he held him in his arms. In Andre's opinion, there was something far too masculine about his fourth son to call him by a name as dandy sounding as Adrian. He even objected to the manner of dress and lack of boyish haircuts in vogue at the time. The dresses and long blonde curls his mother kept him in had been fine for their other son but were out of place for Joey. In an attempt to hurry him out of the dresses and curls, Andre took on the task of toilet training the boy himself. Because only when the boy was toilet trained would his mother allow him to look like the boy he was.

Joey was out of those detestable dresses and into short pants before he was two, and his sheared golden locks were tied with a ribbon and stored away in a keepsake box not long after. He was precocious as his mother had been at his age, and he was eager to know everything he could. He charmed anyone fortunate enough to be in his vicinity with his winning, impish grin and his wide-eyed wonder at all the things in the world there were to know. Anna Marie delighted in teaching him everything she learned in school each day, so by the time he was old enough for school he already knew just about everything that was taught in the first five years. His first year of school he was moved ahead a grade every few weeks, eventually spending just a few days in Anna Marie's class before being sent to his older brother Gilles classroom. Gilles, who had been put back a grade, had chased him and kicked him in the seat of the pants all the way home at the end of the day. Then, after complaining about his treatment, his mother had applied her wooden spoon to the two of them in equal measure; Gilles for being a bully, and Joey for being too big for his britches. And to add insult to injury, she accompanied him to school the next day and insisted that the nuns put him back in the first grade where he belonged and keep him there.

Incensed by the injustice heaped upon him by the school, his brother and his mother, Joey lost interest in learning anything more from books and began prowling the alleys behind the stores in the shopping districts every chance he could. That was the beginning of his real education; the one that would stay with him for life. He discovered that shopkeepers discarded all kinds of useful things in the trash bins behind their stores. There were broken things that could be repaired and made like new, then sold. There was torn or soiled clothing that only needed a wash and a bit of mending to be as good as new that could also be sold. By the time Joey was ten he had set up a small but lucrative business in one corner of the basement in the tenement building, with Anna Marie as his confidant and business partner. He did the finding and the selling, she did the washing and fixing, and they both reaped the profits. Their biggest obstacle was keeping the knowledge of their enterprise from their mother, who would, without a doubt, disapprove. That meant they also had to be extra careful to keep their activity a secret from Gilles as well. They knew he would waste no time tattling on them if he knew, or at the very least, demand a share of the profits to keep his mouth shut.

When he was fourteen Joey decided he was finished with school. He was having to branch out further and further to find suitable items to sell and school was taking up too much of his valuable time. It was on one of his forays further afield that he discovered the bonanza of discarded items that could be obtained in the alleyways of the industrial areas where the goods were manufactured. His father had helped him fashion a wagon that attached to the back of his bicycle, all put together from found items, and he used it daily to transport his booty. While Andre was proud of his son's resourcefulness, Josephine became suspicious of his activities when Gilles informed her he had seen Joey out with his bicycle in the manufacturing district one day when he was supposed to be at school. She determined that a confrontation was definitely in order.

Josephine had always demanded everyone's presence for dinner together at precisely six pm, every evening, without fail. Though Joey often arrived at the last minute, he knew he could never be late for an evening meal without incurring his mother's wrath. Then one evening, as he breathlessly arrived just minutes before six, he opened the basement door off the back alley to stow his loot inside and nearly ran into his mother standing, arms folded across her bosom, just inside the door.

"You have some explaining to do," was all Josephine had said as she pointed toward the stairs that led up to the kitchen in their apartment.

Joey had the dire feeling that, big as he was, he would be doing most of the explaining standing up because in all likelihood he would be finding it difficult to sit with any degree of comfort at various times during the interrogation. He caught the pleading eye of Anna Marie as he and his mother stepped into the kitchen and his look assured her he would be honorable and courageous enough throughout his ordeal not to drag her into the fray.

To his astonishment, his mother insisted that everyone sit down together for the evening meal prior to the inquisition. That gave Joey time to think, to come up with a plausible explanation for all the contraband stacked in one corner of the basement, for his absence from school and for the accountability of his time when he was supposed to be there. He tasted nothing, chewing mechanically as his mind worked, trying to come up with something, anything that would satisfy his mother. His mouth opened wide as the most astonishingly brazen idea popped into his head, and he quickly filled it with another bite of his mother's loathsome liver loaf – smiling inwardly as he realized it just might work. He had decided to tell her the truth. The truth, without implicating Anna Marie, that is.

Josephine listened as Joey talked about being a man now, ready to go out into the world and make his own way. He explained how, ever since he was ten years old he had been doing just that, and could show her his bank book and the grand amount he had been able to accrue from his efforts. He informed her that he was learning nothing useful in school anymore; that more history, geography, spelling or arithmetic wouldn't make him any smarter or more able to make a living. He argued that school merely took up valuable time, time that he could put to far more productive use. When he had finished, his mother, amazingly, just nonchalantly smoothed the front of her apron and looking directly at him had said, "Well, I guess that's that then. Now that you are an adult and earning your own way you can start paying room and board."

Although greatly relieved and grateful for the new freedom his daring argument had afforded him, Joey wasn't foolish enough to think that his mother would now think of him as an adult and treat him as such. He kept her informed of his comings and goings for several months before letting her think he had found employment at one of the factories whose back alleys he frequented. And, when he started handing her five dollars every week for his room and board, while still tending to his regular chore of sweeping down all the stairs in the massive building every Saturday, he felt his mother begin to look at him in a different way and no longer felt inclined to give himself a wide berth around her if she happened to be wielding a wooden spoon. He was aware of Anna Marie's obvious admiration for him as well. She began to treat him as if he were her personal hero. It all went a bit to his head.

When Joey was fifteen he began accompanying his father to the boxing arena three nights a week. Though not quite as muscular as Andre had been at his age, he was nearly as strong and the likeness between father and son was striking. He had the same vibrant green eyes, the same wavy chestnut hair, his father's sculptured chin and close set ears. Only his nose was different; longer, more aristocratic like his mother's. He had broad shoulders and a trunk tapering to a narrow waist and hips, all supported by solid, muscular, incredibly strong legs. He looked as his father must have looked at the same age and Andre proudly showed him off to all his cronies. As Joey began doing some practice sparring, then graduated to Golden Gloves competition, he had visions of becoming a professional boxer. At the time, he couldn't know how his involvement with the kind of people who hung around the ring, and his ever expanding ego, would alter the course of his life. But, at the time, he couldn't have cared less either. He was enjoying himself immensely.

Adele O'Sullivan was seventeen, the same age as Joey, when she made up her mind she was going to hitch her star to his wagon one way or another. She accomplished her goal in the oldest most reliable way by becoming pregnant. Joey, being a gentleman and still deathly afraid of his mother's wrath, sanctified the union with Adele, saying his vows before the parish priest and two hundred guests in a lavish top-hat ceremony orchestrated by Josephine. The young couple moved into one of the smaller apartments in his mother's building where Joey commenced to learn what the term 'hen-pecked' meant. He was allowed out to work to bring in money, but other than that his time belonged strictly to his bride or bridle as he secretly thought of her.

He thought the birth of their infant daughter Arlene would make his situation more tolerable, expecting the baby to occupy much of Adele's time. He had not expected Adele to foist the care of the baby onto his shoulders every moment that he was not engaged in earning a living for them. He would get a chip on his shoulders on those occasions, refusing to care for the child, leaving her to cry herself to sleep in her crib. Adele stubbornly refused to tend to the baby too, shutting herself in her bedroom as far from the sound of the infant as possible. It was after one of those standoffs, when Arlene was five months old, that Adele and Joey discovered their baby daughter smothered to death in her crib one morning.

Josephine convinced Joey that, as tragic as the loss of his child was, it was also an opportunity to rid himself of what she considered to be a totally unsuitable wife. There was just one major hurdle. At that time in Massachusetts, the only grounds for divorce was abandonment for a period exceeding three years. Josephine took care of all the arrangements, contacting a relative in South Dakota who would see to it that Joey had a place to stay and a source of income for the next three years. She bought him a Model T Ford, a new suit and a brown leather valise, then put meat-loaf sandwiches, pickles, apples and thick oatmeal cookies in a tin pail and sent him on his way with a kiss on the cheek followed by a sharp slap and a little shove. Andre shook his son's hand, his eyes shining with unshed tears then patted him on the shoulder.

"Be well," he said. "Write."

"He can't write, fool!" Josephine exclaimed then turned to face Andre. "If he writes we can't say we don't know where he is. We can't have any contact with him for three years."

"What about staying in touch through your relative?"

"That's out of the question. It was risky enough just making arrangements through him in the first place. He knows nothing at all about the circumstances and it must stay that way if Joey is ever to be free of Adele." Josephine had paused, deciding whether or not she wanted to reveal more. Deciding in the affirmative she added, "The cousin I have contacted is a priest. That fact speaks for itself when it comes to the matter of divorce."

With an unfathomable sadness seeming to constrict his heart, Andre silently embraced his youngest son. Joey was the light of his otherwise humdrum life, and he didn't know how he would survive without him for three long years. The death of his son's infant daughter had taken a toll on both of them. Perhaps the only way for Joey to get through that, Andre told himself, was to go somewhere far away so he could forget…and in the process, stop blaming himself.

With all the money he had left tucked into his right sock, Joey set out on what he thought of as the adventure of a lifetime rather than a sad parting. As he drove along he began singing in his pleasant baritone voice, effortlessly switching to a falsetto as he reached the lilting high notes of *'When Irish Eyes Are Smiling'*. When he tired of singing, he began whistling.

He had just turned nineteen; he had a new car, plenty of money and the promise of a job. He was leaving a life he disliked, a wife he loathed, a mother he feared and days filled with tedium. He would miss his father and sister, but felt sure that three years would pass swiftly. He was more than ready for whatever life had waiting for him as he drove from Holyoke, Massachusetts to a small town that was not even big enough to have a dot on the map that sat opened on the seat beside him. St. Onge, a friendly little town nestled in the Black Hills of South Dakota. He liked the solid sound of it, the promise of it. He didn't know that he would be getting a whole lot more than he had bargained for. There was only one thing he knew for sure – he was leaving Joey behind.

From that point on he was Joe

MADELYN EMMA DUBOIS, THE LOVE OF HIS LIFE

MADELYN STOOD BY THE WINDOW SIFTING THROUGH THE essay papers, trying to find one that hadn't been overly smudged with inkblots and was still readable. Distractedly, she glanced through the schoolhouse window once again at the young man out on the road alternately lifting the hood of his Model T Ford for a look inside then kicking a tire in frustration. The bright May sun lit up his head forming a halo of light as it reflected off the unruly tendrils of hair being lifted by the breeze, and the glint of perspiration on his face. As he looked toward the schoolhouse once more, she quickly glanced away not wanting him to see her watching him. Then, when he began making his way toward the building, she glanced at the clock and decided she could dismiss school for the day. The essays could wait. She didn't know why when she had looked the young man directly in the eye for a fraction of a second, a shock had gone through her that felt like a bolt of lightning. But, she was intrigued and titillated enough by the sensation to want to discover the reason.

Charles Dubois and his wife, Emma had bought the tavern and pool hall in St. Onge shortly before their first daughter, Madelyn was born. The money for the purchase had come from Charles's share of his father's estate, and along with his two brothers and their wives, and his two sisters and their husbands, they had purchased various properties and businesses in and around St. Onge. Among them they owned the aforementioned tavern and pool hall, a general store, a creamery, a dance / banquet hall, the two gas pumps in town and a grain storage depot. Emma was one of twelve children, all living in or around St. Onge. Between her family and Charles's family, they made up close to half the town's population. At the time of Charles's father's demise they all had already built substantial houses in town. Charles had enough left over from the purchase of the tavern to invest in five thousand acres of forest and farmland just outside town. He rented out his house in town and moved most of his belongings to the small one room stone house that came with the farmland property. It became the first home for his first child.

Being an industrious type, Charles wasn't long in building a more substantial house in a better location on his farm property and in producing a second daughter, Priscilla. Then he built a barn and a bunkhouse, bought some horses and cattle, hired a hand to help run some barbed wire fences, and he had himself a ranch. Eight years later he had another daughter, Thelma and had added some milk cows and a team of matched work horses, a yard full of hens, a couple of good cow dogs, another barn and a bunkhouse full of field hands at haying and threshing time. He made a success of every endeavor he put his hand to, and could have sat back and watched his empire grow if he had been so inclined.

Living on the ranch, Madelyn and Priscilla almost grew up together on the back of a horse. Just a year apart in school, they rode together on their horse, Blackie to the one room schoolhouse every day. The sisters were always best friends, even though their interests differed greatly. Priscilla loved everything about the ranch and looked forward to helping with the milking and other barn chores after school, but Madelyn had little interest in working around animals. She was more inclined to help with the cooking, cleaning and washing up, relatively mindless tasks that permitted her to indulge in her never ending love of daydreams and make believe. She didn't just read books, she lived them, breathed them, devoured them, imagining herself to be the Cinderella, shrinking violet, forlorn waif or heroine pursued by the handsome, enigmatic hero or prince charming in every book she read.

Although she envisioned herself as the love interest in every story, she was, all the same, a deeply devout Catholic who dreamed constantly of attaining the greatest love of all as the bride of Christ. From the time she saw her first nun at the age of four, and learned what being a nun meant, she was in awe. From that day on there was never any question in her mind what she would grow up to be. She simply had to wait for the day God called her to fulfill her vocation. Her daydreams of love were ecstatically innocent and platonic, physical love being beyond her experience and comprehension. To Madelyn, love had no connection with the things she saw the farm animals doing to reproduce themselves, and she remained blissfully unaware that people did something similar to reproduce themselves, or that it too had anything to do with love, up until she had graduated from high school.

It was Priscilla who told her. One summer evening she had come running into the bedroom they shared, crying and obviously upset. Madelyn had put her arm around her sister's shoulder to comfort her, and Priscilla had sobbed out her fear that she would soon commit a mortal sin with her long time beau, Richard if the two of them weren't soon married. She confided that she was having longings so strong, she didn't know if she could wait another whole year until she was finished with school. It was almost too much of a revelation for Madelyn, too much to know and to digest at the same time. She had been both appalled and intrigued by the things her younger sister had revealed.

Madelyn and Priscilla, though vastly different in their interests and demeanor were inseparable, always wanting to be dressed alike as if they were twins, even sleeping together in the same bed up until Priscilla's wedding night. For Madelyn that was an unimaginably horrible night, filled with hazy visions she couldn't quite conceptualize and a sense of loss and longing that left her sobbing into her soggy pillow until the wee hours of the morning.

Madelyn had finished high school at the age of sixteen, and the Normal School in Spearfish when she was eighteen, and that following fall had begun teaching in the one room country schoolhouse just up the road from the ranch while she waited for God's call. Priscilla had married Richard Ames right after high school, and Charles had talked the young couple into taking over running the ranch. Although Madelyn would have found it more convenient to remain on the ranch to travel back and forth to the schoolhouse every day, she had moved back to the big house in town with her parents and younger sister, Thelma shortly after Priscilla's marriage. She couldn't bear to sleep in the room next to the one shared by her sister and Richard. She could hear them through the wall, their faint gasps and groans and the creak of bedsprings making her breath catch in her throat as if her body willed her not to make even the slightest sound that might impede her hearing, when what she wanted was to hear nothing at all. The sensual nature of what she heard, along with the skulking feeling of eavesdropping, was more than she could bear. On all but the most blustery of winter days, she made the two mile journey back and forth from town to the schoolhouse, pulled along by Blackie in her small two-seat buggy.

Over the years, Madelyn's father and his brothers had acquired the rights to provide both the mail and telephone services for the town. Charles, looking for a more reliable source of water in the often drought stricken region, had a new well drilled on the back portion of his town property. He came up with a gusher. There was enough water to supply the entire town. Ten months later all the lines were dug, the pipes and indoor plumbing installed, and Charles officially became the St. Onge Water Facility. He also needed someone by then to help manage at least one of his enterprises, but was at a loss as to where he would find anyone capable and reliable, other than someone under his own roof. About to suggest to Madelyn that she forego teaching when the next term started in the fall, and instead help manage one of the family businesses, he was spared the necessity of doing so by the parish priest.

Father Brunet's cousin, Josephine in Massachusetts had written inquiring about the possibility of finding lodging and employment in St. Onge for her well educated, industrious son, one Adrian Joseph Tessier, who was eager to experience life in other parts of the country. Charles, used to having things fall into place when he needed them to, welcomed the expediency of the request. He would indeed have a position available for a young man who obviously must come from good stock considering he was second cousin to a priest. He decided to offer lodging as well. He felt he could get better measure of the man if he resided under his roof.

Madelyn was looking forward to having a refined young man from back east coming to stay with them, but Thelma was, quite literally, put out about it. She would have to give up her room to the stranger and move in with her sister. Madelyn thought his name, Adrian sounded sophisticated, but to Thelma it sounded like a sissy name. He was expected around the middle of May, just a couple of weeks before school let out for the summer. Both Madelyn and Thelma daydreamed about what Adrian would look like, and surprisingly they pictured him very much the same, though for very different reasons. They both thought he would have blonde hair and his eyes would be blue, he would be very tall and slender, and he would be handsome in an aesthetic, affected way. But Thelma also thought that he might take after Father Brunet and have a weak chin, crooked teeth, and tend to have a nasal sound to his voice. Madelyn acted horrified at the notion. Handsome, sophisticated men could not have weak chins and crooked teeth, she countered. Although, they could possibly have a cleft chin, wear spectacles, have a high-pitched voice and perhaps even speak with a bit of a lisp the sisters had decided, giggling. Thelma also had decided that sharing a room and a double bed with her older sister might not be so bad after all. She had always envied the closeness between Madelyn and Priscilla, and now maybe this Adrian coming would be a way for her to be close to Madelyn too. She decided right then and there she was going to like him.

The mental image Madelyn had of a tall, fair, aesthete Adrian in no way corresponded with the image of the swarthy, swaggering, rumpled young man making his way toward the schoolhouse that bright, sunny May afternoon. The idea that he could be the expected house guest never entered her mind, especially when he introduced himself as Joe.

MAY, 1927

JOE WAITED AT THE BOTTOM OF THE STEPS WHILE THE twenty or so pupils of various sizes and ages exited the school. He smiled or nodded at each of them in turn, amazed by the difference in size of one tiny raven headed girl followed by two strapping boys in overalls towering over her. Peeking through the door that had been left slightly ajar, he took in the profile of a young woman standing beside a teacher's desk on a slightly raised platform, studiously thumbing through some papers. Her light brown hair hugged her head like a stiff wavy cap which Joe thought was decidedly unattractive. But surveying her further he saw she had a small upturned nose, the kind he found so cute, and a slender neck and shoulders that appeared to be the pattern all the way down to the hem of her loose fitting, knee length shift. It was the shapely legs beneath that shift however that held him spellbound, until the young woman turned toward him and cleared her throat to attract his attention.

Always aware of the effect he had on women, Joe smiled to himself when he saw her cheeks flush charmingly as their eyes met, then was a bit taken back to feel his own flush as well. He introduced himself as Joe, an unfortunate traveler who had taken what he thought was a short-cut and who had misjudged the amount of gasoline he needed to reach his destination. She responded with her own given name, Madelyn, and inquired as to his destination. When he told her he was headed to St. Onge to meet up with a cousin, Madelyn still did not connect the young man standing before her to the expected house guest, Adrian.

"I live in St. Onge," Madelyn said somewhat hesitantly. "I can give you a lift there if you like and you can get some gasoline for your automobile."

Realizing she hadn't offered to drive him back to retrieve his vehicle, Joe asked her how far it was to town.

"It's about two miles."

"Could you perhaps tow my automobile behind yours?"

"Oh. No, I don't think I can tow you," Madelyn replied, frowning.

"Why not?"

"I don't have my automobile here today."

Joe looked out the open door and all around the schoolyard. Seeing no other automobile other than his own stranded vehicle in the middle of the road, he asked, "If you don't have an automobile, how were you planning to give me a lift into town?"

In answer, Madelyn said, "Come with me." She led him around to the back of the school building where a small black horse on a long tether was patiently standing next to a rickety appearing buggy, waiting to be hitched up so he could carry his mistress safely back home and receive his reward for completing another fine day of service.

"A horse and buggy?" Joe asked nervously.

"It's a good thing I decided to bring the buggy today," Madelyn said, laughing lightly. "I often just ride Blackie bareback. I think he can pull the two of us in the buggy, but I wouldn't ask him to carry both of us on his back. He's a very old horse."

"I've never ridden a horse," Joe proffered uneasily. "And I confess, I've never ridden in a horse drawn buggy either."

It was Madelyn's turn to be perplexed. "Where are you from that you have never ridden a horse or ridden in a horse drawn buggy?"

"A city in Massachusetts that is far advanced from that sort of thing."

Madelyn stared, mouth agape at the disheveled looking young man standing before her. Almost without knowing she was going to, she blurted "Are you Adrian? You said your name was Joe!"

"It's Adrian Joseph Tessier," Joe replied, "but, I go by my middle name. Shortened middle name, that is." Then frowning, he asked, "How did you know my first name?"

"You were expected," Madelyn replied bluntly. "But you were expected as Adrian, not Joe. It's my father you will be working for, and you will be boarding at my house," she explained while harnessing Blackie into position at the front of the buggy. Her sudden smile had a touch of incredulity when she added, "What a coincidence you ran out of gasoline on this back road right in front of the school where I teach so I could conveniently give you a lift to where both of us will be going anyway. Now, that certainly *wasn't* expected!"

"Well, I didn't expect I'd find myself riding in a horse drawn buggy either," Joe responded nervously. "It seems like the farther west I travel, the fewer automobiles there are on the road and the harder it is to find places to purchase gasoline, tires and other necessities."

Feeling a bit miffed by Joe's air of superiority Madelyn couldn't resist taking him down a peg or two. "Well, if you kept to the main roads you wouldn't have had trouble finding service stations. We aren't as back-woods here as you seem to think. And you should stop sounding so pompous by saying 'automobile' and 'gasoline'. Around here we started using the terms 'car' and 'gas' long ago. You should think about doing the same if you don't want people around here laughing at you behind your back."

"Car and gas huh? Back east we still use the proper terms for things. I can't imagine you live such a fast paced life here that you need to shorten the names of things to keep from running out of breath."

"Get in the buggy," Madelyn said climbing up into the seat.

Joe watched Madelyn's ascent into the seat, getting a delightful glimpse of thigh above her gartered, silk-clad knee. "I need to get my valise out of my *car* first," he said.

"There's no room for it in the buggy, so you'll have to leave it behind. Don't worry, no one here will take your things. You aren't back east anymore; we're more civilized out here in the sticks."

Joe settled himself in the seat close beside Madelyn, trying in vain not to show his nervousness. He had a white-knuckled grip on the side of the narrow plank seat, but could find no place to brace his feet. To his embarrassment, they came several inches off the floorboard when the buggy began to move, then hung just inches off Blackie's rump before he regained his footing. He tried to act nonchalant, but knew his face had turned beet red and that beads of sweat had broken out on his brow.

Madelyn, aware of Joe's distress, tried to make things easier for him with small talk. She pointed out landmarks as Blackie walked along at a level pace, feeling him gradually relax.

"That's my father's ranch up on the hill on the left. I grew up there with my two sisters, but one sister and her husband live there now, so the rest of us moved back to town. Now, down here on the right is the old stone house where I was born. I don't remember living there because my father built the house up on the hill right after I was born. My sister and I used to ride Blackie to school every day. He would come back to the ranch after he delivered us at school, then my father would send him to fetch us at the end of the school day."

"The school where you teach now? This same Blackie?"

"This same Blackie; I told you, he's a very old horse. But, not the school where I teach. We are just coming up to the school I went to back then. See it there on the left? It has two rooms and two teachers, one for the first four grades and one for grades five through eight. I had hoped to be able to teach there, but the positions were already filled when I finished Normal School, so I had to settle for the one room country school."

"I've never seen a one room school before. Or even a two room school for that matter."

"What kind of school did you have back in Massachusetts?"

"There was a separate room and teacher for every grade."

"It was that way here for high school, but I never heard of such a thing for a grade school. You must have missed out on having older students help you, and missed out on getting a refresher lesson from the younger students. Sorry it had to be that way for you. You must have missed out on a lot."

Blackie made a right turn, seemingly all by himself, just past the two room school house. Madelyn kept on chattering but Joe's attention was elsewhere. The change in direction had brought about a change in the direction of the breeze as well, and Joe was intent on seeing how high the breeze would blow the hem of Madelyn's flimsy shift above her knees, affording him another delectable view of pale thigh above her stockings. His intentions were thwarted when she suddenly tucked the shift between her knees, pressing them tightly together.

"You haven't been listening to a word I've been saying," she accused.

"Yes I have. You were talking about the school."

"That was before. Then I asked you a question and I'm still waiting for your answer."

"I know. I was just pausing to think about my answer instead of just blurting out something without giving it due thought."

"So what's your answer?"

"Well, now you will have to repeat the question because you have gotten me off track."

Madelyn laughed tauntingly. "I didn't ask any question. Caught you! I knew you weren't paying attention to what I was saying. You were paying attention to the breeze lifting the hem of my skirt, that's all you were paying attention to."

"Okay, guilty. But you can't blame a fellow for wanting to look at a pair of nice looking legs." Joe paused for effect before adding, "I like looking at your nose too. You have a very nice nose."

"There's a lot more to me than a nose and legs," Madelyn said huffily.

Joe was liking where the conversation seemed to be going, when Blackie made another right turn and broke into a bone jarring trot along the rutted dirt road. Holding onto the seat as if his life depended on it, he shouted, "What's happening?"

"Blackie's in the home stretch," she hollered back. "He does this every day."

"You could have warned me!"

"What, and miss all the fun of seeing you scared out of your wits?"

"Oh, that amuses you, does it?"

"You aren't in any danger you big sissy. Besides, he'll slow down as he gets near the stable. He wouldn't want to go past it."

"Oh, well now, that's reassuring to know. That he will stop, that is."

Joe was visibly shaken from his first horse-drawn buggy ride, but tried to hide his distress by vigorously brushing the road dust from his clothes. Meanwhile, Madelyn unhitched the little horse, led him to his stall and strapped on a feed bag of oats. She brushed the top layer of dust from his coat followed by a curry-combing that made Blackie quiver with pleasure, then another brushing until his coat glistened. By that time he had finished his oats, and Madelyn removed the feed bag and freed the horse to help himself to hay and water. Joe became a bit impatient at the amount of time she was taking with the animal. He was uneasy about leaving his automobile and his satchel on a back road in the middle of nowhere.

"I am getting a bit anxious about my uh, car and belongings," he stammered. "So, I was wondering when and uh, how I might get some gasoline...gas...and go retrieve them."

"After supper. I have to get cleaned up and changed then help Mama get supper on. Papa will be here by five so that's when we all sit down together. After, I help Mama with the washing up, so it might have to be Papa who takes you to get gas and your car."

"Oh, too bad. I'd rather it was you so I could get to know you a little better...and maybe apologize."

"Apologize for what?"

"For making you feel that the only thing of interest about you was your nose and legs. Obviously, there is a whole lot more about you that is of interest."

"Like my hair for instance?" Madelyn asked coyly.

Joe reddened. "I've never seen hair done that way before," he said diplomatically. "I think though that it may not suit you as well as some other type of uh, *looser* style."

"Well, I happen to think this is the ugliest hairdo I have ever seen in my life!" Madelyn exclaimed. "My cousin, Wilma did this to me last night, then I had to sleep with my head wrapped in a kerchief all night so it wouldn't get mussed, and it's been scratching and itching me all day and has left me decidedly peevish."

Joe couldn't help grinning. "I am in complete agreement that it is the ugliest hairdo imaginable! What did your cousin use to make it so stiff looking? It looks like an iron helmet."

"Egg whites."

"Egg whites?"

"Mm hmm. If I can even get this stuff washed out, I'll probably look like I have the worst case of dandruff imaginable."

Joe's grin turned into a chuckle, which prompted a chuckle out of Madelyn as well. The pair gradually began laughing so hard they slipped in tandem onto the back steps of the house, holding their stomachs in side-splitting laughter. Their eyes streaming with tears, neither of them saw Madelyn's nine year old sister, Thelma approach.

"What are you laughing about?" Thelma asked, soberly.

All she received in answer was Madelyn shaking her head in a renewed burst of laughter.

Thelma, caught up in the mood, chuckled slightly herself. "Is this Adrian?" She pointed at Joe. "Are you laughing because he doesn't look anything like we imagined?" Thelma asked, beginning to laugh too.

Madelyn shook her head then nodded, and Thelma squeezed onto the steps between her sister and Joe, laughing uproariously along with them until she suddenly leaped up and made a run for the outhouse.

Charles Dubois took an immediate liking to Joe. He found him to be affable, industrious and trustworthy after less than a week in his employ. To Charles, the young man was a godsend; obviously in his element in the tavern / pool-hall environment, competent at both the till and in the stockroom, and as a bonus he seemed delighted there was no alcohol in the establishment due to prohibition. Within a month, Joe was given full management responsibility for the facility.

Emma Dubois, however, was slightly wary of Joe from the beginning. He was a little too handsome in a rugged sort of way, a little too charming and flattering, in her estimation, to be entirely above reproach. At times, she caught Joe ogling Madelyn in a way that disturbed her, and she thought that Thelma's obvious crush on him was decidedly out of place.

Joe, however, was so smitten by Madelyn he couldn't take his eyes off her. She wasn't pretty in a conventional way, what with the abundance of freckles she tried to cover up with powder, and her fine, rather limp hair that was neither blonde nor brown nor red but was at times all of them, or none of them, or somewhere in between depending on the light. But there was something about the way her slender body moved when she walked, and the way her whole face lit up when she smiled, and her sudden bursts of infectious laughter that made him want to grab her, and kiss her, and have his way with her. At those times, he had a look of raw passion.

That is the look that Emma Dubois saw; the look that worried her. She asked Charles if it might not be better all- around for Joe to find lodging elsewhere. She argued that Thelma needed to have her room back because Madelyn needed to have her rest and not be bothered by her little sister, and when that didn't work confided that she was feeling overworked by having to provide meals every day for someone other than family. But Charles had pooh-poohed all her arguments, and it wasn't until Joe made a fateful error that she was finally able to get him out of her house.

Joe's eviction was caused by a surprise gift for Madelyn. Had he known of Emma's aversion to having any kind of animal in her house, he never would have given a kitten to the object of his affections. But the scrawny mouser that held reign over the tavern storeroom had given birth to four kittens, and when they were about ten weeks old Joe had decided to take them out to the ranch for barn duty. There was one that stood out from the others though; one all white ball of fluff with blue eyes that was extra friendly and playful, the kind destined to be a house pet. And Joe had decided it would be the perfect pet for Madelyn.

It was a Sunday so the tavern was closed, but Joe drove to the tavern that night to fetch the kitten. He snuck it into the house, past everyone in the sitting room listening to the radio. Once upstairs he headed directly to the big bedroom shared by Madelyn and her little sister, placed the kitten in the center of the bed then exited the room leaving the door just slightly ajar. What he didn't factor into the surprise was the kitten's predilection for exploring, combined with the tantalizing allure of a slightly open door. The resulting surprise was far more than he had anticipated.

Joe had no way of knowing anything about Emma's bedtime ritual. Every night, after slipping into her long nightgown in her bedroom, while Charles stripped down to his long-johns in the bathroom, Emma would turn back the covers on the bed then get down on her hands and knees to peer under the bed and make certain there was no one lurking there. Every night except that one, because she didn't have a chance. The kitten, hiding under Emma's bed, was enticed by the bare toes it saw peeping and moving back and forth under the hem of the bed covers. Crouching, rear end wriggling in intense excitement -- it made a leap for those toes.

The blood-curdling screech that erupted from Emma brought everyone in the house running to her room, where they were all treated to a sight none of them would soon forget. Emma was goose-stepping around on top of her bed, nightgown drawn up into a knot around her waist, screaming *'Under the bed! Under the bed!'* Joe, desperately needing some reason to avert his eyes, was the first one to dive to the floor to look under the bed, and that's where he discovered one pathetically petrified kitten. By the time he had pulled the hapless little thing out from under the bed to show Emma the object of her distress, she had, thankfully, had the presence of mind to release her knotted up nightgown.

The damage done was irrevocable. Emma was not of a mind to listen to any explanations or apologies. She was the mortified victim of a breach of conduct, and she was the judge and jury in the matter as well. Both Joe and the kitten were evicted that very night; the kitten happily reunited with its mother, while Joe spent an uncomfortable night on the pool table. The following day, Charles brought all of Joe's things to him at the tavern, having to scrub at his jaw in an effort to keep a straight face, what with the vision of a bare-bottomed, prancing Emma still fresh in his mind.

"Think you can stay at the rectory with Father Brunet?" Charles asked.

"Oh, probably. Don't know how much I'm going to like that, though. I'm not all that religious, so don't know how that's going to set with the good Father."

"Really? You go to mass every Sunday, don't you?"

"Well, I do because it's expected of me, and because the priest is my cousin and he would probably tell my mother on me if I didn't."

"And it has nothing to do with wanting to stay in Madelyn's good graces either?"

Joe grinned. "Maybe a little. I like her enough to want her to think well of me. And your Missus too." Joe lowered his head in apology. "I sure am sorry about that kitten incident."

Joe realized that if he hoped to see Madelyn at all he had to continue attending church on Sundays. He often arrived early so he could sit in the aisle seat in the back row on the left side of the church. That gave him an unobstructed view of the entire church and everyone in attendance. Everyone that is, with the exception of Emma and the other five tone-deaf, shrill-voiced women who made up what passed for a choir in the loft above him. It was impossible for Madelyn's mother to see where his eyes were focused even if she leaned over the bannister.

For several months of Sundays Joe watched Madelyn's tantalizingly gyrating hips as she walked up to the altar rail to receive communion. He studied her profile as she turned her gaze to the priest giving his sermon from the pulpit. Then as she exited the church he watched her approach, imagining her walking straight into his arms. Sometimes he would catch her eye and she would give him a polite smile. Most of the time however, she would walk past him without a sign of recognition. After that happened three Sundays in a row, Joe never set foot in the church again. He decided he had reached the limit to the torment he was willing to endure.

<hr />

Joe loved to dance and fancied himself to be quite good at it. So he was delighted to hear there would be Saturday night dances all through the winter months in the big open loft above the tavern. Fervently hoping to see Madelyn there, dancing being a socially acceptable excuse for holding a girl in one's arms, Joe attended the first dance of the season dressed in his best Sunday suit and tie. But as the evening wore on it became clear she wouldn't be attending, and he had to be satisfied with dancing with Madelyn's cousin, Wilma.

It was Wilma who suggested they step outside for some fresh air. That's when Joe learned, upon inquiring, that Madelyn would probably not be attending any of the dances.

"Madelyn is going to become a nun. Didn't you know?"

"N no," Joe stammered, stunned. "When did that happen?"

"Well, it hasn't happened yet. She's planning to keep on teaching until she gets the call."

"What call? Who's going to call her?"

"God, I guess."

"God?"

"God!"

"Oh good God!"

"Why '*Oh good God*'? Do you have a thing for Madelyn?"

"Well not any more I guess!" Joe took a good look at Wilma. She was pretty in a blowsy kind of way; buxom, a little too much makeup, her clothes a bit too revealing, but she was fun to be with and felt good in his arms as they danced. "Want to go over to Sturgis Tuesday night to see a basketball game at the Armory? I'm refereeing."

"I'd be delighted!"

"I used to do some refereeing back home and thought I'd try to do some of that while I'm here too."

"How long are you going to be here?"

"Hard to say. I figured maybe only three years, or so."

"A lot can happen in three years," Wilma said, snuggling into the crook of Joe's arm.

"Yeah, maybe a lot can," Joe responded. "Maybe it can."

The three years passed swiftly, Joe busy at the tavern, refereeing basketball, and sparking Wilma. He hardly ever thought of Madelyn again. Hardly ever-- if you didn't count whenever he happened to see her and his breath caught in his throat making his heart skip a beat and his head spin dizzyingly turning him to mush inside. Then he couldn't get her out of his mind for days.

I'm going to pop in here for just a minute to let you know there are gaps in what my father told me because there weren't any significant events worth telling about during those periods. My father did tell me though that remembering back to those three years he had to spend in St. Onge waiting for a divorce were the longest, and in some ways the shortest, three years of his life.

He grew very tired of the monotonous routine of spending his days tending the tavern, eating the bland, heavy meals prepared by the priest's housekeeper, and refereeing the occasional basketball game during the winter months. Wilma monopolized his time at the Saturday night dances and most of his free time otherwise too. He was certain she had designs on him the same way Adele O'Sullivan had and he wasn't going to let himself fall into that trap again. He couldn't see himself spending the rest of his life with her.

The chance sightings of Madelyn every few days, and their brief, casual conversations were what got him through those trying years. Just the anticipation of seeing her, even if she was walking away from him or never acknowledging his existence was enough to make those years bearable. And when his three years were up he waited an extra month before returning to Massachusetts, just in case the next day would be one he would see her on her way to the post office or general store and she would smile at him, or maybe even inquire about his health or comment on the weather. He thought if he left, he would never see her again, and the thought of that was unbearable; even more unbearable than the thought of her becoming a nun.

But he knew he had to leave. There had been no communication between his mother and him, or anyone else, for more than three years. He had given Madelyn's father a month's notice, and when Charles informed him he had found a replacement, he had no choice but to leave.

With his money safely tucked inside the sock on his right foot, he hopped behind the wheel of his car and as he drove off saw Madelyn wave at him from in front of the store, with a sad looking smile on her face before she turned and walked away. He almost slammed on the brake so he could rush to her and take her into his arms and declare his undying love for her. Almost; but didn't.

JUNE, 1930

SEVERAL TIMES ON THE LONG TRIP HOME, JOE THOUGHT about posting a card to his mother announcing his return, or possibly trying to telephone her. He wound up doing neither, deciding it would be more fun to surprise everyone. As he drove along he daydreamed about the reception he would receive as the prodigal son returned, and he busied his mind with stories he would make up about his three year- long adventures in the boondocks. The daydreams were interspersed with singing uplifting songs and whistling, and visualizing Madelyn in his mind's eye walking away from him so he could watch the alluring sway of her hips, then turning and rushing back into his arms, smothering his face with her kisses. He knew he was hopelessly in love with her, but had resigned himself to the fact that she was out of reach for him and that was just a fact that he would have to learn to accept. It was on that trip home that Joe realized he really liked being out on the road, alone with his thoughts. He hadn't known before just how much he enjoyed his own company.

Nothing happened the way Joe fantasied it would. His mother was neither surprised nor overjoyed to see him, giving him a brief hug and telling him to put his valise out of the way so no one would trip over it. Then she motioned for him to follow her out to the kitchen where she began a summary of the past three years while she continued kneading the dough on the breadboard.

"You are finally a free man. Adele let me know two days ago that the divorce came through. And it's none too soon either, by the look of things. She tried to hide her condition by wearing a coat in this hot weather, of all things, but I wasn't fooled." Josephine barely paused to take a breath. "Anna Marie married that Paul Green who lived upstairs on the other end of the block with his folks, and they have a daughter nearly two now that they named Genevieve. And your brother, Gilles married Marie Doucette ... you must remember her, that skinny, homely little waif that used to help her father with his ice deliveries. She's still just as skinny and homely, but your brother is lucky to have her. She's likely the only one who would put up with his infirmities. He's in a wheelchair now, all crippled up with arthritis. Apparently, he was born with it. That's why he was always such a disagreeable child. Since he can't work, Marie supports the two of them by taking over the chore of collecting the rents in this big place for me. They live in that little three room place on the top floor, and your sister lives in the apartment just above me. Oh, and since your father died a little over a year ago, we now have a new janitor too, living in the basement. So you can't be quite as free down there as you used to be in case you were..."

"What did you say?"

"There's a new janitor living in the basement, so..."

"Before that. About my father!" Joe nearly yelled.

"Don't you raise your voice at me, young man! Your father died a little over a year ago in his sleep. He had gone down for an afternoon nap on the couch, as usual, but when he didn't come for dinner at six I went looking for him and found he had peacefully passed away."

"Why didn't you let me know?" Joe asked so faintly it was nearly a whisper.

"What good would that have done? You couldn't have come home, and even if you could you wouldn't have gotten here in time for the funeral."

"But I would have known! I wouldn't have expected to see him, or looked forward to seeing him after such a long time!"

"You ingrate! I saved you a year of grieving over something you couldn't change. I gave you an extra year of happy thoughts, of looking forward to a reunion. I gave you an extra worry-free year while you waited for the time to pass so you could be legally free of Adele. You should be thanking me!"

Joe had often felt rage toward his mother, but never more than he did at that moment. It took every ounce of strength he could muster to calmly ask her where his father was buried.

"He's in the All Saints Cemetery on the north end. Near where my parents, your grandparents, are buried." Josephine's curt answer was punctuated by plopping the dough she had been kneading into the waiting bowl, then covering it with a cloth and leaving it to rise. She brushed her floured hands down the front of her apron then looked directly at Joe. "Go! Go say your goodbyes you didn't get to say. Be back by six. I'll be asking your brother and sister and their families to join us for supper. You need to say some hellos too, you know."

Joe stood at the foot of his father's grave, hands shoved deep into his pockets, tears streaming down his face. The dappled shadow of leaves from the overhanging branch of an Elm tree added to the somber mood as Joe knelt and whispered the thoughts in his mind, assured that his father would hear. *"I've made a mess of things, haven't I Pop? You were always there for me when I needed you, but I wasn't around when you needed me. You were always a good father to me, but I was not always a good son. Every look you gave*

me told me how much you loved me, but I don't know if my look said the same to you. We never said the words to one another because you didn't have to say them for me to know. So I hope you can hear my thoughts now and know how much I always loved you and looked up to you. You were always the most important person in my world. I hope that someday I can be even half the father you were. And now I must say my final goodbye to the finest man I ever knew. Please know it is the hardest goodbye I will ever have to say. My heart is breaking.'

Joe didn't unpack his bags. There was one more thing he had to do before he could let his father go. He knew about his two half-brothers living in Quebec, and that his father hadn't had contact with them since they were in their teen years, but that was all he knew about them. He felt a great need to find out how they had fared all these years, and to inform them of the untimely death of their father. He knew his father would have wanted him to do that.

After spending what seemed like an endless round of small talk and catching up over a stretched out meal, followed by a sleepless night in his old bedroom, Joe set out early the next morning, headed for the Quebec border. At unsuspecting times along the way, he would find his heart feeling heavy in his chest, accompanied by an odd prickling in the back of his eyes, and he would have to pull over and stop on the side of the road until his eyes were cleared of tears. As he drove up through the French speaking countryside, he was thankful he had picked up enough French over the years to be able to converse somewhat intelligibly. The deeper he drove into Quebec, the less chance there was of finding anyone who could speak English.

Joe discovered that his two half-brothers had done quite well for themselves over the years. Both were married, and between them had nine children, all still living on the dairy farm. The elderly couple who had taken them in still lived there too, only the tables were slightly turned.

They were now very old and were being cared for by their two foster sons, one in the original farm house by one of the brothers, and one in the newer farm house by the other brother. They had explained to Joe that the old couple did not seem to know one another anymore, so it was easier all the way around to split them up and share the load.

They seemed truly sorry to hear of their father's death. Though they hadn't known him, they recalled that their beloved Aunt Agnes, also deceased, spoke well of him.

Joe drove back home to Holyoke feeling a puzzling mixture of regret and relief. He wasn't sure exactly what he had accomplished by making the trip to see his half- brothers and informing them of their father's demise. He could have simply written them a letter, something his mother could also have done, but somehow that seemed like the wrong thing to do. It was too crass, too unfeeling, too abrupt and shocking.

It was at that point that Joe began to understand why his mother had not written to tell him of his father's death. It was simply the kindest thing she could do at the time. The most sensible for sure -- but the kindest too. He regretted not knowing sooner, not being there to say goodbye, and not being especially interested in getting to know his two French brothers and all his nieces and nephews. But he was at the same time relieved to finally understand that his mother's seeming cruelty, in this instance at least, was prompted by a true concern and kindness. That is what he chose to believe, because she was his mother.

Back home, Joe tried to reacquaint himself with the boxing arena crowd, but it wasn't the same for him without his father there. His mother encouraged him to get a job, but he discovered that jobs had become few and far between around Holyoke. The hard times following the stock market crash that past fall seemed to be having an adverse effect everywhere. Folks back in St. Onge had hardly felt any effects, but it was another matter in a city the size of Holyoke. He discovered that his mother was feeling the effects too. Several of her tenants had lost their jobs and were having trouble paying their rent. She was letting some of them work it off by sweeping and mopping all the stairs and hallways, or by running errands, washing windows, and doing her laundry, including ironing her sheets and underwear. And from a couple of long term tenants she was just accepting IOU's until things picked up for them.

Joe thought he knew his mother and was astonished to discover that she had a speck of compassion after all. That changed, however, when he realized the true reason for her seeming benevolence toward the newly poor and downtrodden tenants under her roof.

"If I were to evict them there would be little chance right now of finding new tenants that could pay rent anyway," she had informed Joe. "This way, I at least am getting some work out of them that I would ordinarily have to pay someone else to do, and in exchange they get to keep a roof over their heads. When the day comes that I can find new paying tenants, or if my charity begins to cost me too much, they will be out of here."

Joe began spending his time exploring the back alleys of the downtown district the way he had done in his boyhood days. But when he discovered there were a lot of other men doing the same thing, he drove out to the manufacturing districts where there were better pickings. It was on one of those excursions where he came across something out of the ordinary; something he normally would have disregarded as useless. That's what he did at first, but as he searched further among the bins his mind kept returning to the stacks of paperboard boxes he had seen behind the print shop, prompting him to retrace his steps for a closer look.

The flat, unassembled box lids were printed in elegant white script on a stippled emerald green background. *'Lucky Lie'*. 'Lucky lie," Joe said out loud. "What the heck does that mean?" Deciding the boxes had probably been discarded due to a misprint, he had begun stacking all the flat tops and bottoms into a large carton when he noticed the small white print on one of the side flaps of the box tops. *'Premium Golf Balls'* it read. And just as if the idea had been in his head all along, waiting for him to realize it, Joe knew what he was going to do.

Joe counted out seventy - five boxes. At twelve golf balls to a box he was going to need a minimum of 900 balls…make that an even thousand for good measure…, and he was going to need some help too. He knew exactly where to find it. Loading a dozen or so old tin apple buckets into his car, he headed for the boxing arena district where a lot of young boys hung out. Then with boys piled on top of one another and hanging from the sides of the car, he drove out into the countryside where the elite lived and spent their leisure time at the resort styled country clubs, sunning, dining and playing golf.

"Two cents a ball," Joe told the boys. "And any ball that looks brand new is worth a nickel." The results were predictable. The boys started by searching through the roughs at each of the golf courses, then went for the easier pickings of grabbing balls in play, and finally ended up joining forces to distract players while one of the boys pilfered new balls directly from the bags. At the end of that first day Joe had nearly a third of the balls he needed, a skillful and gratified workforce looking forward to the next round of extortion at the expense of the snooty country club crowd, and the satisfaction of knowing he was well on his way to pulling off an even bigger, more lucrative scam of his own.

Back in the basement of the apartment building, Joe spent the evening rummaging through all the odds and ends he had collected over the years, searching for the remnants of fabric he remembered finding several years before. He smiled in satisfaction when he opened the box and saw the folds of jewel colored velvet, then frowned as a musty odor assailed his nostrils. He draped the fabric over a clothesline to air out then continued his search. He needed glue, more paperboard, glossy white paint and some fancy gilded paper. He knew he had all of those things somewhere, and he kept searching until he found them.

Over the next two days Joe drove the boys to the country clubs closer to the shore. Those clubs attracted the upper of the upper crust, and the boys laughingly decreed that the richer the man the dumber. Just six hours of work over those two days netted them a pocket full of top money; there were a whole lot of nickel balls and Joe had more than he needed. The boys didn't ask what he planned to do with all those golf balls. They had grown up in a world where you didn't ask questions and you didn't tell anybody anything. They were just happy to see the look of gratitude and pride in their mothers' eyes as they handed over their contribution to their family's meager coffers.

Joe spent the next several days washing and painting thirty six of the best balls, covering up the name embossed on them. Then he assembled the boxes, making dividers for the balls. He gave special attention to three of the boxes that he would be setting up as samples. In those, he lined the bottom of the boxes with plush green velvet then covered the dividers with the velvet as well. He'd had a stamp made that read *'Lucky Lie'* in the same script as the outside of the box lid, and he stamped the name in gold on each ball before placing it carefully in its individual compartment inside the box. Immensely satisfied with the rich look of the gleaming, dimpled balls in their verdant nests, Joe placed the tops on those three boxes and sealed them shut on two sides with strips of thick gilded paper. He set them aside so they wouldn't get mixed in with the rest of the boxes, then got busy and filled all of them and sealed them shut.

The last thing he did was put together the display box he had dreamed up. He covered a cigar box with the green velvet, complete with a layer of velvet covered cotton wool on the bottom inside of the box. Next, he sawed a top grade ball in half exposing its inner workings, and topped the whole thing off with gilded lettering all over the box. *'Lucky Lie'*

Joe was headed toward the posh country clubs on the outskirts of Boston; in particular the one that was known to serve the upper of the upper crust of Boston society. He wore a brilliant white suit and straw fedora, a dapper looking red, white and blue striped ascot and shiny white shoes. His brown leather valise sat on the seat beside him, the three sample boxes of golf balls and the display box tucked safely inside. The other seventy two boxes of balls were stacked in the rear, on the floor and under the valise, taking up every inch of spare room in the Model T.

During the long drive, Joe rehearsed his spiel over and over in his mind. He felt he knew a lot about people who held servile positions to the rich; his mother being a stellar example. Through her he had seen that the fawning attitude they held toward their employers and their wealthy friends could turn into a snooty contempt for anyone they felt was of a lower station in life. For that reason, Joe knew he had to seize control and remain above whoever purchased supplies for the country club, as well as catering to the snob appeal he was certain to encounter. Sure of himself, Joe drove right up to the front entrance instead of parking in the back lot and using the staff entrance as would have been expected. Carrying the valise, he sauntered nonchalantly through the front door as if he owned the place.

On the long drive back to Holyoke, Joe couldn't stop grinning as he patted the thick wad of bills in his jacket pocket, over and over again. He didn't know what made him happier the five hundred dollars in his pocket, or putting one over on the pompous imbecile in charge of purchasing supplies for the golf shop at the country club. With a satisfied smile, he went over the exchange in his mind, relishing every moment he knew he had the man in the palm of his hand. First he had dazzled him with the cut open ball, displaying the way it was constructed, and what made it different and superior to all other brands. Then he opened the seal on one of his sample boxes, showing the balls richly displayed. At that point he mentioned the price, and seeing the man blanch a bit at the amount, suggested that maybe the new and improved balls were a bit too rich for the club members considering the poor financial situation in the country at that time. Miffed, the man had responded that the price was not too high for club members. And that's when Joe knew for sure he had him in the palm of his hand, and could probably even get him to buy the entire lot of balls. The man had wanted to purchase a dozen boxes to see how club members liked them, but when Joe let him know he had seventy-five boxes on hand, and would be calling on other clubs in the area, the man insisted on an exclusive or no sale.

"The manufacturer in New Britain, Connecticut expects to place all these balls in prestigious clubs around the Boston area," Joe had told him apologetically. "I started with the club I felt was the number one club; the best of the best for the newest and best golf ball being produced. I can't give you an exclusive for just twelve boxes, but I'm sure I can convince the manufacturer to give you an exclusive if you take all seventy five boxes. How long a time period would you need for the exclusive?"

"One full year for seventy five boxes," the man had said.

Joe bit his lip, pretending to think it over. Then, "One full year it is," he had said, extending his hand. "And I'll give it to you in writing. Tell you what, I'll even leave the cut display with you so you'll know I won't be showing it around to anyone else."

Joe had asked for cash since the banks were still shaky and undependable, and the obsequious lackey to the rich had been only too happy to oblige. When the fraud was discovered, Joe knew he would be far away in the opposite direction of New Britain, Connecticut.

⁂

Joe spent the next two years dreaming up, and carrying out, fraudulent schemes that were a way of cheating the wealthy out of their easily earned dollars while putting some of those dollars in the pockets of his loyal band of young helpers, and most of them in his own.

His searches behind the printing warehouse and the textile mill became a daily routine. He was looking for more misprinted boxes, paperboard and rich looking bits of paper; more scraps and roll ends of fancy fabrics, ribbons and laces. And when he found them his mind instantly began conjuring up ideas. One of his favorites had been a stack of silvery unassembled boxes that had a black smear of ink down the center. He felt that was the reason they had been discarded, but that ink stain didn't bother him for a moment. Once they were tied up with the bright pink, blue, green and yellow ribbon he had found, no one would ever see those stains.

Joe involved Anna Marie in the scheme, but didn't tell her what he was actually up to. He bought all the ingredients then asked his sister to make two kinds of her famously delicious fudge for him. "I want to see if this is something we can sell in the fancy confectionary shops," he explained. "I'll pay you well for your work, and who knows? This could turn into a great business for us."

So, Anna Marie made a big batch of creamy chocolate fudge, and another of divinity with black walnuts. Meanwhile, Joe prepared the lavish sample boxes that Anna Marie would help him fill with the real fudge, and checked once again on the boxes of phony fudge he had already prepared. That had been the only part of the plan that had given him trouble. He knew that whatever he put in those boxes had to be the right weight and the right size. It also couldn't move around or rattle in the box. What he finally came up with was mashed potatoes. Once they had cooled he mixed in flour then shaped the potatoes into squares and balls, simulating the two types of fudge, then rolled them in corn starch to seal them into shape. Then he added cocoa to some powdered sugar and iced the squares with the mixture, while dipping the balls into plain powdered sugar sprinkled with finely chopped walnuts.

Joe pulled off his candy scam in the seaside resort of Nantucket. He knew that the very wealthy were always the easiest people to fool, but that the 'climbers' were the quickest to buy, especially if they thought there was a measure of prestige in the purchase. His conscience never bothered him when he pulled his scams because his victims were people who lived a lavish lifestyle, whether or not they could actually afford it, and who delighted in a pretentious display of affluence. He felt they had it coming to them. His scams ranged from flower delivery to coupons for a pick-up dry cleaning service, and anything imaginable that could be put in a box and tied with a pretty ribbon that would have an elitist, snob-appeal.

Josephine did not question her son's ability to pay her a substantial room and board every month. She merely took it as her due, never imagining that it was part of the proceeds of larcenous activity. She suspected that Joe might be frequenting the boxing arena the way his father had, possibly even engaging in strong man stunts, but she was not curious enough to ask. The way in which men spent their time did not concern her, as long as they met their familial obligations.

Meanwhile, Joe spent those years with images of Madelyn popping into his head at unsuspected moments, filling him up with her smiles and her infectious laughter; filling him with a longing that was like a deep pain inside.

JULY, 1932

"A letter came for you today," Josephine said offhandedly, passing the bowl of boiled potatoes to Joe. "From someone in St. Onge. I think the name was Madelyn, something."

Joe nearly bolted from his chair, but sat back down at his mother's command.

"Sit! The letter will still be there when you finish eating. It has traveled a long way to get here so whatever news it contains will be cold by now. Like your meal if you don't start eating it right now."

Joe felt that his mother took an extraordinarily long time finishing the meal. No doubt it was another one of her perverse methods of control over him, he thought; a control she relentlessly tried to exert even though he was a grown man, more than paying his own way. When at long last Josephine lifted the napkin from her lap to dab it delicately at the corners of her mouth, Joe held his breath until she finally placed it beside her plate, the signal that he could excuse himself.

Taking the letter to his bedroom, Joe sat on the bed staring at the envelope in his hand. He ran his fingers over the name in the upper left hand corner, reassuring himself that it actually read 'Madelyn Dubois', and that it was, indeed, addressed to him. The scent of her perfume wafting from the envelope making him giddy, Joe slipped his finger under the flap, careful not to damage the precious missive enclosed.

He read the brief letter through once then read it a second and then a third time, hardly believing what he read. His heart was pounding and he was finding it hard to breathe.

Dear Mr. Tessier,

This letter is to inform you that I will be in Holyoke, Massachusetts for one day, July 5. I am traveling with a theater company that will be giving a matinee performance at the Savoy Theater that afternoon. Father Brunet gave me your address, so I hope you don't mind.

If you are free, and so inclined, I would be delighted to see you once again while I am there. We can meet at the stage door entrance following the performance if that is convenient.

Yours Truly,
Madelyn Dubois

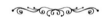

The following morning Joe drove downtown to the Savoy Theater, parking right in front. He was not as familiar with the layout of the Savoy as he was with some of the movie theaters closer to home so he wanted to get his bearings. He went around the right side of the building where he found a door that was not labeled. It was locked. Going back around the front of the building to look on the other side, he passed a poster tacked up on the front of the theater. At first he gave it no notice then something caught his eye and he went up to it for a closer look.

WIN THIS CAR! The poster read, in big block letters. Underneath was a picture of a cream colored 1932 Chevrolet Phaeton with the top down, and a handsome couple laughing gaily as they breezed along a country road, sun shining, and with not a care in the world. Underneath the poster was a playbill announcing the stage performance on July 5th, at which someone attending the performance would be the lucky winner of the car. And right there on that playbill was Madelyn's name.

Joe went around to the other side of the theater but finding the door there locked too he went back around to the front to look at the poster once again. When he saw that the price of admission was a hefty one dollar, his mind began doing some quick calculations. He knew the theater had about 2000 seats, and he guessed the car would have a price-tag around $500.00. If all the seats were filled, once the cost of the car was subtracted, plus whatever had to be paid to the actors and ushers and other help, the theater owner would be likely to have a payday of close to a thousand dollars, Joe reckoned. Even if there were some empty seats due to the high price of admission, he figured the guy would still have a good payday. He stowed all that in the back of his mind the way he stored all his finds in the back corner of the basement in the apartment building. Someday, he knew, everything winds up being useful.

The following day was the Fourth of July. It was a day filled with parades, bands playing, a picnic in the park, carnivals, fireworks and profuse sweating in the summer heat. Joe usually enjoyed the holiday events, but not this year. This year he was impatient for the festivities and noise to be over and for the next day, and Madelyn, to arrive. He walked by the theater several times that day, thinking she might have already arrived, but by dusk he had still seen no sign of her. Disappointed, he returned home that night, his stomach in turmoil and his nerves on edge.

After removing his jacket and hanging it on the back of his bedside chair, Joe barely made it to the bathroom down the hall to rid himself of the hotdogs, pie, watermelon, salt water taffy, corn on the cob, ice cream, cotton candy and lemonade he had consumed that day on top of the heavy breakfast of hot-cakes and sausage his mother had served that morning. After brushing his teeth and splashing cold water on his face, Joe thought to feel his forehead, wondering if he might be coming down with something. It didn't occur to him that he might be having a bit of stage fright from the anticipation of seeing the object of his affections after so much time.

The following morning Joe took special care with his toilette, slicking his unruly hair in place with pomade and dusting his body with a manly scented talc to help keep the sweat from easing through his pores in the ungodly heat the city had been experiencing for the past week. His white trousers and shirt were crisp and clean, but he rolled up his shirt sleeves to let his skin breathe, deciding to wait until it was time to see Madelyn before donning his suit jacket. At the last minute he thought to slip two neatly ironed and folded handkerchiefs in his pants pocket, and another one in the breast pocket of his jacket.

He had intended to buy flowers for Madelyn before the performance, but when he passed the Savoy on his way to the flower shop and saw the lineup of people halfway down the block waiting to get in the theater, he hastily turned around and parked his car, then took his place at the end of the line. *'The car,'* he thought. *'That's what this lineup is all about. Surely they aren't coming and paying a big price just for the entertainment. It's the car!'* Glancing at his wristwatch, Joe saw that it was only five past ten, and the performance didn't start until one. He figured they might open the theater doors an hour or two before that because they had to have time to collect money and hand out raffle tickets, but he found himself bracing for a long, hot wait in the sun anyway.

Shifting from one foot to another, Joe used the index finger of his left hand as a coat hook, relieving his arm of the heat from the jacket draped over it. Then he dabbed at the beads of sweat running down the sides of his face from his temples, removed his straw hat from his head and began using it as a fan. He became aware of a young woman walking in his direction down past all the people in the line, seemingly looking for someone. When she reached him, Joe asked the obvious question, "Are you looking for someone?"

"I'm looking for a familiar face that will let me slip into line so I don't have to go to the end."

"Do you need a particular familiar face, or will just any familiar face do?"

"Any familiar face."

"My name is Joe. What's yours?"

"Doris."

"Well, hello Doris. Now that we are familiar with one another, would you care to get in line in front of me?"

Doris smiled her thanks as well as saying it then slipped in front of Joe. "I was afraid if I had to go to the back of the line they would run out of seats and I wouldn't get in. I just have to win that car! It's my one chance to get out of this place and make something of myself. I want to go to New York, maybe get a job as a secretary and find a rich man to marry... hey, would you mind directing your hat - fan my direction? I'm wilting from the heat!"

Joe spent the next half hour waiting for the theater doors to open regretting his benevolent gesture to Doris. He was certain, however, that it would probably not be the last time he would be the victim of an error in judgment when it came to women. As the line moved along, Joe's spirits lifted. It wasn't long before he had paid his dollar, was handed a numbered ticket stub which he shoved into his pants pocket without looking at it, and had found a seat close to the exit at the back of the theater. He wanted to be able to slip out the door and run around to the stage door as quickly as possible after the show. Placing his now limp jacket across his lap, with the straw hat resting on top, he reveled in the relative coolness of the theater compared to the intense heat of the sun outside. His stomach churning in anticipation, he waited for the show to start.

If asked, Joe couldn't have told anyone what the play was about. He didn't see or hear anyone else on the stage other than Madelyn except for the time the man on the stage with her took her in his arms and kissed her. Joe nearly leaped out of his seat and protested out loud at that, before remembering it was just a play and wasn't real. When the cast members took their final bows, Joe tried to leave but found the exit blocked by a crowd of people in the back who had been sold 'standing room only' tickets. Then he heard a loud screech from a microphone as the theater manager was about to make an announcement.

"The cast members will be in the lobby to greet you shortly," he yelled into the microphone. "But first, we have some business to attend to, don't we!? We have to see which one of you has won that marvelous 1932 Chevrolet Phaeton! So get your ticket stubs out, and here we go!" He made a big show of ripping off the top of the box in which all the torn in half stubs had been placed, then asked a young woman from the audience to come up on stage, stir around all the stubs in the box, then close her eyes and draw one stub out of the box.

"The winning number is ......468. I repeat, 468."

Joe heard grumbling and groans of disappointment all around him before he thought to pull his own stub out of his pocket and take a look. He was waiting to hear a cheer of victory from somewhere in the audience, and when he finally heard it he realized it was coming from him. The ticket stub in his fingers read 468.

"Here!", Joe yelled out, holding the ticket aloft. The crowd made way for him as he headed toward the stage to present his stub to the manager, some people giving him a congratulatory pat on the back, while others looked as if they would like to strangle him. Up on the stage, the manager declared him the winner and handed him the keys to his new car.

Making his way through the crowd exiting the theater, Joe spied Madelyn standing to the side in the lobby along with the other cast members. Dashing over to her, he grabbed her by the arm and dangled the car keys in front of her. "I won the car!" he shouted jubilantly. "Come on! You're coming along for the first ride!"

Madelyn didn't have time for anything but a surprised sounding "Joe!" before being hustled out the theater door and hauled over to the shiny new car parked out front. Joe ceremoniously invited her to get in the front seat then slid in beside her, pressing his body against hers as she inched over to the passenger side. The rest of the theater troupe had chased after them, thinking their leading lady was being kidnaped, but Madelyn assured them she knew Joe and would meet up with them later.

"Where are we headed?"

"I thought I'd show you around a bit. Maybe take a drive out on a country road."

"How have you been?" Madelyn asked shyly.

"Good. Good," Joe nodded perfunctorily. "How about you?"

"Good here too. I had a chance to travel a bit with this theater group for the summer, see a bit of the world, you know. It's been good fun, if a bit tiring."

"Are you still teaching?"

"Yes, my contract was renewed for another year, so I will be back there in September."

Joe glanced over at Madelyn, sitting primly with her knees pressed firmly together, covered by her long cotton skirt. He couldn't help himself; he had to ask, "What happened to your idea of becoming a nun?"

Madelyn gasped. "How did you know about that? I never told you that!"

"Your cousin Wilma told me."

"Oh. Well, she had no business telling you that. If I had wanted you to know I would have told you myself."

"Why didn't you want me to know?"

"I don't know."

Seeing that Madelyn appeared flustered by his question, Joe pulled over to the side of the road and shut off the engine. Turning to her he tenderly asked, "Tell me."

Madelyn sighed, not looking at Joe. "I'm not sure if I have anything to tell you."

"Yes you do. You want to tell me that you felt a shock go through you the same way I did when our eyes first met five years ago. You want to tell me you have never stopped thinking about what that meant all these years the same way I have never stopped thinking about it."

Mouth open in amazement, Madelyn turned to Joe. "You felt it too? I've been trying to figure out what it was all about!"

"I think it was an instant attraction."

"I thought it might have been just the opposite; an instant repulsion like the opposing ends of magnets. But, I wasn't sure."

"Which would you prefer it to be?"

Madelyn blushed and looked away. "I'm not sure about that either. But it's a moot question since I am planning on entering the convent."

"Moot."

"Yes, moot."

"You're -- just waiting for the call."

"I guess you could put it that way."

"Is there any other way to put it?"

"I guess not."

"Well, I can think of another way to put it. It's an excuse for putting off living your life that's what it is."

"What do you mean by that?" Madelyn asked huffily.

"I mean just what it sounds like. I think you are giving yourself an excuse for not being what you are meant to be."

"And just what, in your opinion, am I meant to be?"

"My wife! The mother of my children!" Joe vehemently declared before he was even aware of what he was going to say.

"Your wife?" Madelyn asked faintly. "Is that what you were thinking all these years that I was supposed to wind up as your wife? The mother of your children? Tell me, is that why you spent all your time sparking with my cousin, Wilma? Is that why you scarcely ever gave me a glance? Is that why you left two years ago with no more than a curt nod of your head as I waved goodbye to you, my heart breaking in two?"

"Your heart was breaking?"

"I didn't mean to say that." Madelyn said, flustered once again.

"Yes you did. My heart was breaking too. I was in love with you and didn't think you cared for me at all. I fell in love with you the moment I looked into your eyes and felt the jolt that went from my eyes, down to my feet, then back to my head, making me dizzy with delight. Nothing is more certain to me."

"I always told myself I was waiting for God's call to fulfill my destiny."

"All along I think maybe you have just been waiting for *my* call. I think maybe that's why you wrote to say you were coming to Holyoke with a theater group. Maybe it's even the reason why you joined the theater group."

"Do you really think all that? Do you think I joined the theater group because it was a way to fulfill some kind of destiny?"

"No. I don't believe in destiny. I think it was just a coincidence. Like winning this car. I won it by accident."

"It was a draw. How could you win it by accident?"

"The tickets were handed out in numerical order. I let a woman cut into the line ahead of me, and if I hadn't done that the man in line behind me would have had the winning number, not me."

"And you don't think that maybe fate had something to do with you letting someone cut in line so you would have the winning ticket?"

"No, I just think that my choosing to let that woman in line ahead of me brought me luck, but it was unlucky for the guy behind me. No such thing as 'fate' was involved. It was merely a coincidence."

"The jolt when our eyes met, me joining a traveling theater group for the summer that just happens to have an engagement in the city where you live, you winning this car and taking me for a joyride to declare your love – you think that is all merely a coincidence?"

"Absolutely. It all happened because of choices we made."

"How romantic! I suppose we both chose to have that jolt when our eyes met, hmm?"

"No, that was physical attraction; the kind of attraction that leads to true love."

"And you think everything else was a coincidence?"

"I do. I also think I'm starting to sound really sappy. I suppose being in love and declaring that to the object of your affections can do that to you."

Coyly, Madelyn pointed out, "Perhaps you're right. You haven't even mentioned my legs, or my nose, or the style of my hair. You're slipping."

"Your skirt is too long for me to see your legs, you got your nose out of joint shortly after we started our conversation, and your hair is lovely compared to the way you wore it when I fell in love with you. If I fell in love with you when your hair was so awful, how can you ever doubt my love for you now?" Joe ended with a laugh.

"It really was awful, wasn't it?"

"The absolute worst I've ever seen."

"I'd be laughing out loud with you again if I weren't so tired and hungry right now," Madelyn said apologetically. "It's been a very long day for me and I really do need to be getting back."

On the drive back to the theater Joe and Madelyn made small talk, neither of them inclined to further pursue the topic of their attraction to one another. Finding the theater locked up and deserted, Joe asked Madelyn where she was staying; he would take her there.

"I don't know. Carl, the leading man in the play, is the one who makes those arrangements. He told everyone the name of the hotel, but I don't remember it. I think maybe it started with a G. Or maybe it was an R," Madelyn said helplessly.

"Carl. Is that the guy who kissed you on stage?"

"Yes."

"Why would he kiss you and then in the end wind up with that dumpy girl instead of you? He would have to be blind in real life to do that."

"Then I guess he must be blind in real life. He happens to be married to that girl. Look, this isn't helping us find the hotel where I'm supposed to be staying."

"Oh. You think it might start with a G, huh? Well, offhand I can think of a couple that start with G. There's the Glenholme, the Grand Vista, Grenada – anything sound familiar?"

Madelyn shook her head. "I'm not sure. Would it be terribly inconvenient for you to take me around to some of those hotels so I can check to see if my friends have a room there?"

Joe spent the next three hours driving around the city, first checking out hotels that started with G, then with R, then with any other letter of the alphabet they could find. All to no avail.

Madelyn tearfully shook her head as she climbed back into the car, her brow furrowed into deep lines between her eyes. "I can't believe how foolish I feel!" she declared. "What am I going to do now?"

"You can stay at my place," Joe offered. Then seeing the offended look on Madelyn's face, Joe quickly added, "It's my mother's place, actually. I just have a room there to help her out, and there's a spare room you could use. Besides, neither of us has eaten and the kitchen is always open at my mother's house."

Joe hoped the last little bit he had added wouldn't be a lie, but he never knew with his mother. He had missed supper with her at six. He knew from experience she would be irate about that, but with any luck she would be sound asleep and he and Madelyn would have the kitchen to themselves, undisturbed. It was almost 10 pm. -- long past his mother's bedtime.

Leading Madelyn directly to the kitchen, Joe invited her to sit at the table while he fixed the two of them thick chicken sandwiches, then set out tall glasses of milk and slices of his mother's peach and pecan pies. They ate in silence, Joe enchanted by the movement of Madelyn's jaw as she chewed methodically, then swallowed. Neither of them spoke until they had finished eating.

"I must have been ravenous to have eaten so much!" Madelyn declared.

"You were ravishing to watch," Joe replied, to which Madelyn blushed charmingly.

"Well, thank you I guess but could you please show me where I am to sleep now? Oh, and I guess I should know where your facilities are located as well. My train leaves at ten past seven tomorrow morning, so I need to arrive before that to make contact with my friends. How far is it to the train station?"

"About ten minutes by car."

"And you will drive me?"

"Of course. We can leave here by half past six and you will be there in plenty of time. Do you want me to wake you?"

"Oh no, that won't be necessary. I'm used to rising early and I have a built in clock when it comes to that. Thank you for the wonderful meal, and all your trouble, and I'll see you in the morning."

Once in her room, Madelyn removed her shoes, stockings, skirt and blouse, then stretched out on top of the bed covers in her slip. She slept fitfully, worried that she wouldn't awaken on time after all due to being in an unfamiliar time zone and the late hour at which she had retired. It was still quite dark when she rose and crept out to the kitchen in her bare feet to peer at the clock on the wall. She sighed when she saw that it was only twenty past five, but decided to get dressed anyway. Taking her time in the bathroom, she found some toothpowder in the medicine cupboard, poured some into the palm of her hand, then wet her index finger under the tap, dipped it into the powder, and cleaned her teeth as best she could. Then she washed her face, combed her hair, powdered her face to cover her freckles, and last, applied lipstick to her bottom lip then rubbed her lips together to cover her top lip as well.

Madelyn sat in a chair by the window in her room, waiting for any sound that might indicate there was someone up and about besides her. She found herself about to nod off when she was certain she had heard the bathroom door close. Moving quietly, she peered out into the hall and saw that the bathroom door was indeed closed. But, as she turned to look down the other end of the hall, she saw that the door to Joe's room was also shut, but the door to the room Joe had indicated was his mother's room was wide open. *'It must be Joe's mother in the bathroom,'* Madelyn thought. Not wanting to catch Joe's Mother unaware, she quickly tiptoed out to the kitchen to check the time. It was ten past six. Hurrying back to her room, Madelyn waited fretfully, silently urging Joe's mother to speed up her morning toilette so Joe could get to his and get her to the train station on time. It seemed to Madelyn that she was taking an interminable amount of time.

When she finally heard the bathroom door open, Madelyn waited a few seconds before opening her door a crack to see the back end of a wide-hipped woman shuffling toward the kitchen in a tufted robe and house slippers. Creeping softly over to Joe's bedroom, she pressed her ear against the door trying to hear any sound of movement. Hearing nothing, and by that time desperate, she brazenly opened the door, shut it behind her, and walked over to gaze at the still sound asleep, slightly snoring, undershorts clad Joe reclining akimbo on the rumpled sheets of his turned down bed.

"Psst!" she hissed, leaning over him. Nothing. She tried it again, with a double hiss. "Psst! Psst!" Joe still made no move. Madelyn sat on the side of the bed, leaning over Joe to "Psst!" directly in his ear, while giving his shoulder a shake. That's how Josephine found them when she opened the door to wake her son.

Madelyn leaped away from the bed, frozen in terror as Josephine rushed to the other side of the bed and slapped Joe hard on the side of his head. "Whore - monger!" she bellowed. "You stay out all night then bring a loose woman into my house behind my back! Didn't you learn your lesson the first time? What are you planning to do? Get another chippie in the family way so you have to get married and divorced again? What is it going to take for you to learn – another three year exile in some backwater place like St. Onge?!"

Joe managed to elude more blows by leaping off the end of the bed then simultaneously tried to don his pants and shirt while stopping his mother's screeching invective with an explanation. "You've got it all wrong!" he yelled back. "Madelyn spent the night in the spare room. It's a long story, but I need to get her to the train station and I'll explain later."

Madelyn's eyes were huge as she looked first at Josephine, then at Joe. "No thank you. I'd rather walk!" she said haughtily then nodded at Josephine. "What a pleasure to meet you."

Madelyn dashed from Joe's bedroom, found her way to the front door of the apartment, then slammed it behind her. She turned right when she reached the sidewalk, her angry, deliberate stride matching the rapid beat of her heart.

Joe finished zipping up his trousers, but decided he had no time to waste buttoning his shirt. He slipped his bare feet into his shoes without tying them then ran from his room but not before giving his mother a look of pure hate.

"Let her go," his mother had yelled after him. "You'll be better off for it, mark my words."

When Joe reached his new car he saw that Madelyn was already nearly a block away, headed in the wrong direction. When he pulled up alongside her he hollered for her to get in.

"No thanks!" She had snarled. "I'd rather walk!"

"Well, you'll never get there walking. You're going the wrong way, and your train is leaving in sixteen minutes. So stop being so stubborn and get in the car!"

Madelyn seemed to think it over before hurrying over to the car and letting herself in on the passenger side. She was determined not to speak to Joe, but her resolve was broken when he offered an abject apology for his mother's unforgivable misinterpretation of circumstances.

"Oh, no need to apologize for your mother's misunderstanding," Madelyn said venomously. "Apparently, from what she revealed she had every reason to believe that history was being repeated."

"You know that's not true."

"Oh, do I now? I didn't even know there was a history to repeat!"

"I can explain all that, if you'll give me a chance."

"Well, don't waste your time explaining because I don't plan on giving you a chance. I don't want to have anything more to do with you. At least my time here with you had a good conclusion. I got to see what a cad you truly are. You are a pig! You are a pig if you are!"

When Joe pulled up in front of the station entrance, Madelyn leaped from the car, not wasting a single moment by shutting the car door behind her. While she raced into the station, he drove around to the parking area, found a spot to park his car then dashed after her, tripping twice over the laces of his untied shoes. He stooped to tie them, but one glance at his wristwatch told him he didn't have time. Madelyn's train was scheduled to pull out in less than a minute. Out of breath, and sweating profusely, Joe checked the departure display, realizing too late that Madelyn had never told him where the theater group would be performing next.

Rushing outside to the tracks, Joe saw an empty platform and the tail end of a train that was picking up speed. He hurried back inside the station, scanning the ticket area, waiting area, even waiting to see if someone exited the women's washroom, hoping that somehow Madelyn had managed to miss her train and she would suddenly appear before him. He took a seat in the waiting area, head slumped forward, hands pressed together between his knees, dejectedly waiting for a miracle to happen.

"Your shoes are undone."

Joe didn't realize at first that someone was speaking to him until the man repeated himself.

"I said, your shoes are undone.'"

Joe extended his feet out in front of himself. "My whole life is undone. So my shoes ought to be undone too, I suppose."

"A troublesome affair of the heart, huh?"

"What makes you think that?"

"There's nothing else in this world that makes a man look the way you look right now."

"How's that?" Joe asked, straightening up and looking at the man sitting across from him for the first time.

"It's a look of pure downheartedness. Like you lost the most important thing in life and don't know if you can ever get it back."

"You talk like you've had some experience with that."

"Mm," the man nodded. "Just a couple of days ago, as a matter of fact! My darling wife was going to walk out on me if I didn't find another job that would allow me to be home with her every night now that she's expecting a baby in a few months. And then out of the blue I got an offer to come back to the job at the bank I'd had before the crash, so I can quit this lousy sales job that keeps me away from home for weeks at a time. I'm not cut out for sales, but it was the only work I could find."

Joe immediately perked up. "What were you selling? Selling stuff is right up my alley! By the way, I'm Joe Tessier," he said extending his hand.

"George Miller," the man replied. "I've been selling bandages for a new company in New Jersey; traveling all over Massachusetts by train, calling on doctors and hospitals in every town and city. On foot," he added.

Joe glanced at the leather sample case at George's side. "You don't have a car?"

"Did, but had to sell it to keep on paying the rent before I found this job."

"It must be tough getting around without a car. I've got two of them now. An old Model T and I just won a new car yesterday at a draw at the Savoy Theater."

"Well! Congratulations!" George shook Joe's hand again, and patted him on the shoulder. "Sounds like yesterday was your lucky day!"

"I thought it was too until today happened," Joe said dejectedly.

"I've got some time before my train leaves. Want to tell me about it?"

Joe normally didn't confide in anyone, and it was with a bit of wonder that he found himself relating, in excruciating detail, almost his entire life's history with a special emphasis on the reason he had to go to South Dakota in the first place, the jolt of attraction he and Madelyn had both experienced at first meeting, her wanting to become a nun, declaring his love to her yesterday, and the hateful diatribe concerning Madelyn's morality his mother had heaped upon her just a short while ago. He finally ended his saga with, "I don't know what I can do now to make amends. I am truly at a loss."

"Write her a letter explaining everything," his new found friend, George suggested.

"She would probably return a letter from me or worse yet burn it," Joe responded dejectedly. "She thinks I am a cad. She called me a pig! Her last words to me are still ringing in my ears; *'you are a pig if you are'*."

"Well, I'm not exactly sure what she might have meant by that," George said, scratching his head. "But I do think the only chance you have of turning this whole thing around for yourself is a letter of explanation and apology; one that sounds a lot like a love letter."

"I'm not sure I'd be any good at that. I don't have much experience writing letters."

"Here, let me give you an example," George said while pulling a sheet of paper out of the leather sample case at his feet. "This is my draft of a letter I sent to my wife when she threatened to leave me. It did the trick for me, but you tell me what you think."

Joe read the letter through then glanced at the company letterhead on which the letter had been drafted. "I think I need to have you write the letter for me," he said. "And it needs to be on this company paper so Madelyn won't know right off that it has anything to do with me."

"You want me to write the letter for you?"

"Yes, but not 'for me' the way you might be thinking. I'd like you to write the letter for me, as a friend of mine, who knows what happened and knows how terrible I feel and how much I want to apologize, because I don't think Madelyn would read any letter that was 'from' me personally. Do you get what I mean? Would you write that kind of letter for me?"

George shook his head in apology. "I have a train to catch in a few minutes. There's no time."

"Well how far are you going? Maybe I could drive you instead?"

"I'm going all the way to New Jersey. I have to return this sample case or else I'll be sent a bill to pay for it. Besides, I already have my ticket."

Joe eyed the leather case. "You work on commission, right? You get paid a percentage of sales?"

George nodded.

"Well the company would probably rather have someone else out there selling their stuff than have the case returned, don't you think? And here I am looking for something to sell! And there you are looking to get rid of what you sell! And here I am, in need of having a letter written for me, and there you are with the knowhow to write that kind of letter!" Joe barely paused to catch his breath before jumping to his feet and adding, "And here I am with two cars, and there you are with none, so go get a refund on your train ticket, write that letter for me, along with another one to the bandage company telling them they now have a brand new salesman, then come with me in my new car to pick up *your* new car as payment for all your help."

"You don't need to do that."

"Do what?"

"Give me your old car. Taking over this sales job and saving me a trip to New Jersey is more than payment enough in exchange for writing a letter."

Joe thought about it. "Is your wife a good cook?"

"No, she's a great cook!" George said proudly.

"Then invite me to dinner in exchange for the car." Seeing George about to protest he added, "I'm never going back home for another dinner with my mother, and I need to eat somewhere. Besides, I can't drive two cars at once."

"You could sell one of them."

"Tell you what – if it makes you feel any better I'll sell it to you instead of giving it to you. Deal?"

"Depends. What do you want for it?"

"One home cooked dinner from a 'great' cook, plus whatever you paid for a ticket to New Jersey which you are going to cash in right now, plus a well-worded letter. Have we got a deal?"

George grinned, simultaneously shaking his head in amazement and extending his hand toward Joe. "We have a deal. Something tells me it was a very fortunate coincidence that I chose to sit opposite you and that I noticed your shoes were untied. I don't usually feel comfortable striking up conversations with complete strangers, but it seemed like the right thing to do with you. It felt like I was supposed to do that."

"I think we were both in the right place at the right time," Joe responded. "Come on, let's go cash in that ticket and go get your car. Then you can write that letter for me."

Joe spent the next two days with George and his wife, Margie in their tiny basement flat while George carefully drafted the letter of explanation and apology to Madelyn. Their cramped little place was in one of the poorer sections of the downtown area, the best they could afford after George lost his job at the bank.

"I'll be looking for a better place once I get back on my feet," George said apologetically. "I don't want Margie living here after the baby comes." He peered up through the narrow window slat at the grey boarded up store fronts and litter strewn sidewalks that were his only view, sighing heavily. This is no place anybody should have to live. It makes me feel like a failure."

"If I could find you a nice place, in a nice neighborhood, that you could afford right now...would you be interested?" Joe asked.

"Maybe later -- after I get a couple of paychecks. We're paid up here until the end of the month."

"What if the first month is rent free?"

"You know of a place like that?"

Joe nodded. "The building where I live. The landlord is offering the first month free if you sign a lease guaranteeing you will stay for the next eleven months."

"How much is the rent?"

"Thirty six dollars a month for four rooms and a bath. The kitchen has a gas stove and one of those new refrigerators. And you don't have to share a bathroom. You would even have a separate room for the baby," Joe added, briefly glancing at Margie's abdomen.

"Sounds nice, but it might be a bit steep for me. I'm only going to be making thirty dollars a week at the bank. That's more than I've been making with the bandage company, but still…"

"You wouldn't have to pay for any extras. The heat and water and electricity are all included."

"They're included here too. So is the furniture. For thirty dollars."

"I forgot to mention, the furniture is included in the *nice, safe place with real windows to look out of, a bathroom you don't have to share, and an extra room for the baby,* too. All for six more dollars a month." Joe smiled winningly, looking first at George, then at Margie. "It will cost you about forty dollars a month for food, ten for gas for the car, leaving you with more than a full week's pay to cover clothes and things you will need for the baby. Why, you might even be able to start a savings account in the bank where you will be working. You need a better place than this for your wife and baby, and you *can* afford it," he added convincingly.

Two days later George and Margie moved into their spacious ground floor apartment in his mother's building. Josephine had balked at first about furnishing it, and even more about foregoing the first month's rent, but in the end Joe's power of persuasion had prevailed. He was invited to stay in the spare room until the baby arrived, but he declined the offer saying he wanted to get out on the road and start selling those bandages. His intention was to open up a new sales territory; one that would take him farther west, closer to Madelyn. He took the letter George had written for him to the post office himself, kissing it for luck before dropping it in the slot. Then, after making arrangements with George to stay in touch, he told Margie how much he would miss her wonderful cooking, and set out in his new car for another adventure.

AUGUST, 1932

JOE WAS A DAY AHEAD OF SCHEDULE, BUT HE DECIDED TO TAKE a chance anyway. He pulled up in front of the Post office in Indianapolis before looking for a rooming house where he could stay for the week he planned to be in the city. There was no letter for him from George in the General Delivery file, but the clerk gave him a lead on a rooming house that served good food, so Joe, though disappointed, felt it hadn't been a waste of time.

Joe had bypassed New York, Pennsylvania and Ohio on his trip west on the chance that those states might have already had salesmen there working for the bandage company. Or so he told himself. In reality though, they were simply too far removed from South Dakota which was where he told George he was eventually headed, after making sales calls in major cities beginning with Indianapolis.

The rooming house lived up to expectations as far as the food was concerned, but when he climbed into bed that night Joe's nose told him that the bedding probably hadn't been changed after the last guest had used it. That was the main thing that bothered him about traveling. Most places, he found, would change the sheets for new roomers. But there were always some that didn't unless the sheets had been used for at least a week. Not wanting to make a fuss, especially after the mistress of the house served him an extra slice of gingerbread topped with thick cream, Joe pulled the sheets from the bed, turned them to the unused side then placed them back on the bed. They didn't actually smell any nicer, but he felt better about having the clean side touching him. At least he hoped it was a clean side.

The following day, after calling on all the hospitals in the city and writing orders for bandages in every one of them, Joe again inquired about mail for him at the Post Office. He left disappointed that day, and the next, and the next. On the fourth day he mailed a letter to George asking whether or not there had been any response from Madelyn, and three days later received a thin letter from George. He opened it before he left the Post Office, eager to hear any news, one way or the other.

George had written that he and Margie were enjoying living in their new apartment, truly grateful for the car especially since the baby would soon be arriving, and that his job was going well. He also wrote that he had forgotten to mention that Joe should be collecting a deposit of five percent of the bandage orders as part of his commission, and the company would pay him another two percent once the bandages had been delivered and paid for. Joe grinned at that. He had been collecting a ten percent deposit so he would have to tell the company it needn't bother sending him a check. The news about Madelyn was at the bottom of the letter, almost as a postscript.

Haven't heard back from Madelyn as yet. You mentioned that she would be teaching at her old school again in September so maybe she isn't back from the theater tour and hasn't received the letter yet. If I haven't heard back from her by the end of the month, I'll write another letter. I'll write as many letters for you as necessary to get your desired result. That is my solemn promise my friend for all you have done for me. Warm regards, George

With mixed emotions – disappointment at there being no word from Madelyn, combined with a warm feeling for his newfound friend, Joe decided it was time for him to move on to his next destination.

Joe arrived in Sioux Falls, South Dakota too late to check for mail at the post office. He had passed a seedy looking rooming house on his way into town, but decided to look for some place to stay that was a bit less rundown. He found what he was looking for on the main street, two blocks past the post office. It was a homey looking two story house with a Guests Welcome sign by the front steps and with a pleasant looking little café on one side, and a movie theater two doors down across the street.

At ten dollars a week, the room and board was double what Joe was used to paying. He hesitated at first, considering whether he ought to find another place or sign the register and hand over the money, but the enticing aroma of the supper that was being served in the dining room made up his mind for him. He was invited to sit at the table before he was shown his room and he was only too happy to do so. It was six hours since he had last eaten and he was famished.

Joe took a seat across from a blowsy looking young woman. He smiled and nodded at her, greeted the three men who were also seated at the table, then asked for the one next to him to please pass the potatoes. He was more interested in the platter of pork chops, the applesauce, yams, sweet peas and cornbread than he was in the woman. It soon became apparent to Joe, however, that she was more interested in him than in the food.

"You didn't tell us your name," she said coyly.

"It's Joe," he said, a mouthful of mashed potatoes muffling his speech. Swallowing, he repeated, "Joe Tessier."

"Well, hello Joe Tessier. We are all on a first name basis here. I'm Margaret, and these gentlemen are Henry, Edward and Harold," she informed him, pointing to each man in turn.

The three men merely acknowledged the introduction by raising their forks from their plates, obviously more interested in the delicious abundance in front of them than they were in making Joe's acquaintance.

"Pleased to meet all of you," Joe responded, cutting into a pork-chop.

"Are you just passing through or do you plan to stay a while?" Margaret inquired.

"I'll be here for about a week then I'll be moving on."

"So, you're a traveling salesman?"

"Yes."

"Lots of those around these days. What do you sell?"

"Bandages," Joe said, not looking up from his plate.

"Bandages! That's a new one. What kind of bandages?"

"The kind that doctors and hospitals use for their patients," Joe said rather irritably.

"No need to get your nose out of joint," Margaret said affably. "I'm just trying to make polite conversation over dinner. I'm not trying to pry into your life."

Joe set his fork on the side of his plate then looked over at Margaret. "Sorry," he said apologetically. "I've had a long day. I'm tired and hungry; but that's no excuse to be unsociable, is it?" He smiled at her.

"Well, that's better." She eyed Joe speculatively. "Maybe you'd like to ask a girl to the movies after your supper settles some."

Joe took in Margaret's disheveled straw colored hair that matched the color of her teeth. Her bright red lips seemed to be running into the grooves at the corners of her mouth, and her painted nails made her hands look like blood-tipped talons. He shuddered inside, hoping his distaste didn't show on the outside. "I won't be able to do anything but pass out tonight."

"Maybe another time then," she said flirtatiously.

"Probably not a good idea," he said with a slight chuckle. "I already have a girl I'm engaged to marry over in the Black Hills area and I doubt she'd take too kindly to my stepping out with another young lady." Joe smiled charmingly.

"Oh, so that's how it is. The handsome ones always seem to be taken," she sighed dejectedly, glancing over at the other three men.

Joe was relieved to see that Margaret abruptly lost interest in him and began tucking into her supper with relish. Then, out of the corner of his eye, he saw the unmistakable look of mirth on the faces of Henry, Edward and Harold, barely disguised as they gnawed vigorously, in tandem, on pork chop bones.

Two days later there was a thick letter from George waiting for him at the post office. He ripped it open eagerly then took a deep breath before pulling the contents from the envelope. Joe read the brief message from George before opening the envelope with the letter George had received from Madelyn. It read:

Dear Joe,

Sorry it's not better news. But give it some time and don't give up. George

With hands trembling slightly, Joe slipped Madelyn's letter to George out of its envelope already aware that he would not like what it said. Taking another deep, fortifying breath, he began to read the words that brought tears to his eyes and an agonizing pain around his heart.

Dear Mr. Miller,

My heart is filled with gratitude for your explanation of the unfortunate event that took place concerning Mr. Joseph Tessier. I can see now that there was a misunderstanding on my part as well as on the part of Mr. Tessier's mother.

Please advise Mr. Tessier that I accept his apology, and that of his mother, and bear no grudge over the embarrassment the incident caused.

Please also advise Mr. Tessier that he need not waste his time pursuing any further contact with me. His former marriage and divorce are irreconcilable obstacles to our further association.

Yours truly,
Madelyn Dubois

Joe read the letter over three times, but the feeling was always the same. Her words '*My heart is filled with gratitude*' lifted his spirits, only to be dashed to the ground by the words '*irreconcilable obstacles*'. He drove slowly out into the countryside, abruptly pulling onto a side road, then parking as a searing pain began between his shoulder blades, then settled in his chest. His eyes filled with tears and he gasped from the overwhelming pain. His last thought before losing consciousness was how much it hurt to have his heart broken by the only woman he would ever love.

Joe never realized that he had suffered a mild heart attack. When he came to a few minutes later, belching loudly, he thought he'd had a severe bout of indigestion from the corned beef and cabbage he'd had for his noon meal at a local diner. That, and Madelyn's devastating assertion of '*irreconcilable obstacles*' , he told himself, were the combined reasons for his distress.

When Joe returned to the rooming house that evening, Margaret once again made overtures toward him as she watched him listlessly picking at his supper. She whispered in his ear that she has a little something stashed away in her room that ought to perk him up, but the stale odor of cigarettes and whisky that wafted from her waxy red lips repelled him to the point of extreme nausea. He made a hasty departure just in time to avoid ruining everyone's meal.

Joe spent the last four days of his week at the rooming house lazing around in his room, telling anyone who inquired that he had a touch of something that might be contagious so they would keep their distance. His meals were brought to him on a tray, which he then used as a desk on which he composed long letters to George and his sister, Anna Marie. He was counting on the two of them, he wrote, to help him come up with some ideas he could use to win Madelyn back.

He deposited his letters at the post office on his way to his next destination. He planned to zig-zag north and south through the Dakotas, bearing further westward and drawing nearer and nearer to the Black Hills – and Madelyn. He was in constant touch with George, both posting and receiving letters twice a week. He congratulated his friend on becoming the father of a baby girl he and Margie named Georgette, related amusing anecdotes about events along the way, and thoroughly enjoyed being a bandage salesman; especially the ever thickening wad of bills tucked into his right sock. But in early October, on his second day in Rapid City, South Dakota, he received a letter from George that dashed all his expectations of seeing Madelyn once again.

You need to lose yourself, George had written. *The bandage company wrote to me asking if I knew your whereabouts. The company was sold more than a month ago and the product line has changed. They are not honoring your orders, and they are tracking you as the orders come in. So, you must cease and desist taking orders and deposits for those bandages immediately! And if you don't make restitution to all the doctors and hospitals you have contacted over the last month, you will have the law after you for theft, fraud, or whatever other charges they can think up.*

Joe lost no time getting out of Rapid City. He returned to the rooming house where he had been staying, packed up his belongings and hit the road heading south. He drove all day, stopping only for gas and a bite to eat before realizing that he was carrying around some damning evidence of his larceny on the seat beside him. Pulling off the highway onto a rutted dirt road, he drove for several miles until he reached a wooded area and a secluded spot he could drive into and be hidden from anyone passing by. He carried the sample case of bandages deep into the woods and was about to toss it into a small stream when he had a second thought. It was a fine leather case, very professional looking, with no identifying labeling. It wasn't the case that could indict him, Joe decided; it was the bandages and the order forms and letterhead stationery.

Sitting on a large rock beside the stream, Joe removed his shoes and socks, stuffed the socks safely inside his shoes, then rolled up his pant legs and waded out into the stream with the sample case. One by one he tossed the bandages into the water, regretfully watching them drift away. He hated to waste anything that might one day be useful. He tore the stacks of order forms and letterhead in half, tossing them as far as he could into the center of the stream, before climbing back out of the water onto the bank. He dried his feet as best he could by wiping them on the grassy bank before replacing his shoes and returning to his car.

Joe slept in his car that night just outside a small town in northern Colorado. Then, early the next morning he was frantically hunting for a drugstore and some calamine lotion.

"Looks like poison ivy or maybe oak; likely a few stinging nettles too," the elderly druggist said, looking at Joe's red, blistered left foot. "Got it on your other foot too?" he asked, not waiting for an answer. "Better not touch it, else you'll spread it anywhere else you touch yourself if you get my drift." He placed a bag of Epsom salts and a bottle of calamine lotion on the counter with the instructions, "Soak your feet and any other parts you might have already infected with the salts to get some of the poison out. Then use a wad of gauze or a bandage to apply the lotion. Don't use your bare hand."

'I knew I was going to regret throwing away those bandages,' was Joe's first thought. *'Now that I need them to apply the lotion, I don't have them. Of course, if I hadn't thrown them away in the first place I might not have needed them to apply the lotion because I would have used them to dry off my feet instead of having to rub my feet dry in poisonous weeds.'* Joe decided there was no point in going down the *'if'* road. He had to find a place where he could soak his feet before the itching drove him mad.

He found a service station that had a washroom, and asked if there was a clean bucket he could borrow. After filling the bucket half full of water at the sink, he stirred half the salts into the water with his hand, then perched on the toilet and placed his left foot in the water while carefully rolling down the sock on his right foot. He wasn't sure if the wad of bills that had encircled his ankle would have picked up the poison, but he wasn't taking any chances. He carefully folded over the top of the sock before placing it in his jacket pocket.

Joe was perched on the toilet seat, trying to fit his right foot into the bucket along with his left one, when he was interrupted by someone banging on the washroom door. "Just a minute!" he hollered. Scooting over to the door by dragging the bucket with one foot still inside, Joe opened the door to see a burly, middle-aged man with a greying, unkempt, tobacco juice stained beard and a yellow-toothed grin confronting him. The man took up the entire doorway, and for a brief moment Joe experienced a fearful rush of adrenalin that left him feeling nauseous.

"Just wondering how you're making out?" the man asked congenially. He turned his head to spit out a stream of tobacco juice between his front teeth. "Fella that works for me said you got yourself into some poison ivy and you were in here soaking your feet in a bucket he lent you. Wanted to let you know I've got some calamine lotion if you need some, and a clean rag for you to use to put it on." The man's beady eyes surveyed the tiny room.

Joe smiled his thanks. "I picked up some Epsom salts and calamine lotion at the drug store, but thanks for the offer. I guess I could use one of those clean rags though. Is it okay if I use your facilities until I'm finished soaking my feet?"

"Take your time," the man replied unctuously." I'll just go fetch you a rag." Leaving the door open, he quickly disappeared around the corner of the building.

The uneasy feeling prompted by the appearance and demeanor of the man spurred Joe to move faster than he had ever moved before. In a flash he had pulled his left foot from the bucket, gathered up his shoes and the bag of Epsom salts, and dashed in his bare feet over to his car. In his rear view mirror he saw the man standing there looking after him with a rag in one hand and scratching his head with his other hand. He didn't know if the man had only wanted to be helpful or had meant him harm. And he didn't want to find out which way it was. He'd find his own rag.

Stopping a few miles down the road, Joe applied the calamine lotion to his left foot then wrapped the lotion soaked rag around his right foot, wishing again that he still had those bandages. *'Why is it you always seem to need something just as soon as you throw it away and can't get it back?'* Joe wondered to himself. He drove on until he reached the northern edge of Denver, the crisp early evening air making him shiver. Making one last stop on the side of the road, Joe pulled some cotton socks onto his cold, itchy feet then slipped them into his shoes. He knew he had to look as presentable as possible when applying for a room at a decent boarding establishment.

Once in his room, Joe wasted no time attending to his feet. Then he attended to the bills rolled up inside the sock in his pocket. With clean socks covering his hands, he bathed the money in an Epsom salts bath, scrubbing each bill between his knuckles just as he had seen his mother do countless times on his father's shirt collars. He lay the bills one by one on a towel, then rolled them up inside, pressing firmly. When he unrolled the towel, the money felt almost dry and was only slightly faded and old looking. By morning, it was dry enough to tie inside another sock that he wrapped around his ankle before pulling another sock on over it, slipping into his shoes, and appearing at the breakfast table in the dining room along with the other boarders.

Joe decided it was high time he got on with things. Although he had enjoyed working for the bandage company, he knew it was the selling he enjoyed, not the company job. He was determined to make his own way again, and when the time was right, when the coast was clear, he would be returning to sweep Madelyn off her feet as a self-made man who could offer her the world at her feet; a world and a life so wonderful she would not refuse to share it with him. Joe dreamed on; his dreams and his plans his constant, comforting travel companions.

OCTOBER, 1932

JOE HAD THE BACK SEAT OF HIS CAR FILLED ALMOST SOLID with '*finds*' from in and around the perimeter back alleys and manufacturing districts of Denver. He knew he couldn't comfortably fit anything more in the car, and that knowledge was troubling for him. Either he would have to discard some of the old stuff in favor of new stuff, or he would have to stop looking for any more stuff. And, he had yet to find the one thing that would be the inspiration for a new venture.

He headed south out of Denver, and on a whim turned off the main road to drive through the countryside dotted with small, un-prosperous looking farms. It was along that road, right at a farm gate that separated the road from the dusty, rutted lane that led up to a seedy little timber house setting askew on its foundation, that Joe saw the little trailer with a '*For Sale*' sign tacked to the bumper. He pulled over to the side of the road and looked the trailer over from that vantage point, then got out of his car and walked over to the trailer for a closer look.

It was framed out of wood, with rusty tin roofing tacked all over it. It was nearly the width and length of Joe's car, and had padlocked double doors on the back end. Joe was bent down, checking out the axle and threadbare tires, when out of the corner of his eye he saw a frail looking elderly man approaching him at a leisurely pace. The man cleared his throat and spat before asking, "You looking for a trailer?"

"Didn't know I was until I came upon this one," Joe said affably. "Might be, might not. Depends on what you want for it. Got a key for that padlock so I can take a look inside?"

The man plunged an index finger into a small pocket on the bib of his overalls, withdrawing a key. He handed it to Joe. "Made the trailer myself about a decade ago from lumber I cut off this place and an old wrecked car," he said proudly. "The tin's rusted some now, but it still keeps the rain out. Most of it anyhow. There's a few pinholes, but some tar will fix that. Don't happen to have any tar, or I would of done it myself." He paused as Joe crawled inside the trailer for a closer look. "Used to haul stuff for other folks in it, but there ain't no one wanting stuff hauled any more these days around here. So that's why I'm wanting to sell it – in case you're wondering. Ain't nothing wrong with it at all, just have no need of it anymore."

"How much you want for it?"

The man glanced quickly over at Joe's new car, then back at the young man standing before him wearing a suit and tie. "I'm thinking sixty dollars would be a fair price."

"Oh. I was thinking of offering twenty-five or maybe going as high as thirty. I wasn't even thinking of buying a trailer until I happened to see this one for sale. But, I thought I could maybe find a use for one, for the right price. Sixty dollars though is way too much for me, seeing as how I'd need to get new tires less than a hundred miles down the road," Joe said, kicking one of the bald tires.

Thinking he was about to lose the only prospect he'd had for the trailer, the man proposed a deal. "How about if we split the difference fifty-fifty between what I'm asking and what you are offering. That would be just forty-five dollars." The man gave Joe a tentative smile.

Joe pretended to think it over. That trailer would be the answer to his problems and he knew that one way or the other he wasn't going to leave without it. He also knew the man was asking a price he thought he could get from someone that looked like a rich city slicker, but he figured the poor old guy was desperate and needed as much as possible for it. Joe thought he would probably be lucky to get $25 for the trailer – if that much – but he decided he would rather leave the man feeling like he was a champion bargainer than a loser, even if it meant he would be paying too much. So he surprised the old man by saying, "If you'll throw in a trailer hitch, you've got a deal. Forty five dollars it is." He extended his hand to shake on it.

The old man extended his hand to Joe with an ecstatic toothless grin and the deal was sealed. He walked much faster away from Joe to go fetch a trailer hitch than he had walked when he first approached Joe. While he was gone, Joe went back to his car and removed forty-five dollars from his right sock. Once the hitch and the trailer were attached to the back of Joe's car, the two amicably parted company, each in his own way thinking it had been his lucky day.

Joe decided he'd better get back on the main road in case he suddenly found himself hauling a limping trailer. He knew it was truly his lucky day when the road he turned down that connected to the main highway passed right by the back alley of some kind of manufacturing plant. Pulling over to the side of the road, he saw two men pushing a trolley stacked with boxes over to a pile of other boxes, where they unloaded them. He figured he'd better wait a while to see if the men returned with more boxes. He was glad he did; the men returned a few minutes later with another load of boxes, then again with two more loads. Joe waited twenty minutes after the last load before deciding it would be safe to go take a look at the contents of those boxes.

As he pulled his car and trailer up alongside the piled boxes, Joe could see that they were stacked behind a sign that read BURN PILE in big block letters. More curious than ever, he pulled off the sealing tape on one of the boxes, revealing the spines of a set of twelve books. He pried one out of the middle of the box, studying the cover before opening the book and running his fingers along the glossy, printed pages. Encyclopedias. World Knowledge Encyclopedias was printed on the front of the books. Joe didn't know why the books were scheduled to be burned but he didn't care. He lost no time in loading as many of the boxes he could fit in the trailer, then when that was full, loading a few more on the floor and on the passenger seat of his car. He regretted having to leave more than a dozen boxes behind, but knew there was no way he could take them all.

Twenty or so miles down the main highway, Joe pulled into a service station with two flat tires on the trailer. The gas pumps were in front of a cozy looking diner, and there was a garage on the side with some tires displayed. That's where Joe first discovered what a lucky find those boxes of encyclopedias were, and that he was indeed the consummate salesman he believed himself to be. He left with two new tires on his trailer, a full tank of gas, a belly full of chicken and dumplings and the best chocolate cream pie he had ever tasted, plus twenty dollars in cash. What he left behind was two flat tires and a box filled with all the knowledge in the world in the hands of a man in greasy overalls and a two day beard who had never learned to read.

One week later, Joe arrived in Albuquerque, New Mexico. He had sold two more sets of encyclopedias along the way, which put another hundred and fifty dollars in the sock on his right foot. Since he was accustomed to living on about twenty dollars a week, including the gas for his car, he decided he wouldn't sell more than one set of encyclopedias a week. That way, they would serve as income for a long time to come, give him a lot of free time to explore, and still make it possible for him to live high, wide and handsome if he so desired.

He found a respectable looking boarding house near the center of town. The room and board was a dollar a day; a bit more than he had been used to paying but the bedding was clean and smelled of soap and a fragrant breeze. He found he had to be cautious with the food though. Some of the dishes served set his mouth on fire, then his stomach, and the next day he felt as if his rear end was on fire as well. Talking about it with one of the other boarders, Joe remarked that the fire never seemed to go out of the food. The man had laughed and called him a tenderfoot gringo. The food is what made him move to another boarding house further away from the town center. There, he found the food more to his liking. Plus, the room and board was the five dollars a week he was accustomed to paying. His bed, however sagged in the middle, and the sheets were heavily starched and scratchy. Joe wondered if it would ever be possible to find a place where everything was to his liking.

He spent three days exploring the alleyways behind the stores in the town center, but found nothing he could use there. Chagrined by the lack of 'finds' in those alleys, he concentrated on the back lots of the commercial properties on the outskirts of town. When there was nothing of interest there either, he made his daily check at the post office and came up empty there as well. Deciding he'd had enough of New Mexico, Joe posted a quick note to George saying he was moving on to Texas and that he'd let him know where he was staying as soon as he got settled in. Trying to stay in one location long enough to receive mail from his friend was proving to be a real bother, especially since it looked as if anything worth scavenging had already been scavenged before he got there. He hoped there would be better pickings in Texas.

Joe loved Dallas. There were still some prosperous areas that hadn't been too badly affected yet by what they were calling a 'depression,' especially in big oil country. He found all manner of castoffs he felt would be useful, but lacked any place to stow them. So, in order to make room, he changed his mind about only selling one set of encyclopedias a week and he headed out into the countryside where the newly rich landowners lived. He sold five sets of encyclopedias his first day out, then beat that record by selling seven sets the following day. The space freed up in the trailer by unloading those dozen boxes of books gave him ample room to stow several bolt-ends of fabric he had found discarded behind a notions shop in the high end area of the city. There were remnants of silks, satins, brocades and velvets along with some vibrantly printed woven cottons. Joe had always found ribbon and fabric to be of use, and he never passed up a chance to add to his stockpile whenever possible.

Joe let George Miller know that he planned to spend the winter in Dallas. He felt that staying in one place for a while would be advantageous, especially since he had found a great rooming house, with friendly long time roomers and great food. For six dollars a week, Joe had a comfortable bed, a hearty breakfast and supper daily and his clothes freshly washed and ironed for him. His fellow roommates were avid Rummy and Pinochle players, games that were right up his alley. There was even a shy young lady to keep him company at the movies.

Her name was Rebecca. She was barely five feet tall and could have passed for a twelve year old boy had it not been for her long curly blonde hair and shockingly pink cherub lips. She was not at all Joe's type, but he considered that a good thing. He enjoyed her company at the movies, and the occasional night out dancing, but wasn't looking for anything more than that. He kicked himself later for not realizing that Rebecca had other notions about their seeing so much of one another. To her, they were courting.

When Joe finally received a letter from George telling him that he had given Madelyn his address in Dallas, and that she had said Joe could expect to receive a letter from her soon, he stopped paying any attention to Rebecca. She tearfully confronted him on the front steps of the rooming house, and when he explained to her that he liked her as a friend, but nothing more, she flew at him, fists pounding into his chest, painted lips, tears and snot smearing the front of his pristine white shirt. He pushed her away from him, shouting in disgust, asking her how she could have imagined him to be romantically interested in her. "I never even kissed you on the cheek! I didn't so much as hold your hand unless we were dancing!" Joe loudly asserted.

"I thought you were just treating me with respect!" Rebecca bawled. "I thought you were being a gentleman!"

"I *was* being a gentleman! And I *was* treating you with respect! But I didn't know you would take that to mean I was falling for you." Joe lowered his voice and assumed a posture of abject apology. "I'm sorry if you misunderstood," he explained. "I'm in love with someone else and I have been for several years. Right now she doesn't return that love, but I'm doing everything possible to change that because I know in my heart she is the only woman for me. And I know how you feel right now, because I have experienced the same thing. But for me you were a delightful friend, someone to pass the time with; nothing more. I'm sorry, I truly am. I never expected you to think there was anything more than that between us."

Joe couldn't decide if Rebecca was being contrite or sullen when she responded, "Which one of us is going to move to another rooming-house? You, or me?"

"I guess it should be me, if it has to be one of us," Joe conceded.

"Yes. I'm thinking it should be you too," she concurred. "And the sooner the better."

"Okay, if that's how it's got to be. I'm paid up here for the next three days so I'll be staying until the week runs out. But meanwhile," he quickly added, seeing the angry look on Rebecca's face, "I'll be looking for another place. So don't figure on seeing much of me."

"The less I see of you the better," she said haughtily, then disappeared inside the front door, leaving Joe shrugging his shoulders, wondering if he would ever understand women.

Joe had no trouble locating another suitable rooming house. The food was just as good, the whole place was just as clean, and the price for the week, including laundry was the same. The only difference was there were no female boarders, and the men staying there were mostly pipe smoking, cribbage playing, dyspeptic widowers with flatulence afflictions and an indifferent attitude about when or where they relieved themselves. Joe was still young enough to find that amusing, even adding his own unapologetic musical toots to the aromatic mix himself from time to time. But, he also figured that was the reason for the absence of any female boarders, and it was that absence that made the place almost unbearable after a while.

That all changed for him the day he went to the post office in Dallas, and there in General Delivery was a scented, ivory colored envelope for him with Madelyn's return address in the upper left-hand corner. He literally skipped out the post office door and down the steps, grinning from ear to ear and almost colliding with a young woman pushing a baby carriage. "Sorry!" he sang out, tipping his hat to her and giving her a big smile.

Catching his exuberant mood, the woman smiled back at him. "You must have gotten some good news. Not much of that around these days, so congratulations."

"I got a letter from my sweetheart. Haven't heard from her in a long time."

"Doesn't look like you even opened it yet," the woman said, eying the envelope in Joe's hand. "How do you know if it's good news?"

Joe's smile faded as he looked at the letter in his hand. "I guess I don't," he said in amazement. "Do you think it could be bad news?"

"You say it's been a long time since you heard from her, so I think you won't know if it's good news or bad news until you open it."

"I don't think I could stand it if it's bad news," Joe said, paling slightly. "You see, I am so in love with this woman I can hardly see straight." He held the envelope up toward the sun, trying to see the words written inside.

"Ohhhh!" the young woman crooned, placing her hand over her heart. "What a lucky girl to have such a handsome man so in love with her." She thought a moment before adding, "Would it be better for you if you had someone with you when you open the letter? Just in case? I wouldn't mind doing that for you if it would make you feel better."

Joe looked intently at the woman. Even though she was a mother, she appeared to be more girl than woman, Joe thought. He figured she couldn't be more than nineteen and was still carrying most of the weight she had gained during pregnancy, though she hid it well under her long grey coat. Her strikingly pretty face was framed by a blue kerchief tied in a knot under her chin, making Joe think of a statue of the Madonna in the church back in St. Onge. Tendrils of honey brown hair, the same color as Madelyn's, graced her forehead as she smiled up at him. Joe's impulse was to scoop her up in his arms and hold her close, but fortunately he managed to keep his senses, merely saying, "You would do that for me? Stay with me while I open the letter?"

"Yes."

"Will you come have a cup of coffee with me while I read it?"

"Sure, why not."

It wasn't until they were seated at a table in a small diner that Joe thought to say, "By the way, my name is Joe. What's yours?"

"Catherine."

"Would you like something to eat with your cup of coffee? I'll order us both coffee and doughnuts," he said, not waiting for an answer. He waited until the waitress had brought them refills before taking the letter out of his pocket, holding it in both hands in front of him.

"For the love of Pete, open it! Catherine hissed. "I have to be getting back home. My son will be wanting to eat soon and I can't feed him here. Besides, the suspense is turning my milk sour!"

"Oh!" Joe exclaimed, blushing. "Right."

Running the tip of his index finger under the flap, Joe carefully unsealed the envelope and slipped out the letter. He unfolded it, looking at Catherine before letting his eyes fall to read the words written on the scented paper. Taking a deep breath, he intoned "Dear Mr. Tessier" then paused. "Oh, that doesn't sound good, does it?" he said, looking up at Catherine. "That sounds too formal to be a love letter…or even a friendly letter, don't you think? Here…you read it for me, please," Joe begged, passing the letter to Catherine across the table.

Catherine read the letter silently to herself, studying it carefully to see if it contained anything that would be upsetting for Joe to hear. But, not knowing any of the circumstances, she had no idea what some of the things Madelyn spoke about referred to, and as a result was at a loss to determine whether the letter offered some hope to Joe or was intended to dismiss him from her life forevermore. When she had finished the letter, she looked helplessly over at Joe, giving him a puzzled frown. "She doesn't sound as if she's angry with you, but she doesn't sound as if she's in love with you either. She mentions an 'irreconcilable obstacle.' Do you know what that's about?"

"Yes," Joe said. "Unfortunately I do." Without giving it another thought, he told the young woman sitting across from him what the irreconcilable obstacle was all about. "I was married before and I am legally divorced.

But Madelyn and I are both Catholics, and our religion doesn't recognize the legality of divorce. Therefore, I am considered to be still married to the shrew who tricked me into marrying her in the first place, and according to my church can never be married again or I will be excommunicated and so would Madelyn if she married me in a civil ceremony. How's that for an 'irreconcilable obstacle'?"

"Wow," Catherine exclaimed. "I never met anyone who was divorced. How did you get tricked into getting married?"

"She was…with child."

"She didn't get that way all by herself, huh? So you did the right thing and married her."

"I guess so."

"You have a kid, huh? Boy or girl?"

"Had. Had a little girl. She died when she was about five months old. Found her one morning with her blanket wrapped around her neck and covering her face." Joe stared into space, unseeing as he continued. "Neither her mother nor I wanted to go to her when she started crying, so we let her cry it out and thought she had cried herself to sleep. But in the morning we knew she must have been thrashing around and somehow smothered herself. She was still…and cold. She was always a very fussy baby and I used to get out of the house as much as possible so I wouldn't have to hear her constant crying. But right then I would have given anything to hear her screaming. I left my wife right after that. There was no longer any reason to stay with her. I suppose if our baby hadn't died we would still be living miserably together, but I was able to get her out of my life by deserting her for three years."

"That's what you had to do to get a divorce?"

"Yes. And it was during that time I met Madelyn…and fell in love with her at first sight. That was five years ago," Joe said, his eyes suddenly filling with tears that threatened to spill over. "And even though I have seen very little of her in all those years, she is in my mind constantly. She is the only woman I have ever loved...the only one I ever will."

Seeing Joe's eyes fill with tears, Catherine's eyes filled as well then spilled over , splashing onto the letter from Madelyn she still held in her hand. "Sorry," she said wiping at the teardrops, then handing the letter to Joe. She sniffed back the mucous forming in her nose, looking embarrassed.

"No, I'm the one who should be sorry. I had no right to involve a perfect stranger...a perfectly wonderful, sympathetic stranger...with my problems and get her all upset. I had no right to do that."

"No, you didn't. But I had no business letting you do so either." She looked searchingly at Joe before adding, "I think you have more you need to tell me though so you can get past this setback. And I know for sure there is more I want to hear now that you have dragged me into the middle of things."

"You don't have to do anything more. I appreciate your listening to my problems, but you don't need to involve yourself further."

"Well, *you* don't seem to understand!" Catherine said heatedly. You have told me just enough of your story to make me *need* to hear more. I want to know how the story comes out. You see...you have confided in a hopeless romantic here," she said, thumping her chest, "and now you aren't going to get rid of me until I learn how this whole thing between you and Madelyn plays out!"

At Catherine's insistence, Joe escorted her and her baby down the block and around the corner to a small general store that sold everything from newspapers and light-bulbs, to canned milk and kerosene. On the way there, she learned that Joe was a traveling salesman, currently staying in Dallas for the winter. Catherine's husband, Marty, looked suspiciously at Joe when he was introduced, but relaxed when Catherine said, "You two can talk business while I feed and change the baby. He's looking for a new place to stay," she informed her husband while giving Joe a hard look that warned him not to dispute that.

Marty held his hand out to Joe. "I hadn't expected to find a boarder so soon. Cathy and I just talked about the idea a couple of days ago, to help out with expenses, you know, now that we have a little one to look after. How did the two of you happen to meet?"

"I ran into her," Joe said sheepishly. "Literally. I was running down the post office steps just as she was passing by pushing the carriage, and I nearly knocked her over. I apologized, and told her I was in a hurry to see about a rooming house because I really wanted to get out of the stodgy place I'd been staying. It's more like an old- folks- home than anything, and I was looking for a quiet place with younger people."

"Well, there wouldn't be many people...just my wife and me...and it's pretty quiet except for the baby at times. But he's a pretty good baby... doesn't cry all that much, except at night. Has his days and nights mixed up, I guess. Other than that, your room would be upstairs over the store here, and there aren't a whole lot of customers any more so that shouldn't be a bother."

"Why aren't there many customers anymore?" Joe asked, looking around the store. "Looks like you sell the kind of stuff folks need on a regular basis."

"It's the hard times mostly. Folks can't buy stuff 'cause they don't have any money. All they can do is try to grow stuff or find stuff to barter with so they can get what they need."

"Then why don't you barter with them?"

"Well, I have to buy the things I have stocked in my store, so if I barter for food or things for our baby, where will I get the money to buy more of the things that people need?"

"I see you've given the idea some thought," Joe said. "But maybe with another mind thinking about it...namely mine...there could be a way to make it work for you."

"I hope you're not thinking about bartering your 'idea' for room and board," Marty said pointedly. "Because that's not going to happen. Cathy and I talked about a dollar a day for a room and three meals. Your bedding will be changed and your room swept and dusted once a week, plus you can have a Saturday night bath. You will have to take care of your own personal laundry. There's a laundress about two blocks down."

"Is there a place out in back of the store where I can park my car?"

"You have a car?"

"Yes. And I have a trailer too."

"You some kind of salesman or something?"

"Or something. Maybe you'll get a chance to see. I'll be taking the room."

Joe only planned to spend the winter of '32 / '33 in Dallas, but wound up staying until May of 1934. He spent most of that time running the bartering operation he had set up with his newfound friends, Catherine and Marty Edmond, only occasionally selling a set of encyclopedias when the opportunity presented itself.

Joe referred to himself as a 'Bartering Broker', matching people up according to their needs for a small fee. It didn't take long for him to become well-known in an ever widening area, attracting almost more new participants than he could handle. The business required a good deal of bookkeeping and cross referencing, and that's where Marty came in. The two of them shared the profits equally, enabling Marty to continue to stock the store for the increased volume of customers that visited his store, and for Joe to continually add to the wad of bills in the sock on his right foot.

Catherine not only learned every detail about Joe's unrequited love affair with Madelyn, she also helped him craft increasingly fond letters to her that resulted in return letters from Madelyn, on a regular basis, sounding increasingly friendly with each new letter. At Catherine's urging, after more than a year of regular correspondence, Joe wrote to Madelyn that since they had become such good long-distance pals, he thought it appropriate to come up with a pet name for her. And the name he came up with was… *Pet!* Then he proceeded to write *Pet* across an entire line of the letter. He could fit the tiny word in nine times across the page, grinning with satisfaction as he finished the line. When he mailed off that letter he knew that Madelyn's response might be the most important letter he would ever receive from her. It could be the end… or the start of something new and wonderful.

Joe was ecstatic. The return letter from Madelyn propelled him into an erotic dance with the floor lamp that stood beside the overstuffed chair in his room. Swooping the lamp up in his arms, the plug was jerked from its socket. It whipped around the room at the end of the cord, making a shambles of the toiletries atop the dresser, as Joe twirled round and around the room, singing a made-up love song at the top of his voice, ending with an elaborate dip of the lamp…punctuated by a prolonged kiss to the rim of the shade. Madelyn had chosen a pet name for him too, and had repeated it across an entire line just as he had. *'Pal'*. She was calling him Pal. *'Pet and Pal'*, he thought. *'Two P's together…like two peas in a pod'*.

After pausing to catch his breath, he carefully penned a return letter to Madelyn telling her he would be on his way to St. Onge to see her as soon as he could make arrangements to stay with his cousin, Father Brunet. Only this time his letter did not begin with his usual *'Dear Madelyn'* it began *'Dear Pet'*. He hoped it was not too soon to address her that way, but he knew he needed to take action to advance their friendship toward something more meaningful, or risk losing her to some other man, or worse yet, to the convent.

After anxiously waiting ten days for her reply, Joe almost tore the letter from the agent's hands at the post office's General Delivery window. He breathed in the fragrance of the ivory colored envelope while uttering *please God*, then, hands shaking, carefully unsealed it and removed the folded letter inside. He had to read it three times to be sure he hadn't misread it through his tear-filled eyes. But the words didn't change. She let him know it would be of no use for him to take the long trip to see her, but she would be happy to have him remain her 'pen-pal'.

Joe said his good-byes to Catherine and Marty that day, promising Catherine he would keep in touch since she still had a need to hear how everything with Madelyn would turn out.

"It most likely isn't going to turn out," he told her dejectedly. "But I will certainly keep in touch with the two of you because you have become family to me."

"I'm glad you ran into me that day," Catherine replied. "We were at a point, Marty and I, when we were about to lose the store and everything we owned. Then there you were. You came flying at me like some kind of guardian angel or something and you made everything okay for us. It was as if the fates sent you to us because we both had a need that could only be filled by meeting one another."

"It was just a coincidence," Joe replied, "Just a chance meeting; because we both happened to be in the same place at the same time. I'm glad it was you I almost ran down, and I'm glad we could help one another, but that might have been the case with anyone else too."

"I'll never believe that. I believe we were both in that spot at the same time so that we could meet. You needed to find another place to stay, Marty and I had just decided to take in a border so we might be able to hold off the bank from taking our store for a while longer, then you came up with a plan that saved us...and will keep on saving us and a whole lot of other folks too until things turn around. That couldn't have been 'just a coincidence'."

"If I thought it was anything else I wouldn't be able to stand it. If I believed in fate I would have to believe in its cruelty. I would have to believe that fate brought me to Madelyn and made me fall in love with her, then kept her out of my reach due to a cruel technicality. That's what I would have to believe, if I believed in fate. But I don't believe in it. I believe in coincidence, ...chance. Chance will not keep me forever from Madelyn the way fate would".

MAY, 1934

JOE WAS FURIOUS WITH HIMSELF FOR NOT CHECKING THE water in his radiator the last time he stopped for gas. Now here he was, in the middle of nowhere, with hissing steam billowing out of the front end of his car and nothing in sight except a ramshackle house up a rutted lane with a skinny woman hanging ragged looking shirts and pants on a sagging clothesline. He pulled over to the side of the road stopping under the shade of a towering tree, then raised the hood of the car and took a long look inside, peering around, touching things, as if he knew what he was doing. He didn't. He could change a tire if he had to, he could put gas in the tank and water in the radiator if he had to, and he knew enough not to unscrew the radiator cap while it was hot and hissing if he didn't want to risk getting scalded. But that was about all he knew about cars.

Joe had seen the woman turn and look at him a couple of times as she continued hanging out her washing, so he took that as an invitation to approach her and ask for some water. When he was about fifty feet from her she called out, her voice trembling from fear or agitation, he couldn't tell which.

"No need to come any further! We ain't buying nothing!"

"I don't want to sell you anything," Joe responded, still walking toward the woman. "I just need some water for my radiator so I can be on my way. Should have filled it in Flagstaff, but I didn't know this part of Arizona would have so many hills to climb. The hills overheated my car." Joe stopped about a dozen feet from the woman and gave her a friendly smile. "Could you please let me have some water? I'd be happy to pay you for it," he added, seeing the woman's look of hesitation.

"Help yourself," she said, gesturing toward the well in the middle of the weedy, rock strewn yard. "Wouldn't be very Christian of me to ask you to pay for it," she added, as if she wished she didn't have to be Christian about it.

Joe turned the handle that raised the bucket of water out of the well. He saw there was a smaller pail set to the side of the well, with a spout and a sieve to catch any bugs that might be in the water. Pretending he knew exactly what he was doing, he poured the water into the pail, then released the bucket back down the well again. "Wow! This water is ice cold!" he exclaimed. "I'm going to have to let it sit in the sun for a while to warm up while my car sits in the shade cooling down, before I dare fill the radiator. Mind if I sit on your steps while I wait?"

Not waiting for an answer, Joe sat on the wooden steps at the back door to the house, sighing as if he had been walking for hours rather than sitting behind the wheel of a car. "This place is like an oasis in a desert," he remarked. "Didn't know there was such a beautiful spot in this state."

"You never been around these parts before?" the woman asked shyly.

"No. Just passing through on my way to California. You ever been to California?"

"Never been anywhere but here. Don't see no reason to go gallivanting around the country. Folks that done that tell me there's nothing new to see."

"Oh, they're wrong! There's lots to see. Wonders around every bend in the road! That's why I like being a traveling salesman. Always seeing new places, meeting new people!"

"What do you sell?" the woman asked, cradling the empty laundry basket on her bony hip. "Not that I'm buying nothing," she added. "I'm just curious what you got in that big trailer."

"Encyclopedias, mostly."

"What's ency…what?"

"Books. A big set of books with all there is to know in the world."

The woman appeared awestruck. "Can I see what that looks like? Just curious you know. Like I said, I can't buy nothing."

"Wait here." Joe said as he went to his car, removed his leather case with the sample books from the passenger seat of the car, then returned and placed the case in front of the woman

"Open it," he invited. "By the way, my name is Joe Tessier. I should have introduced myself earlier, but better late than never, I guess."

"Emily. Emily Jensen," she responded, shy once again as she removed one of the books from the case and opened it.

"Read what it says." Joe urged.

"Oh, I couldn't do that," she said, holding the book out for Joe to take from her. "I don't read so good. I might spoil what it says." She hesitated before adding, "My littlest one reads good though. She reads from the Bible to us every night. Is there a Bible here in these books?"

"No Bible. Is your littlest one a boy or girl? How old?"

"A girl. She's twelve. She wants to be a teacher. No Bible? But the Bible has all anyone needs to know in the world."

"The Bible tells you the history of the world up until Jesus. But these encyclopedias tell you the history of the world ever since then. Look," he said turning to a section of the book with pictures. "This is a picture of a city called Athens. It's in a country on another continent called Greece."

"Why would any place call itself grease?"

"It's a different kind of Greece. Spelled different. Doesn't mean the same thing. Look at the pictures and see all the places there are in the world. And that's only some of them. Here," he said, taking the book from her, flipping the pages. "Here's Arizona, where you live. And here's a picture of Phoenix, Arizona. Have you ever been to Phoenix?"

"I've never been there. But I've heard tell of it," Emily said in awe, her worn looking fingers stroking the outline of an enormous church in the photograph. She had an almost frantic look on her face when she asked the question that had been growing inside her as she looked at the pictures in the book. "Could you stay here until my little girl gets here from school? It won't be long now and my man and boys will be along soon too. You can stay for supper if you want. I'll kill us a chicken and I can make some dumplings and open a jar of preserves and maybe cook up a winter squash from the root cellar. Nothing fancy. You're probably used to fancy, but..."

Joe held up his hand to stop her from saying anything more. "I would be happy to stay until your little girl is home from school, and..."

"Jessie. Her name is Jessie."

"...and, let Jessie take a look through the books, and..."

"Can't buy them, remember? They must be very dear!"

"And you don't have to buy them, just let Jessie look at them and enjoy them because I have to wait for my radiator to cool down anyway so I have to stay anyway for that to happen, and..."

"And it will take a while for supper to be ready, so I need to stop talking now and go kill that chicken so you can eat before you have to go," she said handing the book back to Joe.

"Wait!" he said. "If I'm going to be staying for supper, maybe you could make use of some apples I picked up in town. I planned to eat them on the road, but if I'm staying for supper..."

"Pie! I'll make an apple pie!" Emily exclaimed. "And you won't have to eat apples on the road. You can eat them at the table! In a pie! Along with my man, Ben. And my boys, Luke and John," she added, rushing off to round up a chicken.

Joe sat on the steps, watching her as she excitedly entered the chicken pen calling out a sweetly compelling "Here chick-chick-chick. Come and get it." But the sudden frantic squawking of a captured chicken propelled him off the steps and down the lane to his car to fetch the promised apples that would be turned into a pie. He took his time. He had no desire for his ears to witness the thud of steel on wood that signaled the beginnings of a chicken dinner…even if it ended with an apple pie.

While Emily busied herself in the kitchen, Joe remained on the steps browsing through one of the books. He heard the voices of the children before he saw them coming up the hill behind his car. The two boys ran ahead of the little girl, eager to take a closer look at the car and trailer, but the girl was more interested in the stranger sitting on her back steps holding a book in his hands. She approached slowly, her head cocked to one side, taking measure of the man, the book and the leather case in turn. When she was within six feet of him she smiled tentatively.

"Would you like to take a look at this?" Joe asked, holding the book out so it was within her reach. "Your mother told me your name is Jessie. I think that's a beautiful sounding name. My name is Joe."

"Hello Mister," Jessie said shyly.

"You can call me Joe."

"I can't," Jessie said, startled. "Mama says I have to call grownups Mister…or Missus."

"Okay, then you can just call me Mister."

"Mister what?"

"Tessier. But just Mister will do. May I call you Jessie?"

Jessie nodded, giving Joe a shy smile. He held the book out to her once again and she immediately grasped it, sat down on the steps, and almost reverently opened it and began reading on the first page. "I learned at school there were books like these, but I never thought I'd ever get to see them," Jessie said.

"There must be a library in town. Don't you ever get into town to get books at the library? They must have encyclopedias there."

"My Pop and the boys go into town one Saturday every month. Mama and I have to stay here because there are chores to do."

"You've never been in to town?"

Jessie shook her head as if the very idea terrified her. "Pop says town is full of bad things and it's no place for women-folks to be. Mama used to go back before she had kids, but not anymore. She says there are men everywhere drinking, and swearing and trying to grab hold of girls arms or just looking them over and saying rude things and...."

"There might have been some of that a few years back, but it's not like that anymore. At least not that I noticed. I think you'd like going into town, especially going to the library...the way you like books."

"I'll think about it," Jessie said, burying her nose in the book once again. "But if Pop says no, then it's no."

Emily came out on the back stoop and hollered at the boys. "Leave the car be and get on over to the Carter place and help your Pop finish up the chores there. You know you need to get the barn ready over there so your Pop can bring the bull over to Mr. Carter after supper."

"That's tonight?" one of the boys hollered back. "I haven't got him brushed up slick yet."

"Then you best get a move on. And tell your Pop there's company for supper tonight so don't be late."

Joe filed away the tidbit of information about the bull in the back of his mind as assuredly as he stashed tidbits and scraps of everything imaginable in every nook and cranny he could find. To fill in his time until supper, he showed Jessie some of the more interesting sections of the books, pointing out in particular the large pictorial section on New York City. But, as he watched the look on her face and in her eyes as she paged through the books, …a look that could only be described as pure rapture… he knew without a doubt he would be leaving behind a set of encyclopedias for Jessie. And he had no idea how he was going to accomplish that without it looking like an act of charity; a loathsome notion for an obviously poor but proud family.

Joe was offered a seat at the head of the table in the sparsely furnished dining-room; the seat farthest from the oppressive heat of the kitchen cook-stove. He was greeted cordially by Ben, Emily's husband, and the two exchanged formalities while Emily, Jessie and the two boys somberly brought the supper to the table. Joe was offered the platter of fried chicken first, and he looked it over carefully before making his selection. Then, seeing the open-mouth astonishment on the faces of everyone else at the table, he begged their pardon for his bad manners. Looking at the bony piece of chicken on his plate, with the triangular butt end still attached, he explained, "I have always had a preference for this particular piece of chicken, and please forgive me for being greedy and not asking if there was anyone else who preferred it as well. I would be happy to take another piece instead, or share this one if…?"

Everyone spoke at once, assuring Joe he was welcome to his preferred piece of chicken and the somber mood was broken as everyone helped themselves to the most sumptuous meal they'd had since Easter. Then, as Jessie and Emily cleared the table, Ben told the boys to head out to the barn and get the bull all slicked up to take over to his boss, Mr. Carter.

Joe never knew what prompted him to ask the question. He figured later, when he was back out on the road again headed for California that he had just been making small talk, and hadn't planned on anything happening as a result of it. But that question turned out to be the answer to how he would be able to leave a set of encyclopedias behind for Jessie without it looking like charity, and put an extra fifty dollars in both his pocket and in Ben Jensen's too.

"You been taking care of your neighbor's bull?"

"No. He's our bull. Raised him from a calf, him and his mama afore him. My boss, Mr. Carter wants to buy him from us 'cause he's a black bull and they're scarce in these parts…especially a handsome fella like our Best Beau."

Joe chuckled. "Best Beau. That's quite a name." Then, not knowing why he did so, he added, "Must be lots of folks wanting a good black bull. I ran into a rancher back a ways who asked me to be on the lookout for a black bull for him," he lied. "How much you asking for him?"

"I'm asking a hundred and fifty, but my boss is only willing to pay a hundred. He knows that bull is worth a lot more than that…and he could afford to pay a lot more too, the old skinflint… but I guess he's only worth what someone will pay me for him."

"A hundred doesn't sound right. That rancher I told you about was willing to pay two hundred for a good black bull."

"Well, that rancher ain't around here though is he," Ben said dejectedly.

"No, but your boss doesn't know that." Joe narrowed his eyes, thinking. "Why don't you send one of your boys over to your boss's place to tell him there's a man here who will pay you two hundred dollars for your black bull. And tell him that man has a trailer here too and is ready to load him up and take him away. But before you sell that bull to someone else you wanted to give him first refusal at that price because you know how much he wants that bull. And if he matches the deal, the bull is his. You won't be taking a higher offer from the man."

A slow grin appeared on Ben's face as he said, "Better yet, I'll go tell him that myself."

While Ben was gone, Joe used the time to back his trailer up to the barn so it would look as if he were ready to load up the bull and haul him away. He was leaning nonchalantly against his rear bumper when a car turned full speed up the lane, spewing gravel and a cloud of dust behind it. Ben's boss was hollering before he had the car door half open. "That's my bull!" he raged. "He was promised to me!"

"You didn't want to pay my asking price," Ben countered, getting out of the passenger's side. "So, when this fella came along and offered me double what you told me you would pay, I had to let you know that. I can't afford to take half what someone else would pay."

"I pay you good money to work for me, and this is how you treat me?"

"Well, I work hard for what you pay me so that makes us even there. You get to tell me how much you will pay me for my work…don't seem right that you should get to tell me what you will pay me for something of mine that you want, too. Especially since I think we both know my bull is worth a lot more than you want to pay for it."

"And how much do you want to keep your job?" Ben's boss, Mr. Carter was nearly frothing at the mouth with anger.

"You know I need my job, Mr. Carter," Ben said humbly. "But you know you need me to work for you too because I'm the only reliable help around these parts. You've told me that often enough. But what the job pays isn't more than enough to keep us in boot leather, so I need to get a fair amount for what I have to sell. And this man here," he said, gesturing toward Joe, "has offered a fair amount for my bull. If you match that, the bull is yours. Like I told you, I won't hold out for more, even if he offers it. I know you want the bull, and I want you to be the one to own him too, but…"

Joe stepped forward. "If your neighbor here matches my offer, I'll raise it to two hundred twenty five. I want that bull."

"Sorry, I just gave my word I wouldn't accept a higher offer if my boss matched your original offer," Ben said excitedly, seeing that Joe was going in to cement the deal.

"Two hundred fifty!"

Ben looked from Joe to Mr. Carter, scratching his head as if he were thinking it over. He was aware of his boss reaching into his pocket, pulling out a wad of bills and counting. He shoved the money into Ben's hand, and yelled, "Two hundred dollars! There, I met your price! So the bull is mine," he said sneeringly to Joe. "Guess you'll have to find yourself another black bull, but I'll warrant you won't find another one to match Ben's 'Best Beau'. That beauty is going to be siring *me* some top calves, not *you*!"

Ben thanked his boss profusely then went to the barn to put a halter on the bull so his boys could take it to its new home, while Joe and Mr. Carter glared at one another. One man's glare was smugly genuine, while the other man's was theatrically bogus. And all that was left for Joe to do there, he figured, was to get Ben to buy a set of encyclopedias for his daughter, Jessie.

As soon as Mr. Carter had driven off, followed by Ben's two boys leading Best Beau down the road, Joe tapped on the back door of the house. When Emily appeared he thanked her again for the wonderful meal then said he needed to fetch his books and be on his way. Jessie had them neatly placed back in the leather case, and her smile as she handed it to Joe through the open door was all the thanks he needed. But when Ben reached out to shake his hand right there on the back stoop, Joe let him know he had something he wanted to show him in the trailer.

"There's something here you need," Joe said pointedly. "For Jessie." He pointed to a box of encyclopedias.

"Jessie don't need those."

"Yes she does. And you need to get them for her. Because I got you an extra fifty dollars over what you wanted for your bull so you could buy these books for her."

A look of bewilderment followed by a look of realization crossed Ben's face. "You mean you didn't know any rancher willing to pay two hundred dollars for a black bull?'

"I mean I didn't know any rancher wanting a bull of any color, anywhere. You wanted a hundred and fifty dollars for your bull, so I got you that. And I got you an extra fifty so you could give your little girl the best thing you could ever give her in the bargain. I sell these for seventy five a set, but I'm giving you a deal because your wife killed a chicken for me and turned my apples into a pie so I'd stay for supper and Jessie would have some time to see these books."

"I suppose next you'll tell me you're not partial to the south end piece of a chicken flying north, either."

"Did you ever know anyone partial to that particular piece?"

"Never did," Ben said grinning, reaching into his pocket. He handed Joe fifty dollars then helped himself to a box of books in the trunk. "Worth every dollar I guess for the lesson you learned me."

"Wait a minute," Joe said, rummaging in a big box of odds and ends he had collected along the way. He pulled out two rolls of ribbon...one a pretty pink, the other a baby blue...and handed them to Ben. "For Emily and Jessie. To make them feel as pretty as they are, and because this was a lucky place for my radiator to boil over." Joe thought a moment before adding, "And take the two of them into town on Saturdays so Jessie can get books from the library and maybe your wife can get to see a picture show."

"You think these ribbons give you leave to tell me my business?"

"No, nothing gives me leave to do that," Joe said apologetically. "But sometimes it takes a stranger's eyes to see the longing in a woman's. Or a woman's and a girl's. Your little Jessie will do you proud one day for sure if you give her the chance. She's special…and so is her mama. I think you know that. I think that's why you want to keep them all to yourself."

"Maybe you do too much thinking."

"Well, maybe you need to do a bit more."

"I think maybe you're right," Ben said, scuffing the dusty dry ground at his feet. "And I think this was a lucky place for your radiator to boil over too."

Back on the road again, Joe hadn't gone far before he pulled off onto a likely looking side road to park under an outcropping of trees. He walked a few yards into the woods to relieve himself, carefully watching out for any sign of poison oak or ivy, then returned to his car and curled up on the front seat for a bit of shut-eye. He planned to get an early start in the wee hours of morning, so he could make it to the California border with the sun coming up in the east behind him, lighting his way into the golden state.

As Joe approached the town of Needles, he was struck by how accurately the town seemed to live up to its name. He figured it could have been called Boondocks, or maybe even Toheckandgone, and it would still have been aptly named. Dust from the dirt road so nearly obliterated his vision through the windshield that he almost passed the small group of natives at the roadside, hovering around a rickety table, watching him as he drove past. But a glint of something shiny on the table caught his eye, and true to his nature, his curiosity was piqued and he pulled over to see what it was.

The table was strewn with intricate silver jewelry studded with polished turquoise stones. Joe picked up a particularly large necklace, carefully assessing the workmanship of the piece. He had never seen anything like it before, or for that matter, any type of jewelry that even resembled the incredible array of bracelets, brooches, necklaces, earrings, rings, cufflinks and tie-clips before him. The detail on the pieces was amazing -- with filaments of silver twining into images of birds of prey, or scenery, or Indian maidens and braves surrounding the stones.

The excitement Joe felt at his discovery of the remarkable jewelry was surpassed by his discovery of the even more remarkable price indicated alongside each individual piece. He knew instantly that he had found his next big money-maker.

"How much for all of it?" he asked, sweeping his arm in the air across the table and addressing his question to the elder native he assumed was in charge. The man merely nodded in the direction of the lone woman in the group, indicating that she was the person Joe should deal with. Looking at the woman, Joe repeated his question. "How much for all of it?"

"The amount is on each piece," the woman replied, as if Joe were not quite bright.

"So, if I buy all of it I must pay the price indicated for each piece? I don't get a discount for buying all of it?"

"What is a discount?"

"Never mind," Joe replied. The price for each piece was so low that he decided he didn't want to try to bargain for a better price. The jewelry was practically a steal already. He went back to his car and after a bit of rummaging came up with a pad of paper and a pencil. Then returning to the jewelry strewn table, he jotted down the price of each piece in a long column, added it, added it again then showed the figure to the native woman. "This is how much money I will pay you for all the jewelry."

"How do I know this is the right amount?" The woman frowned at Joe.

"Add it up.!"

"What is add it up?"

"Put all the prices together then see how much it is in total."

Looking perplexed, the woman just shook her head. "You must pay the price on each piece."

"Just a minute," Joe said, not wanting to let some native's lack of knowledge of arithmetic deter him. If he had to pay the exact price for each piece of jewelry, one at a time, that's what he would do.

Back in his car, he retrieved the wad of bills from his right sock, counting out the exact amount required for each piece. When he had the amount of bills for each individual piece, plus the correct amount of quarters and half dollar pieces of silver in his coat pocket, Joe returned to the woman and paid her individually for each piece of jewelry. She placed his purchases one by one in a dusty flour sack, smiling her thanks through the whitest, brightest teeth Joe had ever seen. It was only then that Joe actually took notice of her.

"What is your name? he asked. "My name is Joe."

"I am Corrine."

"That's a very nice sounding name. Corrine."

"It was the name of my mother's old mother."

"Are you often in this spot selling jewelry?"

"About once every moon, or so. Only when there are enough pieces made."

"And you sell a lot of them?"

"Not so much as today," Corrine smiled. "Never every piece."

"I might want to buy more from you. How will I know what day you are here?"

"You can ask anywhere in town where to find me. If I am not here, someone will go with you to find me."

Joe nodded his goodbye's to Corrine and the native men then headed ever westward. Due to the purchases he had just made, his next planned stop was in a town called San Bernardino where he hoped to find an accomplished seamstress.

MAY, 1934

THE FIRST THING JOE DID WHEN HE ARRIVED IN SAN Bernardino was scout out a diner that looked to be a local meeting place. That way he could find out about reputable places to stay and get a good cheap meal at the same time. But this time he had another objective as well. He needed to find a seamstress who could turn his hoarded bolt-ends of colorful velvet into various sizes of drawstring bags to hold the silver and turquoise jewelry he had bought from the natives.

He took a seat at the counter, smiling and nodding at the man beside him, then repeating the gesture for the stout young woman who appeared before him. "What'll you have?" she asked, returning his smile.

"Whatever the daily special is, coffee, and a slice of the best pie you've got," Joe said without hesitation. "And you can tell me where the best place is to stay around here and where I can locate a woman who can do a bit of sewing for me. By the way, my name is Joe," Joe said, extending his hand to the woman.

"Eve," she said in return, wiping her hand on her apron before extending it to Joe.

"Eve," Joe said, as if trying the name on for size. That's a name I've always admired."

Eve blushed, her eyes scanning the counter-top as she reached for a rag to wipe off a non-existent spill. "What kind of sewing you need done? I can sew good enough to turn collars and make aprons and stuff like that."

"Do you have a machine that sews? I need some little drawstring bags done as fast as possible."

"Don't have no machine, but I sew fast if it ain't fancy stuff." Eve paused before adding, "You might could get a room where I stay too. It's a good clean place and folks there are friendly and the food is good too. And I could use the extra money for doing some sewing. I have a little boy that the lady that owns the boarding house looks after when I work and I have to pay a dollar a week extra for that. But I don't work at the diner every day so it's hard to come by without some extra work."

"Are you off work tomorrow?"

"Tomorrow and the day after. And after 7 tonight too."

"The job's yours," Joe said, extending his hand to shake on it. "Now, how about fixing me up with the special, starting with a cup of coffee? Then you can tell me where your boarding house is located so I can go get settled in."

"Your grub is coming right up," Eve chirped delightedly. And I'm going to get you the biggest piece of coconut cream pie you ever saw!"

The boarding-house was shabby looking, with peeling paint and wooden stairs set askew, leading up to a front veranda that had seen better days. Joe parked his car and trailer right in front of the house, and as he started up the cracked cement walk he was nearly knocked over by a little boy barreling toward him screaming "No!" at the top of his lungs. Hot on his trail was a beefy, red-faced woman wielding a large wooden spoon screaming "Get back here and take your medicine you little imp." Both were stopped in their tracks as the boy slammed into Joe's legs and Joe grabbed him around the waist, lifted him in the air and spun around to keep the two of them from careening to the ground from the impact.

"Hey, where you going in such a rush? You almost knocked me over!" Joe exclaimed, lifting the boy higher into the air. "Wow! You sure are a hefty one! What you been eating, boy?"

"He's been eating the chocolate cream pies I made for the boarders' supper tonight," the woman wielding the wooden spoon interjected. "Both pies! And I intend to heat up his bottom end so he can't sit at the table with the rest of the folks tonight." She waggled the spoon in the boy's direction.

"No!" the child yelled, wrapping his arms snugly around Joe's neck and burying his chocolate smeared face against Joe's formerly pristine white shirt. "No!"

Joe momentarily had a flashback to his childhood; his mother brandishing a wooden spoon threateningly. "Well, you probably have a good paddling coming to you, and I wouldn't object to you getting your just desserts seeing as how it was *my* dessert you ate because I intend to get a room here tonight and maybe a couple more nights too, that is, if there is room at the Inn," he added, looking up at the woman.

"Oh. You're in need of a place to stay?" the woman asked, hiding the spoon under her apron.

"Yes. For a couple of days anyway. There's a woman named Eve that works at a diner downtown who has agreed to do some sewing I need done over the next couple of days. She stays here with her little boy. I presume this is hers ," Joe said setting the child on his feet, "and she thought you might have a room available. My name is Joe Tessier. I'm just passing through on my way to the coast."

"There's a room, but you would have to share it with another gentleman."

"Oh. That won't do. I need a place to myself."

The woman furrowed her brow. "Well, there's a sun porch that isn't being used right now, but there's just a cot there, not a real bed."

"Could I move the bed from the shared room out to the porch?"

"Well, no. Because it's a shared bed you see."

"Well, maybe a cot would be alright. I'm used to sleeping in my car a lot so a cot would probably be better than that."

"I'll only charge you seventy-five cents a day for the sun porch plus breakfast and supper," the woman said. "You are on your own for the noon meal."

As Joe got himself settled in the sun porch, the wails of the little boy confirmed that he was indeed being subjected to the promised heating up of his bottom end. He momentarily felt sorry for the little guy, then remembering that the greedy lad had demolished that night's dessert, chocolate cream pie his favorite, his sympathy quickly vanished. As he removed his soiled shirt, Joe hoped the boy wasn't going to prove to be more of a problem than he had bargained for. He hoped he hadn't made a big mistake in hiring Eve to make those drawstring bags.

Joe found the location of the sun porch to be a big advantage. The enclosed porch was on the side of the house, with lots of windows and a door that exited out the back, right where there was space to park his car and trailer. He backed the trailer into the spot where he could keep an eye on it. After rummaging around in the trailer to locate all the bolt-ends of velvet he would need for the bags, he rummaged some more for the braided silver colored string, needles and thread he would also need. It took him a bit longer to locate the hook and eye door closures he had salvaged years ago from a junk pile, but he figured he might need them to keep Eve's mischievous child and the other boarders from invading the sun porch since there was no lock on the inside door to the porch. The need for the hook and eye latches was verified when Joe entered the porch from the back door to discover the little boy asleep on the cot, thumb shoved into the mouth of his tear-stained face, with snot on the pillow and the blanket beneath him soaked and reeking of urine.

"Give me strength!" he beseeched the porch.

The landlady, known to the boarders as Miss Edna, had made another batch of chocolate cream pies somewhere between the time she had warmed the behind of the little boy, known as Freddie, and the time she had collected the sodden scamp, washed Joe's shirt, scrubbed the cot and set it in the sun to dry, then fetched him some clean bedding. Joe informed her he would be attaching a hook and eye closure to both sides of the inside door and would be needing the key to the outside door to keep Freddie from invading his privacy again, and Miss Edna told him to put the hooks up high so the boy could not reach them with a chair and she would be grateful if he left them there when he departed. She also informed him that Freddie would be celebrating his third Birthday the following day so she would be making a cake that evening and would appreciate it if she could leave the cake in his care out on the locked up sun porch.

"You're not afraid *I'll* get into it?" he asked jokingly. "You know how we boys are!"

"My wooden spoon is never far away when there are boys about," she said with a straight face. "So watch it! I'll not be hesitant to use it!"

"I'll be sure to remember that," Joe said, having no trouble at all mustering up a sound of sincerity as an image of his mother's stern face surfaced in his mind.

Eve sewed bags that evening after Freddie had been put down for the night then resumed the task after breakfast the following morning. Her progress was hampered by the child's constant demands for attention to the point that she was irritated almost beyond tolerance when Joe appeared mid-morning to check on her work. When he was critical of the amount of work she had completed, the dam broke and she simultaneously smacked Freddie on the back on the head and joined him in bawling out her rage at the indignity. "*You* try getting anything done with a spoiled brat pestering you every second!"

Joe was flustered by Eve's outburst. "Well, can't you get Miss Edna to watch him for you?" he asked lamely.

"She threatened to never watch him again after all the trouble she had with him yesterday," Eve wailed. "How about *you* watch him seeing as how it's *you* that's needing these bags sewed?"

"I don't know anything about looking after little kids," Joe protested. "What would I do with him?"

"Take him for a ride in your car," Eve suggested, brightening a bit. "He's never had a ride in a car and I'm sure he would enjoy it. Besides it's his birthday, and that would be a wonderful present for him. Not that you need to get him a present or anything since you aren't any relation to him, you know, but his Daddy's gone looking for work; he's been gone almost 2 months now and we haven't heard from him in all that time and Freddie's missing him I know 'cause he's been impossible to deal with ever since Jim's been gone and I can't be his daddy for him and I can't bear seeing him hurt so much inside and all I seem to be able to do is add to the hurt instead of helping, and…" she sobbed.

"Car?" Freddie looked at Joe, big-eyed, questioning.

"You want to go for a ride in my car?" Joe asked.

"Ride in car," Freddie confirmed. "Go ride in car." He got up off the floor where he had landed when his mother smacked him on the back of the head, walked over to Joe and slid his chubby little hand into Joe's, smiling up at him. "Go ride in car."

When Joe felt Freddie's hand slip into his, he looked down at the cherubic little face beaming up at him and felt a strange emotion welling up inside him. It was a feeling that erased all the aggravation and annoyance he had felt toward the child, a feeling that gave him a sense of strength and tenderness at the same time. He had never felt that way before, but he decided he liked it. He returned Freddie's smile with one of his own, saying, "We are going for a ride in my car you and I. We are going for a long ride and we will see horses, and cows, and trains and lots of other things and you will have the best birthday you ever had. I will be your pretend daddy just for today, and we will have fun all day so your Mama can sew these bags for me. Okay?"

"Okay!" Freddie shouted, jumping up and down. "We go ride in car, Mama!" he turned and informed his mother importantly. "So you can sew, okay?"

⁓⁓⁓

With Freddie perched solidly on top of a box of encyclopedias in the passenger seat, giving him enough height to see out the windshield, Joe headed for the open road outside of town. He slowly drove past a dilapidated truck loaded with squawking chickens that drew Freddie's rapt attention until he spied another attraction that was even more interesting. A cow in the roadside pasture had jumped on the back of another cow and the two were running piggy-back for a few yards until the cow on back dropped off.

"Where chickens going?" Freddie queried. "What cows doing?"

"Chickens are going to a farm. Cows are playing piggy-back."

"I like piggy-back. Can I play with cows?"

"No. Cows are too heavy for you. They would hurt you."

"Oh. I'm bigger now."

"Not big enough yet. You have to be as big as a daddy to play with cows."

"Oh."

"You have to have a lot more birthdays to get that big."

"How many more?"

"Oh, about twenty I'd say. That's as many as all your fingers and toes together."

"Will they grow too?"

"Oh yes. They will get as big as mine," Joe said, extending his hand in front of Freddie.

Freddie laid his fingers on top of Joe's, measuring the difference. "I will be as big as you," he proclaimed with satisfaction.

As Joe drove along he noticed that Freddie had begun cupping his crotch as he became excited over each new animal he saw or each new truck on the road. Remembering the soaked cot from the day before, he pulled over to the side of the road near some trees and scooped the little boy off the box of books then stood him on the ground next to the car.

"Where we going?" Freddie asked.

"I have to relieve myself so I thought you might want to do that too," Joe explained.

"What's that?"

"Well, there's no toilet or outhouse here, and I have to go pretty bad, so it looks like we are going to have to pee in the woods, you and I."

"I need to go too." Freddie affirmed.

The two boys stood side by side as they relieved themselves before continuing their day's adventure.

Joe drove Freddie back into town and bought the two of them lunch at the diner where his mama worked, then they strolled together around the town, inhaling the pungent odors from the farm feed and fertilizer store, the mouth-watering aromas from the bakery and sweet shop, passing the haberdashery store that held no interest for a small boy, then finally settling on the five and dime to spend the rest of the afternoon looking at, touching and coveting everything in the store.

"If you could have *one thing* you saw in this store, *just one*," Joe asked, "what would that one thing be?"

"I show you," Freddie said without hesitation. He led Joe to the far end of the store where there was a shelf with several large toy trucks displayed. "That one." He pointed to a flatbed truck with a pig in a crate on the back.

Joe glanced at the price-tag, then picked up the heavy metal truck and carried it to the front of the store, with an ecstatic little boy in tow. He was determined that Freddie was going to have his heart's desire that day, his third birthday, from his pretend daddy for the day, even if it cost more than his three day stay at the boardinghouse, with lunch at the diner for the two of them to boot.

That night, as everyone sat down for supper, all eyes were on little Freddie as Miss Edna asked, "Well, young man. Tell us what you and Joe did today!"

Filled with self-importance after experiencing an astonishingly wonderful day, Freddie took a deep breath before announcing "We peed in the woods!"

Joe broke into spontaneous laughter several times on his trip up the newly paved Route 66 to his destination… the Pacific coast. *"We peed in the woods!"* Peeing in the woods had been the highlight of a three-year-olds' day. Peeing was something he could relate to, and peeing in a grown up way in the woods had been the most memorable part of Freddie's day. Joe decided he liked the way the little guy had made him feel although he reminded himself that he didn't really like small children all that much and would probably be perfectly content to never have any of his own. The thought of that quite naturally brought Madelyn to the forefront of his mind, making him anxious to get settled in at the end of the highway at a town called Santa Monica. Joe chose that town purposely for its religious sound. It sounded like the right place to settle so he could resume writing to Madelyn on a regular basis; a place from which letters would not be refused.

Arriving in Santa Monica he found a respectable boardinghouse just a block off the wide Santa Monica Boulevard which appeared to be the main street of the town. After parking his trailer at the back of the house, he unhitched it from his car then took a drive down the boulevard to the shore. He was disappointed by what he saw. He had expected to see crowds of honey colored people lazing about, soaking up the sun and cavorting in the sand. Instead, he saw a few lonely looking souls huddled in their shabby coats, staring listlessly at the grey water and the greyer sand, the sound of the surf adding an additional grey dimension to the scene.

The dismal feeling invoked by the scene at the beach is why Joe decided his first letter to Madelyn was going to have to be a lie.

MAY, 1934

Joe posted a letter to Catherine and Marty in Texas, and another to George in Massachusetts, to let them know that he had arrived in California and found the "golden state" to be a big disappointment…so far. But his letter to Madelyn told of sunny beaches, a lavish lifestyle among the movie stars and an endless array of exotic food available everywhere. *You wouldn't know there is a depression here!* he exclaimed at the end of his letter.

Joe spent his second day in Santa Monica checking out the main street. Several shops were boarded up, with scraps of paper and other debris windswept up against the doors. There was a pungent odor of urine emanating from some of them, making him pick up his stride and hold his breath as he went past. Further down the boulevard he saw a few cars parked along the curb, but there were few people about. He found it to be an odd looking street with all the shops, eateries and professional businesses to be no more than one story high…very different from any other main street in any other town he had ever seen.

The hint of a delectable odor reached Joe's nostrils as he continued down the street, growing stronger with each step. He stopped and surveyed the buildings on his side of the street, then directly across on the other side of the street. The storefront and the sign were both so narrow he almost missed them, but smiled as he jaywalked across the boulevard and opened the door to the minuscule doughnut shop tucked between a grocer and a law office.

Joe took a seat on a stool a couple of seats down from the lone customer in the shop. He ordered a cup of coffee and a doughnut while reaching in his pocket and withdrawing two nickels. "You want two doughnuts and a second cup of coffee?" the man behind the counter asked. "Cup a joe and a doughnut is a nickel."

Joe looked over at the other customer before answering. He saw a young unshaven man in a threadbare coat that probably wouldn't stand up to a cleaning who had just drained the dregs in the cup in front of him. "I just got into town after a long trip and was feeling a bit lost when the aroma of doughnuts drew me right through your door. Then when I saw you had another customer here I thought I might ask him to join me because I could use some company and someone to talk to who can maybe tell me a little bit about the area." Joe looked at the young man seated two stools down. "So, can I buy you a cup of coffee and a doughnut?" he asked. "Back where I'm from it would cost a dime. Might as well get a two for one deal, huh?"

"Sounds good to me," the young man replied. "Name's Howie --short for Howard. But I can't tell you much about the area 'cause I just got here myself and don't know my way around yet. Bout all I can tell you is that folks don't seem so friendly here…not like back home where I come from. 'Cept for you," he said with a grin. "Glad to meet ya!"

"I'm Joe" Joe said extending his hand. "Where you from? Can't quite place your accent."

"Arkansas." Howie then went on to relate to Joe how his Pa had died two years before, then the farmland had turned to dust and no crops could grow, then the bank had taken the farm and he and his Mama and two younger sisters had come to California to pick crops but there was nothing to pick right now so his Mama and sisters were staying in the migrant worker hostel over in Pomona and he had hopped on a freight train and had gotten off in Santa Monica just a couple of days ago hoping to find some way to earn some money to send back to his Mama. But he wasn't having any luck because he didn't have any idea what he could offer to do for someone to pay him to do it. He was eighteen, he had fourteen cents left to his name, no prospects and no idea what he was going to do other than hop on a return train to Pomona, defeated.

Joe placed another ten cents on the counter then held up two fingers to the proprietor who promptly brought them each another doughnut and cup of coffee. "This just might be a lucky day for both of us," Joe told Howie. "Here you are able-bodied and willing but lacking in ideas, and here I am just full of ideas looking for someone able-bodied and willing. Want to team up with me?"

"I ain't doing nothing illegal!" Howie said vehemently. "I hear there's lots of that going on and I don't want no part in that!"

"I'm not going to ask you to do anything illegal. But I've been around and I know there are lots of people who would pay you to do all kinds of things for them that they don't want to do for themselves. And I know where those kinds of people live and how they think. All you need right now is a grubstake…a shave, haircut, bath and some decent clothes, a place to sleep and a full belly…'cause you're skinny, dirty and you don't smell so great. So let's finish up here and get going with that so I can show you what you need to do first thing tomorrow morning."

"What's in it for you?" Howie asked suspiciously. "Why would you get me all set up at your expense if it wasn't something underhanded you had in mind?"

"I guess you don't know you can trust me about that because …you don't know me. I can understand that. But these are tough times and I think maybe I've been one of the lucky ones to get by because I have lots of ideas about things, so if I can be of help to a guy down on his luck… well I think maybe that would be a good thing to do, considering the way things are. Besides, if it makes you feel any better you can pay me back after you start getting paid for the work you do."

"What kind of work?"

"Well, what do you know how to do?"

"Never did anything but farm work and don't look like there's much of that in a city!"

"How about yard work, you know, cutting grass, pulling weeds, trimming bushes…stuff like that?"

"Course! Those are kid chores everybody did afore they were big enough for real work!"

"And how about washing cars, fixing fences, sweeping walks, putting up clotheslines, painting…stuff like that?"

"Course! Anybody can do that kind of stuff!"

"Well that's the kind of stuff I'm talking about."

"People gonna pay for somebody to do kid chores?" Howie asked skeptically.

"Not the kind of people you are used to knowing," Joe said assuredly. "But I know where to find those kinds of people. And that's what I'm going to help you do."

"Is that what you do? Is that how you make your living?"

"No. I'm a salesman. I sell things like encyclopedias and jewelry to the kinds of people who would pay someone to do "kid chores" for them."

"Well, if you just got here, how do you know where to find those kinds of people?"

"I know where because it's the same everywhere you go all across this big wide country, and I'll show you where first thing tomorrow morning. But first, let's get you a shave, haircut and some decent clothes. You're going to need to look presentable where we'll be headed tomorrow."

While Howie was in the barber shop a few doors down from the doughnut shop, Joe scouted out a men's store he had passed before he had been enticed by the smell of doughnuts. He had noticed the 'going out of business' sign on the store window and hoped to find some acceptable bargains there. There were no customers in the store or even a salesperson as far as Joe could see, but as he made his way over to a rack of suit jackets, a very portly, dapper looking gentleman in well-tailored slacks, French cuff shirt, silk vest and bow tie stepped out from behind a curtain in the back of the store. Slicking back his thinning pomaded hair the man asked, in unctuous tones, "May I be of assistance, sir?"

"I'm in need of several things," Joe replied pleasantly. "I'll be needing slacks, a suit jacket, shirt, tie, some work pants, work shirt and jacket, socks and probably a couple pair of shoes or boots too.'"

"Well!" the man exclaimed smiling toothily and removing a measuring tape from his vest pocket. "We better get started then!"

"Oh, it's not for me. It's for a young man I met a few minutes ago who's down on his luck and needs a bit of help. I'm just here looking at what you have while he's at the barber shop getting a shave and haircut. I thought I might find a bargain here because you are going out of business according to your sign. I told him to head down here when he was finished getting cleaned up."

"Let me get this straight," the man said. "You want to buy a full set of clothes for someone you just met…and he will be here as soon as he is "cleaned up" as you say?"

"That's right."

"Why would you do that?"

"Because right now he needs help, and right now I am able to help him…as long as I can get a bargain deal…so I figure it's the right thing to do. I also figure that he will pay me back some day, in some way, when he can."

"You are a very trusting man. I have learned not to be so trusting. But, I can assure you of a bargain price because I am going to let you name the price for any item of clothing you wish to purchase for your new-found friend…and for yourself as well."

"Now it's my turn to ask, why would you do that?"

"Because I have never heard of anyone doing what you are doing before…and I am intrigued."

That evening, after Joe had acquired a room in the rooming house he was staying in for a now very presentable Howie, Joe wondered if he had indeed gotten a bargain price for all the clothing he had bought for Howie, as well as for himself, or…if he, the master salesman, had actually been outsold by someone craftier. But he didn't lose any sleep over it. He merely stored it away in the back of his mind, the way he stored away anything he thought might be of use someday. Because he felt there would always be a someday.

Following a hearty rooming house breakfast the next morning, Joe in suit and tie, and Howie in his new working man duds headed up Sunset Boulevard toward Beverly Hills. They passed several opulent estates before Howie asked, "How come you're not stopping at any of these places? I thought this was where you were planning to sell your jewelry."

"Not here," Joe replied. "The people who live in these houses have already made it. They have finer jewelry than I am offering, and they most likely already have all the domestic help they need too so there wouldn't be any work for you here. We're headed further out where the houses are a little smaller, where the up – and – comers and the climbers live."

Howie gave Joe a puzzled look. "Up- and- comers and climbers?"

"Yeah! The folks who haven't quite made it yet, but would like everyone to think they have. Those are the people easiest to sell to, and they're also the people who will pay more for something than the people who have already made it. They are also usually the most generous people to work for. They pay the most and expect the least."

"Why would they do that? That doesn't make any sense!"

"Because they want everyone to think they can afford to do whatever they want…that price is no object. They think that proves they have "made it". You'll see."

Joe pulled up in front of a house with a wide expanse of emerald green lawn intersected by a brick walk leading up to the front door. He instructed Howie to remain in the car then carried his leather case with the silver and turquoise jewelry encased in velvet pouches up to the front door. He turned and winked at Howie then knocked on the door. Howie saw a woman open the door. She was wearing an expensive looking dressing gown and her hair appeared to be elegantly coifed. He saw Joe remove a piece of jewelry from the case and display it for the woman, but then the woman smilingly opened the door wider and invited Joe inside so he couldn't see or hear any more. Howie waited impatiently for what seemed like a very long time, when finally Joe emerged from the house followed by the woman fondly waving goodbye to him. When Joe climbed in behind the wheel Howie asked him "Did you sell her anything?"

"Of course I did!" Joe exclaimed. "I wouldn't have left without selling her something after she had to see every piece of jewelry in the case! She wound up buying a bracelet and earrings."

"Did you find out if she had any work for me?"

"No. I didn't ask. There was nothing obvious I could see that needed to be done. But we'll find something,…not to worry."

That 'something' was found at the very next stop. The woman who answered the door appeared to be a bit frazzled and upset. She was not very receptive to Joe and told him, rather impolitely, that she had no interest in buying anything unless it was something to tidy up her yard since she had just learned that her in-laws that she would be meeting for the first time would be arriving unexpectedly the next day.

"I just happen to have someone with me," he said motioning to Howie to come join him, "who is just what you need. He will have your lovely estate looking impeccably groomed for your in-laws arrival tomorrow!"

Joe introduced Howie to the woman who was flabbergasted at having her most pressing need fulfilled so unexpectedly. She directed Howie to a shed where he would find what he needed then effusively thanked Joe for being her life-saver.

"I'm going to be your life-saver yet again!" Joe exclaimed. "Because in this leather case is the small but elegant gift you will be giving your in-laws when they arrive for their visit. You'll want one for your mother-in-law and one for your father-in-law. And quite likely it is something they have never seen before!"

The woman, who introduced herself as the new bride of Wilbur Lester, an executive producer at a new studio Joe had never heard of before, bought a brooch for her mother-in-law and a tie clip for her father-in-law, not wanting the gifts to appear too lavish or ostentatious. She treated herself to an expensive necklace as well before asking Joe to please not come back for Howie before five o'clock because she would most likely have more than the yard work for him to do.

When Joe came back for Howie at five, his leather case was lighter by 3 necklaces, 7 bracelets, 2 brooches, 4 pair of earrings and 3 rings. He had also sold a set of encyclopedias. Howie leaped into the passenger seat proudly displaying 8 one dollar bills in his fist and a paper bag full of avocados. "Don't know what these are, but the lady says everyone around here eats them," he said enthusiastically. "She also wants me back there again first thing tomorrow morning, and wants me for the whole day!"

Joe opened the paper bag and took out one of the fruits. "I've never heard of or seen these before, but I guess we could give them to the lady at the boarding house and see if she knows what they are. Don't have much smell to them," he said, holding one up to his nose. "It's got kind of a hard, thick skin too. Must have to peel it like a banana. Maybe if we get right to the boarding house now there would be time to fix some for supper so we could find out how they taste."

The lady at the boarding house was happy to be given the avocados. "These are very dear!" she exclaimed. "I don't have them here often because they are so dear, you know. But you shall have them in a salad for your supper tonight."

Thus, an avocado was served chopped up with a banana and an orange bathed in a honey dressing, and though both Joe and Howie liked the taste of the fruit salad, they both thought the salad wouldn't taste much different without the almost tasteless, greasy texture of that green mushy fruit. They were both unimpressed with what 'everyone was eating nowadays.'

After dropping Howie off at the Lester's house the next morning, Joe decided to forego any sales calls for the day, deciding instead to drive as far out on Sunset Boulevard as he could then return along the Pacific Coast highway and take in the sights around Malibu. It wasn't long before the houses became more spread out, with trees lining the roadway rather than manicured lawns, the occasional graveled lane leading off to what appeared to be mansions nearly hidden from view. Every curve in the road seemed to offer a different, breathtakingly lovely surprise. It was just a few miles past the huge Will Rogers estate, on the crest of a winding hill, that Joe saw a small white house that seemed to be settled into the side of the hill with a winding, red staircase up to the front door and topped with a roof of red Spanish tiles. He stopped to gaze at it from the road below, curious about who might live in such a place and what the view must be like from that front porch. The house was not rich enough looking for him to approach it to try to sell some of his jewelry, but there seemed to be something very special about it. It was like a sentinel there, all by itself, safeguarding something unidentifiable. Puzzled, he continued over the crest of the hill, winding down to the highway that ran along the Pacific Ocean.

After writing his usual daily letter to Madelyn – telling her all about the house he had seen in the Pacific Palisades, he walked to the Post Office and mailed it in addition to the short notes he had written to George Miller and Catherine and Marty to keep them apprised of his whereabouts and what he was up to. It had been three days since there had been a letter from Madelyn, so when the clerk handed him a familiar scented envelope he couldn't wait to tear it open.

Dearest Joe,

I apologize for being so remiss in writing back to you, but I do have a very good excuse. I have decided to travel with the theatre group again this year and have been rehearsing every afternoon and evening for the past few days. We will be performing the same play as we did before, but this time we will be traveling through Virginia, North and South Carolina, Georgia and Florida. I'm absolutely full of excitement about it all because I have never seen that part of the country before and have always wanted to.

I know you thought you might want to come here for a visit this summer, so I'm hoping you won't be too disappointed that I won't be here. I'm sure my cousin Wilma would be delighted to see you again though, and she would also be delighted if you would drop her a line now and then. She was always very fond of you, you know. Thelma would love to see you again too. She had an immense crush on you!

Must rush off to another rehearsal dearest friend, and I promise to do better at keeping in touch whenever possible.

All my love old pal,
Madelyn

Joe leaned against the wall in the Post Office as he refolded the letter and slipped it back into its envelope. The prickling in the back of his eyes told him he needed to make his exit before the tears erupted and he embarrassed himself. Men weren't supposed to cry…especially not in public. He swiftly walked the two blocks down to the tiny hole-in-the-wall doughnut shop where he had met Howie, letting the sun and motion dry his eyes. His mind and his face were blank and it took him a while to respond to the friendly greeting of the man in the back of the shop busy flipping doughnuts in the big vat of grease.

"Good to see you again!" the man called out. "How did you and the kid make out the other day? Saw the two of you leave together and I've been wondering ever since."

"Oh," Joe responded, happy to have something he could concentrate on so he wouldn't have to think about the letter from Madelyn. "Got him a shave and a haircut and some respectable duds, then got him a bed in the rooming house where I'm staying and found him some work yesterday in Beverly Hills. He's there working again today."

The man stood there with his mouth agape for a full minute before saying, "You loaded or something? Didn't rob a bank or nothing did ya? Don't nobody with any money ever come in this joint far as I remember!"

"Not a robber; just a salesman. Same thing to some people, I guess, especially when you're good at it."

"What do you sell?"

"Right now some jewelry made by Indians and some Encyclopedias."

"What's that? That last thing you said, never heard that word before."

"Encyclopedias. That's a set of a dozen books with all the things in the world anybody knows about."

"Sounds important. Sounds like it might cost a whole lot too!"

"Pretty much. It's something mostly rich folks like to have to show off with I figure. I don't know if they use them much once they have them, but maybe their kids do for school work and such. Comes in handy for that I guess. Don't know, don't care."

"Well, for someone who claims to be a good salesman you aren't doing a very good job of selling me! Sounds like you don't much like what you're selling!"

"Oh no, sorry, it's not that. I just got a letter that put me out of sorts is all." Seeing the questioning look on the man's face, Joe decided to explain further. He really needed someone to talk to right then, or at least someone who was willing to listen. "It's a letter from my girl."

"Ah! Woman trouble!"

"Well, yes and no. Not exactly, but sort of…only not the way you might think. You see, I was planning to go see her next month in South Dakota where she lives, but now she tells me she is going to be traveling all summer all around the southeast, clear on the other side of the country, so I won't be able to go see her because she won't be there!"

"Well, that's not the end of the world now, is it? Autumn follows summer, winter follows autumn, then comes spring again followed by another summer. You can still go see her, only maybe not quite as soon as you'd like! Huh?"

"You don't understand! It's already been way too long since I've seen her. I've been counting the days!"

"Well, if there's no changing things looks like you'll have to grow another set of fingers and toes so you can count higher. Or, find another girl close by."

"I'm not interested in finding another girl!" Joe said vehemently. "She's the only girl I want."

"Just making a suggestion! Seems to me you might be a whole lot more interested in her than she is in you…considering the fact she'd rather spend the summer traveling than spending time with you. Did she ever tell you she loves you? Did you ever tell her you love her and she told you the same thing back?"

"She starts her letters 'Dearest Joe' and ends with All my love old pal."

"Joe huh? I'm Ken. Might as well be on a first name basis considering what we're discussing. I don't think what she writes qualifies as an 'I love you'…especially because of the 'old pal' part. You ever ask her to marry you?"

"Not yet. There are some complications we have to get around first."

"Uh oh. What kind of complications? Don't tell me she's already married to somebody else!"

"No. But she says she wants to be. She says she wants to be the bride of Christ. She wants to be a nun."

"You have got yourself some big rival there buddy!" Ken said, slowly shaking his head.

"There's more. It's me who was married before. Married and divorced. No Catholic girl would marry a divorced man unless she wanted to be excommunicated from the Church."

"You know what I think?" Ken offered. "I think you need to recognize that this girl is a lost cause. There are plenty of girls out there who would make you a good wife, make you happy."

"But none of them are Madelyn. No one else ever could be."

"You know what I think?" Ken asked, not caring if anyone really wanted to know or not. "I think maybe you want this Madelyn girl because you know deep down that you can't have her. You know it's never going to be possible. And the more impossible it becomes, the more you want what you want. You need to get over her, find another girl, make a happy life for yourself. A good lookin' smart guy like you shouldn't have no trouble attractin' some beautiful ladies to pick from."

"I don't have any idea where," Joe said apathetically.

"Well I do! You like to dance?"

Joe nodded.

"Ever been to one of them dime a dance joints?"

Joe shook his head, brow furrowed. "What's a dime a dance joint?"

"Oh, they got them places all over now. They're regular dance halls that hire pretty girls to dance with men for a dime a dance. The one I go to you buy as many dances at the ticket booth as you want then look around and find a girl, or as many girls as you want, and hand them a ticket to dance with you. I never saw a girl turn anyone down because she didn't like a guy's looks or the way he was dressed or anything, and if you want to get to know a particular girl a little better you can use a ticket to buy the two of you a lemonade or soda pop or even a sweet tea and sit at one of the little tables they have there and just talk or listen to the music for a while. The girls don't like to sit out the dances for too long though because they get paid at the end of the night according to how many tickets they collected."

Joe listened to Ken ramble on with growing interest. He definitely liked to dance, and the idea of dancing with a lot of different girls definitely sounded appealing. Additionally, there was an intriguing sense of excitement growing in the back of his mind, like an idea trying to form that he couldn't quite grasp…but was frustratingly just inches away. "You planning on going there again anytime soon?" Joe asked. "I might be interested in seeing what it's all about, seeing as how I enjoy dancing."

"How about Saturday night? Think you can wait 3 days? It's a big dancehall called the Starlight Ballroom, 2 blocks east of here then 4 blocks north. I'll meet you outside at eight."

Joe was looking forward to telling Howie what he had learned about dime a dance ballrooms when he picked him up that afternoon, but he didn't get a chance because Howie had news of his own that couldn't wait. "Mr. and Mrs. Lester invited me into their house today for a long talk," he told Joe excitedly. "They wanted to find out all about me since they liked the way I had worked for them for 2 days. And you aren't going to believe this, but when I told them about my mother and 2 sisters over in Pomona they got real excited and happy looking and wanted to know all about them too. The Lesters just moved here a couple of weeks ago and they didn't know where to find any reliable help they told me until I came along and if my mother and sisters are as good workers as I am they want to hire all of us and have us move into their guest house because they don't need it for guests because their house is already big enough for guests but too big without a lot of help with the cooking and cleaning and laundry and gardening and even driving because Mrs. Lester doesn't drive. I told them I knew my family would be just what they needed and they would be happy to work for them and grateful too, and they wanted to drive right to Pomona and pick them up but I asked them to give me a day off to break the news to them and they said okay."

"Why did you want a day to break the news to them?"

Howie's face reddened. "Because I think part of the reason the Lesters like me is because I look presentable. I don't think they ever would have hired me if you hadn't made me look presentable. So I need to make sure Mama and Clarice and Annabelle look presentable too, and I don't know for sure if they do. I need your opinion on that."

"Well, how am I going to know that if I don't see them?"

"I know you need to see them before you can make that judgment. That's what I need the day off for…to ask you for the favor of taking me to Pomona and picking them up so you can tell if they look presentable or not."

Joe could hardly keep a straight face. "Let me get this straight. You want me to take a day off, so you can take a day off, for me to drive you to Pomona to pick up your mama and sisters and determine whether or not they are presentable before they meet their new bosses instead of those new bosses going and picking them up and determining whether or not they were presentable for themselves."

"Yes."

"What if we disagree about whether or not they look presentable?"

"We won't disagree. It's up to you whether or not they look presentable."

"Why is that?"

Howie gave Joe a look that indicated he thought that was a stupid question. "Because… they are my family. I love them. They always look good to me!"

With something new to think about, Joe forgot all about telling Howie about the dime a dance ballrooms…and even about the letter from Madelyn for the time being.

The following morning Joe had driven all the way to a little town called La Puente before interrupting Howie's incessant chatter about the Lesters to ask him more about his sisters.

"Clarice is exactly a year younger than me. We were born on the same day, a year apart, so we share the same birthday. On June 11th she will be 18 and I will be 19."

"That's only a couple of weeks from now."

"Yep! And Annabelle has her 17th birthday on July 29th. As you can see, Mama had us all pretty close together. She said there was a couple of months in there when she had three kids in diapers before I decided to give her a break and finally use the pot."

"What do they look like…you know, color of hair, eyes, tall, short and so on?"

"Well, Clarice is shorter than me and Annabelle. We always kid her that since she was the one in the middle she must've been squashed. She's pretty though with her dark hair and blue eyes but she's a bit too flirty with the boys back home to suit me. Annabelle has dirty blonde hair like me and she's tall and skinny and kinda shy. I don't think it will take much to make Clarice look presentable because she is always pretty fussy about how she looks. But it might take a bit of work to make Annabelle presentable. She'd just as soon wear an old pair of men's overalls and a big old torn shirt as anything!"

"Sounds like we might need to go shopping for a dress for her," Joe said. "Or, did they bring along something other than work clothes when you all came out here?"

"We each just had a gunny-sack of what we couldn't bear to leave behind, plus the clothes on our backs when we hopped on the freight car and headed out here. Mama toted some hard biscuits and jerky she'd made so we had something to eat on the way, plus a lard bucket full of water to wash it down with. I don't think there was a whole lot in the way of clothes…didn't have that many to begin with."

Joe was reluctant to bring up the subject, but decided there was no way out of it so he may as well ask. "Are you thinking about asking me to buy some new clothes for your Mama and sisters the way I did for you? Because if you are…"

"No! Absolutely not! Not at all!" Howie interrupted. "I have sixteen dollars in my pocket. I can buy new clothes for all 3 of them if necessary. I had no intention of asking you for anything more. You've already done enough for me and I'll be paying you back, for everything, just as soon as I can."

"If you hadn't interrupted me, I was about to say I would be willing to do whatever I could to help you get your family 'presentable' for the

Lesters. It might take a lot more than your sixteen dollars, so be prepared to be shocked. They might need a lot more than you think."

"I don't want it to be more than the sixteen dollars. How much do I owe you already…for the clothes, and haircut and room and board and…"

"I didn't keep track."

"If you didn't keep track, how will I know how much I owe you?"

"Maybe someday *I* will need *your* help. That's what you will owe me. Deal?"

"You really don't want me to pay you back?"

"I don't need to be paid back right now. Maybe I never will. But if I do, I want to be able to come to you and ask for repayment…provided you have the means to repay me at the time."

"That's a deal!" Suddenly elated, Howie exclaimed, "If I don't have to pay you back right now I can save up enough to get a ticket for Suzanne to come out here and maybe we can even get married!"

"Who the heck is Suzanne? You never mentioned anyone named Suzanne!"

"My girl! The woman I love and asked to marry me! The woman who said 'yes' she would and would wait for me to get settled out here then she would come be with me! OH!" he blurted, sounding alarmed. "I'll have to discuss that with the Lesters I guess. I don't know how many folks they would want living in their guest house."

"Well I'll be darned!" Joe exclaimed. You've got yourself a girl who wants to marry you. Wish I was you right now. I've got a girl I want to marry too and I love her so much I can hardly tell you, but I have no idea if she even loves me back."

"I surely didn't know you had a girl either so you surprised me with that too! But as far as knowing whether or not she loves you back, that's easy!"

"How so?"

"Well, she'd probably act like my Suzanne. She'd come running when she saw you coming and fly into your arms and cover your face with kisses. Then she'd hug you tight and giggle and couldn't stop touching you. Does your girl do that?"

"No. Are you sure that's how girls are supposed to act when they're in love?"

"That's how Suzanne acts…and I know she loves me. She tells me she does, over and over again. Of course, not a day goes by that I don't tell her I love her too. Do you do that? If you don't, don't expect her to ever tell you she loves you. The man has to say it first. My Mama told me that."

'The man has to say it first.' Joe mulled that over inside his head, trying to remember if he had actually ever said it to her or only implied it. One minute he was sure he had said it, then the next minute not so sure at all. The only thing he was certain of is that Madelyn had never said it to him.

The first thing Joe noticed about Howie's mother and sisters is what each of them, obviously, considered to be something they could not leave behind. His mother, neatly dressed in a faded cotton housedress that reached nearly to her feet sat on a wooden bench surrounded by neatly folded bits of cloth, embroidery hoops and numerous skeins of brightly colored embroidery floss, completely absorbed in what she called her 'fancy work'. She nodded perfunctorily at Joe when Howie introduced her then resumed her intricate stitching without offering any form of greeting or acknowledgement to her son. The sister with the long dark hair tied back with a blue ribbon and wearing what looked like a Sunday best dress with a fancy lace collar had to be Clarice, Joe decided. She smiled at him through lips heavily plastered with lipstick, making her rouged cheeks look pale by comparison. And the remaining sister that had to be Annabelle had her long hair in pigtails and was wearing what must have been her dead Pa's old work shirt, pants and boots. Joe didn't know exactly what it would take to make the trio look like what Howie meant by 'presentable'. But it didn't look to him like it was going to be easy.

He sat, quietly observing, while Howie explained the situation to his mother and sisters, seeing Howie's mother seeming to come to life as the information sank in. Clarice began squealing and jumping up and down like a small child at Christmas, while Annabelle collapsed to the floor and began bawling in relief, and in the middle of all the bedlam that ensued, with everyone talking at once, Joe found himself being kissed soundly on the mouth by a pair of slippery, sweet smelling lips, then hugged from behind by strong arms in a vile smelling, scratchy shirt. He grinned in embarrassment, then quickly decided he better take charge if they all expected to 'get presentable' then get back to Santa Monica before dark.

All three women thoroughly enjoyed shopping at the Orange Belt Emporium on the main street in Pomona. They each got a simple, no nonsense cotton dress, plus a head-scarf for Mama to wear to hide the grey in her hair and white cotton gloves to hide her ragged looking fingernails. Annabelle needed gloves for the same reason, plus white socks and some girl shoes in addition to the dress. And when Clarice crossed Annabelle's long pigtails over the top of her head and pinned them in place for her then added a bow, and a bit of color to her lips and cheeks, Joe decided she looked very nice indeed. Clarice also looked very sweet and demure in her plain cotton dress and white gloves, but it took quite a bit of convincing for Joe to get her to remove most of her lipstick, and he found he had to do it for her with his handkerchief. She smiled at him coyly as he did so then, eyes twinkling, coquettishly said, "Now go remove *your* lipstick!"

That Saturday morning Joe dropped by the Lester's house to see how Howie and his mother and sisters were doing. He found Howie in the side yard pushing a lawnmower around, and whistling off-key. "Getting all settled in?" he asked.

"Not that much settling in to do." Howie replied. "Everything is furnished here for us so all we had is our gunny-sacks to unload and put away. Mama put out the pictures she had of us growing up to make it feel like home and put some of her doilies out on the backs of chairs and on the tables. Made it look right nice!"

"So, did the Lester's think your mama and sisters were presentable enough?"

"Took right to them!" Howie said heartily. "Mama will be doing the cooking, baking and cleaning up and shopping…the kitchen is all hers Mrs. Lester said. Annabelle is to do the laundry, bed making, ironing and keeping things tidy upstairs, while Clarice is responsible for downstairs and for answering the telephone and keeping track of appointments and such. Sort of like a secretary / maid combined. And I will be keeping up the grounds and keeping the 2 cars polished and driving Mrs. Lester wherever she needs to go."

"You know how to drive?"

"I've been driving since I was ten. Tractor, old pick-up truck, car …all over the farm and out on the roads and into town. Did lots of things… until my Pa died and the bank took everything we ever had."

"That's happened to a lot of people. It's maybe why I never wanted to own anything I didn't have the money in my pocket to pay for. It's also why I don't ever plan to work for anyone but myself. No job working for someone else is forever, but when you make your own way for yourself you will always have a way to make a living as long as you are alive. And you can keep changing what you do whenever the need arises; you aren't stuck with doing the same thing for your whole life. Right now I'm selling Indian jewelry and encyclopedias, but before that I was selling surgical bandages to doctors and hospitals, and before that it was golf balls and candy."

"But it's all selling, so how is that different? It's just selling something different."

"You have a point there," Joe conceded. "But selling something different means you are into a different market. With the bandages I was selling to doctors and hospitals, the golf balls and candy was sold to stores and small shops, and the jewelry and encyclopedias are sold directly to the consumer. Big difference."

"Not so big. It's still all selling."

"Everything is selling!" Joe exclaimed. "Every single kind of work or job involves selling, so I figure I might as well do it directly and not have to bother with any middle-man who dictates to me how much I'm going to get paid for doing his selling for him."

"How is everything selling?" Howie argued. "I'm mowing the lawn here…how is that selling?"

"You are selling your labor for a price!" Joe exclaimed. "And your employer is buying your labor at a price he is willing to pay. Also, do you think you would even have this job if your employer hadn't been *sold* on the idea that you had something worth buying?"

Howie stood, alternately looking at the handle of the push mower he held in his hands, then the yard around him, then back at Joe, mouth agape. "*Dang!*" he exclaimed. "I never thought about it like that before. *I reckon you're right!*"

Joe met Ken outside the Starlight Ballroom that night, genuinely looking forward to a night of dancing with pretty girls. He watched Ken plunking down fifty cents, and then picking up and counting his five tickets. But, knowing he wanted to dance more than five dances, Joe handed the clerk a dollar bill and boldly said "ten please."

"You didn't need to buy that much right off," Ken said. "You can start with just a few then come back and buy more if you want them."

"Can't I use these tickets another night if I don't use them all tonight?"

"Nope! They change them every day so they are only good for the night you buy them. The girls all line up at the end of the night hoping men will give them some leftover tickets so they can cash them in."

"So, I am buying a dance for a price I am willing to pay, and the girl is selling a dance with me for an amount she is willing to accept as payment. Is that how it works?"

"Pretty much. Except, the girl doesn't get a dime for every dance, she only gets a nickel. The other five cents is split between the band and the owner of the ballroom."

"So, the more girls there are, the more men are attracted, and the more money there is for the band and the ballroom owner because they get half of what every girl makes. So, the more girls, the better."

"I guess so. Never thought about it that way, but I suppose that's the way it would work."

"Whoever thought up this idea is a genius!" Joe remarked.

"How's that?"

"Well, what lonely guy wouldn't pay a dime to hold a pretty girl in his arms for the length of a dance? Guys pay that much for a cup of coffee and a greasy doughnut they can swig down in half the time it takes for a dance, and that's not anywhere near as satisfying! So, thanks for letting me in on this my friend. I plan on having myself a great time tonight!"

Joe and Ken found themselves a small empty table surrounded by 4 small wooden chairs. Joe thought of that spot as his 'base of operations' as he surveyed the room. Girls were lining up along the far wall, some sitting demurely with their hands folded in their laps while others were loudly conversing and openly flirting with the men seated on their side of the hall. Some were still entering the hall from the back rooms or were just standing about waiting for the band to begin playing and their work night to begin. Some looked excited, some looked bored, some looked expensively done up and some looked like the girl next door. Joe saw that some even looked like his 4th grade teacher, and to his horror, like his mother as he remembered her from his childhood.

"Is there a particular girl here that you especially like to dance with?" Joe asked Ken.

"See that one, 1,2,3,4...the 6th one down over there in the yellow dress?" Ken asked. "She's the one. So, she's off limits for you, okay? I already have enough trouble trying to keep her to myself without a good-looking young guy like you after her too. Her name is Gladys...and she smells like Ivory soap and clothes starch and honeysuckle all mixed together."

Joe looked at the girl in the yellow dress. She was one of the ones demurely seated with her hands folded in her lap and her knees pressed firmly together, discretely covered by the hem of her dress. To Joe, she looked like the dangerous kind, the kind he wanted to avoid. Because she looked like the kind of girl who didn't belong working in a dime a dance joint...she looked like the kind of girl men wanted to marry. "You serious about her or just think she's a great girl to be dancing with?" Joe asked.

"Both, I guess." Ken had been keeping an eye on her ever since they arrived, and at just that moment he saw another regular at the dancehall approach Gladys and begin talking to her. "Be right back," he called to Joe as he leapt up to charge across the dance floor.

Joe watched as Ken intervened on the other side of the room, seeing him fish out all his dance tickets from his coat pocket and hand them to the girl. He saw the other man back off, clearly not as entranced with Gladys as Ken was, and not at all interested in an altercation. After all, his demeanor implied, there were other fish in the sea just as tasty and satisfying.

Joe discovered that his wandering eyes kept going back to a girl with light brown hair, a dainty nose and slender, shapely legs. His breath caught in his throat when he first saw her, startled by how much she resembled Madelyn. He felt he was under some kind of spell until he saw the girl smile at something another girl said to her before she remembered to cover that smile with her hand. The poor girl was missing several teeth in the front and the smile looked like a dark, gaping hole. Feeling sorry for her, but repulsed at the same time, Joe decided he would just hand one of his tickets to the first likely looking girl he came to once the music started.

His first pick was a petite girl named Trudy who looked like she would be light on her feet but was more like trying to haul a truck around the dance floor. Next was Eleanor who proved to be more of a leader than a follower, then came Marion with a shrill voice who wanted to chat in his ear the whole time. The fourth girl he chose to hand a ticket to, proved to be the one he chose to hand the remainder of his tickets to. Her name was Lorraine, she fit nicely in his arms, followed his lead flawlessly, smelled of rosewater, had a pleasant sounding voice and conversed about the right amount; not too much or too little. Joe decided she was very pleasant company and used one of his tickets to sit out a dance with her and another one to buy them both a glass of lemonade. "How long have you been doing this? This kind of work I mean," he added.

"Not long. About 3 weeks now is all."

"You like it?"

"Yes and no. I like to dance, but I don't always like the men I have to dance with. But that doesn't include you!" she quickly added. "You are a gentleman…and a very good dancer."

"So are you…a very good dancer, that is. Unlike the first three girls I danced with tonight. I like to dance too, so I was wondering if you would allow me to monopolize you until I run out of dance tickets. Unless, of course, you would prefer…"

"No!" she laughed. "I would be very happy…grateful even, if you were to monopolize me for as long as you want! You would be saving me from all the clods out there with two left feet, not to mention having to put up with their halitosis and having my face whisker burned and my nose shoved into their pomaded hair when they try to lock me into their unwelcome embrace."

Joe was bemused. "Why do you do it if it's that bad?"

"For the money. I have a bad habit. I like to eat and keep a roof over my head."

"Isn't there anything else you could do?"

"I can make about sixty cents an hour here doing something I like to do so much I would do it for free. Can you tell me another kind of job a girl could get for that kind of money?"

"I don't know much about the kind of jobs there are for girls."

"What kind of job do *you* have?"

"I work for myself. I sell jewelry and encyclopedias. For right now, anyway. I sell different things at different times."

"Can you make good money selling stuff?"

"Depends on what you're selling; sometimes yes, and sometimes no."

"So, give me an example. What's a good thing to sell so you make a lot of money, and what's a bad thing to sell that won't make you all that much."

"Well, don't take offense, but what you are selling is a dance with you for five cents, so you have to sell a dozen dances every hour to make sixty cents. That means you have to have someone want to dance every dance with you if you want to make that much an hour. Could get mighty tiring after a while, huh? A little hard on the feet night after night? Plus, you have to put up with dancing with a lot of men you'd rather not let anywhere near you. So, seems to me like selling dances is not a very good thing to be selling if you're looking to make money…even if you like to dance. Now me, I make seventy five dollars for every set of encyclopedias I sell…that's seventy five dollars clear…and sometimes it doesn't even take an hour to do it!"

"Where are you going to find anybody to buy a set of encyclopedias every day?"

"Nowhere that I know of, but at seventy five dollars a sale I don't have to! Selling just one set of those books a month will give me as much money as you make dancing here 5 nights a week for a month."

"Okay, but where are you going to find anybody with that kind of money to buy those books?"

"I do it regularly! If you're interested in learning how I'd be happy to show you. How about I meet up with you first thing Monday morning and show you where and how to sell something that can make you some real money…not just a few dollars to get you by."

"How do I know I can trust you? How do I know you won't be getting me involved in something illegal? There's a whole lot of that going around!"

"You don't know. I guess you'll just have to decide whether or not you think you can trust me. If you decide you can, I'll be over at that little hole-in-the-wall doughnut shop on Santa Monica Boulevard at 9am on Monday morning. Meanwhile," he said, reaching for her hand, "let's earn you another nickel."

Joe wasn't surprised to see Lorraine come through the door of the miniscule doughnut shop precisely at 9am carrying what appeared to be ancient looking hatboxes, one in each hand. After all her questions about selling at the dancehall on Saturday night, he figured she had something to sell besides dances and was dying to find out how to go about doing it. "I see you decided you could trust me," he said, smiling at her.

"I decided I would trust you enough to show me how I could sell something I've been making as a hobby for several years now. I have no idea how to go about it."

"So what have you been making for a hobby?"

"Ladies hats," she said shyly. "Want to see?"

At Joe's nod, Lorraine opened the first hatbox and took out a floral concoction that looked like a flowerpot with red geraniums potted inside. She placed it on the counter then reached into the hatbox again and withdrew what looked like another potted plant in a flowerpot full of pink peonies.

"I thought you said you made ladies hats!" Joe exclaimed.

"Just wait a minute…they *are* ladies hats…as I will show you!" Lorraine then took a U-shaped metal band wrapped in cloth to match the flowerpot, slipped it through a slot on the bottom of the pot of geraniums, placed the band across the top of her head, arranging her hair over it, then slipped the pot slightly over to the right side of her head so it sat at a rakish angle, then turned to smile at Joe. "What do you think?"

Joe leaned in for a closer look. "Cute, but…isn't that a bit heavy for a lady to wear for a hat?"

"It's not heavy at all! The whole hat is just made of light cardboard and felt and scraps of material and fine wire and some of them with a bit of straw. I've made these in every kind of flower imaginable, from asters to zinnias. And in the other hatbox I have hats I have crocheted in all different shapes and colors. They are very elegant and dressy looking, whereas these flower-pot hats are just for fun!"

Joe put his hands on the hat on Lorrain's head, feeling the flowers and the pot. "The flowers feel stiff," he remarked. I can see they are made of cloth, but they feel like heavy paper. How did you do that?"

"Starch, of course!" Lorraine explained as if that should have been self- evident.

"Oh." Joe said lamely.

"So, what do you think? Do you think I could sell them?"

"Absolutely!"

"Do you think maybe I could ask as much as three dollars for them?"

"I don't think three dollars is what you should ask. I think you should be asking more like five dollars."

As Lorraine sat there with her mouth open, staring in wonder at Joe, Joe was busy looking through the crocheted, and obviously starched, hats in the other hatbox, declaring "And I think some of these are worth as much as seven dollars, and some maybe as much as nine! Okay," he said abruptly, "we need to get over to my place. I've got some stuff over there you're going to need to get started and we've got a lot of work to do."

Lorraine looked startled. "You want me to go over to your place? Where is that?"

"A boarding house a couple of blocks from here. I have my car and a trailer full of the stuff you will need to get your hat selling business off the ground over there." Seeing her hesitation, Joe added, "You trusted me enough to come here, now you need to trust me a little further. I'm telling you that what you are making as a hobby is good and very salable. You don't have to believe me if you don't want to. But the question is, do you believe in yourself? If your answer is 'yes' then follow me."

Joe was several doors down from the doughnut shop when he heard Lorraine running behind him to catch up. "You could have been a gentleman and held a door for a girl," she said, handing him one of the hatboxes. Then she added, "This better be good!"

"Oh it will be!" Joe assured her. "You will never dance for a nickel again. And that's a promise!"

Joe went through the entire inventory in his trailer with Lorraine oohing and gasping at his side, stricken with envy by all the treasures he had amassed. Finally finding what he had been searching for, he withdrew a small box, telling the girl "Now let's hope the lady of the house here has a few minutes to give us."

Since his first day at the boarding-house, Joe had noticed how elegantly scripted all the house rules for boarders had been written, and had complimented the owner on her artful calligraphy. He figured she might be willing to use her skill making an advertisement and calling card for Lorraine's hats in exchange for a hat of her choice. She proved to be more than willing, even delighted to be asked, and Lorraine was very impressed with the name and drawing she came up with. It was a simple and elegant 'Hats by Lorraine', with the name Lorraine drawn out in the form of a wide-brimmed hat with letters made to look like flowers.

While the artwork was receiving finishing touches, Joe drove Lorraine out to the edge of the shopping district in Beverly Hills where he had previously noticed several vacant stores with "For Rent" signs posted on the windows. He found the owner sweeping out one of the smaller stores and inquired about the rent, a perplexed looking Lorraine hovering behind him.

"The rent is sixty dollars a month. In advance."

"That's a bit steep for me," Joe said, sounding regretful. "We are just getting an exciting new business started that should bring more customers to this end of the street, but our money is tied up in inventory and money will be tight until we can open up shop and start selling."

"What are you selling?" the man asked, more interested now.

"Ladies hats! Hats by Lorraine! This is Lorraine," Joe said, effusively presenting her to the man. Lorraine smiled and nodded then Joe introduced himself. "Let me introduce myself. I'm Adrian Joseph Tessier, dealer in fine jewelry and other finery for the sophisticated woman. I have discovered the talents of the lovely Lorraine whom I believe will become the most sought after designer of Ladies hats in the entire area. My jewelry sales are directly to the customer, but for this venture Lorraine will need a shop in which to display her wares as well as in which to design new ones for the many customers she is certain to have. So, do you know the owners of some of these other unused stores that might be willing to defer the rent for her, or preferably, reduce the amount of rent required? I would imagine that most would think even a reduced and/or deferred rent would be better than no rent!"

"I don't think anyone else could give you a better deal than I would," the man said.

"Are you offering a deal?"

"I can offer you the first month at half price, just so you can get yourself started."

"Is that thirty dollars in advance?"

"Yes."

"That's going to be hard too. Would you consider accepting something instead of cash?"

"Well now, that depends on what you have in mind."

"Well, let me ask you. Are you married?"

"Yes," the man said, drawing out the word.

"Does your wife have a birthday coming up? Or is it maybe your anniversary soon? Or do you have something you need to apologize for, or just want to give her something that says 'I love you' for no reason at all? Then, how about accepting a one-of-a-kind hat by Lorraine and an elegant turquoise and silver hatpin to pin it on with from me, in place of that half price first month rent? That could even pay off in dividends from your wife, if you know what I mean!"

The store owner didn't take long thinking it over. "Let's see the hat and the pin," he said, then the little lady can sign a rental agreement."

"Now what?" Lorraine asked as soon as she and Joe were back in Joe's car.

"Now we go back to the boarding house and get the address and phone number put on the advertisement and calling card then it's off to the library and their mimeograph machine. That's not as good as taking it to a printer, but we don't have 2 weeks to wait for that. Those advertisements are going to announce a grand opening a week from today. And first thing tomorrow I'm going to take you, your hat-boxes full of samples, your calling cards and advertisements out to the area where we will find the most likely buyers for your hats. We might wind up selling some of them on the spot, but we will mostly be introducing you and your unique line of hats."

"I don't think I'm ready to be selling hats!" Lorraine said nervously.

"Don't worry. I'll be right there showing you how it's done. Actually, I think you'll be a natural at it. The way you put that first hat on your head in a "voila!" sort of way certainly sold me! Plus, your hats are something new and different. And everyone wants something new and different. They will practically sell themselves!"

Joe's words proved to be prophetic. Nearly everyone they called on the following day was delighted with the hats, and the grand opening of Hats by Lorraine proved to be successful beyond Lorraine's wildest dreams. The advertisements that were left at all the houses they had called on were actually worded as special invitations to a premier showing at the new shop, with the recipient invited to bring along as many as three friends. There was also a door prize of a lovely silver and turquoise necklace to be won by a lucky buyer of a hat at the premier showing. Lorraine proved to be so adept at selling her millinery creations and coming up with new ideas all the time that it wasn't long before she needed to hire an assistant. Joe helped her out with that too, introducing her to Howie's sister, Clarice who proved to be very talented at finishing touches as well as bookkeeping and sales. All of which had a side-effect for Howie when Clarice moved out of the Lester's guest house and took up residence in a genteel boarding house, making it possible for Howie to bring Suzanne out on the train, marry her, and move into the guest house and take over Clarice's duties.

Joe and Lorraine stood up for the happy couple, Howie wearing the slacks and jacket Joe had bought him just a few weeks before, while

Suzanne wore a white linen suit she had brought with her on the train and a hat of white velvet roses with a veil that reached down to her nose that Lorraine had made especially for her. As they stood before the judge, solemnly repeating their vows to one another, Joe felt the prickling behind his eyes as they filled with tears. Then he felt a sudden tightness in his chest he thought of as heartache for the wedding he longed for that might never be a reality for him when everything suddenly turned black and he felt himself tumbling to the floor whispering her name, Madelyn, as the darkness overwhelmed him.

Joe came around quickly and everyone tended to take the whole incident lightly, including Joe, making fun of his lovesickness at witnessing the marriage of two young friends.

"You and Lorraine ought to consider tying the knot!" Howie chided him. "The two of you look good together and I really think she has a 'thing' for you, you know?"

"I don't think so. I think she just appreciates the way I helped her when she needed it."

"I think it's more than that."

"But it's not on my part!" Joe said adamantly. "It's not on my part."

Howie eyed Joe, concern written all over his face. Joe had recently confided in him about the irreconcilable obstacle between him and Madelyn. "Give it up, Joe. You need to stop wasting your life wanting something that can never be. Just give it up, friend."

"I can't; not yet," was all Joe could say.

OCTOBER, 1934

MADELYN'S LETTERS TO JOE HAD BECOME MORE FREQUENT ever since she returned from her summer-long theatrical tour and resumed teaching in the little one-room country school. They still weren't as frequent as Joe's daily letters to her, but he happily received a letter from her at least every other day. Although she was no more encouraging of a visit from him, saying nothing more promising than an admission that it would be 'nice' to see him again if he happened to get out that way, Joe chose to define that admission as provocative rather than simply promising. Her ramblings about her sister, Priscilla's little daughter born the previous year, the antics of her various students and the idiosyncrasies of her dear, sweet mother passed through Joe's mind like water through a sieve; and all that registered with him was any hint of encouragement he could discern in her words.

Realizing that his stock of Indian jewelry was running low, he made another trip down to Needles to find Corrine and replenish his supply. But the trip proved to be a waste of time. Corrine told him she could not sell to him anymore because a dealer had contracted to buy all the jewelry made by local tribes to sell in his chain of stores, so they were not allowed to sell to anyone else. Not knowing what else he could do, Joe merely turned around and headed back to Santa Monica. He spent that evening writing a letter to Madelyn letting her know he was on his way to South Dakota to see her, then writing another to the parish priest, Father Brunet, letting him know that he was headed there too, telling both of them not to bother writing back because he would not be there to receive their letters. He packed up his belongings, told the owner of the boarding house not to hold the room for him, mailed his letters then went around to say his good-byes to Lorraine and Howie, telling them he didn't know when he would be back…but promised to write.

With plenty of cash to sustain him, Joe decided he didn't need to haul his trailer all the way to South Dakota and back because he didn't plan on making any sales or foraging stops along the way. He made arrangements with Lorraine to stow the locked trailer behind her shop, taking with him only the remaining silver and turquoise jewelry to use as peacekeeping gifts for Madelyn and her mother, if necessary, as well as his valise with his personal effects.

Saint Onge had not changed one iota, Joe saw, as he slowly drove down the one main street, his vision blurred at times by smoke from autumn leaves set afire in the roadside ditches. He stopped where the road ended at a T that melded into a worn footpath snaking toward a miniscule white house where an elderly aunt of Madelyn's lived. He could see her sitting in a rocking chair on the tiny porch, looking back at him, so he waved at her, marveling that the ancient woman was still sitting in the exact spot he had last seen her several years before.

Then he turned his eyes to the right and looked down the road to the two handsome houses that stood side by side, separated by a wide swath of verdant grass raked clean of leaves, the open sky above outlining the stark branches of the oak trees surrounding the houses. The smaller of the two, on the right, was home to Madelyn's maternal grandmother familiarly known to everyone as "Tooty". Joe recalled how both her house and her person smelled of scallions, those little green onions she ate at every meal from spring into fall; a smell that permeated the flowered wallpaper and braided rugs and heavy velvet drapery in her parlor, releasing their pungent odor year round. He recalled with amusement the way he had learned how she had gotten her nickname on the day he had accompanied her and Madelyn on a tour of the garden and had heard a muffled poot-poot from time to time, and the way Madelyn had tried to cover the sound by clearing her throat or stooping to pluck a weed with a tsk-tsk sound. He smiled at the memory. He found the elderly woman to be utterly charming and a delight to be around. He wished he could say the same for her daughter, Emma—Madelyn's mother.

Joe directed his gaze toward the house on the left, trying to detect any movement around the place. When he saw none, he sighed then turned the steering wheel of his car to the left, toward the church, and the rectory and Father Brunet. After getting settled in and spending what he felt was an appropriate amount of time filling in the priest on his intervening years away, Joe excused himself to drive out to the ranch where Madelyn's sister Priscilla lived with her husband, Richard and young daughter, Linda. He had been hoping that Madelyn would be staying at the ranch instead of going all the way into town so he wouldn't have to face her mother just yet. But that was not the case. Then when he told Priscilla that he would head on up the road to the schoolhouse where Madelyn taught and she told him that school let out early during harvest season so Madelyn would have already left and would be back home in St. Onge, he realized he had missed her by spending time with Father Brunet.

Seeing the down-hearted look on Joe's face, Priscilla said, "Why don't you come for dinner tomorrow? School lets out at noon because it's harvest season, and Madelyn plans on being here tomorrow."

"Dinner is at noon?"

"Of course! The main meal of the day is always at noon. Have you forgotten? How could you forget that!?"

"I guess I've been away long enough for that to slip my mind. Madelyn will be here for dinner tomorrow?"

"Yes. And Mama and Papa will be here too. Mama will be helping me with the canning all day and Papa will be helping with the threshing. Madelyn will be helping in the kitchen too, so you won't get to spend a lot of time visiting with her…unless you want to put on an apron and ladle preserves into jars by her side," Priscilla said mischievously.

"I would be happy to be doing anything by her side," Joe replied. "But are you sure it won't be too much having me here when everyone is so, uh…busy?"

"One more plate to set out doesn't take much effort," Priscilla assured him. "And I'm sure Madelyn is just as anxious to see you as you are to see her."

"Do you think so? Did she say something to you about me coming back here?"

"Well, just that you were coming back. And it would be nice to see you again since she hadn't seen you for a long time."

There was that word 'nice' again, Joe thought ruefully. "We last saw one another in Holyoke, Massachusetts when she was traveling with the theater group in that area. Did she mention anything to you about that?" Joe asked tensely.

"She told us how you had won a draw for a new car at the show, and how you had taken her for a ride in it. And…oh yes, how the two of you had spent so much time driving that she missed going back to the hotel with the rest of the troupe and couldn't remember which hotel they were staying at so she stayed at your mother's house then had to rush to get the train in the morning and didn't even get to say a proper good-bye."

"That's it?"

"I think so. I can't remember anything else."

"She didn't, by any chance, tell you that I told her I thought I had fallen in love with her the very first time I had laid eyes on her?"

Priscilla laughed. "No, she didn't mention that. Did you really tell her that?"

"I did," Joe said vehemently. "And I meant it too. I felt a jolt when our eyes met for the first time. There was an instant attraction. She felt it too! She said as much!"

"Are you trying to convince me—or yourself?"

"I don't need convincing. I know! But I'm not sure Madelyn knows. She thinks she is destined to become a nun, and somehow I have to convince her that her destiny is to be with me—as my wife, the mother of my children, *our* children. I love her and being apart from her is killing me!"

"I don't understand," Priscilla said. "Why did you ever leave here if what you really wanted was to be with Madelyn?"

Joe searched for an easy answer, but knew there wasn't one that would be truthful or that would ensure that Priscilla would be on his side. So he merely said, "Sometimes, I guess, we don't know what we want until we realize we might lose it if we don't do something about it. I want to convince Madelyn that what she really wants is to spend her life with a man who loves her and wants to take care of her and be with her always. And that man is me."

"And you are telling me this because you want my help. Am I right about that?"

Joe nodded. "Any way you can."

Priscilla smiled at him then said the words that Joe most wanted to hear. "I'll do my best to convince her, because I have never liked the idea of my sister becoming a nun. I have always thought she should be a wife and mother…like me." She paused, furrowing her brow, before continuing.

"Tell me though, just what is it about Madelyn that made you fall so in love with her and makes you continue to pursue her after all the time that has passed?"

Joe didn't even have to pause to think about it. "She laughs out loud!" he affirmed.

Priscilla snickered. "Everybody laughs out loud! That's what laughing is, isn't it?"

"For most people, yes! But to me Madelyn is laughing out loud every minute of every day, awake or asleep, no matter where she is or what she is doing she makes me feel as if she is laughing out loud! She makes me feel the way laughing out loud makes you feel; warm and happy and welcome and…loved. We laughed together the day we met—sitting on the back porch steps of your folk's house in town—laughing over the hideous hair style her cousin had foisted on her. And ever since then I have felt her laughing out loud every time I think about her, which is almost every minute of every day anymore."

"Have you ever told Madelyn that?" Priscilla asked breathlessly.

"I haven't had the chance to tell her yet. I'm waiting for just the right time, you know, the timing has to be just right so I don't look like a fool or something, pouring my heart out, unless I'm sure I'm saying what she wants to hear. I have to be sure she's ready to hear what I have to say."

"Oh for heaven's sake just find a quiet time together and say it! I dare say it won't be something she has ever heard before and it is something any girl would be thrilled to hear! I was thrilled just hearing you say it, and it wasn't even directed at me!"

"You think I should just come out and say it to her? Really?"

"Really. And you will have the perfect opportunity to do so tomorrow when you come for dinner. I'll personally see to it!"

Joe arrived at the ranch a few minutes before noon the next day. He wanted to be there, waiting to greet her, when Madelyn walked through the door. He had pondered the idea of presenting gifts to everyone, trying to visualize when the best time would be—before dinner or after—changing his mind several times before deciding to wait for another opportunity. Perhaps at another dinner, or maybe never, just in case he might seem pathetically intent on winning everyone over with bribery or worse yet, look like he was showing off.

As he nervously waited, inhaling the delectable aroma of roasting chicken and pumpkin pies cooling on the windowsill, Joe watched the grinning Priscilla and scowling Emma as they set the table and filled glasses with iced tea, refusing his offers of help. Waiting, and pacing from the kitchen to the dining room and back again, he became aware of a nervous gurgling in his stomach, followed by a warning cramp. In a sudden panic, he excused himself while heading for the door, and made a mad dash for the outhouse. Then, as luck would have it, he exited the outhouse just as Madelyn pulled up beside it in her car.

Seeing her again after all the time that had elapsed was not the scene he had imagined and planned for. Red-faced in embarrassment, he mumbled a hello and an inane apology seemingly all at once, then escorted Madelyn into the house where he wasted no time before washing his hands then returning to her side to shake hers. His planned embrace and kiss on her cheek wasn't going to happen due to the perversity of an unruly belly and untimely nature call. *'This is off to a bad start,'* he told himself ruefully.

Following what felt to Joe like an almost gluttonous meal, he meandered into the living room to take his belt out a notch, unnoticed. The room was decorated in some very primitive looking antiques, with the centerpiece of the room being a slick, uncomfortable appearing horsehair couch. But it was the framed drawings and watercolors adorning the walls that caught his attention. The perspective of the artwork was so well rendered, Joe had the feeling he could walk right into the scenes. Stepping up to each painting, he saw that every single one of them was signed *Madelyn Dubois*. *'Artist, actress'* he mused. *'A girl of many talents. I wonder what other talents I will discover!'* Joe decided to take a stroll around the farm yard while the women did the cleaning up. The kitchen, where they had eaten, was overheated by the wood burning stove which was laden with boiling vats of water for the dishwashing, rinsing and sterilizing of the jars that would be used for the canning of peaches, pickles and jam, and the heat had permeated throughout the house. Outside, Joe soon found himself being followed by a bevy of hens pecking about his feet, intent on scoffing down any morsel he might unearth. But it wasn't long before the resident rooster took exception to his harem bestowing so much attention on a strange human, and ruffling his feathers to make him appear larger and more ferocious, he flew at Joe screaming out his fury, spurs digging, ineffectually, into Joe's leather belt. Joe hollered out his surprise and alarm, kicking out at the rooster and striking it squarely in the breast. More furious than ever, the bird charged at Joe again, and Joe ran screaming for the closest refuge, which unfortunately happened to be the outhouse. He managed to get inside and slam the door just a fraction of a second before the rooster flew at him again, spurs extended.

Breathing hard, Joe leaned his ear against the door, trying to discern whether or not the rooster had departed in defeat to join his flock. Hearing nothing, he decided to open the door a crack and take a peek, but what he saw almost made his heart stop. The rooster was positioned, ruffled and red-eyed, ready for war just outside the door. And he didn't look like he had any intention of leaving. Deciding there was nothing he could do other than wait out the rooster changing his mind about the situation, Joe decided he might just as well take advantage of his situation and relieve himself of some of that iced tea he'd had for dinner, and maybe, just maybe his gut was making those noises again and he was actually in a good place…if he didn't have to be there too long, that is. With no ventilation or light other than that afforded by a tiny sliding panel on the back wall of the outhouse, the rank odor was beginning to get the best of him. And by the time he was finally rescued nearly two hours later by a giggling Priscilla, he was painfully aware that the odor had permeated his clothes as well, as she laughingly held her nose walking beside him all the way to the house, then refused to let him enter until he had been sufficiently aired out.

"But what if that rooster comes back," Joe protested.

"Here," Priscilla answered, handing Joe a small pitchfork situated beside the door. "If he comes back just show him this pitchfork and he will be on the run away from you. He has flown into this trying to attack enough times to know he doesn't want to try it again."

"Well, why didn't someone tell me about that rooster before I came outside?"

"I don't think anyone saw you go outside. But even if they did it might not occur to anyone to warn you about the rooster. Especially not the men. They get a kick out of seeing unsuspecting strangers get attacked by that rooster."

Indignant, Joe stammered, "I spent almost two hours cooped up in that dark, airless, smelly outhouse. Didn't anyone see that rooster all fluffed up and angry, guarding that outhouse door all that time?" Joe asked, following Priscilla back toward that hateful outhouse.

"We were all a bit too busy to be looking out the door, wondering where you were or, quite frankly, caring where you were," Priscilla explained, trying unsuccessfully not to smirk. "You're just lucky I felt a need to use the outhouse or you'd probably still be in there!"

"How did you get the rooster to leave? You weren't carrying the pitchfork."

"Don't have to use the pitchfork any more. I got him so good with it one time that he is scared to death of me now. He runs when he sees me, except, of course, when I am emptying out the dishwater or tossing out scraps. Then he is right there with the hens getting his share of the pickings."

"I thought you were going to help me with Madelyn today," Joe said petulantly.

"The day isn't over yet," Priscilla retorted. "But you are seriously going to have to spend some time airing yourself out before you will be able to get anywhere near Madelyn. I suggest you take a walk down by the crick and strip out of your jacket, pants and shirt and hang them to air out on some tree branches. Then you can wash yourself off and let yourself air dry."

"What do I use to wash myself off?"

Priscilla gave Joe a dumbfounded look. "Water and your hands."

"I know that. But where do I get the water from?"

"From the crick, of course!"

"What's a crick?"

"A stream, you big dummy! Haven't you ever heard of a crick before?"

"Oh! Okay! You mean a creek!"

"Around here it's a crick! You need to learn to speak the language! Now get going, and don't forget to take that pitchfork with you." With that, Priscilla opened the door to the outhouse, entered, and closed the door behind her, effectively dismissing Joe to go air himself out.

Joe went around the side of the house holding the pitchfork threateningly in front of him. He traipsed slowly down the incline to the well-worn dirt path that led to the creek, pausing several times to check on the whereabouts of the rooster and his flock. When he spied the detestable bird on the far side of the house, vigorously scratching up the earth then pecking at it with his sharp beak, he sneered at it, uttering an oath of contempt. At the same time, he felt a sense of safety and relief, the pitchfork becoming a walking aide as opposed to a weapon.

He walked along the bank of the creek until he came to a grassy knoll surrounded by a copse of trees. It looked like a perfect place to strip out of his clothes and air them out, hidden from view as it was from the house and even from the path along the creek. He thought it looked like a good place for other things too…like a picnic, or…a place to profess his love. Quickly stripping down to his undershirt and shorts, he hung his smelly jacket, trousers, shirt and necktie on low hanging branches where the autumn breeze could cleanse them of the pungent outhouse odors, then removed his shoes and socks, carefully rolling his money into the toe of one sock and shoving it securely down into a shoe.

Joe waded into the water, but no more than three steps in found the ground dropped down and he was in above his knees. He reversed his direction, climbed back onto the grassy knoll and slipped out of his shorts and undershirt, hanging them on branches next to his shirt, then ran back to the creek and walked out into the middle of it. He gasped as the chest-high, frigid water surrounded him, but he dove down to submerge his head then erupted from the water with invigorating laughter, shaking it from his head with glee, loudly hollering "Whooh!" Dashing out of the creek, Joe clambered onto the knoll and stretched out in a spot in the grass, sun-washed through a break in the trees. He lay there shivering, but exhilarated, one arm extended as if he were reaching for the sun, waiting for it to dry him.

Had Joe known that Madelyn had gone looking for him, and had heard him loudly holler "Whooh!" divulging his whereabouts, he might not have been so complacent about lying naked in the grass on a sunny knoll, waiting for the sun to dry him. But for her part, Madelyn kept the knowledge of what she saw to herself, and held it in her heart. What she saw was, to her, a real-life re-creation of Michelangelo's painting of Adam, the first man, on the ceiling of the Sistine Chapel in Rome. And the sight had a striking impact on her feelings about Joe. She stared in awe at his naked body glistening in the sun until she saw him stir slightly. The movement breaking her trance, she quietly turned and retreated back along the creek and up the path toward the house.

Joe swiftly donned his underwear then thoroughly sniffed each remaining article of clothing, giving it a final shake in the cool air, before putting it on. He sat precariously on a small rock to put on his socks and shoes, gazing out over the creek he would now have to learn to call a crick, marveling at the serenity of the place while simultaneously wondering what his hair looked like. He figured he might be able to check himself out if he could get a mirror effect from the water in the stream, but the water near the edge was moving too fast for that to be possible. Resigned to the idea that his always unruly hair was going to be a mess regardless of whether he saw it or not, he raked it back with his fingers, pressing it to his head, and began the short trek back to the house. He would have forgotten all about the pitchfork if he hadn't had to go around it to access the path, but he pulled it from the ground, tines covered in dirt, right where he had planted it. All the way to the farm yard, he hoped he would encounter that blasted rooster and have occasion to use that pitchfork.

Joe found Madelyn, Priscilla and their mother, Emma seated on chairs they had hauled out doors from the kitchen, fanning themselves with the bottoms of their aprons, when he rounded the corner of the house. Priscilla's little daughter, Linda was toddling around in the sparse grass outside the door, hauling a bedraggled looking rag doll behind her, clucking like a hen calling to her brood. She smiled a toothless smile up at Joe making her lose her balance, and promptly fell hard on her bottom and began to wail.

Priscilla immediately jumped up to comfort her baby, explaining to Joe, "It's too hot to be inside right now. Just go in and grab a chair and bring it out here. We have to let the house air out for a while."

'Lots of airing out going on around here today,' Joe thought as he carried a chair outside and set it across from Madelyn so he had a full view of her. He didn't consider the fact that his positioning himself that way would give all three women a full view of him as well.

"What in the world happened to your hair?" Emma asked bluntly.

"Mama!" Priscilla exclaimed, reddening even more than her overheated face had already been. "That's not a very polite question!"

"I'm not looking to be polite, I'm just looking for an answer to my question. And don't lecture me on proper etiquette young lady. He left here with his hair neatly combed, and has come back with it all disheveled, and there has to be a reason for that, which makes it a perfectly reasonable question."

All eyes were on Joe, awaiting a response from him. "Well," he began, "it was getting pretty hot in the kitchen several hours ago so I came outside. And I stuck around here pretty close for quite some time then decided to take a walk down by the 'crick'. I found this grassy knoll and decided to sit there for a while, but the water in that 'crick' looked so inviting that I just couldn't resist taking a dip in it. I realized that was a bit risky…it's been a long time since I've been skinny dipping…but I figured I was well hidden and nobody would be coming around, so I chanced it. When I got out of the water…which was pretty quick since it was freezing cold…I lay in the sun on the knoll until I dried off. I hadn't figured on what getting my hair all wet, and me being without a comb and my pomade would do to my appearance, and for that I apologize. Ladies!"

Joe's impish grin combined with his unruly hair nearly obliterating one of his eyes made Madelyn start to laugh. "You look almost as ridiculous as I looked the first time we met," she giggled. "Remember that stiffly starched helmet of hair I was wearing?"

"Do I ever!" Joe laughed. "And I remember how we sat on the back steps of your house in town and laughed until our sides ached. Too bad we don't have a photograph of the two of us together…you with your starched helmet and me with my fluffed up mop dangling in my eyes… we'd make such an attractive pair!"

The embarrassing silence that followed hung like a dark cloud over everyone until Priscilla suggested to Madelyn that she take Joe for a little tour of the farm. "Show him the milking parlor, and the cream separator, and the chicken coop and setting hens," Priscilla chirped invitingly. "And don't forget that pitchfork to protect yourself from Clyde."

"The rooster's name is Clyde?" Joe queried. "Do the hens have names too?"

"Some do, some don't," Priscilla answered, as if the reason for that should be patently obvious. "It's only the one's you can tell apart from the rest that have names."

With the pitchfork slung over his left shoulder, Joe offered his right arm to Madelyn. She tentatively placed her hand inside the bend of his elbow, as if trying it on for size then, quickly withdrew it to remove her apron, handing it to Priscilla. "Let's go down the path to the well first," she said a bit too loudly. "Then you'll see how steep the path is to tote those buckets of water back up to the house several times a day. I used to have to do that for more years than I care to remember!"

Joe followed Madelyn down the path which was too narrow for them to walk side by side. But he didn't mind following her at all. He enjoyed the view of her side to side swaying posterior, marveling at her ability to produce such an astoundingly enticing stride without anything breaking or seeming to come apart. He decided right then and there to make certain to follow her back up the path when they returned to the house.

He had to see if she could be as loose-jointed walking uphill as she was going downhill. One thing he knew for certain…he would be content to walk behind her forever if he had to…because her behind was the most entertaining and thoroughly enticing and enchanting thing he had ever seen in his life!

"This is the well," Madelyn said in her best 'school-marm' voice as they reached the bottom of the path.

"Yes. I surmised as much," Joe said in a deadpan. "The pump was a dead giveaway."

"Oh, so you're going to be a smart-aleck are you?"

"That wasn't my intention."

"Well it sounded like it was. I know what smart alecks sound like because I'm subjected to them every day in the classroom. And what you said was definitely a smart-alecky remark."

"I didn't mean it to be. I was just trying to bring a bit of levity into the conversation."

"We weren't having a conversation. I was simply pointing out to you that we had reached the bottom of the path and had arrived at the well."

Joe took a deep breath, exhaling loudly. "Can we start over? I don't want us to be having an argument over nothing."

"Oh, so you think it's nothing do you? Is that why you are huffing and puffing?"

"How am I 'huffing and puffing' as you call it? I just took a deep breath!"

Madelyn gave Joe a stern look then, ever so slowly, the sternness turned into a grin. "You should see yourself," she chuckled. "Your face is all red and your hair is blowing all over the place and hanging in your eyes and you look like you are getting ready to throw a fit or something! You look too funny for words!"

"Then stop looking at me!"

"How can I stop looking at you when you are right there in front of me? Should I look at the ground, or maybe turn around and face the other direction, or..."

Madelyn suddenly found her words halted by Joe's mouth covering hers in a violent kiss. He pressed his lips hard against hers, his hands pressing against the back of her head making it impossible for her to pull away. She struggled at first, more out of shock than offense, relaxing as Joe's lips gradually softened against hers and his hands began caressing her cheeks and the back of her neck. In wonder, she leaned into him, her arms encircling his shoulders, her hands grasping his hair, her breath catching in her throat. Suddenly abashed by her own reaction, she pulled away, whispering "Why did you do that?"

"Because it's what I have wanted to do ever since I first laid eyes on you years ago!"

"I mean right now. Why did you kiss me right now, here, in this particular spot?"

"Because you were close enough for me to do it...and to shut you up!"

"Shut me up?"

"It worked, didn't it? Pressing my lips against yours stopped you from saying another word...at least temporarily. But it didn't stop you from doing something unexpected."

"What did I do that was unexpected?"

"You kissed me back."

"I did not. I did?"

"Uh huh! You did, and you seemed to like it!"

"Well, if that was unexpected, what did you expect me to do?"

"I don't know...shove me away...slap my face...bite my lip..."

Aware that their arms still encircled one another in a close embrace, and their lips were just inches apart, Joe did the most natural thing he could think of and planted his lips firmly on Madelyn's once again. And once again she kissed him back, melting against him, enfolded in his arms.

"I can't be doing this," she protested lamely, pulling away from Joe.

"Why can't you be doing this? It's the most natural thing in the world for you to be doing."

"There's no point to it. Nothing can come from it. There's no way there is anything that can ever be between us!"

"You're referring to the fact that I've been married before. And divorced…don't forget that fact!"

"But that doesn't change anything as far as the church is concerned. A civil divorce isn't recognized by the church. The only thing the church would recognize is a legal annulment of your marriage approved by the Vatican, and there's probably not a chance of that happening. So, anything between us is impossible…and I shouldn't be kissing you. Maybe even kissing you under these circumstances is a sin. Not a mortal sin, maybe, but just a venial sin. Even so, I shouldn't be doing it…much less liking it!"

"And you *were* liking it, weren't you!"

"Well I'm not supposed to be, so I don't know why I did."

"I do. You are attracted to me the same way I am attracted to you. I know we need to be together for the rest of our lives, and you must know that too!"

"All I know is that it's not possible. I won't go against my church, my beliefs!"

"What if you don't have to? What if I apply for an annulment? What if I can prove I was forced into a marriage I didn't want? Is that grounds for an annulment?"

"I don't know what the grounds for an annulment might be. Can you find out from Father Brunet?"

"Um…the good Father doesn't know I've been married before. He may be curious as to why I am asking about grounds for annulment and ask questions I'm not prepared to answer."

"Why wouldn't you be prepared to answer them?"

"Maybe for the same reason you never told anyone about your experience when you stayed at my mother's house when you were in Holyoke. Maybe there was a reason you didn't want anyone to know about what you think of as my wicked past. Maybe, deep down, you wanted to keep it hidden so there would be a way, some day for us to be together."

"That's a lot of maybe's. And maybe some of them are even irrefutable… but how are you going to find out about the grounds for annulment if you don't ask the priest?"

"I'll ask another priest…one I'm not related to, one who doesn't know anything about me." A slow grin appeared on Joe's face. "Irrefutable… huh? You said the reasons I gave were irrefutable!"

"I said maybe. Maybe they are irrefutable."

"You don't know?"

"Not for sure I don't. I'm really confused about everything." Madelyn looked at the ground while saying, almost in a whisper, "I saw you earlier today."

"I know you saw me earlier today. We had dinner together."

"That's not what I meant. I meant I saw you down by the crick."

Joe felt his face reddening. "Just exactly what is it you saw? And how long were you watching?"

"I saw you lying in the sun, naked. I had gone looking for you and when I heard what sounded like a whoop of pure joy coming from the direction of the crick I followed that sound and discovered you lying on that knoll we use for picnics and you were stretched out naked and still…like a painting. I was mesmerized by the beauty and tranquility of the scene, but came out of it when I saw you move and then I knew I was seeing something I had no business seeing and I quickly turned around and fled back up to the house."

Joe studied Madelyn for a long time before replying, shuffling his feet from side to side and running his fingers through his hair like a comb, as if those movements would help him formulate exactly the right thing to say. He laughed softly to himself at one point when he realized he never seemed to say the right thing to Madelyn, making her look at him questioningly. "I don't know what to say," he admitted, shrugging his shoulders. "Seeing me in the buff today obviously wasn't the reason for you not divulging my situation to your family, because you knew about that several years ago. But seeing me in the buff today seems to have had an effect on you in terms of how you would respond to my advances. Am I correct about that?"

"I don't know" Madelyn said, blushing charmingly and with a trace of a giggle in her voice. "Maybe it did. I guess it must have. But I really don't know for sure."

"I'm going to drive over to Sturgis tomorrow and see if I can't talk to the priest there at St. Martins and get some answers about grounds for an annulment. Will that help clarify things in your mind for you?"

"You need to see if you *can* talk to the priest."

"That's what I said."

"No, you said you wanted to see if you *can't* talk to the priest. That's a distinct difference."

"Are we always going to have stupid little arguments about everything? Are you always going to turn into a school-marm when it comes to everything I say?"

"Do you want me to not do that?"

"Darn right I want you to not do that! It's very annoying, and besides that it interrupts my thought process. I just told you I was going to go talk to the priest in Sturgis, and instead of discussing that further you choose to give me a grammar lesson."

"It wasn't exactly a grammar lesson, it was…"

"It was a diversion!" Joe said a little too loudly. "Do you not want to discuss the possibility of my obtaining an annulment?"

"In all honesty, I don't know what I want, Joe." Madelyn's eyes filled with tears. "I thought I had my life all figured out and I felt content about it…and then here you are and I don't know any more about anything. I feel euphoric about the idea of becoming a nun, but then find myself dreaming of being in your arms and you kissing me and I know those two things don't go together and I feel so befuddled by the whole thing I don't know what to do or what to think. Am I making any sense to you?"

"To me, the only thing that makes sense is being with you for the rest of my life. I am in love with you, Madelyn Dubois, and I'm going to do whatever it takes to make you realize you are in love with me too and your future is with me by your side. And the first thing I am going to do is check out those grounds for annulment…and then I am going to court you."

"Court me? That sounds old-fashioned and fun!"

"I hope courting never goes out of fashion. I will bring you bouquets and bon-bons, I will escort you on strolls through the park, take you for teas and ice cream, and church suppers and country fairs. And I will dance with you under the stars and kiss you in the moonlight and hold you safely in my arms so you know you never have anything to fear ever again. And we will laugh together the way we did when we first met, every day, for the rest of our lives."

Without another word, Joe took Madelyn by the hand and led her around the side of the barn, pitchfork slung over his shoulder, then back up the lane to the house. As much as he would have enjoyed the view following her back up the path they had just come down, he enjoyed the feeling of her hand firmly and trustingly clasped in his far more.

Joe's meeting with Father Cartier in Sturgis the following day didn't go well. The priest was not at all reassuring about his grounds for annulment based on a forced marriage to a girl whose child he had fathered. He didn't feel that doing the right and honorable thing constituted grounds for an annulment no matter how much Joe felt he had been forced into it. "You are certainly free to try for an annulment," he said offhandedly. "But I think it will be a wasted effort and the results will not be to your liking. The Church is very exacting in matters of marriage."

Joe didn't know what he was going to tell Madelyn about the prospects for an annulment, but he knew he would, without a doubt, have to convince her that an annulment was indeed possible if he were to stand a chance with her. Lost in thought, he nearly drove off the road and into the ditch twice before deciding to pull into a farmer's lane and park. Not having to concentrate on driving made it possible for him to think more clearly, so when the idea popped into his head after just a few minutes he wasn't all that surprised. It had been there all along, just waiting for the right moment to reveal itself. But there was just one problem. He would have to reveal to Madelyn something she didn't already know about his situation…and he didn't know how she would react to that.

Joe timed his arrival at the Dubois family home in town to coincide with the time it would take for them to finish with supper and the cleaning up afterward. He bowed slightly to Madelyn's mother, Emma as he handed her a small box of chocolates then presented Madelyn with a flower for her hair. Seeing Emma's questioning scowl, he explained, "I am officially courting your eldest daughter…with her permission, of course."

"Madelyn gave you permission to court her?" Emma gave her daughter a questioning look. "Why? I thought you were intent on entering the nunnery when school lets out next spring!"

Flustered, Madelyn blushed. "Well, when Joe told me he wanted to court me, I thought it might be a good idea to let him so I could determine, for certain, whether or not becoming a nun was the right thing for me to do. I've put it off for quite some time now, supposedly waiting for a call that never seems to come, and I need to make sure it's the right thing so maybe this is the way to do that. Being courted, that is."

"Well, I know your father and I are very pleased to hear that you are finally allowing yourself another option…but I, for one, find your selection for a suitor to court you…questionable to say the least!"

"Why do you find it questionable?"

"Well you hardly know him! He's been away for years, and when he was here years ago he was insufferably rude to the point that I had to evict him from my house! And now this is the man you want to have court you so you can see whether or not you truly want to be a nun?"

"Yes Mama…Joe is the man I want to have court me."

Emma tossed her hands in the air, shaking her head in consternation, and exited the room leaving Joe and Madelyn grinning at one another.

"She'll come around," Madelyn reassured.

"I'm not so sure of that. Your mother has not taken a liking to me from the very first day I arrived here…and the unfortunate incident with the kitten way back then probably made it impossible for her to ever think of me as a worthwhile candidate for your hand. People generally take a liking to me right away…but your mother is the first person I have ever met who disliked me…seemingly out of principle…before we even met!"

"My mother doesn't like any man…out of principle…that she considers a potential suitor for one of her daughters. When Priscilla's husband, Richard started coming around, Mama wouldn't let him in the house!

And it was the same with any of the boys who wanted to come around to see me too!"

"That doesn't make any sense! She just said she was happy to see you were looking at options other than becoming a nun…and the other option is courtship and marriage!"

"I think the option she would truly prefer is to have me remain a spinster!"

"Isn't being a spinster almost the same thing as being a nun? Seems to me there is not that much distinction between the two!"

"Well, yes…in a way, I guess. But if I became a nun I would have to move away from here and probably wouldn't get to see my family very often. Remaining a spinster, however, would mean I could stick around here forever and just keep on teaching school or, better yet as far as Papa is concerned, take over the management of some of his various enterprises. He and Mama would both like that idea very much."

"And you? What would you like 'very much'?"

"That's what I don't know, Joe. But it's what I really want to find out."

"Then let's go outside so we can talk," Joe said, taking Madelyn by the hand.

Joe led Madelyn to the bench that was set on top of a concrete pad covering the cistern, far enough away from the house to be out of earshot from any nosy listeners. As they sat down, he took the flower he had brought her from her hand where she still held it, and placed it in her hair just above her left ear. Then he kissed her on her neck just below that ear. "You are so beautiful!" he told her, softly.

"I'm covered in freckles. You find freckles beautiful, do you?" Madelyn giggled.

"I do when they're covering you!" Joe insisted.

Sobering, Madelyn asked, "Did you get to see the priest in Sturgis today?"

"Yes!" Joe exclaimed, feigning excitement. "That's what I needed to talk to you about!"

"It sounds like you were happy with what he told you!"

"Yes! Very happy," Joe lied. "And a little bit afraid too because there's something you don't know about my situation and I don't know how you are going to take it when I tell you."

"Well, now you have me afraid too! So what is it you have to tell me?"

Joe took a deep breath for effect, trying to appear as if he were struggling to collect himself before a big revelation, which in actual fact it was, he told himself ruefully. "Okay, you know I was married before, and that I was forced into that marriage because the girl was in the family way and I was supposedly the father, right?"

"Right. Oh, you mean, you might *not* have been the father and you were tricked into marrying her? Is that a possibility?" Madelyn asked, excitedly.

"Well, that's *one* possibility," Joe said, wondering why he hadn't come up with that idea himself because it was a darned good one! "But there's a second possibility as well. I assume you must know that there was a baby involved."

"Oh! I guess I never really thought about that. So you are telling me that you have a child!"

"No, that's not what I'm telling you," Joe said, with not a little exasperation. "If you will just stop interrupting and listen, perhaps I can get through telling you about my conversation with the priest. Anyway, there *was* a baby involved, but there's not anymore. The baby, a girl, accidently smothered to death in her crib when she was five months old."

Madelyn opened her mouth to speak, but Joe held up his hand to stop her. Unabashed, she spoke anyway. "I just wanted to say I'm so sorry for you that the baby died," she explained.

"Thank you, I'm sorry too…but the baby dying was also the reason for the divorce and is now the reason why I could be eligible for an annulment.

Not only was I forced into a marriage when I was only seventeen, to a girl whose baby I might not even have fathered, that baby is no longer a living bond between me and her mother, so it is highly probable that the marriage can be annulled. So sayeth Father Cartier. It's going to take some time of course…these things do…and I'm sure there will be some expense involved as well…it seems there always is when it comes to church matters…but the end result will be my freedom to marry you, under the full sanction of the Catholic Church…if you will have me."

Madelyn smiled her most charming smile for Joe. "When that time comes, I guess we will see!"

"And meanwhile, I will be courting you, and doing my utmost to make you realize you are as in love with me as I am in love with you. Because I believe that, deep down, you already are and you just have to discover the certainty of that."

"Do you think that's why I haven't entered the convent after all these years?"

"I do. And the two words I just said are words I hope to be saying to you again very soon."

"There's a lot that needs to happen before that," Madelyn said resolutely. "I won't be able to make a decision about anything until you are able to obtain an annulment. And it won't matter at all if I discover I love you if an annulment is not possible."

"I intend to keep in touch with Father Cartier about the progress of that," Joe said, his sudden feeling of anxiety evident in his voice. He didn't know how he was going to be able to maintain the charade of attaining an annulment without a continuous deception and obfuscation of the progress toward that end. He knew he was engaging in the most immense and personally consequential con of his life…and that it could backfire on him as easily as it could work in his favor. The thought of that happening terrified him.

Picking up on the tremor in Joe's voice, Madelyn sought to reassure him. "Everything will happen as it should. You'll see. Just have faith that justice will be done and the Church will decide in your favor."

Joe put his arms around Madelyn's shoulders, drawing her close to him, and kissed the top of her head tenderly. "I have to believe that's the way it will be," was his fervent response. "Anything else is absolutely unacceptable. There can't be any other resolution of the matter."

They sat on the bench in a quiet embrace, both deep in their own thoughts, until the chill night air led them to say their good night's to one another, with a vow to see one another the following day after school let out at noon.

As the days grew shorter and colder, plodding along relentlessly toward the end of autumn and the onset of winter, Joe and Madelyn filled their time together attending country fairs and harvest dances, church bazaars and pot-luck suppers, interspersed between strolls around the town, the farm, and along the creek. It was on one of these strolls, just before dusk, that the two of them settled on the grassy knoll by the creek, wrapping the blanket around them that they had brought along to help ward off the evening chill. For a time they sat quietly, arms wrapped around one another, content to just be, and each immersed in their own thoughts.

Joe was the first to break the silence. "I wish I could stay here like this forever! I wish I hadn't left my trailer and everything in it that I need to make a living back in California. And oh how I wish I didn't have to leave and go back there and retrieve everything!"

They had discussed that the day before, and the urgency that Joe felt about making the trip before winter set in. Madelyn understood, but that didn't make things any easier. "I guess if you go back there right away you will be able to return right away too. You know…before it decides to snow and makes traveling difficult. But, how is that going to impact your discourse with Father Cartier and your progress toward an annulment? Will that set it back?"

"I don't think so. Are you worried about there being a setback?"

"I guess not,…not if *you're* not worried about the possibility of a setback."

"I think I kind of like you being worried about it. That means you really want this annulment to happen as soon as possible."

"Well, yes! The sooner we know, the sooner I will be able to make a decision about things!"

"Are you sure that's all it is?" Joe asked teasingly, kissing the tip of her nose.

Madelyn sighed. "When you do that I'm not sure of anything at the moment."

"Do what?" Joe murmured, nipping gently on her bottom lip then kissing it softly and sensually, the tip of his tongue tenderly brushing her slightly parted lips. He felt her body seem to relax and come to life at the same time, and he drew the two of them down onto the grassy knoll until they lay side by side, locked in an embrace, neither of them aware of anything in the world other than the intense desire of the moment, compelling them toward an end that ordinarily would have been unseemly.

Madelyn's sudden cry of alarm brought them both back to their senses.

"What's wrong?" Joe whispered, rolling onto his side and elevating himself so he could look Madelyn directly in the eye. "Did I hurt you? I'm so sorry if I…"

"What we're doing is what's wrong!" Madelyn whispered back. "It hurt, and that made me realize I got carried away and we were committing a mortal sin in the eyes of God."

"I readily admit to getting carried away…but I don't buy the idea of making love to you being a mortal sin when I am so in love with you."

"I'm ashamed of getting carried away like this. It can't happen again. It is purely and simply fornication," Madelyn said with a sob in her voice. As she continued talking, Madelyn readjusted her clothing under the blanket. "I can't take Communion this Sunday without going to confession, and I can't go to confession with Father Brunet because he will know who I am and I could never face him again if I confess that to him. I'll have to go over to Spearfish and visit my Aunt Leona, Mama's sister, and go to confession there." With a sudden intake of breath, Madelyn cried out in what was almost a whimper, "How could Christ ever accept me now as his bride? And what if what we did makes me with child?"

"It won't Madelyn. I can promise you that. We didn't get far enough for that to happen."

"We didn't? How can you be sure?"

"Well, I've had some experience with this, and I can tell you with certainty that we didn't get far enough with things for that to happen. And it's even possible that we didn't get far enough along for it to be considered fornication, so it probably wasn't a mortal sin either."

"Really? Are you telling me I haven't actually been defiled?"

"You haven't actually been defiled!" Joe assured her with as much fervor as he could muster. "Your virginity is intact and it is not possible for you to be with child as a consequence of what happened between us."

"But if I hadn't stopped us…if I had allowed things to go further…I would have lost my virginity and could have run the risk of getting with child. Is that right?"

"I suppose that that would have been possible, the virginity part anyway. But 'getting with child' as you put it is not that simple. I think it takes a lot more than one time, a lot of times actually, for that to happen."

Madelyn looked at Joe as if she were trying to come to terms with something that she found troubling. "So what you are telling me is that you would have had to make love with your wife many times before she could get with child. And if that's the case, why would you have any reason to believe that the child was not yours?"

"You're confusing the issue! It *can* happen the first time, but that isn't usually the case!"

"But is that the way it happened? Did she get with child the first time? Or, were there *many* times?"

"There was more than one time, I guess," Joe said haltingly and with a touch of anger. "I didn't keep count." In exasperation he enclosed Madelyn's face in the palms of his hands, looking directly into her eyes. "I didn't love her. That's the main point. I just took what she offered to me. And I don't know how many others she may have offered the same thing to. She just wanted to be married and I was handy. But I won't ever make that mistake again. From the moment I knew I was in love with you, I have kept myself for no one but you. I have been as celibate as a priest or a monk in a monastery. Until now…and nothing really happened now. And it won't as long as you don't want it to. You have my word on that. I love you more than you could possibly ever know Madelyn. And maybe even more than I know myself."

Madelyn looked back at Joe, silently digesting his impassioned words, judging their veracity. After an extended silence she said, "Well then , I guess you need to get back to California and collect your things and get back here as soon as possible so you can make further progress toward your annulment."

Two days later, Joe was on the road heading for the Wyoming border and the route he would be taking toward California. His last night in St. Onge was spent at the farm, where he dispensed the silver and turquoise jewelry he had brought for Madelyn and her mother and sisters. It was the last of the jewelry he had and he regretted there would be no more…it had been a very good way to gain entrance to the upper class neighborhoods, as were the encyclopedias, and he was running low on those as well. So the day before he left he went over to the tiny town of Lead where he heard they were making some jewelry they had dubbed Black Hills Gold. And what he saw took his breath away.

Never before had he seen such intricately designed pieces. The theme was the same on each piece of jewelry…grapevines and leaves, all of gold and alloys of silver and copper intermingled…rendered with a delicate perfection. He negotiated a price for as many pieces as he could fit into his black leather case, which had first seen duty as a receptacle for bandages, then for sets of encyclopedias, then for silver and turquoise jewelry in hand made velvet pouches, and now for exquisite gold jewelry, each piece in a gold box, padded inside with various shades of silk. He knew he could sell each piece, in select neighborhoods, for ten times what he had paid.

On the morning he left, he arrived at Madelyn's back door to say his good-bye's before she left for her school house. He had kissed her long and hard, and had held her in his arms for an extended time, aware all the while of a frowning Emma in the background watching disapprovingly with folded arms. Madelyn's father, Charles however, clapped him on the back and shook his hand, encouraging him to have a safe trip and return soon.

This time, on leaving St. Onge, it was different than it had been when he left several years before. Then, his rear view mirror had been of Madelyn walking indifferently away from him. Now, it was of Madelyn walking slowly toward his departing car, wiping away tears with a linen hanky.

Joe smiled at the vision…his eyes filling with tears as he did so.

NOVEMBER, 1934

JOE MADE IT ALL THE WAY TO PROVO, UTAH WITHOUT INCIdent before his progress was halted by a late fall snow storm. Cursing under his breath at the perversity of nature and its propensity for throwing a monkey wrench in the middle of his plans without regard for his need for haste, Joe reluctantly searched for a boarding house where he could wait out the storm and get a hot meal.

The place he found, Greene's Boarding House, looked reputable enough on the outside, but as Joe later discovered after the snow melted, its dilapidated exterior had been well camouflaged by a dressing of clean, white snow. Inside, the shabbiness was so overwhelming Joe thought the décor must have been intentional. The rugs on the floor were worn through to the floorboards in places, springs were poking up through the seat at one end of a seedy looking green couch, a small table in front of the couch sat on three legs with a stack of old books serving as the fourth leg, and a floor lamp to the side was as bent and fragile looking as a very old man with a bad back.

Joe very nearly turned around and walked out of the place, but a sudden gust of wind and swirling snow outside changed his mind for him. That,...

and the odor of something baking in an oven, fruity and seasoned with cinnamon. That smell made his stomach growl and his mouth water, and blinded him to the shabby surroundings.

The woman who greeted him at the door was very plain looking, but neat and clean. She showed him to an upstairs bedroom that he would be sharing with another gentleman, and advised him that supper would be at 6 PM sharp and he would owe her $1.50 for the room and supper, with breakfast in the morning included. Joe saw that, thankfully, there were two twin beds in the tiny room so he would not have to share a bed with a stranger. He'd had to do that a few times before in his life, and it had not been a good experience for the most part. Scooting as far as possible to the edge of the bed, and hanging on for dear life to avoid falling out was not his idea of a way to get a good night's sleep. But then, neither was trying to sleep in the same room with a stranger.

Deciding to try to make the best of it, he turned down the covers on the bed the woman had indicated would be his and was pleasantly surprised. The crisp, clean look and smell of the sheets did a lot to allay his fears about the place, so he made himself comfortable and tried to get in a bit of a snooze before suppertime – just in case sleep might prove to be impossible later on. But that snooze time proved to be short lived.

The door suddenly banged open to a loud "Well now! Frankie, the lady that runs this place, told me I had me a roommate! Name's Ralph Turner, what's yours?"

"Joe Tessier," Joe answered groggily, having been awakened so suddenly. "Pleased to meet you. Hope you don't mind me sharing your room with you on such short notice."

"That's okay. Don't mind a little company once in a while. It kind of breaks up the monotony, if you know what I mean."

"Yeah, I guess," Joe answered non- committedly. "Not sure what you consider to be monotonous though."

"Oh, pretty much everything anymore. Just the same old stinking job, the same old tacky boardinghouse, the same old girlfriend that don't seem to know any word but 'no', and the same old nothin' much to look forward to anymore. How about you?"

"Well, I guess there was a time I found life monotonous a few years back, but not anymore. Now I wake up every day anxious to see what the day is going to bring."

Ralph sat on the side of his bed and leaned in as close as possible to Joe, as if he expected him to reveal something secretive or magical. "How did you make that happen?" he asked solemnly. "If I'm not being too personal."

"No, not at all!" Joe said affably. "And there's no secret at all to breaking your monotony. You just have to decide you want to make a change…then make it!"

"But what does that mean!" Ralph asked, exasperation very evident in his voice. "What is it, exactly, that I have to do to make that change?"

"Well first, quit your 'stinking' job, then find yourself a new place to stay and maybe even a new girlfriend that knows how to say something more than 'no'."

"I can't do that!" Ralph protested loudly. "I need my job so I can pay room and board, and Frankie's place here is the best I can afford. And my girlfriend, well…she's sweet and kind even if she tells me 'no' when I want more from her than she is willing to give me right yet…without a ring on her finger…and I guess I love her and don't want no other girl. So what can I do besides all of that?"

"Beats me!" Joe exclaimed, shrugging his shoulders. "But it sounds to me like your life might not be as monotonous as you think. So maybe what you need to do is focus on what you need to do to get a ring on that girl's finger then work from there."

"I've been saving every little bit I can for that, but it's been so slow going I've gotten impatient I guess. If we could be together under the same roof our money would go a lot farther. Two can live as cheaply as one, or so they say."

"So they say!" Joe said agreeably. "Keep plugging away with what you're doing, and you may find that everything falls into place for you and your sweetheart before you know it."

Joe had to spend three days in Frankie's boarding house in Provo waiting for the snow squall to play itself out and enough snow to melt to make the roads passable. He spent most of his time writing letters to Madelyn and his various other friends even though he had no news to tell them. And the fact that there was a mailbox conveniently placed across the street from the boarding house, and that Frankie kept a roll of postage stamps on hand for her guests, made Joe feel obliged to write every day whether or not he had anything worth telling.

He also got to meet Ralph's girlfriend, Gwendolyn and decided she was indeed a very sweet girl. She was small boned, pale and delicate looking even though she was nearly as tall as big, beefy, florid-faced Ralph. In their quiet moments alone in their room, Joe told Ralph about his friends Howie and Lorraine, and how they had ideas they put into motion and how they changed their lives for the better. What he didn't tell Ralph was anything about his involvement in their success because he didn't want Ralph to think they couldn't have done it completely on their own. He had been there to help Howie and Lorraine, and he wasn't intending to stick around to help Ralph. He was in a hurry to get to California and pick up his trailer then get back to Madelyn before winter set in.

Following breakfast on his third day at the boardinghouse, Joe packed up his valise then wrote a short farewell note for Ralph, leaving it on his pillow along with a small gold box. When Ralph returned from work that afternoon he would find a note that read *"A Ring for Her Finger,* and when he opened the little box he would find a Black Hills Gold ring…about the right size for a small boned, feminine finger.

Joe felt it was the least he could do.

As he neared the outskirts of San Bernardino, Joe debated with himself about whether or not he should stop and see how Freddie and Eve were faring. He was curious about whether or not Eve's husband, Jim had returned, and whether or not Eve and Freddie were even still there. Changing his mind every few seconds about whether or not he should stop, he finally decided to stop in at the diner where Eve had worked if there was an empty parking spot right in front, and if there wasn't he would just keep going. But, there was an empty spot right in front of the diner – so Joe pulled into it.

It was as if six months had not elapsed since Joe had first walked into that diner. He took a seat at the counter next to the same man who had been seated there back in May, and the same young woman behind the counter who had greeted him then, greeted him again. Only this time the young woman was considerably less stout – and the greeting was considerably more effusive.

"Joe!" she chirped. "How nice to see you again! You need some more sewing done?"

"Not this time," Joe told her, reaching out and grasping her shoulder and giving it a squeeze. "Just passing through on my way back to Santa Monica and thought I'd stop in to see how you and Freddie are doing and whether or not you've had any word from your husband. I know you were worried about him when I was here back in May."

"I got a letter from Jim about a month ago. He sent me ten dollars which was a big help."

"So, did he tell you where he was? Did he find a job? Are you and Freddie going to be joining him?"

Eve looked embarrassed and considerably distressed, turning to look at the cook in the galley behind her who was eyeing her intently. "Do you want to order something?" she asked, turning her gaze back on Joe.

"I'll have the special, coffee, and a slice of pie. I take it you aren't supposed to fraternize with customers, according to the look on the cook's face," Joe added.

"Well, only if the customer is a good looking guy," Eve responded while writing on her order pad. "He's decided I should leave my husband and take up with him."

"Is that what you want to do?"

"No. Maybe. I don't know." Her eyes bright with unshed tears, Eve asked Joe if he could stop by the boarding house and see Freddie then wait there for her shift to be over so she could tell him all about what had been taking place with her. Joe had no idea why he agreed to do so since he was so near to his destination and he definitely didn't need any more delays. But he told her he would, partly because she seemed so distraught – and partly because Eve's situation had piqued his interest.

Miss Edna greeted him effusively, settled him on the settee in the parlor then loudly hollered "Freddie! You have a visitor in the front room!"

Freddie came halfway down the stairs, saw Joe, then in open-mouthed astonishment fled back up the stairs. Seconds later he returned carrying the big metal truck with a pig in a crate on the back of it. Joe had wondered if Freddie had been too young back in May to remember him six months later, but fetching that toy dispelled any question in his mind in that regard. He also saw that Freddie was taller and a good deal less pudgy than he had been six months ago.

"Hey there big guy!" Joe said, tousling Freddie's hair. "It looks like both you and your mama lost all the baby fat at the same time! And you got bigger – just like I said you would!"

Freddie smiled at Joe then sat on the floor next to his truck and began pushing it along the pattern in the carpet, carefully watching so that the wheels didn't go out of bounds on the imaginary road. He looked up at Joe every few seconds to make sure that he was watching, seemingly shy in his presence.

"Would you like to take a ride in my car again?" Joe asked.

Freddie nodded, shyly breaking into a grin.

"I don't have a big box for you to sit on this time so we'll need to get some pillows for you to sit on so you can see out the windshield. But you're bigger now," he added, "So maybe we only need one or two pillows. You grew a lot – and you look older too!"

Freddie held his hand out for Joe to see, and Joe placed his hand next to Freddie's. "My hand got bigger too!" Freddie said solemnly.

Perched on top of two pillows Miss Edna had provided them, Freddie eagerly chattered away, seemingly remarking about every fence, power pole, billboard and piece of discarded litter on the side of the road in addition to every animal he saw. It was obvious to Joe that the little guy didn't get to spend much time away from the boardinghouse, so he was determined to give him as much of an adventure, once again, as time would allow. After driving down several country roads, and once again standing side by side and peeing in the woods, Joe drove back into town and found an expansive public park. He and Freddie swung on the swings, slid down the slide, climbed the monkey bars and got dizzy and giddy on the merry-go-round. They ran races, played hide and seek, and furtively peed in the woods around the park a second time. Exhausted from all the activity, they sat side by side on a bench under an enormous oak tree, content to just be still for a while in one another's company.

"I'm thirsty!" Joe suddenly exclaimed.

"I'm thirsty too!" Freddie declared.

"Let's go get us a soda pop!"

"Mama doesn't let me have soda pop."

"Well, I'm not your Mama!"

Freddie smiled up at Joe, open-mouthed in wonder that he and his big friend were going to do something forbidden. "We won't tell Mama."

"We won't tell Mama!" Joe affirmed.

The two of them hopped in the car and drove into town and stopped in front of the drugstore. Once inside, they perched on the swivel seats at the counter and Joe ordered two nickel cokes. Freddie tentatively sipped at his through a straw, his eyes growing big as the sweet acidic bubbles bounced on his tongue and ticked his throat in a delightful way. He gave Joe a shamelessly exuberant grin, exclaiming "I like this!" as he greedily gulped then noisily drained the glass, sucking up every last drop of his coke through the straw.

"It's time to get you back so you can have supper with your Mama," Joe said, checking his watch.

"Mama don't eat supper at Miss Edna's."

"Oh. Does she eat her supper where she works now?"

Freddie nodded. "With Uncle Bob now."

"Uncle Bob," Joe repeated. "She stays at work and eats with Uncle Bob now."

Freddie nodded again. "But I still eat at Miss Edna's. Are you going to have supper there too?"

"I hadn't planned on doing that, but it looks as if my plans have changed. That is…if Miss Edna has room for one more plate and something to put on it!"

Miss Edna did, refusing to let Joe pay for his supper after taking Freddie off her hands for the entire afternoon. But she didn't have a room for him, not even one in which he would have to share a bed. The sun porch with the cot was available, but it got cold at night she informed him, and he might find that just a tad uncomfortable even with several blankets. Since it was getting late, and already dark out before Eve finally arrived home, Joe decided the cot on the sun porch was a better option than driving further that night and trying to find a place to stay in Santa Monica at a late hour.

After getting Freddie tucked into bed for the night, Joe and Eve sat in wicker chairs on the sun porch, wearing their coats and covering their knees with the blankets Edna had set out on the cot. Eve nervously made small talk, asking Joe what he had been up to for the past six months, even asking about the weather everywhere he had been, as if everything about Joe was what was important to her, until Joe decided he'd had enough of that and blurted out "Okay Eve, tell me why you wanted me to stay here so you could talk to me."

Eve immediately burst into tears. "I've made a mess of everything and I don't know what to do!" she sobbed.

"What kind of mess?"

"It's a big one -- the worst kind possible! I've been unfaithful to my husband!"

Joe's breath nearly exploded from his mouth. "Wow! That *would* be what I'd call a big mess. How could you let that happen?"

To Joe, Eve sounded as if she were bawling out a whiney excuse for her indiscretion, attempting to place the blame on everyone but herself. She blamed her husband, Jim for being away for so long describing it as abandonment, then blamed Freddie for crying for his daddy and making her life miserable, and finally her boss, Bob for being so lonely he wanted to steal another man's wife and make her his own. It was everybody else's fault she declared, and she simply couldn't bear it anymore so had succumbed to what everyone else wanted from her; Jim, his freedom, Freddie, a daddy, and Bob, a bed partner.

"It was your choice to make," Joe told her solemnly. "You are really the only one who forced herself to make that choice. No one *made* you do it."

"I couldn't take the pressure any more. The pressure made me make that choice."

"I guess that's a way to justify your actions –but why did you feel you wanted to tell me and what do you want to do about it now?"

"I told you I got a letter from Jim," Eve sobbed. "He told me he hadn't been able to find work for a long time and had been living in hobo camps, stealing chickens and digging up potatoes in backyard gardens in order to eat, only sometimes getting to use soup kitchens and sleep on a cot in a hostel. He says he didn't write to me because he didn't want me to know, but also because he didn't have any money for paper to write on or to buy a stamp to mail a letter. But when he was discovered digging through a garbage can behind a restaurant looking for food, the man who owned the place gave him a job washing dishes for his food and a place to sleep in a storeroom. That was just at first. Later, he got Jim all cleaned up and began paying him some too. Then he had him clearing tables, and Jim says the man is showing him how to wait on tables too. He says he has now saved enough and is being paid enough to have me and Freddie come live with him. He sent me ten dollars for our bus fare. That was over a month ago, and I didn't write back to him. I don't know what to do. Jim hasn't written me another letter so I don't know if he still wants me to come to him or if he has changed his mind, maybe met someone else or something – the way I have. Besides, I already spent the ten dollars he sent for bus fare. I owed almost that much to Miss Edna."

Eve paused for a few seconds, waiting for some kind of response from Joe. But when it appeared there was none immediately forthcoming, she asked "How far is Hollywood from where you are going?"

"It's almost next door. Why?"

"Just wondering. That's where Jim is living. He's working in a place where rich folks come to eat. Maybe even some movie stars eat there. I suppose that's possible, don't you?"

"Yes, I suppose that's possible. Are you asking because you want me to take you there, seeing as how you no longer have any money for bus fare?"

"I don't know yet. What if I get there and he doesn't want me anymore because I let another man have his way with me?"

"Well, how is he going to know that unless you are foolish enough to tell him?"

"I don't have to tell him that?"

"Sometimes what people we care about don't know about us is doing them an act of kindness. Telling him you have been unfaithful to him while he has been going through a torturous existence for months so the two of you can be together again will do nothing but hurt him. Is that what you want to do?"

"I did something unforgivable," Eve wailed. "I shouldn't get away with that so easily."

"Well, if it will make you feel any better, you can go get Miss Edna's wooden spoon and I will put you over my knee and gladly give you the punishment you feel you deserve. That may put your mind at ease, but the ease of your backside would be another matter. Or, you can just let me know your decision in the morning, following breakfast, by having your bags all packed and being ready to leave this place and go be with your husband in Hollywood."

"Do you think he really wants me?" Eve whispered.

"Do you think he would have written and sent you bus fare if he didn't want you with him?"

"No, but it doesn't make sense that he hasn't written again wondering why I didn't come."

"Eve, I bet he is going to the post office every day looking for a letter from you, wondering why you haven't written back to him telling him when you will be coming to him, bringing him his son. He is probably fearful of hearing that you have found someone else after all this time, and he wants to know and doesn't want to know at the same time."

"You think so?"

"I know so! And what's more, if you aren't prepared to come with me tomorrow morning, I promise to put you over my knee in front of everyone and give you the spanking you deserve – not for being unfaithful to your husband, but for breaking his heart – with or without the benefit of Miss Edna's wooden spoon. Now go to your room and let me get some sleep. I've got to be fit to hit the road in the morning."

A contrite Eve shared the back seat of Joe's car with all of her, Jim's and Freddie's worldly possessions, while Freddie rode beside Joe on the front seat. Unable to see much out the windows, he was soon lulled to sleep from the motion of the car. Eve re-read her letter from Jim then read it aloud to Joe as they drove, sniffling back her runny nose and wiping at her eyes with the back of her hand. "Have you got a handkerchief I can borrow?" she pleaded. "I'm making a mess of myself! You could at least be a bit of a help!"

Sighing, Joe removed the neatly folded, clean handkerchief from inside the breast pocket of his jacket and held it back over his shoulder for Eve to grasp. "You could at least say *thanks* seeing as how you are going to get your snot all over my nice clean handkerchief," Joe remarked. Then he added, "Why is it that women never seem to have a handkerchief handy when they burst out bawling, and if they do happen to have one it is so tiny and lacy it can't mop up even a fraction of the snot and tears they produce?"

"Why are you being so mean to me?" Eve wailed.

"I'm not being mean to you. I'm just feeling disgusted by your self-pity, when it's your poor husband who's deserving of the pity. These are not easy times and he went through a lot looking for a better future for his wife and son. Maybe he could have made a better effort at staying in touch with you – but he most likely felt you were okay where you were, you had a job and a roof over your head and someone to look after the kid when you couldn't – and it was a lot better than what he could give you at the time, which was nothing. A man wants to feel that he can provide for his family, and when he can't he feels like a failure. So he waited until he knew he could provide for you and Freddie then sent you that letter and the money for bus fare so you could all be together again."

"But not letting me know where he was or if he even wanted me anymore was cruel!" Eve sobbed.

"Yes it was," Joe agreed. "But it was understandable under the circumstances. And it wasn't nearly as cruel as you not getting back with him and letting him know whether or not you and Freddie would be on your way to be with him – especially after learning all he had been through to make that possible. That smacks of intentional cruelty on your part. Being vindictive – like wanting to hurt him back because he didn't let you know what was going on with him."

"But Joe, not hearing from him is what made me take up with my boss!" Eve wailed. "Don't you see? And that happened just before I got that letter from Jim. I didn't know what to do! I would never have been unfaithful to Jim if I had known he still wanted me, if I had known he hadn't just deserted me and his son too. I was alone – with a child to care for – and no one to help me as far as I knew. Then all of a sudden there was someone there who wanted to change that so I felt I was just doing what I had to do. And when I got that letter from Jim I couldn't answer him or go to him because I didn't know how I could tell him what I had done and because I thought he wouldn't want me anymore since I had been with another man."

Joe pulled the car over to the side of the road then turned around to look at Eve with a look of solemn remorse on his face. "I think I need to apologize to you," he said. "And I am truly sorry for not understanding your side of things. It took me a while, but I think I can see now why you did what you did. It must have been very hard for you – the not knowing part – but now it is Jim experiencing the not knowing. I guess it all comes down to this – do you still love him and want to be with him?"

"I never stopped loving him or wanting to be with him."

"Then I'm going to take you to him and you are never going to tell him that you have been unfaithful to him. Is that clear?"

"You don't think that's something he deserves to know?"

"Your unfaithfulness was caused by him in a very real sense. It was like an act of self-preservation rather than an act of deception. You were never deliberately unfaithful in your heart out of a feeling of lust, were you?"

"NO! Oh, good heavens no!"

"Then let's get you and this big guy here reunited with his daddy in Hollywood," Joe said as he pulled the car back out onto the road.

❦

The *La Palisade Restaurant* where Jim worked was situated in the business district on Sunset Blvd. in Hollywood. It was small but very nicely kept, with fence stakes artfully painted along the front of the building, giving the restaurant its name. There were no patrons inside, and the establishment had been tidied up after the noon meal and readied for the dinner crowd. As Joe, Eve and Freddie entered, a bell on the door signaled their presence, and a handsome young man appeared from a back room.

The young man hollered out "Eve, Freddie" at the same moment Eve hollered out "Jim" and Freddie hollered out "Daddy!" Then all three of them were in one another's arms, hugging, kissing, laughing and smiling through tears of joy.

"What a wonderful surprise!" Jim exclaimed. "But why didn't you let me know you were coming?"

"We couldn't," Eve said. "It was a spur of the moment decision this morning. Joe here," she said, pointing at Joe, "stayed at Miss Edna's on his way to Santa Monica, and offered to bring us here because it wasn't out of his way. So I got us all packed up really quick and we were on our way to give you a big surprise.!"

Jim eyed Joe suspiciously then asked Eve if she had thought it wise to take a long drive with a stranger. Joe, not fully trusting Eve to say the right thing, intruded.

"We aren't strangers," he explained. "I stayed at Miss Edna's place for a couple of days about six months ago, and I hired Eve to do some hand sewing for me – I needed some fancy little bags for jewelry and she did a fine job making them for me – and then it was Freddie's birthday so I treated him to a ride in my car and lunch at a diner so his mama could sew."

"Joe got me a truck and we peed in the woods!" Freddie enthusiastically interrupted.

Seeing Jim frowning at Freddie's revelation, Joe quickly added, "And, I was on my way back here to collect my things after visiting the young lady I am courting in South Dakota so I can get back there and settled in before winter and ask her to marry me, and I decided to stop at Miss Edna's because it was getting late, and I was surprised to see that Eve and Freddie were still there. Then when Eve told me you had sent her money for bus fare so she could join you out here, but she hadn't had enough work to cover what she owed for her room and board so had to use the money to pay Miss Edna and was trying to save up enough for bus fare, I offered to bring the two of them out here to you – provided she could get all packed up and ready to go first thing in the morning. So she did – and here we are!"

"And here we are!" Freddie piped. "I got bigger, daddy! And my hand got bigger too!" he exclaimed, holding his hand out for Jim to see. "It will get as big as yours!"

"You sure did get bigger!" Jim agreed. "And your Mama got skinnier. I don't want you to go get Hollywood skinny now," he admonished Eve. "You know I like you with some meat on your bones!" he said, giving her a bear hug.

"Well, I need to get going," Joe said, "so I guess you need to tell me where I can offload your stuff so I can be on my way."

"I'm renting a little house on the street just behind this restaurant, so we'll go out the back way, Eve, Freddie and me, and I'll let my boss know I'll be out for a while and you can drive around and meet us outside there. It's not much of a place, but it doesn't cost much and it's handy to the restaurant here."

"A house!" Eve gushed as she walked to the back of the restaurant, arm in arm with Jim. "A real house – not a boarding house?"

"A real house, but like I said it isn't much, just a little more room and privacy, that's all."

When Joe drove around the block, he saw that the place indeed wasn't much. The one bedroom was furnished with a lumpy looking bed and a dresser with a cracked mirror and most of the knobs missing on the drawers. The kitchen had a two-burner stove with a tiny oven, an old style refrigerator that was little more than a box with a big coil on top, a chipped sink with a peeling linoleum countertop and a small wooden table and two chairs, painted a sickly looking pea green. There was a tiny bathroom with a rusty looking tub and faucet, and an equally rusty looking toilet and sink, with a faded blue towel beside it hanging on a large nail. The sitting room was large compared to the other two rooms, the sparse furnishings of a shabby couch, matching chair and a small table set on top of a dusty looking braided rug making the room appear barren and uninviting. Joe found himself fervently hoping that some of the boxes being removed from the back seat of his car would contain something that could make the place look more like a home.

He said his good-bye's, promising to stop by for a final good-bye on his way back to South Dakota. Then he headed for Santa Monica and was overjoyed to be able to get his old room back where he had stayed before. He unloaded his valise and the leather bag with the precious Black Hills Gold jewelry, and just had time to get to the post office to retrieve his mail before it closed. He planned to read the letters from Madelyn he was sure would be waiting for him, then enjoy a fine meal, followed by a visit to see Howie, then a visit to see Lorraine and pick up his trailer, then write a letter to Madelyn, get a good night's sleep and get an early start back out on the road.

But Joe soon discovered that even the best laid plans have a way of getting messed up. And what was astounding was just how messed up they could become!

NOVEMBER, 1934

THERE WERE THREE LETTERS FROM MADELYN WAITING FOR Joe at the post office. He waited to read them until he was back in the solitude of his room at the boarding house, the wait building up his anticipation to a peak. He opened the letter with the earliest postmark first, beaming in delight at the opening words. *My Dearest Pal,* he read, barely absorbing the rest of the missive of day to day activity that represented Madelyn's life as those three words burned into his mind. He couldn't decide if *'My', 'Dearest' or 'Pal'* was his favorite word, or if the flow of the three words together created the substance of Madelyn's regard for him. He only knew that those three words filled him up like the best holiday meal he had ever eaten, and the ending *All My Love Old Pal,* followed by her name, put whipped cream and a cherry on top of it!

The second letter was more of the same, and affected Joe the same way. As a result, he eagerly opened the third letter and read the same delightful greeting, *My Dearest Pal,* but then the letter went on to tell him the very last thing he ever wanted to hear. He reread the short letter twice through tear-filled eyes, not wanting to believe the words written there.

My Dearest Pal,

I have been doing a great deal of thinking about what occurred between us, and have come to the conclusion that it would be better for us to be apart until you have obtained an annulment. I'm sure you can continue that process in California as easily as you could here – perhaps even easier, and certainly much safer for the two of us, morally speaking.

I think the best thing would be for our courtship to be long distance. I will miss seeing you every day, but ask that you please honor my request.

All My Love Old Pal,
Madelyn

Out of habit, Joe went down to supper when he heard the dinner bell ring, but he couldn't bring himself to eat anything or converse with the other roomers. Excusing himself by saying he was exhausted from his long drive, he retired back to his room where he lay on his bed, wide awake, thinking. His mood alternated between vengeful anger toward Madelyn and a sorrowful self-pity; between anguish over Madelyn's change of heart and his overwhelming determination to never give up —never, ever stop trying. Thus, he decided to honor her request as she wanted, and seek the advice of a priest in Santa Monica concerning the possibility of an annulment. And he would continue on as before, doing what he had to do, until the day came that he and Madelyn could be together—for as long as it took!

The following morning Joe drove up into the outskirts of Beverly Hills to the house where Howie and his family worked. Howie was busy pushing a lawn mower over the grass in front of the house, but stopped and broke into a wide grin when he saw Joe. "Got your letter yesterday!" he called out. "You're back to get your stuff and head back to the Black Hills, huh?"

"There's been a change of plans," Joe said, trying hard not to let Howie see his distress. "I need to stay here for a while. It's going to be easier for me to get the process of getting an annulment going here rather than in South Dakota so Madelyn and I can be married."

"What's an annulment?"

"It's a way to declare a marriage void so the Catholic Church will allow a previously married Catholic to re-marry. A divorce isn't enough for the Church."

"You can do that?"

"Probably not," Joe admitted, "but I've got to try. It's my only hope."

"What do you have to do to get an annulment?"

"File some papers with the Diocese here, make some declarations I guess."

"What kind of declarations?"

"Claims as to why the marriage should be voided." Joe paused then sighed deeply, shaking his head. "My claims are not the truth, and yet I am shamelessly going to make them because I don't have any choice if I ever want to be with Madelyn. And that's what I *do* want! It's *all* I want!"

"What are those claims?" Howie asked almost reverently.

"That I was forced into a marriage with a girl who claimed to be carrying a child that I had fathered."

"And that's not a possibility?" Howie asked expectantly.

"No. I know it was my child, and I was not forced to marry the girl. I did so freely, even had a big fancy wedding. It was not a happy marriage though – we fought a lot – and when the baby died I knew I wanted to be free of her. I could only get a divorce in Massachusetts by deserting her for three years, so that's how and when I met Madelyn and fell so hopelessly in love."

"Do you think those claims will be believed?"

"I don't know – I only know I've got to try because it's all the hope I have. So I'm going to be staying here for as long as it takes, one way or the other."

"What if the answer from the Church is 'no'? What if they won't give you an annulment?"

"I won't even think about that right now," Joe said vehemently. "Because that possibility is unthinkable!"

Half an hour later Joe pulled up in front of the little shop topped by an attractive sign. *Hats by Lorraine* it read, and the windows below were filled with colorful hat boxes topped with a variety of hat styles. There were several expensively dressed women inside, and Joe had to wait until they had finished trying on hats and finally making a purchase before Lorraine could focus her attention on him.

"How have you been? So good to see you're back, even if you will be leaving again right away. I'm hoping you will let me fix you some dinner tonight. I've never properly thanked you for all you did for me, and…"

"Your obvious success is all the thanks I need," Joe interrupted. "And I would love to have you fix me dinner tonight. My plans have changed just a bit, so I will be staying here for a while – not sure yet just how long."

"Well I'm glad you will be around for a while, but I thought you said in your letter that you wanted to get back to St. Onge before the snow started to fly."

"It's already started, apparently. That's what held me up in Utah for three days. But, my plan is to pick up my trailer right now and get it out of your way, then go check up on a young woman and her little boy that I gave a lift to from San Bernardino and dropped off in Hollywood."

"Huh?" Lorraine said, frowning. "You want to run that one by me again?"

"Not right now," Joe chuckled. "But I'll fill you in on everything tonight at dinner."

"Aw, come on! Don't leave me hanging here!"

Joe grinned. "I have to leave something for a dinner conversation, don't I? What time?"

"How does seven suit you? I close up here at five, so I'll need a little time to fix something unless you want to settle for canned beans and wieners."

"Is that beans with molasses or with tomato sauce? I like molasses, don't like the kind with tomato sauce."

"Get out of here!" Lorraine said, giggling. "I'll see you at seven!"

Joe pulled his car and trailer up in front of the little house on the street behind the *La Palisade Restaurant*. He saw Freddie at the front window, nose pressed against the glass, his face breaking into a broad smile of recognition. He could clearly see Eve standing behind her little boy, and realized that living in that little house, so close to the street, made it possible for anyone passing by to see inside.

Once inside, he saw that Eve had made an attempt at making the place look like a home with a couple of framed pictures of Jim holding Freddie when he was a baby, and one of the three of them, when Freddie had just learned to walk. There was a folded blanket over one arm of the couch – where Freddie, or maybe Jim, had slept for the night since there was only one bed in the bedroom. But the early afternoon sun filled the room, illuminating the myriad flecks of dust in the air as well as the three of them – Joe, Eve and Freddie, -- as they stood shading their eyes from the glare.

"You need some curtains on this front window!" Joe exclaimed. "And not just to keep out the glare of the sun, but to keep anyone passing by from seeing in here."

"I know," Eve said. "And I'll get some as soon as I can."

"Soon, as in right now!" Joe said. "Come with me."

He led Eve and Freddie out to the back of his trailer, where he had Eve look through the bolts of material he had stored there, telling her she was welcome to take anything she found to make curtains for her front window. She had no trouble deciding what she wanted after she spied some yellow cotton dotted with white daisies and green leaves. "Oh!

This will be perfect!" she gushed. "Are you sure you want to let me have this, Joe?"

"I've never been as sure. I need to get rid of some of this stuff to make room for other stuff I'm bound to find, that I'd rather have. You are probably going to need some clothesline wire and a couple of big nails to wrap it around so you can hang those curtains after you get them sewn," he added, searching through his wares for the necessary items. "Also, these needles and a good supply of thread," he said, handing Eve a packet of sewing needles and two large spools of white thread. "Anything else you might need that you can think of?"

"A way to thank you for everything is all," Eve said through tear-filled eyes.

"Seeing some bright curtains on that window instead of a blindingly bright sun will be all the thanks I need when I stop by for a visit next time," Joe told her. "Without curtains, you might just as well be living in a fish-bowl here."

"I'll get right at it!" Eve vowed. "And the next time you come around this place is going to look more livable!"

※

Joe arrived at Lorraine's little apartment promptly at seven. She greeted him with "I got delayed at the shop with a late customer, so it's canned beans and wieners after all...with molasses!" she added, tittering. "I could sure use some help besides Clarice when it gets really busy. It's getting hard for me to keep up with things at times."

"What is it exactly that you need help doing?"

"Mostly hand sewing, some starching, things like that. But I only need someone once in a while, not all the time."

"I think I know someone who might be able to help you out on occasion," Joe said, then proceeded to tell Lorraine all about the young woman and boy he had given a ride to from San Bernardino, how he had met them, and how he had reunited them with Jim who had been absent from their lives for eight long months. "Eve is good at hand sewing," he told her. "And she would probably like to earn a bit of money doing some sewing at home."

With that out of the way, Joe proceeded to tell Lorraine that he would be staying in California for the time being and that he would be seeking an annulment. He had told her before about his marriage and subsequent divorce and, about Madelyn as well. Lorraine had been sympathetic, but being a Catholic herself had told Joe there was likely nothing he could do about his situation unless he and Madelyn could abide being excommunicated from the Church in order to be together as husband and wife.

"What makes you think you could get an annulment?" she asked Joe. "What grounds for an annulment could you possibly have?"

"Adele, the woman I was forced to marry, claimed that the child she was carrying was fathered by me. I will never know if that is in fact true because the child died when she was just a few months old. So, the forced marriage, the fact that I may not have been the father, and the death of the child breaking the bond between the two of us could conceivably constitute grounds for an annulment"

Lorraine stared at Joe in open-mouthed astonishment. "Wow!" she exclaimed. "That paints a whole different picture of things. But isn't that all going to be very difficult to prove?"

"It's not going to be easy, and I don't know yet what all it's going to take, but I've got to give it a try because it's the only hope I have for a life together with Madelyn. And that is all in this world that really matters to me!"

⁕

Joe regretted having to lie to Lorraine, but with her being a devout Catholic he could see no other choice. He was determined to continue the ruse by contacting a parish priest, to whom he would also have to lie, in the hope that he could, by any means possible, obtain an annulment. And he would have to keep that ruse alive in Madelyn's mind to keep her from deciding to become a nun. But there was another plot budding in the back of his mind to achieve his heart's desire, and he stored it away, the way he stored away everything he thought would one day be of use. And it would be there, if, and when, he needed it.

Christmas that year was spent with Howie and his family in the Lester's guest house, along with Lorraine and also Eve, Jim and Freddie since Eve was doing some part time sewing work for Lorraine's hat business. They thought of one another as family – because they were all the family any of them had. Freddie, being the only child, was the center of attention and was lavished with gifts from everyone. Joe got him a bed of his own and a fuzzy brown teddy bear to share it with, and *Santa* put a kaleidoscope, a set of blocks and a little red wagon under the tree. The rest of the extended family gave him socks, underwear, a knit cap and suspenders to hold up his first pair of long pants his mama had made for him.

Joe spent his days occasionally selling his wares, making enough to keep him comfortably well off, and spent his nights occasionally joining Ken at the Starlight Ballroom and dancing the night away. The remainder of his time was spent in the company of the various people he considered to be his extended family. They filled the void for him, cheered him, vexed him at times, puzzled him at others; but they were always there for him when he felt a need for their company. Madelyn's daily letters sustained him, even though they were at times filled with nothing but uninteresting prattle or inanities between *My Dearest Joe* and *All My Love Old Pal*. That was better than the serious letters asking about the progress toward an annulment, requiring Joe to reply to the love of his life with a pack of lies that did nothing but make his heart ache.

He had met with the parish priest at St. Boniface's in Santa Monica, telling him the lie that he hoped would result in the granting of an annulment. The priest had not offered him much in the way of encouragement. He would need a sworn statement from Adele, he was told, witnessed and signed by a justice of the peace, that she knew unequivocally that he was not the father of her child and had tricked him into marriage. And in addition he would need signed statements from both her parents and his parents attesting to the fact that he was subsequently subjected to what amounted to a shotgun wedding. Joe knew, without even trying, that there wasn't a hope in hell of that happening. But in his letters to Madelyn, he pretended to be working toward that end, even telling her after a long wait that some of the necessary paperwork had been signed and delivered and he was just waiting for the remainder of what was needed in order to proceed further. He hated himself at times – but at others he half believed the lies he was telling – because he wanted to believe them with all his heart. It was as if he believed them enough they would come true.

Life proceeded for everyone, never seeming to change, yet with change being the only certainty. Eve produced a baby sister for Freddie, who became a doting big brother, Jim became the head waiter at the *La Palisade Restaurant*, and moved his family to a bigger, better house, Howie and his bride, Suzanne were expecting a baby and Clarice had become engaged – all by the spring of 1936.

Joe had gone down to the shipping district in Long Beach thinking he might find some discarded goods behind the warehouses there to replenish the somewhat depleted store in his trailer. He thought it was mostly a waste of his time, finding only a few useful items, when he opened a big bag that at first appeared to be stuffed with kindling wood. On closer inspection he saw that the wood had been carved into gun shapes. Not the kind of guns you saw in the cowboy movies, but the kind you saw in gangster movies. He was about to dismiss them as being anything of value, until a picture of them, with a polished, finished look appeared in his mind. He could imagine them sanded smooth, painted black, with painted on markings and triggers to make them look real. Then a picture of Priscilla's living room at the farm, with the perspective drawings done by Madelyn filled his head, and putting the two images together he quickly packed up the four bags of discarded fake guns he found, whistling a happy tune all the while.

The following day he said his surprising good-bye's to everyone and was headed back to the Black Hills of South Dakota – back to the love of his life – and where he would put to use the plan that he had stored in the back of his mind to finally win her for his own.

MAY, 1936

ST. ONGE ALREADY HAD AN OVERBLOWN LOOK IN EARLY MAY, the kind of lush green that wasn't usually seen until late June. It was hotter than usual too, and Joe found himself mopping the sweat from his brow at regular intervals, his handkerchief turning a dirty yellow from the road dust as he drove with his window rolled down, along the back road toward the farm.

Although achingly tired from his nearly non-stop drive, seeing Madelyn was the one and only thing on his mind. He had considered getting settled in with Father Brunet, and getting himself freshened up first, but as he neared the little town he knew that would have to wait. He had stopped at the tavern, and Madelyn's father, Charles had informed him that she was at the farm helping her sister with some spring planting in the garden. And that was where he was headed, adrenalin pumping through his veins making him breathe hard and break into a sweat, his mind filled with a vision of her, head thrown back, laughing out loud in boundless joy when she saw him. He had driven long and hard – and was arriving a day earlier than expected.

To his surprise, he was greeted by a large, angrily barking dog of indeterminate breed circling his car as he pulled up into the yard at the ranch. The dog stood his ground, his vicious sounding growls daring Joe to step out of the vehicle. "Hey there fella!" he said in a chipper sounding voice that he hoped would make the dog think of him as friendly. "Now, where did you come from, huh? Got a name?"

"Buster!" he heard a female voice yell from over in the garden. "Go lay down!"

"Buster, huh?" he said to the dog. "Go lay down like your missus told you. That's a good dog," he added when Buster didn't go lay down as instructed, but instead moved closer to the car and sat down blocking Joe's exit. "No, go lay down!" he insisted, to which Buster let out a low, menacing growl.

"It's okay Buster," Joe heard Priscilla call out as she rushed up the hilly rise that surrounded the garden, over to his car. "So get away; go lay down!"

"Your animals sure don't seem to like me much!" he told her curtly.

"He'll be okay once he gets used to seeing you around," Priscilla assured him, resting her forearms tiredly on the window opening of the car and peering in at him. "You got here sooner than expected. Madelyn is going to have a fit!"

"Why is she going to have a fit?" Joe asked in sudden alarm.

"Because she's been out in the sun for the past couple of hours, she's all red in the face and sweaty and all her freckles have popped out! And she has dirt under her fingernails and covering her knees, and her hair is in tangled knots, and…"

"She sounds just beautiful to me!" Joe beamed. "I can't wait to see her!"

"Well, what you'll see is her running in the opposite direction if she sees you're here!" Priscilla exclaimed. "So be a gentleman and get out of here and come back tomorrow, when she's expecting you, so she can be all fresh and clean and presentable! And you could stand to make yourself a bit more presentable as well!" she added, giving Joe the once over. "You look like you were rode hard and put away wet!"

"Huh?"

"Never mind! Just scram before she decides to come up over the hill looking for me!"

"Is she happy I've come back? Do you know?"

"That's all she talks about, if that's any help. But you are going to ruin the reunion for her if she is a mess when you see her. She picked out a new dress for when you get here – tomorrow – ," Priscilla added with emphasis, "and she got a fresh bottle of her favorite perfume and new shoes and lipstick. So please don't spoil it for her!"

"I wanted to surprise her," Joe said, sounding apologetic.

"Well, sometimes surprises aren't taken too well," Priscilla admonished. "Now get out of here, and make it snappy!"

Joe drove back to St. Onge with both his spirits and his ego deflated. Father Brunet's housekeeper wasn't happy either to see him arrive a day early, and she let him know in no uncertain terms. "Arriving a day ahead of time is an imposition. I don't have your room ready for you and I only have enough supper for the good father. So I guess you will have to pay for your lack of courtesy by making up your own bed and either finding something to eat on your own or going hungry," she huffed.

Joe hung his head and shuffled his feet as he offered a lame sounding apology. "I was just so anxious to see the wonderful girl I am courting – it's been way too long since I've seen her – so I wanted to get here as soon as possible and surprise her. But that didn't work out too well," he said despondently.

"I don't suppose it did!" the housekeeper admonished. "Surprises often have a way of backfiring. Most folks don't like surprises…unless they know about them beforehand and are prepared for them. But then they aren't really surprises, are they!"

"I guess I won't be planning any more surprises," Joe replied laconically. "I've learned my lesson about surprises – especially now that it means I will have to make my own bed and figure out what to do about getting some supper for myself, plus wait another day before I can see my sweetheart. Looks like I'm the one who got surprised!"

Joe's affected 'little boy look' of helplessness worked its charm on the middle-aged housekeeper who interrupted his attempts at bed-making with a "tsk, tsk, you don't tuck the sheet in that way!" as she took command of the task. "Go get your bag unpacked while I do this the right way!" And that look was still working at suppertime, because there was a place set for him at the table across from Father Brunet. She had added an extra potato and carrot to the leftover chicken stew from the night before, and had even topped it with some enormous raised dumplings she had cooked in the stew. "It's chicken with dumplings tonight Father," she had announced heartily, "rather than leftover chicken stew."

Father Brunet chuckled. "Anything you make for me Miss Mabel is better than dining with the Crosby sisters as I was supposed to do tonight. I was sorry to learn that Isabelle is feeling under the weather today so her sister, Candice came by to inform me that our usual supper engagement would need to be cancelled," he said for Joe's benefit.

"I hope it's nothing serious," Joe said solicitously.

"Just a touch of the vapors, according to Candice," Father Brunet said, stifling a grin.

"I don't think I know what that means," Joe said helplessly.

"She's going through the change," Mabel the housekeeper announced. "Hot flashes, vapors – same thing!"

Father Brunet cleared his throat in embarrassment. "Well, whatever it is, it gave me a reprieve from dining on cucumber sandwiches, lady fingers and peppermint tea."

It was Joe's turn to chuckle. "I was a supper guest at the Crosby girl's table a number of times, and it was always cucumber sandwiches, served on bread with the crusts cut off, and sliced so thin if you held the bread up to the light you could see through it. And the cucumbers were sliced paper thin too. They were tasty though, with that special spread the girls made with the dill, poppy and celery seeds, but they wouldn't feed a bird!"

"Those two are a lot like birds," Father Brunet mused. "Don't you think?"

Joe pictured the two small-boned, frail looking sisters in his mind. They were indeed bird-like he decided, with their tiny stature and ankles not much bigger around than his thumbs. And their high-pitched, twittering voices, accented by their rapidly gesturing hands and fluttering fingers as they chirped away for anyone willing to listen. They were like fixtures in the little town and he always thought of them as delightfully entertaining oddities. Joe thoroughly enjoyed their company and their supper invitations, even if he had to raid the icebox in the middle of the night afterwards due to an angrily growling empty stomach. "I agree," he concurred. "They are a lot like birds. But the question is – what kind of birds?"

Thus, the mood for the dinner conversation was set, with the different peculiarities of various species of birds being compared to the individualities of Isabelle and Candice Crosby, two of St. Onge's most interesting personages. Joe was grateful for the distraction from the conversation he had expected to have with the good father. The diversion kept him from having any personal questions asked of him that he did not want to, or could not, answer.

Early the following morning, Joe set out walking down the dusty road that led from the rectory behind the church and around the bend to Madelyn's house. At the turn in the road, who did Joe meet but the two sisters who had been the topic of discussion the previous evening at the rectory dinner. They rushed at him with high-pitched, twittering laughter, wildly gesticulating fingers punctuating their vociferous greeting.

"Oh, look who is back!" Isabelle gushed.

"Oh, it's Mr. Handsome himself, back to court his lady love!" Candice exclaimed. "But Madelyn left a while ago -- so you missed her Joe!"

"Oh, aren't we poetic this morning, Isabelle!" Candice giggled. "You made a rhyme!"

"I did? Oh yes, I guess I did! Well, you just missed her anyway," she said, wriggling her bony fingers toward Joe's chest. "She was driving her Papa's car and I think she might have been on her way out to the ranch. But I can't be sure of that you know, so don't think of that as the gospel truth! She could just as easily be headed somewhere else as far as I know, but I couldn't say where. I honestly wouldn't know, you understand!"

"Well then stop prattling on about it!" Candice huffed. "Just say you don't know where she was headed and leave it at that! You do tend to go on and on about things you know!"

"And you don't? I don't think I have any exclusive when it comes to prattling on about things! You may think that's so, but you should hear yourself sometime! You can get carried away with an idea like it's nobody's business and it's impossible to get a word in edgewise once you get started!"

"Me! You're the one who doesn't know when to stop! I, on the other hand…"

Joe tuned out the two 'girls', a misnomer if ever there was one since they were both more than twice his age, laughing inside at their inanities. He brought their uproarious tirade to a halt by wrapping his arms around the two of them, Isabelle in his right arm and Candice in his left, and drawing them close to him in an embrace. He kissed both of them on the cheek in turn, telling them he found them to be the most delightful residents of St. Onge and to never change. The sisters were not astonished by his sudden embrace because it was not the first time he had made such a maneuver, nor was it the second or even the third. And Joe suspected that the two adorable spinsters even maneuvered the conversation into a confrontation every time they saw him in order to be the beneficiaries of some manly attention.

"You two behave yourselves now!" he admonished them. "Looks like I need to head back to the rectory and get my car so I can try to locate Madelyn."

"Are you here to propose something to her?" Candice asked with a hint of salacious innuendo.

"Candice!" Isabelle exclaimed. "That didn't sound very nice!"

"I was referring to proposing marriage – not something naughty!" Candice retorted. "Now you're starting in all over again and …"

"And I'm leaving," Joe declared, hugging the two sisters one last time.

"We're glad you're here!" Candice told Joe resolutely. "We don't think becoming a nun is the right thing for Madelyn. We aren't Catholics you know," she acknowledged, "and we don't have anything against Catholics per se, but we don't think being a nun is the right thing for a girl to do. We just don't think that was God's plan when He created both a man and a woman. Oh, I'm saying this badly!" she said, sounding distressed.

"No you're not. I don't think it's the right thing for her either," Joe agreed. "And I'm here to make her realize that – for as long as it takes. I think the right thing for her is to be by my side, as my wife, for all the years to come."

He left the two Crosby girls, twittering and hugging one another in the middle of the road.

After unhitching his trailer and stowing it in the side yard between the rectory and the church, Joe arrived at the farm and was greeted by

Madelyn running out the back door of the house and straight into his arms. He lifted her off her feet and swung her around and around, kissing her face wherever his lips landed, ecstatically astounded by her greeting. The only thought in his mind at the time were Howie's words, asking him if Madelyn came running into his arms when she saw him, and if she did, that was when he would know she loved him.

Joe set Madelyn back down on the ground his arms still snuggly around her, and hers just as snuggly around him. They kissed lingeringly with eyes open, not wanting to take their eyes off one another for a second. "I've missed you so much!" Joe whispered with a catch in his voice when their lips parted briefly, then connected once again. Then, hearing the back door open, Madelyn reluctantly pulled her lips from his, and instead snuggled her head under his chin, squeezing him tightly.

"I've missed you so much too!" she ardently whispered back. "It seems as if you have been gone forever. There hasn't been a day I didn't think about you and long for you to be here."

"Looks like you two long-lost love-birds will be needing a chaperone!" Priscilla chided jovially as she walked over to greet Joe. "That is *some* impassioned reunion I just witnessed!"

"He's been away such a long time!" Madelyn declared, blushing charmingly while releasing her hold around Joe's waist. "And I'm just so very happy to see him! I promise you I will conduct myself from hereon with more decorum."

"I don't think I want you to conduct yourself with more decorum!" Joe objected. I fully approve of every second of your decorum from the moment you flew out of that door and catapulted yourself into my arms. And I would not be the least bit upset with you if you conducted yourself in that manner every time I see you, from now on!"

Madelyn threw her head back and laughed her laugh that seemed to come from the center of her being, and Joe could not take his eyes off her.

Her laugh, her embrace, her kiss, her very presence filled him to the point of bursting with happiness. Joe's head spun dizzily with that sensation of joy then without further warning, he felt his knees melting into a boneless mush as the world turned black and he slipped to the ground, unconscious.

The force of the impact brought him around just a few seconds later, and he opened his eyes to see Madelyn's startled face as she dropped to her knees beside him, frantically calling his name. "Joe! Joe! What happened? Are you all right?"

"I'm fine, I guess," he managed to say as he sat upright. "This is just something that seems to happen when I get really excited and happy, or really down in the dumps and unhappy. And right now it's the *really* excited and happy reason."

"But I don't think that's a normal response to being excited and happy," Madelyn declared. "You say this has happened before? Are you sure you don't have some sort of affliction that could be causing this to happen? Don't you think we should be getting you to a doctor?"

"Do I look like I need a doctor?" Joe asked, briskly getting to his feet. He shadow-boxed the air around him then grasped Madelyn around the waist and planted a noisy kiss on her cheek.

Madelyn gave him a measured look that gradually melted into a condescending kind of look she might give a mischievous little boy trying to show off. "Okay, if you say so. But if it happens again, you're going to see a doctor! You got that?"

"Yes mam," Joe said, trying to keep a straight face.

Joe took Madelyn by the arm, directing her toward the house, with Priscilla following. But suddenly Priscilla was howling with laughter and telling Joe to go no further – he wasn't going in her clean house and sitting on any of her furniture. "I guess you can't see it without a mirror," she tittered, "but when you swooned you sat down right in a big pile of chicken doo-doo and it's completely covering the seat of your pants!"

Madelyn checked out Joe's backside, trying unsuccessfully to stifle her giggles. "You better go get him a pair of Richard's pants to change into," she directed Priscilla between peals of laughter.

When Priscilla returned promptly with a pair of her husband's dungarees, she handed them to him and pointed toward the outhouse. "Your changing-room awaits you!" she snickered. "But be careful…I noticed a polecat lurking around there earlier!"

As he trekked despondently toward the outhouse, Joe wondered if Clyde, the rooster, hadn't gotten the best of him after all! Then, his eyes scanning around the outhouse, Joe muttered "What the hell is a polecat?"

Joe opened the outhouse door a few inches and shoved his soiled trousers out through the crack straight into Madelyn's waiting fingers. Then all he heard was Priscilla telling him to come on into the house when he was ready. When he entered the kitchen all he saw was Priscilla's wriggling behind as she reached into the bottom depths of her new refrigerator searching for something. When she emerged she told Joe that Madelyn was in the wash-house cleaning and drying his trousers with a flatiron so he should make himself comfortable in the dining room.

Spying a huge dictionary on a side table, Joe looked up the word 'polecat' but could not find a listing. So he went back out to the kitchen to tell Priscilla that polecat was not a word listed in the dictionary, and he'd like to know what it meant.

"Skunk," she stated without any further explanation.

He was about to make a comment when Priscilla vehemently said "Look, we need to talk, you and I. I'd like to know why you were just going back to California to get your trailer and then come right back, but you stayed away for many months leaving Madelyn wondering and grieving and crying herself to sleep at night. That's something a cad would do, not something a man in love would do!"

"I didn't come back because Madelyn wrote and told me not to," Joe said, seriously perplexed. "Didn't she tell you that?"

"No, and I don't think I believe she would do that. If she had told you that, it wouldn't be something she would keep from me. She tells me everything."

"Well, maybe she felt she had a reason not to tell you."

"And just what could that reason possibly be?" Priscilla fumed.

"She told me in her letter that she felt we were getting dangerously close to doing something we shouldn't be doing, so it would be best if we took a break from one another for a while. And that's what I kept on hearing from her until I just couldn't take it anymore. So I just packed up everything and let her know I was on my way back here no matter what because I couldn't bear another day away from her, consequences be damned!"

"If what you say is true, I don't understand why she wouldn't tell me."

"Neither do I…but then, there are lots of things I don't quite understand about Madelyn. She's a hard one to figure out."

"She's a romantic at heart. Always has been. As a child she liked stories about forlorn maidens rescued by handsome princes and "happy ever after" fantasies. And then there's that becoming a bride of Christ thing which I could never figure out. Me, I couldn't abide those stories or ideas. My taste ran to tales of heroic animals and farm life."

"I was amazed by the way she greeted me!" Joe confessed. "Absolutely delighted, but amazed just the same! I really didn't know what to expect."

"Well, I did! Madelyn was breathless with excitement, but I was worried that you were going to let her down somehow, that you weren't really in love with her at all."

"I hope you realize that's not the way it is. I have never stopped thinking about her, or being in love with her from the moment I set eyes on her. But I was told back then that I could never have her because she was going to be a nun, so I never pursued her. Then when I saw her again when she came to Holyoke with the theater group, I knew I would never stop loving her, and wanting her, and I told her so. She is never out of my mind, but I am growing impatient…and not getting any younger. Help me, Priscilla. Tell me what I need to do to convince Madelyn that we were meant to be together as man and wife," he added pleadingly.

"Tell her. Tell her the way you feel the same way you have been telling *me* the way you feel about her. I'm not the least bit a romantic, but if it were me you were professing your love to I would be all over you!"

"Just tell her? I thought I had been doing that all these years!"

"Well maybe you haven't been telling her in the same way you have been telling me how you feel about her. Maybe you need to be telling her in person, not in a letter. And there's no better time than now to start. I've put together a picnic lunch for the two of you. So take her somewhere where the two of you can be alone and undisturbed…and figure out how to be the most romantic you have ever been…sweep her off her feet!"

Driving along the country road, with his arm around Madelyn's shoulder as she snuggled against him, Joe responded to her chatter in monosyllables and chuckles, his mind on trying to figure things out rather than the present moment. He began to realize that there were lots of things Madelyn was keeping from her sister, her lifelong confidant, but he couldn't figure out why, unless…unless she was reluctant to reveal any incident involving him that would shed a bad light on him in her sister's eyes. But, if that were the case, why? Could it mean that she felt as strong an attraction to him as he did to her…and there was no way she wanted that to end? Or was it nothing more than a need to keep her options open while she waited for her 'calling' to the convent?

He was snapped out of his reverie by a sharp slap on his thigh and an admonishment from Madelyn. "Pay attention! What are you daydreaming about anyway? Turn around…there's a lovely little spot for a picnic you passed by, even though I told you twice to stop!"

Apologizing profusely for his momentary lapse of brain function, Joe turned his car around and pulled off onto a dirt track in a small orchard as Madelyn indicated.

"What were you thinking about that shut down your ear's ability to hear?"

Joe didn't give it a thought before answering ."I was wondering why you never told Priscilla you asked me not to come back when I went to California to get my trailer."

Madelyn looked away, busying her fingers with the hem of her dress. "What makes you think I never told her that?" she asked, trying to sound nonchalant.

"Because, while you were out in the wash house cleaning my trousers, your sister jumped all over me for breaking your heart by not coming back and giving no good reason. I told her I didn't come back because you had written to me asking me not to."

"Did she believe you?"

"Not at first. She said there was no reason for you to do that. But I think I finally convinced her that I was telling the truth."

"What did you say to her to convince her of that?" Madelyn asked apprehensively.

"I told her the reason you gave me. I told her you felt we were getting too close to doing something we shouldn't be doing…and she seemed to understand that."

"She did? Because I'm not sure I even understand that. So many times I wanted to tell you to get back here as quickly as possible because I missed you so much, but it was as if my mind and my heart were in conflict with one another and my mind wouldn't let my heart win."

"But you wanted your heart to win?"

"I think I did one minute then the next minute my mind wouldn't let me write the words 'come back to me'." Madelyn sobbed.

"I'm sorry, I didn't mean to make you cry my love," Joe said, wrapping Madelyn tightly in his arms.

"Am I your love?" she sniffled.

"Yesterday, today and always…runny nose and all…forever and ever, amen!"

"Are you sure, beyond any doubt?"

"As sure as the fact that your beautiful face is covered with sun kisses and I want to kiss every one of them and claim them for my own. Then I'll claim the ones on your shoulders and your arms and go searching for any I might find anywhere else. I'll kiss them all because they are all a part of you and I love you beyond belief!"

"There are a lot of freckles," Madelyn said softly. "Hundreds…maybe even thousands."

"I'm hoping for millions!" Joe declared, loosening his hold on Madelyn so he could gaze into her face. "Millions of freckles would mean it would take me a lifetime to kiss them all, and I would have to keep on kissing them as new ones appeared…as freckles tend to do."

He saw Madelyn's eyes brim over with tears again and heard the sighing sound of a sob as she whispered, "Why do we always seem to want most what we can't have?"

"I don't know what you mean," Joe said, perplexed.

"I know I have fallen in love with you too, she sobbed, "and I want to spend the rest of my life with you but I most likely can't unless you can get an annulment. And I don't know how long I can wait for that to happen!"

"Can you wait just a little longer," Joe begged. "It takes time to get everything signed and validated, then to be reviewed by the Cardinals in Rome, and a decision to be made. But it is moving along."

"Is it? You haven't kept me very well informed about the progress you are making."

"That's because the progress is slow. But it *is* happening…and you can trust me on that!" Joe added emphatically, the lie slipping through his lips with an ease that astonished him. "There's nothing in this world I want more than to one day…soon, I hope… marry you and take you away from everything and begin the rest of our lives together."

"That's what I hope for too," Madelyn affirmed. "But meanwhile we have to be very careful not to jeopardize our chance of maintaining the integrity of our relationship in the eyes of the Church. We can't be careless…and my greatest fear is that we will be if we spend too much of our time alone, together."

Seeing that his hope of a romantic afternoon with Madelyn, away from the prying eyes of her family, would be out of the question for the present, Joe changed the subject. "How about taking a drive with me over to Sturgis?"

"What do you want to do in Sturgis? I already saw the movie they're showing there, but I wouldn't mind seeing it again. It's 'Captain January' with Shirley Temple, but I'm not sure what the second feature is."

"I'm not thinking of going to the movies. I want to go to the Armory there to see some of the handguns they always have on display.

"Whatever for?" Madelyn exclaimed.

"Well, I think there's a project the two of us can do together," Joe explained. "I found a whole bunch of wooden toy guns out in Hollywood that had been discarded behind a warehouse. They are in pretty rough shape, but I figured if I sanded them, made them sleek and smooth then painted them and painted on the details, they could be sold for toys. So I'd like to see if I can find some pictures of guns at the Armory, or maybe the library, that would show how the real guns look so we could make them look like the real thing."

"You say 'we', but where do I come in with this? What is it you want me to do? Madelyn asked, suddenly interested.

"Paint on the details," Joe said matter-of-factly. "Those paintings you did that are hanging in your sister's dining room show me that you would be an expert at painting fine details. But, that's if it's something you would want to do with me that would be a safe way for us to be together, you know, side by side with one another, but our hands busy with paint and brushes and smelly turpentine and stuff."

Madelyn's only response was to throw her head back and release her deep, throaty laugh, while Joe's longing-filled eyes never left her face. He was fully aware that his intentions were definitely not honorable.

The following morning, laden with the gunny sacks filled with carved wooden guns plus paint cans, brushes, art brushes and paints, and books on firearms from the library, Joe set up shop in Charles Dubois's workshop attached to his carriage house. The workshop was surprisingly messy and disorganized, not at all what Joe would have expected of a workplace owned by Madelyn's rather distinguished father. He spent most of the morning clearing a space for the gun shapes to be laid out and compared to the pictures in the book. He sorted them out as to types, but then was stymied as to how he was going to go about painting them. Then an idea hit him as he remembered some of the things he had stowed away in his trailer, but rather than going back to the rectory where his trailer was parked he decided to look around the workshop for what he needed. And he found it! He also found heavy nails protruding from the walls in various places that would serve the purpose very well, and when Madelyn arrived at noon with some thick egg sandwiches and sweet tea, she saw lines of toy guns strung on taut wires through their trigger slots running in every direction throughout the workshop, just waiting for some sanding and painting.

"Good heavens! How many are there?" Madelyn exclaimed.

"About five hundred, I think."

"What do you suppose they were made for? And why would they just be thrown away and not used for firewood or something instead?"

"Well," Joe drawled out, "there's not much use for firewood out in California because it's mostly always warm there. And my best guess is that they were made for the movies, and were going to be painted the way I want to do, but the movie people didn't want them for some reason so they were tossed out."

"I think I might know the reason for that," Madelyn said smugly. "If there was shooting going on, wooden guns, even those painted to look real, wouldn't have any sign of smoke or fire coming from them so they would come off as fake in the movies. I saw a gangster movie last month and they were using real guns in it, because there was smoke and flashes of fire coming from them, so they must have some way of shooting bullets that aren't real."

"Yes, I think you've come up with the answer!" Joe exclaimed, sticking his tongue as far as he could into his cheek to keep from snickering out loud. "These guns were intended for the movies, but the studios rejected them. They might have used these years ago, but now they use real guns that fire blanks."

"It's too bad they are all the type of guns gangsters would use rather than the kind of gun used by cowboys," Madelyn lamented. "They might be a little hard to sell to stores as toys for kids, don't you think?"

Rather than let Madelyn in on how he intended to sell the toys, Joe merely said "Well, maybe kids will decide it's as much fun to play cops and robbers as it is to play cowboys and Indians."

"Maybe," she said with a sigh. "But I really wouldn't know because I was never interested in playing cowboys and Indians growing up. I never was much of a tomboy, I guess."

239

"Well I'm glad of that!" Joe said emphatically. "With my background I don't think I'd know what to do with a tomboy type of girl!"

"So you prefer a girl who can crochet doilies to one who can climb trees?" Madelyn asked coquettishly. "Or a girl who can iron starched bed sheets and bake apple pies to one who can milk a cow and chop off the head of a chicken for supper?"

"Oh, most definitely!" Joe said, wincing slightly. "I can appreciate the amount of work that goes into crocheting doilies. And I love crisp, freshly ironed bed sheets and apple pies. But I couldn't care less if you could climb a tree or milk a cow, and I probably might not even love you as much if you went around chopping the heads off chickens! I would make an exception however to your sister's rooster, Clyde."

"So you don't like doilies."

"I didn't say I don't like doilies!" Joe objected.

"You said you *appreciate* the amount of work that goes into making them. So you might as well have just said you don't like them."

"Now you know darn good and well that's not the same thing!" Joe said vehemently.

"So you *do* like doilies!"

Joe shrugged. "Not especially."

"See! I knew it! You need to learn to say what you mean, and mean what you say!"

"Okay. I said what I did to get a rise out of you, because you have a way of turning the most trivial of things into an argument."

"I do not!"

"Yes you do. You do it almost every time we are together and I have to grab you and kiss you to get you to stop arguing."

"So, what is it about doilies you don't like?"

"Okay, keep on starting stupid little arguments so I can keep on stopping them."

Joe did what he had to do to get Madelyn to shut up. She pulled away from him after that first lingering kiss, saying, "We can't be doing this," before smashing her mouth against his in an even more passionate kiss. "You have to stop it," she implored, "because I don't seem to be able to."

"What makes you think *I* can!" Joe managed to exclaim before Madelyn's lips covered his once more. '*Or what makes you think I would ever want to*' he thought as his tongue snuck past her lips, exploring her mouth as his hands explored her breasts then slid down her sides and around to her back to caress the fleshy mounds of her oh so enticing bottom. '*If this is going to stop, it has to be her that stops it, because there's no way I can do that. I want to be doing this until the moment I die.*'

Startled by her own lack of restraint, Madelyn reluctantly pulled away from Joe, her face reddening in embarrassment. "We better get to work on those guns," she said, breathlessly. "How about we both do some sanding to start then paint a few to see how they look. That way I can figure out how to finish them off to make them look real."

Joe avoided looking directly at Madelyn, the tension in both his body and in the very air of the workshop making his head spin. He sat on a high stool in front of the workbench, grasping a sheet of sandpaper in one hand and one of the hanging guns in the other before his eyes met Madelyn's, the discomfiture they both felt compelling them to grin shyly at one another at first, then gradually changing to peals of unrestrained mirth.

"What are we going to do?" he asked helplessly. "Good lord, what are we going to do!"

Joe and Madelyn worked tirelessly on sanding, painting and adding the finishing touches to the guns all that week: shading and burnishing them until they couldn't be told from the real thing unless they were held in the hand and their light weight gave them away, prompting a closer examination. "What you did to make these guns look real is truly remarkable," Joe said, turning one of the specimens over and over in his hands. "They are absolute perfection!"

Madelyn smiled in appreciation of the compliment. "So, now what?" she asked.

"So now we let the guns all completely dry, we go back over to Sturgis, return the library books, go shopping at the dime store for a whole bunch of tissue paper to wrap the guns in, get a sandwich and a coke at the drug store, go see a double feature movie then get some supper at the Dakota restaurant then go see the Rhythm Wranglers stage show at the Armory and stay for the dance that follows. That's what!" Joe said.

"Sounds like you have it all planned!"

"Yup! Just go grab a sweater…it still gets cold at night this time of year…and we'll be on our way!"

On the drive over to Sturgis, Madelyn tried to get Joe to divulge his plans for selling the toy guns, but Joe kept evading her questions. He didn't know if what he planned on trying would work, or even if she would approve of his plan, so felt it would be better to keep it to himself for the time being. "Why are you so curious?" he asked. "You admit you don't know anything about sales, but you want me to give you a condensed lesson on salesmanship tactics that you probably won't understand anyway since it's not part and parcel of your experience."

"You don't think I am smart enough to comprehend something so complex if it is explained to me?" Madelyn huffed.

Joe decided it was time to set his ego aside and let Madelyn win this one. "No," he said sorrowfully, "It's that you are educated far beyond what I am, and I don't feel I have the ability to adequately explain the methods of salesmanship to you because I lack the necessary vocabulary." He surreptitiously glanced in her direction out of the corner of his eye, and was relieved and gratified to see a look of remorse on her face. In fact, was that a tear in her eye, he wondered.

"Don't ever think you aren't as smart as I am just because you have less formal schooling!" she said vehemently. "You are much smarter than I am in so many ways! And don't you ever doubt that!"

As Madelyn snuggled closer to Joe, and he placed his arms around her shoulders feeling her simultaneously kiss the lobe of his ear, he grinned to himself in contentment. He felt certain he had set the right mood and was on the right track for a very delightful day and for what he hoped would be a most eventful night. He knew he still had a bit more planning to do, but he also felt confident in his ability to come up with whatever was needed, when it was needed. He was, after all, a consummate salesman. And he was convinced that everything in life... be it love or hate, war or peace, fame or fortune... was just a matter of salesmanship. The product sold was whatever one desired it to be, and that desire was the true essence of the product. And right then what he desired was Madelyn, and his mission was to sell himself to her...all of himself, unrestrained.

The day went as planned, even better than Joe could have hoped for. The second feature movie had no appeal for Madelyn, so the two of them spent the time seated in the loges at the back of the theatre doing a lot of kissing and as much petting as Joe could get away with. They enjoyed a simple supper of meat-loaf, mashed potatoes and cooked carrots washed down with milk, followed by a slice of apple pie. Then they headed down the block to the Armory for the stage show and the dance, holding hands all the way. The country songs at the show were interspersed with a cowboy roping and acrobatics act, a ventriloquist act, and a very entertaining tap-dancing on roller skates act that both Joe and Madelyn found exceptional. And Joe two-stepped the evening away with the love of his life in his arms thinking that life couldn't get any better. He still hadn't come up with a plan for after the dance ended, but decided that didn't matter. He knew from past experience that most of the time the best things happened when there was no plan.

They were half way back to St. Onge when Joe's car blew a rear tire. Cursing under his breath so that Madelyn could not clearly hear his words, he pulled over to the side of the road and got out of the car to examine the damage. It was only by feeling the rear tires that he discovered the flat tire was on the rear, passenger side of the car. He had a spare in the trunk, but no flashlight, and as luck would have it the moon was in the 'new' stage and there was not light enough to see anything, even with the headlights on.

"We're going to have to wait it out until sunrise, I'm afraid," he told Madelyn dejectedly. "I can't see my hand in front of my face out there. It's black as pitch!"

"What time is it?"

Joe walked to the front of the car and held his wrist in front of the headlights then went back to slide into the driver's seat and report to Madelyn, "It's twenty past one."

"It's a long time yet until sunup... especially at this time of year. We're going to run out of things to talk about, and it's getting cold too," Madelyn grumbled.

Joe turned off his headlights. "I guess we could catch a bit of a snooze," he suggested. "Climb into the back seat while I get the blanket out of the trunk. We can snuggle together and keep one another warm until the sun comes up."

Hi there, remember me? The seventy-something daughter of Joe and Madelyn telling their story? I'm cutting in here because, although my father told me "it" (as you probably already surmised) happened that night, and in that place, he

understandably did not relate any of the details to me. I was, after all, just seventeen, and the mid-fifties was still somewhat the age of innocence. Having no experience of my own with the backseats of cars at the time, I could not even imagine what transpired.

However, this is no longer the fifties and I have experienced enough in the sixty years that have elapsed since then to have a fairly accurate idea of what must have taken place. But that doesn't mean I will indulge your prurient interest by writing out a salacious scenario for you. If you feel you must have an image in mind of what took place, I suggest that you close your eyes and let your own mind depict the event for you, keeping in mind that Joe and Madelyn loved one another passionately and there could be no other outcome for them. To them, it was just a matter of time, convenience and circumstance. So, your own depiction of what took place would be as accurate as mine…since I have no idea exactly how, or with how much passion, Joe and Madelyn consummated their love for one another.

Also, with you being the one imagining it, you will be saving me from having to do so in order to move the story along. There's a part of me that is still seventeen when it comes to my father, since that is the age I was when he died, and I'm sure you are aware of the way seventeen year-olds think of the idea of their parents having sexual relations. That ranges from complete denial to the ultimate "yuck" factor. So, you do whatever you think you have to do regarding what took place in the back seat of Joe's car, and I will get on with the story from that point on. And I will try not to interrupt again. Deal?

At first light Joe was busy changing the rear tire on his car, still basking in the ecstasy of his first carnal experience with Madelyn. He was fearful though about what her reaction to the incident was going to be. His breath caught in his throat when he saw the back door of the car open, and Madelyn step out. His body tensed as their eyes met, his filled with a timid apprehension while hers were shining with glee. Then in an instant his foreboding was obliterated by her shy smile that told him volumes. "Did you sleep well?" he asked solicitously.

"Very well..., if not quite long enough," she said, yawning. Frowning, she took a step toward Joe. "I committed a mortal sin last night," she said blandly, "and I can't figure out why I'm not upset about that."

Joe was at a loss as to what to say about that. He merely gave Madelyn a sappy grin and went about picking up his tools and the flat tire, stowing them in the trunk of the car before he thought of something to say. "Real love has no regrets."

"I think you must be right about that. Because I'm feeling something truly strange! I think maybe I regret not having done what we did sooner!"

"Oh, you wonderfully, naughty girl!" Joe exclaimed, astonished and delighted at the same time. He swept Madelyn up in his arms, and glancing toward the open door to the back seat of the car asked, "Would you like to do it again? Right now? Because I sure would! I've been waiting years for this to happen!"

Joe almost couldn't believe Madelyn's response. "Yes I want to do it again! I sure do! But not here on the side of the road because there will surely be some cars coming along soon. We need to find some place out of sight."

His mind numbed by anticipation of the delight intimated by her pronouncement, Joe flooded the car by giving it too much gas when he tried to start it and he was forced to wait another few minutes before trying it again. When they were finally on the road, it wasn't long before they came to a turnoff that led through a well-treed area on the way to a large ranch. Joe pulled off to the side at Madelyn's behest, his car invisible from either the road or the ranch. Giggling, Madelyn reached into the back seat, grabbed the blanket and was spreading it out by the side of the car almost before Joe knew what was happening.

"You are surprising me!" Joe exclaimed, joining Madelyn on the blanket. "I thought you would be upset about me taking your virginity, and I have to say I am so thankful you aren't. But I also have to say, I don't understand why."

"I'm not upset because doing what we did means that we belong to one another now. We can't undo the taking of my virginity and I wouldn't have wanted anyone else to take it. It hurt some, but the hurt didn't matter because it felt like the most right thing in the world to do and I wouldn't want to take it back for anything! I love you, Joe. And now I'm yours… completely. Does that sound maudlin or silly to you?"

"If that's what silly sounds like, I'd like to hear more of it. Some guys might be a little bit scared by that, but it is music to my ears because it is you who said it to me. I love you Madelyn, and I want you in my arms anytime and anywhere for the rest of my life."

"So get going on that annulment a little harder!" Madelyn exclaimed, rolling over on top of Joe. "I want the day when I can be your wife to come as soon as possible."

They spent the next two hours wrapped in the blanket, making love and marveling at the wonder of it all, whispering and giggling as they explored one another's bodies and as Joe started in on his quest to kiss every freckle, starting on Madelyn's face. Their plan was to arrive at the farm at about 9am so it would appear as if they had both spent the night in town, she at her parent's home and he at the rectory with Father Brunet, and they had simply driven out to the farm together. Then, if asked by her parents or the good Father, they could say they had been at the farm. Not a lie, actually, Joe had assured Madelyn; it was just a matter of creative semantics.

But no one questioned anything…quite possibly because no one could imagine Madelyn ever compromising her chastity for any reason whatsoever. Only Joe knew the minx dwelling inside that prim and proper slender body with a spectacularly articulated behind supported by a pair of astonishingly gorgeous legs all topped off with a halo of light brown hair with gold and red highlights. Add in the million freckles she unsuccessfully tried to conceal with powder on her dainty turned up nose, and her joyous laugh, Joe decided, and Madelyn was almost enough to make a man lose his sanity. He wondered how she had managed to keep the sensual side of herself so well hidden for so many years…perhaps even hidden from herself. And when he came to the conclusion that it was he, and he alone responsible for her wondrous transformation from a chaste school-marm into an enchanting paramour, he couldn't help but feel he was walking a little taller…and with a strut at that!

But it turned out that Joe was a bit premature in his thinking that Madelyn's ardor would continue unabated. She was still the devout Catholic girl later that day when she announced to him that she had a problem with things. "I can't take communion at Mass tomorrow," she stated solemnly. "I have to go to confession first, and I don't want to go to Father Brunet because he will know it's me!"

"Do you have to take communion every Sunday? Couldn't you skip it once?"

"How would I explain that? I take communion every Sunday, without fail."

They sat quietly together on a bale of hay, basking in the sun just outside the barn. They had accompanied Priscilla as she set out to milk the two cows, using her as a chaperone so they wouldn't be tempted to get carried away. They were both deep in thought, trying to come up with a way to solve Madelyn's predicament, when Joe pulled a thick blade of hay out of the bale and placed it between his teeth. Eyes widening, with a grin erasing her furrowed brow, Madelyn pointed to the blade of grass, exclaiming "That's it!"

"What's it?" Joe asked, taking the blade of hay from his mouth and studying it intently.

"I need to eat something…or maybe drink something before Mass. You can't take communion if any food or drink has passed your lips after midnight, remember?"

"Won't you still have to explain the reason why you aren't taking communion?"

"Yes, of course."

"Well what if someone asks why you ate or drank something? Won't you have to tell a lie?"

"I guess I'll just have to hope no one asks me why." Madelyn paused then added, "If someone does ask me that and I just shrug my shoulders in response and not say anything, would that be a lie?"

"Probably not as much of one as saying you were hungry, or you were thirsty, or you just forgot."

"That's not much help. Is that all you've got?"

Joe shrugged….which led to Madelyn bursting out in laughter, and the infectious nature of the laugh making Joe laugh, the sound transferring all the way over to Priscilla who sat on a stool with her head pressed against the flank of her Guernsey cow, laughing in helpless mirth along with them, without having any idea why.

Joe turned up Junction Blvd. in Sturgis, nearly halfway to Rapid City. Leaving behind a sample of each of the 3 kinds of guns, he had three big gunny sacks of toy guns wrapped in tissue paper stowed in the back seat, plus one gun tucked into a holster under his left armpit, and two more unwrapped guns in his leather case. He rehearsed his sales spiel out loud as he drove along, but for perhaps the first time in his life he felt a bit unsure of himself. He knew that what he planned on doing would work in Massachusetts, but South Dakota, with its large Sioux population on the reservation near Rapid City, might be a different matter. He decided he would have to be very careful.

He had no trouble finding the boxing arena. As in every other town he had ever been in, they were always located in a somewhat seedy and isolated location. The one in Rapid City was no exception. He noted the prevalence of expensive new cars parked outside the back entrance, and instantly felt more at ease. Those cars told him what kind of men he would find inside…the kind he wanted to deal with.

The five men seated at a ringside table smoking cigars all turned to look at Joe as he entered, swinging his leather case at his side and whistling as if he owned the joint.

"Can I do something for you?" one of the men asked gruffly. "We're not open until this evening."

"Oh, I know!" Joe said affably. "I used to do some Golden Gloves boxing back east in my younger years."

"Then what do you want?"

"I have something I think will be of interest to you gentlemen," Joe said seriously. "Because I know it would definitely be of interest to the people I used to know in the prize-fighting business back east."

"What is it you think you have that would be of interest to us?" the same man scoffed.

"Guns," Joe announced, opening the left side of his suit jacket and pulling the fake pistol from the holster. "All made right here in the USA… this one is a Colt 45 automatic pistol, and there's a 32 caliber Savage and a 38 Smith & Wesson revolver in my bag."

Joe was delighted to see the men noticeably flinch when he pulled the gun out of the holster, and even more delighted when the man who had done all the talking so far warily asked him to not point that thing at him. "Oh, it's not loaded," he assured them. "In fact, it's not even a real gun."

"Whatta ya mean it's not a real gun!" the man hesitantly asked.

"Here," Joe said, extending the gun handle- first toward the man. "Check it out for yourself"

The man gingerly took the gun from Joe, the disbelief on his face turning to amazement, then amusement, as he turned the gun over and over in his hands, testing its heft and the way it felt and looked. "Well you sure fooled me!" he exclaimed. "I'm holding it in my hands and it sure looks real, but the weight and the feel of it tells me it's not made of any kind of metal. What is it, wood?"

Joe nodded. "Wood. Expertly painted to make it look so real it would fool anyone, even close up."

"Well what makes you think we would be interested in buying fake guns? No matter how real they look, they aren't good for anything!"

"Sure they are!" Joe exclaimed. "They're even better than real guns in lots of ways! Look, you gentlemen got just a little bit wary of me when you thought I had a real, loaded gun. And I probably could have gotten away with robbing you or something and you would have been none the wiser. But if it was the other way around, if you were the guy with one of these guns, I'll bet no one would want to mess with you. Just having what looks like a real gun on you is a big deterrent. I know there can be some pretty shady types hanging around fight -arenas, that's why I figured I would offer these guns to you…for your protection." Joe opened his case, offering to let the men help themselves to a close up inspection of the merchandise. "If you don't want them, I know there are plenty of people who will!"

"I guess whether or not we want them depends on how much you want for your three *toy* guns."

"I'm only asking two dollars apiece. But there are 524 of them…and it's an all or nothing deal."

"Five hundred and twenty-four of them!" the man shouted. "What in hell are we supposed to do with 524 fake guns?"

"Well, since you are most likely going to live longer with that kind of preventive sort of protection, you will have a lifetime of replacements when the guns get scuffed or the paint gets chipped off, as it surely will over time. And you may each, all five of you and maybe some of your close acquaintances as well, want to carry one or more on you at all times, plus have them in strategic locations such as your cars and houses, etc. They will all find a use, believe me."

"Maybe, but 524 guns at two dollars apiece, why that's over a thousand dollars!"

"Hey, I know that's peanuts for guys like you! But tell you what I'll do… call it a thousand even, and the guns are yours. You will have an exclusive on them because there aren't any more, and I can take a thousand bucks home to my sweetheart who helped me paint them to look so real."

The man who was the only one who spoke to Joe shook his hand. "Deal!" he said, snapping his fingers at the other four men, indicating that each of them was expected to pony up two hundred dollars. Grinning lewdly, he slapped Joe on the back declaring, "Maybe you'll be getting a little bonus when you hand over that thousand bucks to your honey back home!"

Joe shrugged, grinning back at the man. "Maybe so!" he said. "Maybe so!"

"So, where is home?"

The question made Joe decidedly nervous as he pocketed the money for the guns and the five men accompanied him out to his car to help him unload the gunny sacks. "Home is near Boston. That's in Massachusetts," Joe added.

"What are you doing here in Rapid City?"

"Just here to offer you these guns," Joe said by way of explanation. "I heard on the news there's been some Indian trouble here, plus there's been a lot of outlaw activity in the region lately, so thought this might be the place they were most needed."

"Where'd you get them? You make 'em?"

Joe grinned, shaking his head. "Nooo!" he exclaimed. "I found them in a pile of junk in a lot behind a studio where they make movies out in

Hollywood. They were probably leftover stuff from the silent movie days and got tossed because they were of no use because movies need sound now. So I just bagged them up and took them back home with me, and my sweetheart and I sanded them, and painted them, and then did the hard work of painting the details on them to make them look like the real thing. I planned on selling them to the five and dimes as toys for kids to play cops and robbers, but my girl told me they looked too real and might give kids bad ideas so I figured I'd sell them to folks like you who sometimes have a need for protection and could put them to good use."

"Why didn't you sell them back in Boston?"

"That's a stronghold for the Mafia, Boston is!" Joe exclaimed. "I don't want to have any dealings with the Mafia!" He was starting to sweat and wondering if he had said too much, or not enough; if the men thought he was on the level or was a wise guy or an idiot; and he was beginning to wonder which it was himself. He watched as the men unwrapped random guns, examining them closely and assuring themselves that all the guns were indeed real looking. "I went to the trouble of wrapping all of them so the paint wouldn't get chipped," he explained. "I wanted them all to remain perfect."

"You could have gotten more than two dollars for them," the man said, removing the cigar from the side of his mouth for the first time.

"I know. But sales isn't a business I want to be in. Too much traveling and too many lonely nights away from my lady, if you know what I mean."

Chuckling, the man's eyes narrowed as he slapped Joe on the back and sent him on his way.

Instead of heading toward the road that would take him back to St. Onge, Joe took the road that would lead him east across South Dakota. He kept his eye as much on his rear-view mirror as he did the road, watching for any sign of one or more of the cars that had been parked in the back of the boxing arena. Not wanting to take the chance of being waylaid out in prairie-dog territory between towns, Joe pulled up in front of a small diner near the edge of town where he felt it would be unlikely to be ambushed and took a seat at the end of the counter where he had an unimpeded view of the road and parking area. He ordered a ham sandwich and a vanilla milkshake and his order had just been placed in front of him when he saw a shiny black Cadillac pull up next to his car. He recognized the two men in the car as two of the silent cigar smokers at the boxing arena. Keeping them in view out of the corner of his eye, he took a bite of his sandwich, chewing methodically then followed with a sip of the milkshake through a straw. He made a point of smiling and nodding at the waitress, giving her a thumbs-up gesture and carefully avoiding looking out the window. The men had not moved. They sat still, stonily watching him through the windshield of their car.

As he finished his sandwich and milkshake, Joe gestured to the waitress, fishing in his pocket for a fifty-cent piece to pay for his lunch, telling her to keep the change. Then he asked for directions that would take him east to Sioux Falls, making sure there was plenty of gesturing going on from both him and the waitress to assure the men in the car that he was intending to continue on in an easterly direction.

As Joe slid off the stool he saw the men back out of their parking spot and speed east down the long, straight stretch of road. He waited until they were out of sight then went out to his car and headed west, turning down a back street lined with modest clapboard houses and bypassing the boxing arena before once again getting back on the main road. He imagined the two men waiting in their car for him to come by so they could force him off the road and retrieve the money they had just paid him for the guns, and he wished he could share the laughter that was bubbling up inside him with Madelyn. But he knew it was something he would have to keep to himself, because he could never tell her. Instead, he satisfied himself by patting the big wad of bills in the breast pocket of his jacket… right over the spot where the fake gun had rested in a holster.

NOVEMBER, 1936

JOE LOOKED THROUGH THE MAIL THAT FATHER BRUNET'S housekeeper had left for him on the breakfast table. Among the usual letters from George Miller in Holyoke and Howie out in California, he was surprised to see a letter from his mother. Letters from her were a rarity, so he opened that one first to get what he expected to be bad news out of the way. His mother had written to tell him that his brother, Gilles was at death's door and that he should come home immediately if not sooner to be of any assistance to her that he was capable of. The tone of the letter was insulting…as letters from his mother generally were… but since the insults were expected, he was never actually insulted. What he felt instead was a combination of worry and annoyance. His mother's missive suggested he consider taking an airplane rather than driving, because speed was of the essence.

Joe knew there was no way he would be getting on an airplane. Deciding he would have to leave immediately, he wolfed down his breakfast, packed up his few clothes and other belongings, scrawled a note to Father Brunet then drove over to Madelyn's house to let her know he had to leave immediately for Holyoke. "I'll be back as soon as I can," he promised her, "and I will miss you every second I am gone!"

Madelyn didn't feel well that morning. Her stomach was queasy and her head ached, no doubt, she thought, from all the candy corn and popcorn balls she had eaten the night before at the Halloween party she and Joe had attended. She hoped that Joe wasn't feeling out of sorts too because he had a long drive ahead of him. She watched the back end of his car as he drove away until he turned the corner and disappeared from sight. Then she dry-heaved right there by the fence where she had waved her good-byes.

Traveling light, without the trailer hitched to his car, Joe made good time. He only stopped for gas and to relieve his bladder and pick up a few items he could munch on while driving. He considered stopping in Sioux Falls for the night, then changed his mind, driving all the way to Sioux City, Iowa before resting. He mailed a rapidly written letter off to Madelyn before setting out again the next morning, letting her know he would keep in touch every day and wishing he could hear her voice on the telephone.

Chuckling to himself, he recalled how they had all been so excited about the fact that Madelyn's mother, Emma had finally relented and had allowed a telephone to be installed in her house that summer. But the telephone hadn't lasted long. Being a party line, the phone rang several times a day, and every time it did Emma would scream as if a cannon had been fired inside the house and she would holler for someone to 'get it'! even if it wasn't her ring. And if it *was* her ring, she was even more frantic! She would pick up the receiver and bellow "hello!" into the mouthpiece as if she were certain she had to make her voice travel all the way to China. The whole experience had been too much for everyone to take, and the telephone had been disconnected and removed from its place on the dining room wall after just 3 weeks of its torture.

Emma's reaction to the ringing of the phone, however, didn't compare to her reaction to the many thunderstorms they'd had that summer. The lightening, followed by loudly rumbling thunder, sent her screaming for cover under her bed, where she screeched in panic until the storm played itself out. At first it was a source of amusement for Joe, but that soon changed, becoming a source of extreme annoyance instead.

There had been another change as well. Madelyn had declined to renew her contract to teach at the country school that fall, and instead had taken over much of the bookkeeping for her father's various enterprises. To Joe's delight, that gave her more time to spend with him since he began working in the pool hall once again, and it pleased her father as well. It meant that Charles had more time to spend at the ranch, helping with the livestock and the harvest, the things that were closest to his heart.

For Madelyn's part, the extra time she had proved to be both an opportunity to spend more time with Joe as well as a curse when it came to her sense of moral integrity. The constant confliction between desire and morality kept her in a state of anxiety that manifested itself in moodiness that ranged from anger to outright wantonness. Her erratic behavior kept Joe on guard, never knowing what the disposition of his beloved, enigmatic Madelyn would be from one minute to the next. But he reveled in the changeability and the ardor that transformed her into the tempestuous minx that made his mundane world disappear in the circle of her arms, and increasingly, her legs as well.

• ⁘ •

Joe arrived in Holyoke to discover that his brother, Gilles had recovered from his bout with pneumonia, as his mother referred to it, but as his sister, Anna Marie insisted had been just a slight cold. Incensed, Joe had turned on his mother demanding to know why she had forced him to return home at breakneck speed on a trumped up emergency, even suggesting that he should risk his life on a tube flying through the air high above the clouds, when it was clear that there was absolutely no good reason to do so.

"You are needed here!" she said emphatically. "Your days of gallivanting all over the countryside in pursuit of who knows what are over! It's time you took on the responsibility of an adult instead of wasting your time on a frivolous life, doing nothing more than selfishly gratifying yourself while you have family that needs you here!"

"What is it you need from me?"

"I need your time and attention to this property for one thing!"

"Be more specific."

"There are things that need to be seen to. Repairs need to be made in several of the apartments and you need to be here to oversee that. There will be workmen to schedule and general maintenance, and so forth."

"Why do you need me to do any of that? You have a maintenance man and two of your children here to see to those things, as well as yourself. Isn't that enough?"

"When I die you will be inheriting this place along with your brother and sister," his mother stated vehemently. "Do you think it is fair for them to do everything while you do nothing for an equal share?"

"Who says I want a share?" Joe yelled explosively. "Why would I want any part of this place when all I ever wanted to do was get away from it?"

"Are you telling me, young man, that you are not at all interested in your inheritance? Do you even know what this place is worth?"

"No. And I'm not sure I care either. I'll bet neither Anna Marie nor Gilles would care if I give my share up to them," Joe said emphatically. He looked directly at his mother, staring her down, as he asked "Why are you doing this right now. I've been away for several years and there's been no suggestion that I should come back where I belong, so why now? Are you planning on dying right away or something?"

"Don't be impertinent! Of course I'm not planning on dying soon. That's not something you can plan on doing with any degree of accuracy unless you are planning on taking your own life, and let me assure you I am not planning any such thing! I have simply come to the realization that it is not fair that the burden of managing this property is on the shoulders of your brother and sister while you play the dilettante and do not take on your share of the responsibility while expecting to reap an equal share of the value."

"I expect no such thing! It has never even occurred to me that I would be inheriting anything from you,"

"Ah, but you will be. And don't be too quick to relinquish your inheritance without giving it a great deal of thought. You wouldn't want to live to regret a foolish, hasty decision now, would you?"

Joe took a leisurely walk around the square block the huge brownstone apartment building occupied, surveying it, estimating its value, and making a decision about its worth to him. It was indeed an impressive looking building, but it was also identical to several others along the street so it did not stand out in any special way. On the plus side it was a reminder of the father and sister he loved, but on the other side it was a reminder of the mother he loathed at times, but generally respected, and the brother he pitied and who mostly disgusted him. It was also home to his dear friend George Miller and his growing family, so that definitely counted for something. But when it came to a list of things he could easily give up, and a list of things he could never bear to part with, that big building easily made the first list but wasn't even thought of for that second list. That second list of things he could never part with had just one word on it; Madelyn.

Joe spent the next few days catching up on things with George and Anna Marie while also tending to some of the things his mother felt needed his attention in order to placate her. He had told her he would stay for a month, under one condition. She was not to open any of his mail or come in his room for any reason. She had begged him to stay for the holidays, but he insisted he would not be doing that because his place was with the woman he loved at Christmastime.

But Mother Nature must have been in cahoots with Joe's mother, or maybe God had left instructions for her to fulfill the fervent prayers of one Josephine Tessier to make the roads impassable due to a massive winter storm, so that the poor woman could retain the presence of her youngest child for the holidays…and for as long as possible after that as well.

Joe listened to the weather report on the radio every morning, and day after day the news was unbelievably disheartening. The snow was relentless, with blizzard conditions followed by freezing rain topped off with more blowing snow and white-out conditions. He spent his days shoveling the walkways out to the main sidewalk. And every night those walkways were filled back in so he had it to do all over again. The walkways began to look like tunnels through the banks of snow, and when those banks became too high to toss more snow on top, Joe began tromping them down by walking back and forth over them until they eventually became long blocks of ice. His car, along with the cars of the other tenants, was defined as one of the huge white mounds strung all along the impassable roadway. It was impossible to tell which one belonged to him.

Despondent, Joe resigned himself to the fact that he would have to be content with daily letters from Madelyn…until he received one that informed him she was taking a train up to Montreal and would be there for a month-long retreat at a convent along with her cousin, Celeste and she would not be able to correspond with him for that entire month.

'The retreat is for meditation and reflection on your life,' she explained in the letter. *'So, there can be no outside communication that would interfere with that process.'* She asked him to please understand that she needed

the retreat because she had some very big decisions to make and she needed inner peace and solitude to do so. Anguished by the knowledge that it would be more than another month before he could be with her again, and filled with fear at what the long absence might mean, Joe felt himself losing consciousness as the world around him turned black. He attempted to sit on his bed, but missed, landing on the floor with a loud thump instead.

Josephine heard Joe fall and rushed to his room thinking he might have collapsed due to exhaustion from all the shoveling. His door was ajar and she could see him lying on the floor beside his bed so she rushed to his side and knelt next to him. She could see he was breathing and did not seem to be in any distress, so she decided she would take the opportunity to read the letter that lay on the floor near his hand since she surmised it was most likely the cause of his fainting spell, or whatever it was that ailed him. She smiled to herself when she read the letter, mentally calculating how much longer Joe would be there with her and thanking providence for her good fortune. Why, he might even still be there on his birthday!

When she saw Joe begin to stir then take a deep breath of air and exhale loudly, Josephine quickly got to her feet and exited the room. As far as she was concerned she had never gone into his room or read his letter, nor had she seen him collapsed on his bedroom floor. She decided she would also keep her tongue when Joe surprisingly remained at home even when the snow had melted away and he could have easily navigated the cleared roads. She would merely count her blessings and offer her thanks for once again being rewarded for her prayers.

MARCH, 1937

JOE HAD DREAMED SO MANY TIMES OF OPENING THE DOOR TO find his beloved Madelyn standing there, that on the afternoon of the 24th of March when he answered the ring of the bell and opened the door and saw Madelyn standing there he could only stammer "I'm going to close the door then open it again to see if you are still there or if it's only a dream."

And that's what he did. "Is it really you?" he asked inanely.

Madelyn dropped the suitcase she was carrying then reached out and wrapped her arms around Joe. "Does it feel like it's really me?"

Lightheaded, Joe took several deep breaths then softly placed his lips against Madelyn's, breathing in the smell and the taste of her. Then he hastily released her, grabbed her suitcase and ushered her through the apartment to his bedroom where he kissed her longingly once again then collapsed with her in his arms onto the bed.

"We need to talk," she gasped.

"Indeed we do!" he affirmed. "I need to know what comes next. What did that retreat in Montreal make you decide? The way you are kissing me back right now makes me think I'm winning this one, but I need to conclusively hear it from you."

"I now know I want to be with you, that I *need* to be with you, no matter what."

Not wanting to jinx anything by asking the hundreds of questions that plagued him, Joe kept his silence and simply held Madelyn in his arms, kissing her softly, content to just revel in her presence after so long an absence. But when he heard his mother return from her twice weekly game of Bridge in one of the third floor apartments, he was immediately set in motion. Whispering to Madelyn as he drew a large suitcase out of his closet, he said "Help me pack. Empty out my drawers and put everything in the suitcase while I gather my toiletries and things in the bathroom. We are going to get out of here…right now, today! I don't want to spend one more minute than I have to here ever again!"

"Where are we going?" Madelyn asked, with a gleeful smile lighting up her face.

"To a hotel for tonight. Then anywhere you want to go in the morning."

As Joe and Madelyn exited Joe's bedroom, each carrying a suitcase, there was no way to avoid his mother who was seated in the living room browsing through a church bulletin. Startled, she leaped to her feet and demanded to know what was going on.

"Madelyn arrived here today and we are leaving right now, Mother," Joe informed her. "I've packed up everything I want from here, so don't expect me back."

"You're leaving without even having the courtesy to say goodbye to your brother and sister, or to your friends, the Millers? And without due notice to me as well?"

"My due notice is to Madelyn."

"Yes, I can see that," Josephine said, derisively, looking intently at Madelyn. "I can see that very clearly you have done it again. What a shameful fool you are."

"I guess I have been a shameful fool for putting up with your abuse my whole life. But that ends right now. I'm out of here for good."

"For now maybe; but probably not for good. You will come to your senses one day and realize which side your bread has been buttered on all along. And that will be the day you have finally become a man I can respect."

"I couldn't care less if you ever respect me. It's my self-respect that has any meaning for me. And my self-respect tells me that the best thing I can do right now is leave this place and this life behind me. I don't share your ambition for me, and I don't relish living under your thumb any longer. Please tell Anna Marie and Gilles they are welcome to my share of your estate, whenever that estate may be available to them, for I want no part of it, now or ever. This is goodbye, Mother."

<hr>

That night at the hotel in Holyoke, Joe and Madelyn talked at length about Joe's animosity toward his mother. Joe poured his heart out and Madelyn sympathized with him but couldn't fully understand how he could feel such loathing for the woman responsible for his existence.

"I guess I don't really hate her," Joe confessed. "Maybe the more appropriate term is that I intensely dislike her," he grinned impishly. "But I'm tired of talking about something that matters so little to me. I want to talk about you; what you experienced during your month at the retreat, and especially why you are here now. I want to know everything!"

"*Everything* might be a bit much to take," Madelyn said, avoiding Joe's eyes. "First, I didn't go to the retreat. That was a lie I told Mama and Papa and repeated to you because it was the easiest thing for me to do at the time. I merely visited my cousin, Celeste who lives in Montreal. She's a nurse in one of the big hospitals there, and works on the maternity floor helping in the delivery room. I wanted to learn everything I could from her about childbirth."

"Why? Are you thinking about becoming a midwife or something?"

"No, and don't interrupt me! Madelyn admonished, "or, I may never get through telling you what I have to tell you. Your mother knows what it is I have to say. She could tell, I know, because of what she said. She said '*I see you have done it again.*' You know what that means don't you?"

Joe shook his head, puzzled. "No, I don't know what that means!"

Madelyn's eyes brimmed with tears as she said, "It means I think I am carrying your baby." She studied Joe's face to see his reaction as the tears spilled from her eyes and rolled down her cheeks leaving streaks in the powder she had applied to cover her freckles. When she saw his smile and the love in his eyes, she smiled too and burst out alternately sobbing and giggling in response.

"You *think* you are carrying my baby? Don't you *know*?"

"Well, no. Not for sure anyway. I think so, but…I've never carried a baby before so how can I be sure? I thought I might just be getting fat!"

"I love you, you silly goose!" Joe declared. He placed a hand on Madelyn's stomach and was soon rewarded with a light kick at his palm. "Let's see, we were last together in October, and it's now close to April, so you must be at least five months along now, maybe a bit more. My guess would be a July birth. That's not that far off. Do you think we can find a place in St. Onge? It wouldn't have to be much with just the two of us and a baby, and…"

Alarmed, Madelyn yelled "NO! I can't go back home! I can't face anyone there right now!"

"Well, they have to know sometime, don't they? A baby is not something you can hide forever!"

"They already know…at least Priscilla and some others in town for sure. But I don't think Mama and Papa know yet."

"How do you know that anyone knows?"

"Well, it was Priscilla who told me I was pregnant…because I didn't know…not for sure anyway. She said I had all the signs so asked me if I had been intimate with you and if it was possible that I could have a baby growing inside me. So then I thought maybe I was. Then one day when I brought some of my fancy work to a 'Bring and Brag' get together the women in the community have to show off their quilts and sweaters and embroidery and such, I saw a bunch of the ladies looking at me and whispering and Priscilla told me she had been asked if I was in the family way and she told them I had just been eating too many pies and cakes and sitting around doing bookwork for the past few months and to wash out their dirty minds. But I know they know, and so does Priscilla. That's when I told everyone I was going on a retreat with my cousin, Celeste in Montreal. Celeste knows, of course. She took me to see a doctor there and he says everything is okay. But I'm scared, Joe. Scared, and ashamed, and embarrassed and I don't know if I'm ever going to be able to face my parents again. I must be such a disappointment to them!"

Madelyn was sobbing profusely by the time she finished her confession to Joe, and though he offered her soft words of comfort and understanding, inside he was smiling and jumping for joy. He was going to have Madelyn, and a baby thrown in for a bonus, without having to go through the pretention of obtaining an annulment, the possibility of which he knew for a fact would be impossible. And he was saved from having to carry out his nefarious plan of getting her pregnant on purpose so she would be forced to marry him, because miraculously that had already happened.

"Let's get some sleep then get an early start tomorrow," he murmured while kissing the tears from her face. "We'll have a few days on the road to make plans."

And plan they did. Joe left Madelyn at a boarding house in Spearfish while he doubled back alone to St. Onge to pick up his trailer. He picked up a few of Madelyn's things she had left at the ranch as well, telling Priscilla that he and Madelyn were headed for California and that they would be married there. Then he picked up Madelyn at the boarding house and they drove to Santa Monica, arriving four days later after stopping to rest frequently along the side of the road. Three days later they stood before a judge, with Lorraine and Howie for witnesses, and repeated their vows. And they kissed one another for the first time as Mr. and Mrs. Adrian Joseph Tessier.

Joe was disappointed to find there was no vacancy at the boarding house he had stayed in before, but the one he found was just as suitable, except that he had to park his trailer further down the alley behind the boarding house than he would have liked. The only place for it was next to the barrels where the trash was burned. He and Madelyn had been there no more than two weeks when sparks from the burning trash escaped and set his trailer on fire, destroying all the encyclopedias he had left as well as everything else he had managed to acquire and stash away for future use. The trailer and its entire contents was a total loss, he had only three items of Black Hills Gold jewelry left, and the wad of bills stuffed in the sock on his right foot was sorely depleted due to all the months he'd had no income while in Holyoke. So he went back out, day after day, searching the alleys in the commerce and manufacturing areas, looking for anything that would inspire him to create something, anything, that would put a few dollars in his pocket so he could keep a roof over Madelyn's head and pay for the cost of childbirth in a hospital, at the most critical point in her life. It was on one of those frustratingly fruitless excursions that he once again lost consciousness, and when he came to he discovered that his feet were bare and his pockets had been emptied…and his empty socks had been discarded in a puddle of water.

Joe was thankful he was paid up a week in advance at the boarding house, but he didn't know how he was going to tell Madelyn he had been robbed of every cent he had. He did wind up telling her, but he led her to believe he had been knocked unconscious by a thief who had snuck up behind him, not wanting her to know he had passed out again. She might insist that he see a doctor, and he knew he couldn't afford to do that. But then she argued with him that he should see a doctor anyway because he could be seriously injured from a blow on the head, and he had to prove to her that his head showed no sign of abuse.

Deciding he had to change the subject, he asked "Do you have any money?"

"All I have is fifty cents," she replied. "I have some money in my bank account back in St. Onge though, so it shouldn't take too long to transfer it here."

"How much do you have?"

"Not a lot after spending so much on train fare to Montreal, then down to Holyoke. Maybe I still have a couple hundred dollars. Teaching doesn't pay much, you know."

"Give me the fifty cents," Joe said, holding out his hand.

Madelyn fished in her purse for the coin then handed it to Joe. "What are you going to do with fifty cents?" she asked.

"I'm going to take you to the movies, and buy us some popcorn and a soda pop."

"Why would you want to do that? Shouldn't we keep that money to buy a loaf of bread and a bottle of milk or something instead of wasting it on a movie and popcorn?"

"I'm taking you to a movie, woman, so powder your nose and grab your sweater, and let's get there before the show starts…and I don't want any argument about it!"

So they went to the movie…and Joe had the winning ticket stub for the $10 door prize.

When they returned to their room at the boarding house later that evening, Joe handed the ten dollar bill to Madelyn telling her "That was a pretty good investment you made with your fifty-cent piece, I'd say!"

Madelyn looked embarrassingly contrite. "I thought maybe God was punishing us for our sins when the trailer burned down then you were robbed, but maybe He decided to help us out of a jam anyway by seeing to it that you had the winning ticket for the door prize."

"You don't honestly think God had anything to do with it, do you?" Joe asked in amazement. "My wooden trailer was just too close to the burning trash, and I was just in the wrong place at the wrong time when my money was stolen, and I was in the right place at the right time when my number was drawn for the door prize. It's nothing more than that! Divine intervention or punishment had nothing to do with any of it!"

Madelyn shook her head. "It's all too much of a coincidence!"

"Nothing is ever *too much of a coincidence!*" Joe exclaimed, shoving his hands deep into his trouser pockets, and pulling out a dime that had been hidden in a crease. "Oh look! I found a dime that the thief overlooked! Now I can grab a coffee and doughnut while I'm out pounding the pavement looking for a job tomorrow. What a coincidence!"

"Why are you yelling at me?" Madelyn wailed, her eyes filling with tears.

Joe quickly pulled her into his arms, gently stroking the back of her head. "I'm not angry at you sweetheart. I'm just angry at myself for letting us get in the situation we're in. I'm supposed to be taking care of you and I'm not doing a very good job of it."

"None of this is your fault, and I'm prepared to be of help too. The school-year will be ending soon so I don't think I can get a job teaching, but do you think I could get a job as a typewriter?"

"You want a job as a typewriter?" Joe asked, sticking his tongue in his cheek to keep from bursting out laughing. "Do you know how to type?"

"No, but I've seen one of those machines and watched how it's done; and it doesn't look like it would be very hard to do. So what do you think?" she asked expectantly.

"The machine is called a typewriter, and the person doing the typing is called a typist," Joe explained, trying not to sound like he was talking down to her. "It's probably not that hard to learn, but learning how to do it really fast might take quite a while and businesses want to hire people who can type really fast and who don't make mistakes or have to look at what they are typing. I think it would take quite a while to master that."

"Maybe I could be a clerk in a store?" Madelyn suggested, questioningly.

"Or maybe you could just let me take care of us for now. It's not long before you will have a baby to care for and that will take up most of your time. Even if you could find some sort of job right now, you would just have to quit it anyway when the baby comes."

"But I feel so useless!" Madelyn lamented. "And you wouldn't be in the situation you're in right now if it weren't for me!"

"Well, that's just a ridiculous notion! Things happen that we don't have any control over, and we just need to go along for the ride wherever it takes us. And my ride took me to you, and your ride brought you to me, and now we are going to ride our way through this setback together, and we will make it because we have one another to lean on. Everything is going to work out because I have always been able to make things work out. So don't worry. Promise me you won't worry. That's not good for either you or our baby."

"You promise that everything will be okay?"

"I promise," Joe said solemnly.

"Then I promise to trust you and not worry about it anymore."

First thing the next morning, Joe kissed a still sleeping Madelyn on the forehead then leisurely strolled over to the doughnut shop on Santa Monica Blvd. to make good use of the dime in his pocket. The proprietor, Ken greeted him profusely, and the two men spent several minutes on small talk, catching up on things after a long absence. But when Joe got around to his second cup of coffee and second doughnut, he told Ken about the fire that destroyed his trailer and about being robbed.

"Right now I'm thinking I need to do something I swore I'd never do," he confessed.

"What's that? That doesn't have a good sound to it!" Ken exclaimed.

"Oh no, I don't mean anything illegal; nothing like that! What I mean is getting a job. I have a real aversion to working for anyone but myself. But it looks like I'm going to have to for the time being. So, have you heard where there might be any hiring going on or anything?"

"As a matter of fact there's an article about them looking for men to work down at the docks in Long Beach in the morning paper!" Ken exclaimed, fishing under the counter for the newspaper he had folded up and placed there earlier. He handed it to Joe, stabbing the paper with his index finger. "Read about it right there!"

Joe quietly perused the notice in the paper and read the accompanying article.

"Says they're going to be taking names and experience tomorrow and telling men they might consider that they'll have to come back the next day for an in-depth interview. They'd have to join the longshoreman's union and provide their own work boots. I guess they expect to have a lot of men show up tomorrow."

"They most likely will. Seems like all there is around here anymore is men looking for work. They come here from all over the country thinking this is the land of milk and honey or something, and jobs are being handed out left and right to all comers. But this is really the place to get your dreams shattered is what it is!"

"That doesn't sound like the way you used to talk about life here in the golden state! What happened to make you change your outlook?"

"Gladys, the lady I danced every dance with at the dime-a-dance ballroom, moved back to Carolina to look after her Grandma is what happened. I'm trying to find a way to head east and ask her to marry me. I know she would if I asked her to."

"So what's stopping you?"

"I need to sell my business here, but it don't make enough money for anyone to be interested in buying it. I don't own the building, I just rent the space for $25 a month and I live in the back there."

"Then what is it you're looking to sell? Just your equipment, and supplies, and…"

"And the counter and stools I put in, and the bit of furniture and stuff in the back. None of it is worth much, and I'd let it all go for a couple hundred bucks, just so I could buy a train ticket to take me to Gladys. My God how I miss her!"

"I know what it's like being apart from the woman you love," Joe stated. "It's about the most awful thing in the world. But I took care of that. I married my girl, and we are going to be adding to our family round about July, and…"

"You married that girl who was planning on being a nun?" Ken asked, stunned by Joe's revelation. "How on earth did you accomplish that?"

"I'm not even sure myself, except that maybe she was more attracted to me than she was to a life without me. But right now my string of bad luck has me in a pickle and for the first time in my life I am at a loss as to what to do about it." Sighing, Joe added, "Guess I'll be headed for Long Beach first thing tomorrow to see if I can get on as a longshoreman…at least for now."

The following morning, Madelyn woke when Joe kissed her, and puzzled by the way Joe was dressed, she asked "Why are you wearing a suit? I thought you said you were going for a job as a longshoreman. Wouldn't it be better to be dressed for that kind of work?"

"I suppose it would be if I had any work clothes…but I don't. All I have is suits and shoes like a businessman would wear. So there's nothing I can do other than dress the way I am." He blew her a kiss as he closed the door behind him, wearing his dark brown suit, polished brown shoes and his fedora, with his black leather case in his left hand. On the drive over to Long Beach he tried to come up with an idea that would make his attire seem appropriate, but he still had no idea what that would be until he saw the long lineup of men standing in front of a table where two men in suits were taking down names and work experience. Then Joe knew exactly what he was going to do.

He marched past all the men standing in the two lines waiting for their turn, went around to the other side of the table and announced to the two men seated there "Help has arrived! It looks like there was a bigger turnout than originally expected. Just tell me what you want me to do, and I'll grab another chair and get started."

Neither of the men questioned Joe, thinking that someone higher up must have sent him to help out. After they gave him some brief instructions, he placed his chair a couple of feet away along the table, arranged the pad of paper and pencils he had been given in front of him, and in an official manner waved some of the men over to his line. There was a frantic scurry at first, and a couple of scuffles as some of the men were accused of cutting-in, but that soon subsided and Joe set to work taking names and writing down qualifications.

Joe had to hand a card to the men who were to come back for an interview the following day. The card had the name of the applicant, as well as Joe's name as the interviewer. He felt that the hardest thing he ever had to do was to refuse a card to men who were not likely to be hired. Sometimes it was easy; the shifty-eyed liars who obviously exaggerated their qualifications, the boozy smelling men with slurred speech and the shiftless looking who would just as soon sleep in a box-car and eat at a soup kitchen as work. But it was the skinny, emaciated men with a desperate look that bothered him, and he found himself handing many of them a ticket for an interview, especially if he discovered they had a family to support. At the end of the day, as he went over the list of applicants who would be coming back for an interview, he saw that every man he had given an interview card had a family to support.

The following day Joe was told to escort all the men he had given a card to into one of the warehouses near the dock. He was joined by a union foreman who briefly looked over each applicant then told the men what the job would entail and where they were to report for work the following morning before excusing them. "You are all hired." He stated.

"That's it?" Joe asked. "Why did I need to come back here today if I didn't have to do anything?"

"You want to get paid, don't you?" the man asked. "The pay office is over there in that green shack, and you need to give them this voucher," he said, handing Joe a slip of paper. "We're going to want you again for interviewing in a couple of weeks, so leave your contact information with the clerk when you pick up your pay."

"Do you know that I wasn't hired to do any interviewing...that I just walked up to the front of the line like I belonged there, and...?"

"I know. I hired those other two men, so I know you weren't supposed to be there."

"Then why?" Joe asked, holding up the pay voucher.

"You did the job, didn't you? So you earned that money. Besides, every man you gave a card to has a family. They're the ones who need the jobs the most, so are most willing to do the hard work. That's why I hired all of them, even though some of them looked downright puny!"

"Puny looking can be wiry strong! It can surprise you!" Joe said as he headed for the green shack to pick up the $20 pay listed on the voucher. That $20 was going to give him some breathing room while he discussed with Madelyn the idea that was brewing in his head. It would be a long shot for sure, and he wasn't sure he could pull it off, but he wouldn't know unless he tried it. And if he could make a go of it, he'd be setting up his new little family for the long run, and doing an old friend a favor at the same time. He just had to convince Madelyn…and he figured that might not be so easy to do.

Instead of discussing his idea with her that evening, he told her he wanted to take her to meet an old friend after breakfast the next day. And, rather than take the car, they strolled hand in hand over to Santa Monica Blvd., stopping to look into the show windows of the businesses that were still operating, interspersed between boarded up shops. "It isn't going to stay this way forever," he said. "Things are starting to pick up and pretty soon you'll see all these stores open again, and the streets so full of cars there won't be any places to park. I know that's hard to believe right now, but it was that way once and I know it's bound to be that way again."

"I think you are more of an optimist than I am," Madelyn responded solemnly. "Right now you could park in front of any store you wanted to, provided you could find one still in business hidden among all the boarded up and empty windows."

"Well, we have arrived at the one owned by the old friend I brought you to meet," Joe said, as they both lifted their smiling faces and inhaled the delectable aroma emanating from the miniscule doughnut shop. Once inside, Joe nervously introduced Madelyn to Ken then plunked a dime on the counter for coffee and doughnuts for the two of them. "So, what do you think of the place?" Joe asked jovially.

"I don't know! Are you going to tell me what I'm supposed to think?" Madelyn replied in an equally jovial tone. "There's not really enough 'place' to have an opinion about!"

Right then, Ken placed two cups of coffee and two little plates with warm, freshly made doughnuts in front of them, giving the two of them a broad smile. "She sure does look like she was worth all the effort it took to snag her!" he told Joe. "No wonder no one could ever get you interested in any gal here in California when you had this one tucked away in the Black Hills. You are one lucky guy, and I hope you know it!"

"Thank you for your assessment of me just by looking at me," Madelyn said blushing. "But what if it turns out that I'm really a bossy old shrew?"

"Well I guess that would mean Joe is in love with a *beautiful* bossy old shrew!"

Madelyn laughed her throaty, infectious laugh, and both Ken and Joe joined in, Joe losing his nervousness and jumping right in to address the matter at hand. "Ken wants to sell this place and head back east to the Carolinas to be with his girl, Gladys…and he doesn't know it yet, but I've decided I want to buy his doughnut shop business, provided you are in agreement with that," he said smilingly to Madelyn. "I'm hoping you like the idea," he added.

"Are you kidding me?" Ken asked. "What do *you* know about running a doughnut shop? I'll bet you don't know the first thing about running a business, and you for sure don't know how to make doughnuts or probably even a pot of coffee!"

"No, but I figure you could show me how! I'm a quick learner! And I have a partner here who probably knows how to make coffee, and maybe doughnuts too, and we could make a go of it provided it would be something she could see us doing," Joe said, looking at Madelyn with his eyebrows raised questioningly.

"This place isn't making any money right now. I'm barely getting by," Ken said helplessly. "You've got a baby coming, and there's going to be doctor bills and the hospital too, and the baby's gonna need stuff…"

"I know…but I think we can do some things that will bring in more business, and if we can live in the back of the store like you do, for a while at least, I think we have a chance of making it work for us. What do you think, sweetheart?" he turned toward Madelyn and asked expectantly.

"Show me the back of the store where we would live," she ordered Ken.

For the next week, Joe and Madelyn spent every day with Ken, learning how to mix the batter for the doughnuts, how to fry them and flip them in the oil, and generally how to operate a business. They both had some experience doing that, since they had both done some work for Madelyn's father, so the business end was not that big of a challenge for them. Neither was dealing with customers or keeping things tidy. It was the doughnut making that proved to be the biggest challenge. Timing was the important factor in making doughnuts, and to Joe's dismay he discovered that timing was not instinctual for him or for Madelyn either. But by the end of that week Joe discovered, by accident, that whistling a tune all the way through was just the right amount of time for the first side of the doughnut to cook in the oil, then with a wooden stick he would begin turning them in the same order he had put them in the big vat while whistling the tune for the second time, and when he had gotten all the way through that it was time to remove them from the oil and put them out on a clean towel to soak up some of the oil while they cooled.

"You are going to be known as the whistling doughnut man," Ken professed. "You could probably charge extra for the entertainment!"

Joe also called on Howie to see if he was in a position to help him out with the money he needed to pay Ken for his business. With few expenses to spend his money on, Howie was flush and told Joe he could have whatever he needed because he wouldn't have anything if it hadn't been for his help a few years ago. Joe asked him for $250…that would be $200 for Ken, and the $50 left over was for supplies for the shop… and for paint.

"Paint?" Madelyn asked, as Joe set more than a dozen pint-sized cans of different colors of paint on the floor in the back room. "What is it you want to paint?"

"Not me…you!" Joe exclaimed. We need a name painted on the window out front so people will know we are in business."

"I guess I can do that. Do you have a name in mind?"

Joe grabbed a paper napkin from under the counter and scrawled something on it then handed it to Madelyn.

"The Hole in the Wall Donut Shop," she read aloud. "You spelled doughnut wrong."

"That's how I want to spell it." Joe was busily drawing on another napkin, and when he was finished he handed it to her. "Put the two napkins together," he instructed, "and you will see how I want the window to look. I'm going to get Howie over here after we close today to help me move the vat up to the front window so passersby can see as well as smell the doughnuts being made. And I'm going to put up a screen door so we can leave the door open and people can hear me whistling too. I'm darned proud of the way I can whistle! Maybe that can help draw folks in here and lift everyone's morale too!"

Madelyn looked at all the cans of paint and said, "You got way more paint than I'm going to need for that sign on the window. Do you have something else in mind as well?"

"Oh, guess I forgot to mention. That same picture I drew that I want you to paint on the front window, well, I'd like you to paint it on the side wall there too."

"Where on the wall?"

"The whole wall. A great big version of the little one on the window. I plan on building another narrow counter along that wall and set out some wooden stools too. That way we can get maybe a dozen or more people in here at once and give them something nice to look at too."

"A dozen people at once!" Madelyn said, raising her brows. "You really are an optimist!"

"I don't like to dream small, baby," Joe said in the best brusque, nasal Cagney impression he could muster. "Stick with me kiddo! We're going places!"

Madelyn painted the name and logo on the store window during the daylight hours for the next two days, resting frequently at Joe's insistence. She enjoyed his whistling and the aroma of the doughnuts cooking in the oil, and was delighted to see that an increasing number of people did as well. By the third day the 6 stools along the counter were filled every morning, and refilled again and again with new customers, nearly up to their five o'clock closing. That's when Madelyn set to work on the mural for the long wall across from the counter. Anyone sitting at the counter would have their backs to the wall, but if they turned on the swivel seats they would have a breathtaking view of her artistry.

The mural, which was also the smaller version logo on the window, was of a large hole looking out of a rocky cave onto a perspective drawing of a railroad track arcing into the distance under a blue sky studded with fluffy clouds and surrounded by lush greenery and a refreshingly inviting stream.

And if you peered closely, you could just see the rear end of a caboose as it rounded a bend in the far distance. It was the hole in the wall that took you away to a better place.

⁂

When it was finished, Joe asked Madelyn to sign her work of art, and the two of them stood with arms around one another's waists, smilingly admiring its beauty and the way it made the tiny shop look three times larger. Within a week the little doughnut shop had been transformed, with another narrow counter attached to the back wall, and 6 more stools for customers.

"We have to start charging more for a cup of coffee and a doughnut," Joe announced. "At a nickel, I calculate that we are only making a penny profit on each customer, if that, so we need to raise the price to a dime. No wonder Ken was just getting by!"

"Won't we lose customers by raising the price?"

"Well, we don't really have a choice. If the price of any of our supplies goes up by even a cent we could be losing money, so how could we even pay the rent on this place?"

Madelyn looked speculatively at Joe. "I can almost see your mind churning. Did you know you get a faraway, vacant sort of look when you are hatching up an idea? What have you got in mind this time?"

"We're going to start charging a dime for a cup of coffee and a doughnut," Joe enumerated, "but I'm going to make the doughnuts noticeably larger at first so regular customers will think they're still getting their money's worth. Then in about a week I'll gradually scale them back to the size they are now, and at that point we can offer another doughnut and a refill for a nickel. That amounts to two cups of coffee and 2 doughnuts for fifteen cents instead of the dime we're getting for them now. But I'm also wondering if we could get some people coming in at lunchtime if we had some sandwiches here too, and we could get a quarter for a sandwich, doughnut and coffee."

"Where would we get the sandwiches?"

"We could make them at night, and wrap them in waxed paper, and keep them in the refrigerator here. We have plenty of time at night to do that. It would give us something to do and make us some more money too! What do you think?"

"What kind of sandwiches do you have in mind?" Madelyn asked, frowning.

Joe shrugged his shoulders. "I don't know; something simple maybe like baloney or chopped eggs. I don't know a whole lot about sandwiches. We didn't have them much when I was growing up. But people seem to be eating sandwiches a lot anymore, so I figure they might come here for a sandwich and a doughnut instead of going to a diner for a regular meal."

"If I had some kind of a grinder I could grind up some bologna with some sweet pickle relish and add some mayonnaise so it is like a smooth spread. Mama used to do that for our school lunch when we were kids since none of us liked bologna all that much. She called it minced ham, even though there wasn't any ham in it. But it tasted like there was. And sometimes she would grind up hard boiled eggs too, and add some mayonnaise and salt and pepper to it, and she said that was egg salad. Does that sound like the kinds of sandwiches you have in mind?"

"That should do it. But maybe you could try grinding up some of that new ham stuff that comes in a can instead of bologna. I hate bologna."

The Hole in the Wall Donut Shop proved to be an almost instantaneous success, especially with the extended menu. So much so that Joe and Madelyn were able to move into a small house with 2 bedrooms and a real kitchen rather than the makeshift setup they had at the shop. And as the time approached for their baby to be born, Joe realized he would need to hire someone to replace Madelyn in the shop. And he knew exactly who he wanted that person to be.

The house that Madelyn and Joe rented was just a ten minute walk to the one where Eve, Jim, Freddie and their youngest, Danielle lived. With school out for the summer, Eve was happy to help out at the shop in exchange for a small paycheck and Madelyn watching her kids for her. Besides, she missed having other adults to converse with, and thoroughly enjoyed the banter and light-hearted flirting that was the essence of the job that made it worthwhile for her.

❦

Joe closed the shop for a week when their baby daughter arrived. They had a hard time deciding what to name her, and even broke into a fairly heated argument right there in the hospital.

"I want to name her after my brother, Gilles," Joe insisted. "It will be the feminine version of the name…Gillette."

"Do you realize that's the name of your razor blade!?" Madelyn fumed.

"Oh. But it's pronounced a little different; more like *Jeel* rather than *Jill*."

"It's spelled the same though. Do you think that people won't pronounce her name the same as the razor blade?"

"Well, we can make it feminine in a different way. How about Gillesinia?"

"With the S still there?"

"Yes, but the S is silent."

"It's a made-up name. How would anyone reading it know the S is silent?"

"Well then, how about Gillessa? No silent S in sight or in pronunciation. Gillessa Marie, that way she's named after my sister too."

"I still want her name to be Annette Louise," Madelyn pouted.

"I draw the line at Louise! I knew someone by that name years ago and she was, well, not the nicest person you would ever want to know. How about a different middle name?"

"What about Carole?"

Joe thought about it then said "How about we draw for it?"

Joe wrote out the two names on separate slips of paper, folded them and put them in his hat.

"You get to draw out the name," he told Madelyn. She did…and that's how their first-born daughter got stuck with the made up name Gillessa Marie.

Madelyn was nearly three months pregnant again by the time Gillessa had her first birthday. She hadn't been back to work at the doughnut shop, but was watching Eve's kids for her during the day and still grinding up bologna and spam together and mashing hard boiled eggs every night then making sandwiches and wrapping them in waxed paper. Sometimes Joe had some leftover sandwiches he brought home, and the two of them occasionally dined on minced ham or egg salad sandwiches, laughing together and making jokes about their gourmet fare. But at Easter time that year, Madelyn had baked a large ham and rather than eat ham every night for a month, she decided to make some ham and cheese sandwiches, telling Joe she figured he could sell them for a quarter. She had figured right, so she began roasting chickens and cutting them up for sandwiches too, and Joe could hardly keep up with the demand for sandwiches at the shop. Since there wasn't any space to accommodate more customers, Joe turned the back room he and Madelyn had occupied when they started out into a sandwich making area, hiring a young man in need of work that Howie had referred to him, as well as another woman to take orders for sandwiches and donuts that customers would take out of the shop and consume elsewhere. Joe kept busy mixing batter and frying the doughnuts in the front window, puckered up and whistling, and sometimes even shuffling his feet in a make-believe tap dance as he flipped the doughnuts in the vat of oil. He was enjoying every minute of his life, and his bank account was growing nicely.

The Hole in the Wall Donut Shop was always closed on Sundays, and was only open until noon on Saturdays. It was on one of those Saturday afternoons that Joe and Madelyn decided it would be nice to take a drive up through Beverly Hills to see some of the beautiful houses where the beautiful people in the movies lived, then go up past Will Rogers Park and on through the Pacific Palisades, making a return trip along the Pacific Coast Highway. With Gillessa napping in the back seat and the windows rolled down to collect the cooling fall breeze, Madelyn slid over to snuggle next to Joe, and they held hands and snuck in some quick pecks, like teenaged kids out on a date, away from the prying eyes of their parents, all the while ogling all the lavish homes of the rich and famous. Then suddenly Joe slammed on the brakes and nearly sent Madelyn flying into the windshield.

"Why did you do that?" she asked, frightened. "Did you hit something?"

"No! I just almost missed something is all!" Joe exclaimed, pointing to a sign on a lawn. "I can't believe it! It's for sale!"

Madelyn looked at the small white house with the red tile roof, situated on a knoll with steps the same color as the roof leading up to the front door. "Is there something special about that house?" she asked.

"I'm not sure if there's anything really special about the house itself, or if it's just special to me. I stopped and looked at this house a few years ago when I was driving through the area just like we are today. I think maybe I wrote to you about it, remember? There was something about the house that seemed to call to me. It's not really remarkable looking when you stop to think about it, but just the way it's sitting there on that knoll, looking proud as a peacock on a pedestal; and all those red stairs leading up to it…I count twenty-two…well, it just has a kind of presence that really appeals to me. "Does it say anything to you?" Joe asked Madelyn expectantly.

"It says it's for sale," Madelyn said jestingly. "But it doesn't say how much it wants."

"Hmm…looks like it's not going to tell us anything more. Maybe we should climb those steps and find out if there's anyone inside who can tell us what we want to know."

"Is there something we want to know? Are you interested in buying the house?"

"It all depends on what they want for it, and whether or not we both like it on the inside," Joe said, suddenly serious. "I've thought about this house a few times since I first saw it, and now that it's for sale I can't pass up the chance to see what it's like inside."

"It's awfully far from the doughnut shop!" Madelyn protested. "If we lived here it would mean a long drive into town every day, and even in to church on Sunday. Right now we can walk wherever we need to go and…"

"And, we are paying rent instead of owning our own house. Wouldn't you like for us to own our own house?"

NOVEMBER, 1938

JOE AND MADELYN MOVED INTO THEIR NEW HOME IN THE Pacific Palisades just in time to celebrate Thanksgiving there with Eve and Jim, Lorraine, Howie and Suzette and their families. Madelyn roasted the turkey and stuffing, while everyone else contributed to the feast with mashed potatoes, sweet potatoes, fresh baked rolls, five kinds of vegetables, four kinds of salads, and three kinds of pies, plus a chocolate fudge cake.

When they had looked at the house, Joe and Madelyn were delighted to see there was a large dining room off the kitchen at the back of the house that overlooked a flower garden surrounding a cement pool with a fountain in the center. The fountain no longer worked, but that didn't seem to matter to either of them. It was elegant to look at anyway, and was the focal point guests would see when they came for dinner. There was also a large living room open to the dining room, a large solarium on the front of the house, and a west wing with two bedrooms and a bathroom tucked between them. The large yard was surrounded by towering cedars, several fragrant lilac bushes, a lemon tree and even a grand avocado tree bearing fruit. It was perfect, and even though Madelyn had argued that the $6,700 asking price for the house was too much for them, Joe convinced her they were doing so well at the doughnut shop they could easily afford it.

Near the end of January, 1939 they welcomed a second daughter into their family, and though Joe was disappointed the baby wasn't a boy, he nonetheless fell in love with her from the moment he first held her in his arms. He'd had trouble doing that with Gillessa, fearing that if he became too attached to her he would find her lifeless in her crib one morning the same way he had found his first child. But that hadn't happened; Gillessa was now a lively toddler, running them ragged at times, so he wasn't fearful that anything would happen to his second child. And he bonded with her the way he had been afraid to with Gillessa. Once again there was an argument over what to name the baby, and there was a repeat of putting the names in a hat, this time with Joe getting to draw the winning name. And this time Madelyn won. Their second daughter was officially named Annette Carole rather than Adrianna Celine – the name Joe wanted.

That second daughter was me!

Shortly after the birth of her second child, Madelyn received a letter from her mother letting her know that she and Madelyn's father would be driving out in May for a visit, and to get acquainted with their two granddaughters. Nothing could have been more upsetting for Madelyn, who alternated between bouts of tearful frenzy and a depressed melancholy at the prospect of facing her parents. The months between the letter and their arrival were almost more than Joe could bear. Even though he assured Madelyn her perceived transgressions would have long ago been forgiven as well as forgotten by her parents, he could not persuade her to forgive herself. Her sense of guilt at what she considered her betrayal of their trust consumed her, and more often than not he felt his presence was what instigated much of her distress.

Joe began making excuses to stay late at the shop, or to run errands and pay visits to old friends he felt he had been neglecting. Weekends were the worst…that's when they usually had time to spend together, but he felt he had to find ways to be away from one another so that Madelyn's mind could be more at peace. In an effort to find something else to occupy her mind, he bought her an all-white kitten that she named Fluffy, and went to the pound and picked out a little white terrier with brown spots that she named Tiny. The pets helped by taking her mind off her parent's arrival when she was busy tending to them, but it never lasted for long. The only time Madelyn seemed truly at peace was when she was nursing her new baby, Annette.

Joe couldn't figure out any way he could help Madelyn through what she thought of as her 'good girl gone bad and now suffering remorse and acute embarrassment and regret at the choices she'd made' self-assessment. The presence of the man she loved and two babies she adored, all living the sweet life dreams are made of together did little to assuage her perception that she had no right to be happily living a sinful life.

One day in early April, Lorraine invited Joe to join her for lunch at a new restaurant that had opened two doors down from her hat shop. She had become concerned about Madelyn's demeanor for the past several weeks, especially her curt refusal when Lorraine suggested they all get together for Easter, attend Mass together and maybe have a bonfire cookout at the beach rather than a more formal dinner. "Have I offended Madelyn in some way?" she asked solemnly.

Joe launched into a hesitant explanation of Madelyn's behavior at first, assuring Lorraine that she was not in any way the problem. But then, remembering that Lorraine already knew all about his and Madelyn's past together, he told her how his beloved was feeling about herself now that she would be facing her parents, and that she had assured herself that their judgment could be nothing other than condemnation of her and her wanton actions. "The problem is, I don't know what her parent's attitude will be…and I surely don't know what to do to put Madelyn's mind at ease."

"Do you have any more news about how the annulment is progressing? Some news in that regard might be really helpful, especially if the news is good. Things seem to be taking an awfully long time!" she added.

"Yes, they do!" Joe exclaimed, giving himself time to come up with some kind of excuse for such an extended delay. "Actually, I haven't been to see the priest here who's working on it since we moved into our new house, and if he had some news for me he wouldn't know where to get in touch with me! So…I need to get in touch with him, right away, and see what he has to tell me!"

"Well, if he has anything to tell you, let's hope its good news!"

"If it isn't good, I won't tell Madelyn anything. She doesn't need any bad news right now. And we should plan on getting together for Easter, just maybe not the Mass part. I know she's really affected by the fact that she can't receive communion, and it's probably not a good idea to make her feel bad about that any more than she already does." Joe hung his head shamefully for a moment before adding "Is it a sin to wish that the woman I had been forced to marry would miraculously just kick the bucket so I could put an end to Madelyn's misery? Because, her dying would solve everything!"

The priest at St. Boniface's echoed those last words Joe had spoken in his conversation with Lorraine, only his words were said with even more finality. "The only way you will ever be able to marry the mother of your children in the Catholic Church will be at the death of your wife. In the eyes of the Church you are still married to her, no matter what the state says. For the sake of your souls, you and the woman you are now living with must live apart. That does not mean you are not required to financially support your children as well as their mother, but it does mean that you must refrain from any intimacy with that said mother. You have no grounds for an annulment, and I believe you have been told that before. You have put yourself and the unfortunate object of your affections in moral jeopardy with your fornication and complete disregard for the sinful nature of your actions! And unfortunately you have caused two innocents to be born as a result, who must now be impoverished by the absence of their father."

"We were married though, nearly a year ago before a judge here in Santa Monica!"

"The state may recognize your marriage, but, rest assured, the Church does not! In the eyes of God you are not married to the woman you are living with…in sin, I might add!"

Driving home after meeting with the priest, Joe was furious with the Church's stance that made it necessary for him to lie to Madelyn once again. He had to make her think that the annulment was still in the works, that it was going to take some time, that there were bureaucracies in Rome to go through…and Rome wasn't built in a day. He had to make her believe that, because he couldn't tell her the alternative that the Church demanded. There was no way he would ever tell her they must live apart; because that was unthinkable.

And at that moment he felt certain he knew what he had to say to Madelyn to rid her of the angst she felt at the prospect of facing her parents…even though it was an outright lie!

Helping her make sandwiches in the kitchen, after the children had been fed and tucked in bed for the night, Joe broached the subject of the parental visit. "I bought a bed and dresser for your folks to use while they are here," he said nonchalantly. "I figured we could move Gillessa's crib into our bedroom or maybe into the dining room if you think it would be better, and your parents could have the other bedroom to themselves. The furniture will be delivered in a couple of days."

"I guess we needed to get them a bed," Madelyn replied morosely. "But I really feel like writing and telling them not to come."

"You know what I think?" Joe said, turning and wrapping his arms around Madelyn's waist, forcing her to face him. "I think you are going to be pleasantly surprised by your parent's reaction to being grandparents to two beautiful babies…so much so that they won't care one little bit that we eloped and got married here in California rather than put them through a big wedding and all that fuss right around spring planting time."

Madelyn shoved Joe away. "And I suppose they will have forgotten all about the fact that I was obviously pregnant and that we *had* to get married!"

"Yes, they will know that," Joe agreed. "But I also think they will find that forgivable when they see those babies, and this lovely house, and the fact that we have a successful business. What they don't know…and what we *won't* be telling them, for now at least…is that we were married before a judge, not in the Church, and that I was married before. They don't need to know about that, maybe *never* need to know about that, until the annulment comes through. The paperwork is in Rome right now. I thought I'd surprise you with that news. I had a meeting with the priest today. He said there was a liturgical protocol to go through, but everything was progressing."

Madelyn tearfully hugged Joe. "That is good news! It's taking so long I almost forgot about it! But how do I explain to Mama and Papa the way I just ran off without telling them anything?"

"Why would you have to explain anything? I think they've probably gotten it all figured out for themselves by now, don't you? You were embarrassed by your condition and wanted to keep it hidden from all the gossips in St. Onge, so we eloped and made everything as right as it was possible to make it. There is no shame in doing the right thing after a mistake has been made."

Madelyn looked at Joe, wide-eyed and with furrowed brow before her face erupted in a joyous smile. "Do you think we should make some peanut butter and jelly sandwiches to see if they would be a hit at the doughnut shop?" she asked. "I've been thinking about doing that."

"And I've been thinking about getting a new car! Our hole in the wall is doing so well we can easily afford it, and it would be a good idea for you to have a car here so you could get out and around more in case you want to, or need to."

"What kind of car do you have in mind?"

"I'm looking at either one of those new Plymouth road-kings or a Ford four door sedan. I'm leaning more toward the Ford, I think. But, since it's going to be your car to drive, maybe you would like to come with me tomorrow and you can decide which one you'd rather have."

Madelyn laughed her infectious laugh. "Why, I think I would love to pick out my car!"

Joe shook his head in wonder at the delightful enigma that was his Madelyn.

Joe drove the new Ford sedan into Beverly Hills, with Madelyn's father, Charles in the front passenger seat and her mother, Emma, Madelyn and the two children in the rear seat. Madelyn's parents had agreed to stand up as baby Annette's godparents at her christening, and would be meeting Gillessa'a godparents, Lorraine and Howie, at the church where she had been baptized. Madelyn had wanted Annette to be baptized at St. Boniface's, since that was where she attended Mass every Sunday, but Joe had convinced her that it would be much better all-around if the baby could be baptized in the same church as her older sister. He couldn't let her know that he didn't want them to be seen together at St. Boniface's for fear the priest there might say something that would reveal his lies to her. Madelyn was used to him not attending Mass with her, begging off instead to tend to the children at home so she could concentrate more fully on her religious experience, uninterrupted. But she did not know the true reason he didn't want to be seen at the church, and Joe wanted it to stay that way.

The three week visit with Madelyn's parents went without a hitch, all except for one thing. Two days after they arrived, Joe, at Madelyn's whispered pleading, had the telephone at the house disconnected. Whenever the phone rang, Emma would shriek and loudly demand that someone answer it as if she expected the instrument to leap out and strangle her if it was ignored for so much as a split second. And, as luck would have it, the phone inevitably seemed to ring whenever one, or both of the children were sleeping. The ring didn't waken them, but the shrieks from Emma certainly did!

Other than that, the visit was very pleasant...even though Emma couldn't fathom why Joe and Madelyn would allow both a cat and a dog to roam throughout the house, something she would never have allowed in her own home. But she decided they *were* kind of cute, and maybe even a bit sweet to be around, and she was seen to pat both of them on the head occasionally and talk baby talk to them in the same tone she spoke to her grandbabies, but…she kept the door to the bedroom she and Charles used, shut at all times. That space was off limits to animals.

To Madelyn's relief, there was never any mention made of her indiscretions, even at moments when she was alone with either her mother or her father. And she came to the conclusion that they might both be so relieved she hadn't made the decision to become a nun…a profession which she knew neither of her parents were in favor of for her…that they could overlook her unprincipled transgressions, and perhaps even be thankful for them in a way.

Joe had had some trepidation at the prospect of being under the same roof with Emma, a woman whose presence elicited a certain amount of instinctual groveling in him, until one afternoon when he arrived home from the shop and saw her engaged in something that clearly dumbfounded him. She was alone in the living-room, with the radio loudly blaring out some ragtime music…and she was dancing! Her back was to him, and Joe watched her gyrate her ample, corseted behind in an energetic shimmy that looked as if it might snap her garters free. Then, hiking her skirt up to mid-thigh she kicked her legs, one after the other, so high in the air he feared she would shatter the ceiling light fixture. When he saw her arms begin to flail, as though she were about to break into a lavish pirouette, he quietly tiptoed backwards, out of sight, stifling a guffaw that he was finding hard to contain. He wondered if everyone had some secret persona inside them that only came out when there was no one looking. And from that moment on, he viewed her in a different light, no longer suffering an abysmal fear of Madelyn's dour mother.

JANUARY, 1942 TO JANUARY, 1945

I'm going to jump in here again because I have some memories during this period of time and I can tell them to you directly instead of as a narrator. My father, Joe wanted to serve his country after Pearl Harbor was bombed by the Japanese, but when he went for his medical he was turned down due to a heart murmur. So he became an area warden instead, making sure everyone in the neighborhood had their lights turned off when the sirens rang, warning of the possibility of an air raid along the California coast. Though I was only three years old at the time, I remember those sirens, the black-out blinds on all the windows and the feeling of fear of the unknown all the while those sirens blared. I remember one of those times my older sister and I were in the bathtub when a siren sounded and the lights were turned off, and I remember slipping down into the water and the frightful fear of drowning before being pulled to safety and wrapped in a towel.

I remember the dog, Tiny and the cat, Fluffy and riding a tricycle along the walk in the back yard. I remember a fat girl babysitting us on the days when my mother went to help my daddy in the doughnut shop. I think her name was Patsy but I'm not sure. The only thing I was sure of was that I didn't like her all that much. I remember being out somewhere with my father; he was carrying me in his arms, and he introduced me to a friend of his and told me to shake hands with him. I remember stage-whispering in my father's ear that I didn't want to because his hands were dirty. That was the first time I had ever been up close to a black person. I remember my sister Gillessa's problem with pronunciation. She seemed to have a language all her own in her pre-school years that was nothing like our parents, or mine, for that matter. She referred to herself as Zee-Zoo, and she pronounced my name as Toddy. I remember lying beside her in the double bed we shared when I was four and she was six, coaxing her through the recitation of the Pledge of Allegiance that she had difficulty learning, but that I had picked up quickly. She was in the first grade, and although her pronunciation had gotten better by then, I distinctly remember that her best attempt at pronouncing 'indivisible' was 'inzy-zee-zee-boo.' I remember the Christmas just before I turned five, when my sister and I both received identical dolls from Santa. They had cloth bodies, but their heads, hands and feet were molded from what must have been sawdust and glue, then their facial expressions were painted on. We named them B-Ann and S-Ann, and we sandpapered off their noses then painted the scars with red nail polish. And I remember my Dad urging me to do "The Shimmy" in front of company, and everyone laughing and asking me to do it again and again. When I think back to the hodge-podge of memories from back then, one thing seems to be perfectly clear. There is apparently no rationale or accounting for the things that stick in young minds!

I also remember my mother being ill not long after I turned five. I remember her gasping for air, and wheezing, and hating to have to smoke some powdery green, stinky stuff rolled in cigarette paper that her doctor had prescribed. I remember her crying a lot, and generally being unhappy and not wanting to be around anyone or go anywhere or do anything. And I remember wondering if it was my fault because I wasn't old enough to be away all day at school yet, and she had to stay home with me instead of going to work at the doughnut shop with daddy. Then ... everything changed.

All of a sudden we were all in the car, driving for what seemed like forever, for a place called St. Onge, where we would live with grandparents I didn't remember. But it would be fun, I was told, because there would be snow.

Now, I'm going back to my role as narrator to explain what happened.

Joe remembered Madelyn's cold, accusing stare when he returned home from the doughnut shop one fateful afternoon. Her look told him more than words could have that he had been found out; his lie had been revealed. He stood numbly before her, afraid to hear what she had to say, and knowing what her words would be when she finally spoke.

"I went to see the head priest at St. Boniface's today," she said, her words sounding more like an accusation than a statement. "The priest you told me you have been conferring with about an annulment."

Joe didn't blink or divert his eyes from hers for even a split second, belying the churning in his stomach and the increase in his heart rate. He felt the best thing was to face her head-on and own up to his deception, damn the consequences. "I couldn't let you know the reality of the situation," he said sincerely. "I couldn't take away your hope; I love you too much."

"He said you've known from the beginning! And you've been lying to me all along! And that's not all he said! He as much as told me I'm a tramp, bound for hellfire and eternal damnation if I don't ban you from my life and do penance all the rest of my days to atone for my sinful ways!" Madelyn sobbed as if her heart were breaking.

Joe went to her, wrapping his arms around her and drawing her close, but she pushed him away, slapping at his arms, tearfully scolding him not to touch her. "The priest said I must never let you touch me again!" she wailed, backing away from him.

Joe stood helplessly, hands at his sides, his eyes pleadingly locked on Madelyn's, begging her to understand. "I'm sorry you had to listen to a priest say such awful things to you; for that I am supremely sorry. I'm sorry for lying to you; but I'm *not* sorry for giving you hope all these years. And there *is still* hope! That vile woman I had hoped to have an annulment from will set us free when her life ends. And there is always hope that will happen, the sooner the better."

"That's a terrible thing to say! How can you wish someone dead so you can relieve your own conscience? I don't think I know who you are anymore! Maybe I never did!"

"I'm hoping I'm still the man you fell in love with; the man who loves you more than life itself! I'm still that man, Madelyn. And it works both ways; that love wasn't just on my side. I know you fell in love with me too."

"Because you kept the truth from me! If I had known the truth from the beginning, I wouldn't be married to you now! We wouldn't be here – there wouldn't be any innocent children involved, there wouldn't be any 'us'!"

"Is that really how you would rather it be?" Joe asked softly. "Do you really wish there were no Gillessa, no Annette, no Tiny or Fluffy, no house in the Palisades, no 'Hole in the Wall' doughnut shop with your beautiful painting, -- no me?"

"Yes! No! I don't know! That's not a fair question!"

"It's a fair question. There's just no fair answer. All of those things are real – they exist. And there's no way to wish them away. They aren't going anywhere. So there's really nothing either of us can do other than accept what *is*."

Madelyn gazed aimlessly around the kitchen where she had been occupied with getting supper started before Joe's arrival and her expected confrontation with him. She was at a loss as to how to respond to him. What he said made sense, but it didn't make the kind of sense she thought she needed to hear, so she simply said "I don't know if I can accept what is, because I don't have any idea how I'm going to be able to do that. Right now I hate you."

Joe held onto the first two words of Madelyn's declaration, 'right now', as a lifeline, because they were the only lifeline she gave him. Later that night, she wordlessly let him know how it was going to be as he watched her remove her pillow and the spare blanket from the foot of the bed and carry them into the living room. She was done with sharing his bed – for 'right now'.

Since they were both always up before the children, there were no questions about why Mama was sleeping on the couch instead of her bed, because there was never any trace of her new sleeping arrangement when they arose. That ended, however, after about 10 days, when Gillessa was sent home from school with the German measles. Joe and Madelyn decided that Annette should not sleep in the same bed with her sister, and instead should sleep between them in their bed. That arrangement gave them separation, but it had its drawbacks as well. For the week that Annette shared their bed, they got very little sleep and frequently found her in some contrived position between them…her head on her mother's stomach, one leg across her father's torso and the other with the foot planted across his mouth…or some other contortion. They were relieved when Gillessa was over the measles and Annette could resume sleeping with her sister.

Madelyn didn't bother going back to sleeping on the couch…she just scooted far over to her side of the bed so that she and Joe wouldn't be touching. Another week went by then Annette had her turn at the measles. She was itchy and out of sorts, but she said something on about her third day with the ailment that made them laugh together, changing the 'right now' to 'not right now'. "Why did those mean Germans have to give us their measles?" she asked, pouting.

Though the effect of their child's words only lasted a few minutes, they assured Joe that Madelyn was still capable of laughing, and the joy that sound gave him outlasted the return of her silence. Her laugh had been a forgiveness of sorts, a brief reprieve from the austere demeanor she affected in his presence whenever the children were not there. That laugh was a gift of hope.

Madelyn's illness started with a bad case of influenza that left her coughing for weeks. She was just beginning to feel much better when, one Sunday at Mass, the priest at St. Boniface's gave a sermon about the sin of adultery. She sensed his eyes blazing directly into hers, and his words of condemnation searing into her like a physical blow. She felt as if the wind had been knocked out of her; she couldn't breathe and it seemed as if the lights went out in the church. Leaning forward, she put her head between her knees and tried to breathe deeply as the Crosby girls in St. Onge had once told her to do if she ever felt like she were about to faint.

The effect of that sermon never seemed to leave her. The contemptible words of the priest toward both the act and the adulterer filled her with an anxiety the nature of which she had never known before. She alternated between a desire to flee from Joe one minute, and fling herself into his comforting arms the next, and at such times she felt she couldn't breathe; there was never enough air anywhere.

Her doctor diagnosed her ailment as asthma, along with a touch of the vapors common among women. She was given medication, and among those remedies was a powdered form of a noxious weed called marijuana that was supposed to calm her nerves and prevent the anxiety caused by difficulty to breathe, while expanding her bronchial tubes as well. Madelyn didn't like the lightheadedness she experienced from the weed, and she complained that smoking it actually made her cough worse. But

Joe insisted that she follow doctor's orders, mostly because she was in a far mellower mood, and even smiling after she had smoked the stinky stuff.

Sundays always seemed to be the worst days, and the reality of that didn't get past Joe. It obviously had something to do with church, but asking Madelyn to skip going to Mass was out of the question. To her, skipping Mass was every bit as much of a mortal sin as adultery. He knew he had to get her away from St. Boniface's, but when he got her to attend the church in Santa Monica where Lorraine and Howie went, things didn't get much better. She was still morose most of the day, and uninterested in doing anything with either her husband or her children. She busied herself with her fancy work, embroidering more pillow cases and crocheting more doilies than they could possibly have used in a lifetime.

After enduring months of this, Joe was at his wits end. Thinking that maybe what she needed was to get away from the sea air for a while, he said, "I've been thinking it would be nice to go see your folks, spend some time breathing the clean air in the country there ...what do you think?"

Madelyn looked up from her embroidery work, eyes suddenly moist with unshed tears. "I think I would like that very much. But it's such a short time now before school starts, it's just 2 weeks away, and..."

"You'd really like to go see your folks?"

"I really would! I miss them so much, and it's been so long since I've seen Priscilla and Thelma, but..."

"Then we should go!"

"But what about school? We'd just get there and have to turn around and come right back!"

Joe never knew exactly what made him say it, but say it he did. "Well then, how about if we don't have to come back? How about if we pack up and move there?"

Madelyn stared at him, open-mouthed. "What about this house? The doughnut shop?"

"I don't think we would have any trouble selling either one of them! So, what do you say?"

"Why would you want to do that? You love this house; you dreamed of owning it! And you love your little 'Hole in the Wall' doughnut shop too!"

"Yes, but I love you more. And being with you, wherever it is that makes you happy is what will make me happy too."

"Do you really mean that? You'd give up everything you've worked for so I could move back home and be near my family?"

"I would do anything, anywhere, anytime for you," Joe said with every ounce of ardor he could muster. His eyes, along with Madelyn's had filled with tears. "The *"For Sale"* signs are going up on both the house and the doughnut shop first thing tomorrow morning."

Everything about Madelyn's demeanor changed following the decision to move back to South Dakota. Even her physical condition seemed to improve dramatically, compelling Joe to come to the conclusion that her illness was more an ailment of her mind rather than her body. The children still had to be enrolled in school while they waited for the two properties to be sold; Gillessa in the second grade at St. Boniface School, and Annette starting kindergarten. The house didn't have to be put on the market. Lorraine, who was a frequent visitor, and who often said she wanted first refusal if Joe and Madelyn ever decided to sell the house, was thrilled to make the purchase. A firm offer for the doughnut shop was made by the middle of October and everything was packed up and ready to go by the end of November. Following a big Thanksgiving get-together with Lorraine, Eve and her family, and Howie and his family, with a glut of too much to eat and what seemed to be a never ending rehash of memories and tearful good-byes, on the first of December, 1944, Joe, Madelyn, and their two daughters, 7 year old Gillessa and 5 year old Annette piled into their black Ford sedan and set out for South Dakota.

JANUARY, 1945 TO JUNE, 1950

THEY HAD MADE IT ALL THE WAY TO PROVO, UTAH BEFORE JOE had to stop and have chains put on his tires if they wanted to go any further. The snow had become fairly well packed on the roads, but chains would make the going much easier as well as safer. It was slow going the rest of the way to St. Onge, interspersed as the trip was with frequent 'rest stops' for the girls, summoning in Joe's mind a fond memory of the ease of 'peeing in the woods' with Freddie.

Lorraine had made the transition much easier for them. She would be having the moving company come and pick up all their household goods in a couple weeks, giving them time to find a place to call home before all their worldly goods arrived. She also adopted Tiny and Fluffy so they could remain in the only home they had ever known.

But when they arrived at Madelyn's parents' house in St. Onge, cold, tired and hungry, they were kept on the cold porch rather than being let into the warmth of the house, because Madelyn's father, Charles had the mumps. "He's still contagious," Emma had informed them, "so you'll have to go up to the ranch and stay there, for a few days anyway. Your papa got the mumps from Priscilla's boy, Danny, but Danny's been over them for a while."

"Seems like there's lots of catching up to do over the past few years. And there are also lots of kids for everybody to get to know!" Madelyn exclaimed. "Only you and Papa have ever seen Gillessa and Annette, and they're so much bigger now than when you saw them. And I'm dying to see Danny, the first boy in the family! And Thelma… married and with a year old baby girl!"

"And we just learned that Priscilla is expecting again in the spring!" Emma added.

When they arrived at the ranch, Priscilla had a wide array of leftovers, roasted chicken and beef mostly, with thick slices of homemade bread and jam laid out in the kitchen in case Madelyn and her family were hungry after their long trip. The food was as welcome as the welcoming hugs and greetings of Priscilla and her family. Priscilla's daughter, Linda, now a very grown up eleven year old, took charge of Gillessa and Annette, getting them out of their coats and boots and settling them at the table along with their parents.

That night, and the next four nights after that, Joe and Madelyn slept in the bed in the room next to Priscilla's and Richard's, where Madelyn had spent many nights in the past, straining to hear and trying not to hear at the same time, the things that transpired in that room. The children all slept in a cozily warm room above the kitchen, Linda sharing her bed with Gillessa and four year old Danny sharing his with Annette who asked him if he wet the bed, to which he shyly did not reply. So Annette looked to Linda for an answer to her question, and it wasn't until she was assured that Danny had not wet the bed for more than a year that she climbed in next to him.

Joe and Madelyn found a house to rent in Sturgis. Since there was nothing available in St. Onge, (other than with Madelyn's parents, which was out of the question as far as Joe was concerned), they had decided that Sturgis would be ideal for them since there was a Catholic school there, which Madelyn preferred to a public school. Gillessa attended the little two-room school in St. Onge for a couple of weeks; just until their furniture arrived and they could get settled in their new home in Sturgis. Since there was no kindergarten, however, Annette could not start school until next fall because her birthday fell just past the deadline. They had to listen to her fume about the unfairness of it all, because she could already read better, and spell better, and add and subtract better than her sister who got to go to school. Joe tried to comfort her by telling her about his own experience with school being very much like hers. "You are just too smart, too young like I was," he told her. "But you'll get over it."

In late January Joe went to Lead to buy more Black Hills Gold jewelry. Although he now had most of his money from the sale of the house and business in the bank there in Sturgis rather than in the sock on his right foot, he knew that amount would dwindle quickly if he didn't do something to keep adding to it. He was planning on trying out a different area of the country where there might be plenty of well-to-do neighborhoods he could canvass…Chicago. It meant leaving Madelyn and the kids alone for the first time, but it was something he had to do until he could figure out what kind of business he could make a go of in Sturgis.

He was gone for five long months, making it back in time for the 4th of July celebrations and family picnic at Madelyn's parents' house in St. Onge. He was there for Gillessa'a birthday as she turned 8 years old, and there to welcome Priscilla's two month old baby girl she named Roberta. But the best part of his returning home was Madelyn. She hung onto him, kissing him on the neck just beneath his ear, snuggling next to him wherever he managed to seat himself, smiling and …laughing out loud. And their quiet hours in the dark of night, in the bed they shared, on the opposite side of the house from their children, were the best of all. That was where they became one person, locked together in an ardor that erased all their worldly cares.

That fall, when it was time for school to start again, Joe had not yet found any kind of business he could get started in Sturgis. He discovered that living in a small town was a lot different than living in a city. Their neighbor on the corner owned the bakery in town, and he made doughnuts and also supplied the little diner in town as well as the lunch counter in the drug store with a steady supply of baked goods. So opening a doughnut shop, which was something he knew about, was out of the question if he wanted to be on friendly terms with his neighbors.

He knew he needed to get back out on the road again, but Madelyn nearly always burst into tears at the mention of that. There was no alternative that either of them could come up with except…Madelyn coming with him and leaving their children behind. When the suggestion first came up the idea was vehemently dismissed. But, with further discussion, they soon both felt it was the most workable solution. The school Gillessa and Annette attended was both a boarding school and a school with day students. It would be easy enough for them to become boarder students, and they could be picked up on Fridays after school and taken to stay with their grandparents on weekends so they wouldn't feel as if they had been deserted, and they could be brought back on Sunday nights. And it *was* a long walk to school from their rented house, and if the winter was like it had been last year, when Gillessa had to be driven there so many times, well… As the idea grew, it was discussed with the children and with Madelyn's parents, and on the day before the first day of school, Joe and Madelyn said goodbye to their two little girls in the day room at the convent boarding school of St. Martin's Academy.

There had been no tears from either Madelyn or the children, leading Joe to believe that the best, most workable solution had been made for everyone concerned, under the circumstances. But he had not accounted for the immutable fact that young children do not dread separation from their parents unless they have had previous experience with an unsettling episode of abandonment. And as the weeks and months progressed, Gillessa and Annette felt that abandonment acutely, becoming fearful of the strict nuns and worrying whether or not they would make mistakes that would mean they would be subjected to chastisement or would be deprived of 'candy time' after school, the one tiny connection to their parents, when they could be ushered into a room with a locked closet, in which treats were kept that had been supplied by the boarders' parents… that's if the parents had remembered to send anything. And more often than not, there was nothing in the cupboard for Gillessa or Annette, furthering their conclusion that their parents no longer wanted them.

Grandpa picked them up every Friday after school though, and Grandma read them the letters their mother sent, letting everyone know where they were and what they were doing. It sounded like they were having a wonderful time without the burden of having their children around, but their ending words of affection and good wishes in their letters felt like hollow comfort and didn't do much to make it better.

Christmas was a dismal affair. It was the first year without the excitement of Santa or the expectation of some wonderful, wanted toy. Not that either of the girls truly believed in Santa anymore…but they truly wished that all the adults thought they still did. Joe and Madelyn had sent money for their grandparents to buy them gifts, and Emma, being ever practical, had bought them new winter underwear and garter-belts to hold up their long, tan winter stockings. They also received knitted hats and mittens and peppermint sticks. There was not a toy or a chocolate, or an ounce of joy in sight. At the ranch, Annette was grateful that Danny shared his pair of six-shooters with her, and he even showed her how to load the caps in them then draw back the hammer and pull the trigger, resulting in a loud pop and a whiff of smelly smoke. The two of them had a great time chasing around the house together, giving those cap-pistols a real workout, while Gillessa was intent on learning how to use the embroidery kit that her cousin, Linda had gotten for Christmas. It was hard to tell which of the two girls had a better time with their cousin's Christmas presents, but one thing was sure…they had to leave them behind when they went back to their grandparents house…and their new underwear.

The day that school pictures were taken, both Gillessa and Annette were sick with colds. Gillessa had learned to braid her own hair, more out of desperation than for any other reason. If she didn't take care of her own hair, she would have to submit to the harsh combing of her long hair by Sister Dora, the short, round nun who was in charge of the younger children. So her hair was very inexpertly braided for her school photo. Annette's hair was combed, but it always looked a mess shortly after combing because she had very long, fine textured, flyaway hair. So the combination of being sick with a cold and messy looking hair resulted in photos of the two girls unsmiling, glassy-eyed and unkempt looking. And weeks later, after the photos had been processed and the pictures sent to Joe and Madelyn, they prompted the immediate return of a profoundly dismayed and regretful Madelyn on a train to rescue her two little girls.

Joe and Madelyn had spent their time away from their daughters in Dallas. While there, Joe did more than renew his friendship with Catherine and Marty Edmond whom he had lived with there, he also discovered the upcoming business he wanted to get started in Sturgis.

The discovery was accidental; Joe just happened to be there when the man from the water softener company had arrived to install the system in Catherine and Marty's living area above their store. Intrigued by something he had never seen before, Joe watched the installation process, even helping in any way he could, and asking a myriad of questions about the product, what it did, how it worked and why it was necessary for Marty to have it installed.

"Hard water," was the reason a water softener was needed, he was told. Because hard water stains your bath fixtures, leaves lime and calcium deposits that are almost impossible to clean, and that clog your pipes so that almost no water can get through. It also dulls your hair and makes your skin dry and flaky, and lord knows what damage it does to your teeth and your insides. And a water softener is the sure-fire solution to all those problems. It will save you money in the long run and it might even help you live longer; but for certain it will make your life better.

Joe was sold. If nothing more, it would at least remove the smell and taste of iron in the water back in South Dakota and eliminate all that scrubbing trying to remove those iron stains under the taps. He contacted the company, proposed opening a dealership in Sturgis then signed all the papers, made all the financial arrangements and shook hands on the deal. Following that, he spent several hours a day in an apprenticeship role with the company's installers, learning all there was to know about the product while helping with installations. When he returned to Sturgis, he rented a small store on the main street, three doors down from the Armory and directly across the street from the drug store. There was a loft area at the back of the store he could use as an office, and the main floor would be for a display of the various sizes of water softeners that would be visible through the big plate-glass window at the front of the store.

Following his return home, Joe spent the first week spending as much time as possible with Madelyn and his two daughters. Then, after seeing the girls off to school, Joe, with Madelyn tagging along, went to the store he had rented, armed with brooms, mops, buckets, rags and white paint and brushes. They needed to get the place spic-and-span clean and all spiffed up for their store opening the following week…if the water softeners arrived on time, that is. The store had been boarded up for several years and was in a despicable state. Joe immediately saw that the first thing he was going to have to do was tackle the removal of a wasp nest up in the corner of the front window. Although he didn't see any activity around the nest, thinking it might still be too early in the spring for the wasps to be active, or to even be alive at all considering how long the nest might have been there, he proceeded with caution when he took the broom and swept the nest from the window trim. That action sent the nest flying, and it landed in a small pile of debris near the center of the room, where the sun beamed in its warmth through the window, and where Madelyn was vigorously adding to the pile of debris with her broom. Joe paid no more attention to the small nest, and Madelyn wasn't even aware of its existence.

But, as she continued her sweeping, constantly bombarding the nest with debris, the nest suddenly came alive with indignant buzzing, with the wasps flying out one after the other in search of their offensive intruder. Madelyn felt the first sting in her left armpit as she lifted her hand to push back her hair from her sweaty brow. She let out a yelp that sounded like a puppy that had gotten its tail stepped on, followed by a scream and a flailing of her arms all around her head as she was stung on her upper lip, then her left eyelid and her neck.

Joe came on the run, grabbing Madelyn by the arm and hauling her out the front door. The wasps followed, but the sudden chill air was more than they could take. They began dropping to the ground, unable to fly, and Joe lost no time stepping on them, one after the other while Madelyn brushed vigorously at her clothes, shaking them loose in the chilly air and stamping her feet. When they could no longer see any wasps moving, Joe told Madelyn to stay put while he went back inside to see if there were any more wasps there. He spied a couple of them crawling on the floor and he quickly stepped on one, but when he turned to trounce on the second one he couldn't find it. Suspecting it had hidden under some of the debris, he pushed it around with his foot, searching for that last wasp. But it was nowhere to be found. Carefully sweeping up the nest into a dustpan, Joe stepped outside with it, dumped it on the sidewalk, and thoroughly stomped on it until it was little more than papery dust. Then as Joe was ushering Madelyn back inside the store he simultaneously yelled out an expletive while slapping himself hard in the groin. Shaking out the leg of his pants, he saw a dead wasp hit the sidewalk. That last wasp he couldn't find had crawled up inside his trousers and gotten its revenge in the most delicately tactile spot it could find.

No longer in the mood for any more cleaning, even though they had barely gotten started, Joe and Madelyn returned home where, after applying ice wrapped in washcloths to their stings to ease the pain and reduce the swelling, they could do nothing but laugh at the whole episode. "You have a face that belongs in a comic strip," Joe told Madelyn.

"And you probably have a third nut!" Madelyn lisped through her swollen lip.

"Pet! Watch your language!" Joe snickered, delighted to hear Madelyn say something on the risqué side for her. "I can hardly believe that word came out of your mouth."

Madelyn giggled. "It's better than calling it by its real name. Testicle sounds kind of nasty," she whispered. "You got stung in a nasty sounding place."

"You are making me want to see what it would be like to kiss you on that swollen lip."

"Do you think it would hurt?" Madelyn asked, tenderly touching her lip.

"We won't know unless we try!" Joe said, taking her by the hand and leading her into their bedroom. "And we've got more than four hours until the girls will be home from school to find out."

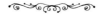

The rest of that week Joe, with a bit of help from Madelyn, finished the job of cleaning and painting the small store. Madelyn scrubbed the hardwood floors on her hands and knees then applied floor wax, which Joe buffed with thick rags tied to the bottoms of his shoes. His offer to Madelyn to tie rags onto her shoes so they could dance their way around the room together while polishing the floor was soundly rebuffed.

"Anyone walking by here would be able to see us and would wonder if we are of sound mind! So, just keep doing what you're doing and the job will get done faster. I'm done here for today; you're on your own."

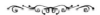

Madelyn had spaded up a sizable area of the back yard of the property they were renting, and was intent on putting in a garden with onions, carrots, radishes, corn, cucumbers, tomatoes and strawberries. There was already an asparagus patch and rhubarb growing along the garage next to the back alley, plus an apple tree and some choke-cherry bushes in the side yard. She figured that, since she would have time on her hands, she would at least be contributing to the household with a store of fresh and preserved food the way Priscilla did for her family. Not on as big a scale of course; her garden was a good deal smaller and she wouldn't be milking any cows, but she would at least be doing her part to help out.

They all settled into a routine. Madelyn was up first in the morning cooking the hot cereal for breakfast and packing school lunches, then seeing the girls off walking to school and kissing Joe goodbye before he drove to his store for the day. Then Madelyn would tidy up the kitchen and the rest of the house, followed by some weeding in her garden before going back inside to fix sandwiches in time for Joe's return so they could have lunch together. On Saturdays, Madelyn did the week's laundry in her wringer washer that was set up in the bathroom then hung everything on the line outdoors to dry. Gillessa, who was big enough to use the vacuum cleaner, vacuumed all the floors and carpeting throughout the house while

Madelyn tended to the wash, and Annette dusted off the furniture. This was all accomplished before noon.

The water softener store was closed at noon on Saturdays, and Joe spent those afternoons with Madelyn while Gillessa and Annette, each with their fifty-cents allowance in their pockets, attended the double feature matinee at the local movie theater. Every Saturday they each spent seventeen cents of their allowance to see two feature movies, a serial, a newsreel and a cartoon, viewed while devouring a big box of buttered popcorn.

Saturday night was bath night and hair washing time for the girls, followed by Madelyn wrapping their damp hair around her finger and pinning it with bobby pins into long ringlets. And Sunday morning Madelyn, Gillessa and Annette attended Mass while Joe slept – in late, and when they returned, Madelyn fixed bacon and eggs and toast...and sometimes pancakes... for breakfast instead of the cereal they had every other morning. Sunday was special. The girls had the day off to play, or read, or go to the park, while Joe and Madelyn retired to their bedroom together for a "nap" as they told their children. They did not wish to be disturbed. And in the evenings, before bedtime, they all sat together in the living-room focused on the console radio, enjoying listening to the Luigi Bosco serial, Fanny Brice or the Arthur Godfrey Amateur Hour.

The years in that house in Sturgis were also interspersed with visits with relatives in St. Onge, or with their visits to Sturgis, and with holidays and summer vacations when Gillessa and Annette entertained themselves by making southern belle dolls out of hollyhocks for dresses and with snapdragons for heads, held together by toothpicks. There was also the occasional excitement of buying a new car, or Joe making a big sale, or everyone going to see a live show at the Armory on Friday nights and staying for the dance. But for the most part, life was very simple and ordinary for the times. Madelyn freshened herself up every afternoon for Joe's return home from his day at the store. She changed out of her housedress into a skirt and blouse, stockings and high-heeled shoes, made sure her hair was well coifed, her nose powdered and her lips and cheeks rouged. And she was always at the door when he opened it – there to greet him with a kiss.

In May, 1949 – when Annette was ten and Gillessa just two months shy of twelve, Madelyn gave birth to a third daughter they named Jeannette Therese. All was well until they made plans to have their new daughter baptized, and that's when Joe and Madelyn's world began to fall apart once again.

The decision to have baby Jeannette baptized at St. Martin's Church in Sturgis proved to be an enormous mistake with far-reaching consequences. Old Father Cartier remembered Joe from when he came to him inquiring about the prerequisites for the granting of an annulment of a marriage. He also remembered informing Joe, after a fairly intensive probing, that in no uncertain terms did he have any such grounds for an annulment. And, in addition, he could never re-marry as long as his wife was living or else he would be excommunicated from the Church.

Thus, when all the family was assembled around the baptismal fountain; Priscilla and her husband, Richard who would be the godparents, Madelyn's parents, Charles and Emma, and Gillessa and Annette along with Joe and Madelyn with their newborn baby – when Father Cartier asked Joe when his wife had passed away, everyone had looked at the priest, puzzled. Everyone with the exception of Joe, that is – who decided to brazen it out. "My wife is very much alive!" he said, gesturing toward Madelyn.

"I see. Then you have re-married this woman you previously divorced?" the priest asked.

That's when Emma interjected with, "What are you talking about, Father? Joe was never married to anyone before Madelyn, were you Joe?" she asked turning to Joe to affirm her declaration.

When Joe just looked helplessly at Madelyn, who looked as if she wanted to find a hole she could crawl into to get away from everyone, and time stretched out silently, interminably without a reply, Emma screeched "I *knew* from the first time I met you that you were bad news! I had you pegged as a charlatan from the beginning, up to no good! And I was right! You deceptively charmed an innocent girl and led her astray, and you have selfishly caused her to commit the most grievous of sins, destroying her life forever and shaming her in the eyes of God and her family! How could you do such a thing? Explain young man!"

Priscilla had the presence of mind to usher Gillessa and Annette out of the church, preventing them from hearing anything further. It was some time before all of Joe and Madelyn's confessions were made. The disclosure that Madelyn knew about Joe's marriage and divorce prior to the two of them marrying somewhat ameliorated Emma's vitriol toward Joe, but Emma immediately turned on her eldest daughter with vile sounding accusations like whore and tramp escaping her lips in cringing whimpers that both Joe and Madelyn felt to the core.

"Why?" Emma asked pleadingly. "Can you please tell me why you could let this happen?"

"We fell in love with one another," Joe said, wrapping an arm protectively around Madelyn's shoulders. "We simply fell deeply in love and there is no other answer."

It was nearly an hour before Gillessa and Annette were allowed back in the church for the baptism of their baby sister to commence. What was supposed to have been a happy, celebratory occasion had turned into a debacle of glowering silence and shame.

That feeling hovered in the air to some extent for the next year. It was never spoken about, but it was there in the silence that said more than words could convey. It affected Madelyn the same way the damnation of the priest at St. Boniface's had affected her. She had trouble breathing and was morose and uncommunicative. When the school-year was finished, Joe arranged for an auction of their furniture, packed up the rest of their household goods along with the remaining, unsold water softeners, and moved his family back to California in his 1950 Chevy. There was no stopping for the night anywhere. He and Madelyn took turns driving straight through, alternately sleeping on the go, while their three children suffered through the ordeal in the back seat. They arrived in Pomona, the town they would call home, in just two days.

JUNE, 1950 TO OCTOBER, 1956

JOE SELECTED POMONA AS THE IDEAL LOCATION FOR HIS water softener business. Located as it was, about halfway between Los Angeles and San Bernardino, and surrounded by other smaller towns, it was an up-and-coming area with tract-home developments seemingly going up everywhere. He and Madelyn fell in love with a house that was located mid-way between what had been older semi-rural housing or small farms and a large tract-home development of stucco houses with large yards and wide, straight streets. And even though it was a very pricey $11,000 dollars, Joe felt it was well worth it. It was on a half- acre lot with an elegant redwood fence enclosing it, a cement driveway and parking area and a two-car garage. But best of all, the house was surrounded by several acres of walnut groves and it faced a pasture full of cows lazily munching grass on a large dairy farm stuck smack dab in the middle of things. The dairy was an obvious leftover from a previous era – and it stubbornly wasn't going anywhere.

The move had introduced Gillessa and Annette to a more modern world than they had known growing up in Sturgis. They tasted their first homogenized milk, their first root-beer float, their first experience riding a bus to school, their first telephone where theirs was the only ring and you didn't need to give a number to an operator to make a local call, you could just dial it yourself. But best of all was that wondrous thing called a television that brought Tom Mix into their house every Saturday afternoon so they didn't have to spend any allowance on going to the movies. And they actually got to *see* Arthur Godfrey and his talent show and lots of movies, so they didn't even mind all that much when their daddy monopolized the television on Friday nights, watching his Friday Night Fights.

The girls were enrolled in St. Joseph's Catholic school, Gillessa in eighth grade and Annette in sixth. On the very first day of school Annette discovered that she was the only girl in the entire school who had her hair in long ringlets – not even the first-graders wore their hair that way anymore – and on her second day of school she had her long hair in braids, and by her second week her hair was cut short, and worn in a bob like the other girls. Both girls were happy with their new school situation and generally content to have left their old life behind.

The same was true for both Joe and Madelyn as well. The church congregation at St. Joseph's was large so Madelyn did not feel as if she stood out during Sunday Mass by not going up to the altar rail to receive communion. And since no one other than a handful of her children's friends knew who she was, and no one knew anything about her background, she did not feel as if anyone wondered about her or judged her in any way. It was even easier for Joe, as it always had been. He never cared what anyone thought of him the way Madelyn did, because people generally had no reason to think badly of him. The only person whose opinion of him he cared about was Madelyn's.

Joe's business didn't thrive quite as easily as it had in Sturgis; he'd had no competition there, while there proved to be a lot of competition in Pomona. He was still a one-man operation, both salesman and installer, when a devastating event occurred in January, 1952 that nearly caused him to lose his business, his house, and the small savings he had managed to accumulate.

Joe had a full-blown heart attack.

It happened on a Monday morning just after breakfast. Gillessa and Annette had dashed out the door in time to catch the bus for school and Madelyn was in the kitchen admonishing two and a half year old Jeannette for once again climbing onto the table, grabbing the stick of butter and dipping it into the sugar bowl. She caught her just as she was about to take a bite, and Jeannette, enraged at being caught before she could relish her treat, loudly wailed out her frustration at having her plans foiled -- drowning out Joe's anguished pleas for help. It was several minutes later when Madelyn found Joe supine on the floor in the hall, breathing laboriously. She tried in vain to rouse him for several minutes before rushing to the phone to call their doctor.

Joe was taken by ambulance to the hospital where he remained for a week then was on bed-rest at home for the next month. During that time he had several painful episodes for which he made good use of the nitroglycerine tablets his doctor had prescribed. He referred to those episodes as the aftershocks of his earthquake; painful and scary, but without that much damage.

It was nearly three months before the doctor told him it was okay to go back to work again, so long as he didn't overdo. Financially, he was at a point where he had to make a choice between making a payment on his mortgage or pay the rent for his office and showroom...and there was no way he could pay the tuition that was due at Gillessa's and Annette's school. He made the decision to close down his water softener business and take a job with a housing development firm, selling houses. It was a straight commission job; there was no salary. But that did not prove to be a problem for Joe. He wrote up a sales contract on his very first day on the job.

Joe really took to the idea of fulfilling young couple's dreams of home ownership, but he didn't care that much for the design of the houses he was selling, or the manner in which the company he worked for was operated. He had ideas of his own, which he discussed with Madelyn at length, and between the two of them they came up with their idea of a great functioning home along with an ideal business and sales plan. But they lacked the financial backing to activate their ideas, and without that, it remained nothing more than an idea, a someday dream.

Joe worked for the housing company for nearly a year, making steady commissions and keeping up with the bills while putting a little bit away in savings every month too. Frustrated by the length of time it was taking to do little more than just get by, he took a side-line job with a novelty company selling their line of plastic gimmicks such as soap dishes, card holders for Canasta fanatics, colorful bracelets and a myriad of other tacky adornments and non-necessities. He spent his evenings and weekends calling on mom-and-pop store clients for less than a month before giving up on the job. He found he was embarrassed to be selling things no one should ever want to buy in the first place.

Then one day Madelyn received a letter from her father with a check enclosed for $5,000 – and an explanation. Charles had decided it was time for him to retire, so he had sold the ranch to Priscilla and her husband, Richard for $5,000 *less* than its value as a gift to them. So, in order not to play favorites with his three daughters, he had given Thelma and her husband $5,000 and was giving Madelyn and Joe $5,000 as well. All he asked was for them to use it to further themselves rather than use it frivolously.

It was Madelyn who immediately suggested that Joe use the money to purchase a building lot and build a model home on it; a model of the home they had designed together. And Joe lost no time doing just that. He had gotten to know many of the contractors who did the foundations, house-framing, plumbing, roofing, electrical, tiling and finishing work and he got together with them and laid out his plans. The houses he would build would be on the client's lot, and would have two bedrooms, one bathroom, kitchen, living room and dining area, laundry room, plus an attached one car garage. They would have walls of lathe and plaster, hardwood floors and all ceramic tile kitchens and baths, would be complete and ready to move into in 60 days, at the price of $4,995.

Using samples of blueprints from the company Joe worked for, Madelyn learned how to draw up construction house plans for her and Joe's house design. While she was busy working on that, spending every hour she could at the task while still fulfilling her role as wife and mother, chief cook and bottle washer, Joe had the lot he had purchased cleared and leveled, and had the footings for the house and garage poured.

Each element of the building process was carefully timed, with each trade completing its part so the next trade could begin in a well- organized, efficient manner. To the amazement of everyone concerned, the house was finished in just 51 days, leaving 9 days to sweep the floors, wash the windows and clean up any construction mess remaining in the yard. Landscaping was not included in the price, but the lot would be free of weeds and debris when the keys were handed to the new owner.

"We can do this!" Joe proudly crowed to his work crew as they dug into the now famous sandwiches and ice cold bottles of root beer and orange soda that Madelyn was passing around. It had been her job to keep the men 'fed and watered' throughout the building process. Although the sandwiches, coffee and cold drinks she supplied were always much appreciated, she knew it was her cream puffs and fried apple turnovers that kept the men on the job, rain or shine. And this was the final day for the cleanup and celebration. "Are you all in for this? Will you all be there with me on this venture? To make this work I need the same kind of dedication you showed on building this model home, for every house we build.

We proved we can do it in 60 days, with time to spare if need be. So, what do you say?"

One by one the men nodded and affirmed their commitment to Joe. But it was the short, beefy tile installer, Leon who held up a ham sandwich in one hand and a creampuff in the other, exclaiming "Keep feeding us like this and we'll be here working every day, standing on our heads if that's what you want us to do!"

Joe had had a sign made from Madelyn's drawing of the house as it would look when finished, complete with landscaping and a mom and dad in the front yard playing with their two children. To the left of the picture was a description of the house and that it would be built on *your* lot in 60 days for $4,995. He placed the sign at the corner of the road where the model home was located, with a smaller sign beneath it reading '*Model Home*' and an arrow pointing down the road. Then he placed another *Model Home* sign in the front yard of the house.

There was a lot of traffic on the road where the sign had been placed, but even so it had been almost a week before anyone stopped by to look at the house other than several of the neighbors in the area. They weren't in the market for a new home, but were just curious enough to want to see what you could get for $4,995. The first person to want a tour of the house who saw the sign while driving by proved to be just a tire-kicker too. Joe was feeling a bit discouraged when friends of one of the neighbors in the area stopped by, and after viewing the house they sat down with Joe and signed a contract for him to build a house just like the model home on their lot in a new area that was being developed between Pomona and Ontario. The only thing they wanted different was the color of the tile in the kitchen and bathroom – and they were ready for the building to begin immediately.

That was the start. Lots were being sold in the wide expanse of acreage between Pomona and Ontario, an area that was to be known as Montclair, and Joe had a good share of the house building contracts. It was at about this time when Madelyn received a letter from her younger sister, Thelma that she and her husband, Lionel and their eight year old daughter, Ginger would be moving to California. The creamery in St. Onge where Lionel had worked as general manager had closed, and there was no other suitable work available for him anywhere in the area. They had visited Madelyn and Joe the year before, shortly after Joe had recovered from his heart attack, and felt that California was where they wanted to be, so to expect to see them within a week.

"I'm thrilled I will have at least one member of my family living here," Madelyn told Joe excitedly. "But they will probably expect to stay here with us until Lionel can find work and they find a place to live. We can let them have the girl's room, and the kids can all sleep on the couches in the living room the way they did when they visited last year. But school is going to be starting again soon, and I'm so busy keeping all the workmen fed, and you have to be on the job site every day – it's going to be hectic, to say the least."

"Well, I think I have a solution to everything, provided it's okay with Lionel and Thelma. How about we get the model home furnished and let them move in there? Then I can hire Lionel to show the house to prospective customers and run the office that's set up in the garage there. All Thelma will have to do is keep the place spiffy." Joe said, extending his hands in a 'ta-da' gesture.

"Will they be paying rent?"

"Mm; I suppose they could if I'm going to pay Lionel to take charge of the office for me. But maybe I could just make his pay a little less and tell him the house is part of his pay. I think maybe he should pay his own gas, and electric, and water though, don't you?"

Madelyn laughed. "You would make a lousy landlord, you know that?"

"Why do you think I would make a lousy landlord?"

"Because you would probably always be trying to figure out a way for no one to have to pay you rent, even if you bought all the furniture they were using and paid all the utilities too!"

"But it's your kid sister we're talking about here, not some stranger!" Joe protested.

"Yes. But my kid sister also got $5,000 from Papa so she can pay her own way. You don't have to be the one to do it. And it's just possible she will feel insulted if you try to!"

"Well okay, if you think that's how it will be I'll pay Lionel a salary and he can pay rent and his own living expenses out of his pay, I guess."

"As it *should* be!" Madelyn laughed. "You really need to get over the idea that you need to take care of everyone you think may need some help. It's a very admirable quality, and it's one of the things I love about you, but sometimes you *do* take it a bit too far."

"Can you tell me something I have taken too far?" Joe asked, mildly incensed.

"Oh, feeding all the workmen every day comes to mind!" Madelyn answered flippantly. "It is not only very expensive, but it is actually quite a burden on me too. It was okay, and likely a very good thing to do when the model home was being built because it gave the workmen a feeling of being partners in the whole thing. But now they expect it to continue and that's putting the burden directly on me. I'm expected to shop for the food, make loads of sandwiches and do a whole lot of baking every day, as well as delivering everything to the job site!"

"You never complained about doing that before! Back when we had the doughnut shop you made even more sandwiches every day, and delivered them to the shop!"

"We were selling those sandwiches; they were part of our business! This is different. We are bribing the workmen with free food to do the job they are being paid to do! And believe me it's costing us more than you might think. I know – I'm the one keeping the books."

"But what if we stop feeding them and that means they stop showing up on time and it takes longer than 60 days to finish the houses? What then?"

"Then you have to learn how to tell them if they don't show up and complete their work on time you will find a replacement that will! But I really don't think you will have a problem with anyone just because their wives have to pack their lunches for them again, instead of me."

Joe frowned. "You really think they will be okay with that after getting used to having everything catered for them?"

"I do!" Madelyn said solemnly.

"Do you have any idea how much I love to hear those two words come out of your mouth?"

"Yes, I do!" she said, wrapping her arms around Joe's neck and kissing him softly and sensually. "I sure do."

"I'll have a talk with the men tomorrow, first thing," Joe promised. "But do you think I might be able to tell them there will be some home baked cookies, or some of those fried apple turnovers or creampuffs at unexpected times, and if they don't show up when they should they just might miss out on them?"

⁂

Madelyn's sister, Thelma and her husband, Lionel were delighted to move into the model home, and take care of showing it to prospective buyers and generally taking care of the place, answering the phone, etc. whenever Joe couldn't be there. But they let him know it was only temporary. Lionel wanted to find a position at one of the big local creameries in the area, and they also hoped to find a house to purchase close by.

The dairy across from Joe and Madelyn's house wasn't hiring any help because they were strictly a family-run operation. But Lionel found a good position making ice-cream at the large creamery in Ontario in very short order, and since the model home was in a convenient location for them, they remained there, with Thelma taking over showing the model home to prospective buyers.

Their daughter, Ginger had her 9th birthday a week before school started. It was decided that Thelma would drive her all the way over to St. Joseph's school in Pomona every day so she wouldn't be quite so frightened by what was to be an enormous change for her. She had been used to a classroom with 12 students ranging from grade 1 through grade 4, and if she had remained in St. Onge she would have been in the highest grade in her classroom. Instead, she would be experiencing a 4th grade classroom with more than 30 other children, with a nun for a teacher. It didn't help at all that she arrived for her first day of school wearing a bright kelly-green corduroy dress highlighted with shiny gold buttons down the front, and with her long hair in a double row of tight ringlets. She stood out like a sore thumb in the group of girls wearing navy blue jumpers over white blouses, with their hair in braids or short bobs. Annette, who was in the 8th grade at the same school, took her younger cousin under her wing during recess and the lunch hour, doing her best to comfort her. Ginger adored her older cousin, and for the first couple of weeks she would search for Annette and cling to her for dear life.

But then Annette had an idea. Remembering her first day of school when she was in the 6th grade, Annette told Ginger to ask her mother to braid her hair for her the following morning, and then she would feel as if she fit right in with all the other kids once those long ringlets were gone. "You're wearing the school uniform now but those curls make you look old-fashioned and the other kids don't know what to make of you," Annette told her. "Wearing your hair in pigtails will make all the difference in the world!"

And she was right, it did! A pigtailed Ginger found Annette at recess the next morning, with two other girls from her class in tow. And after briefly introducing her new friends to her cousin, she ran off with them headed for the swings.

By the close of the school year in May, Thelma and Lionel were convinced that moving to California had been the right move for them. Ginger was getting along very well in her new school situation, Lionel had found work he genuinely took an interest in and had already been promoted, and miracle of miracles, Thelma was, *finally*, expecting another baby. In June they bought a building lot in Montclair, and after waiting a month for Joe to finish the two houses he was building before he could get started on one for them, the foundation for their new house was laid on the first of August. It was exactly the same layout as the model home they had been living in, except that the one car attached garage would no longer be a garage, it would be a third bedroom, and an unattached two car garage would be built in the big back yard.

It was a hectic time for everyone; building a new house with new specifications, Ginger's tenth birthday, new responsibilities at work for Lionel, a new school year – and the birth of a son – all within a two month period. And that was just for Thelma and Lionel's family. Joe and Madelyn also had the responsibility for the house building, and they took turns taking Annette to the model home every day to help run the office and help Thelma however she could with her new baby. But then, as if that wasn't enough, Annette's appendix ruptured right in the middle of things and she had to be rushed to the hospital for emergency surgery. She was there for an entire week, and they had to somehow fit in visiting her every afternoon and evening while getting everything else done too. Both Joe and Madelyn were glad they were no longer feeding all the workmen. It would have been an impossible task! And all the while Madelyn kept a close eye on Joe for any sign that things were just too much for him. She lived in a constant state of fear for him, even if he never appeared to have that concern for himself.

Things began to quiet down after school started in September, but it wasn't until October, after Thelma and Lionel and their two children moved into their new home, that everything returned to a manageable routine. Gillessa was an 11th grade Junior in high school, Annette was a 9th grade Freshman, Ginger was in the 5th grade, Jeannette was a 4 year old nuisance and Thelma's new baby boy, Rory was the center of everyone's attention. Annette took over duties at the model home on weekends, showing the house to prospective buyers, while Gillessa helped Madelyn with the household chores and watched Jeannette whenever her mother needed her to. Annette loved being given the responsibility for showing the model home, even though it often meant spending many hours alone with nothing to do. But, in all truth, she would have been happy to do just about anything that didn't involve housework or babysitting her spoiled brat little sister.

Two summers later Thelma surprised everyone with another baby boy that left Jeannette whining about everybody getting to have a baby brother but her. If she didn't get to have a baby brother she insisted, she should at least get to name this one. "His name will be Bobby," she decreed, which was quite all right with Thelma and Lionel since they had decided to name their new son Robert.

Madelyn made certain that Joe had his little bottle of nitroglycerine tablets in the breast pocket of his shirt at all times. "You never know when you are going to need it, she admonished, "and it needs to be right there where you can reach it in a moment's notice." The only exception to that was at night, when she insisted the tablets be placed within easy reach on Joe's bedside table. He had needed them several times following his heart attack when he had felt a growing weight pressing against his chest along with a dull ache. Placing one of those tablets under his tongue gave him rapid relief, so he had no objection at all to following Madelyn's wishes.

Joe and Madelyn's family was changing, growing up. Almost before they knew it, their oldest daughter, Gillessa was in her first year of college, Annette was in her junior year of high school and their youngest daughter, Jeannette was in the 1st grade. Though they always seemed to manage to take life events in stride, there were three events during that school year that had a tremendous impact on them, so much so that Joe found himself reaching in his breast pocket for the nitroglycerine tablets several times, and Madelyn prayed for no more surprises, welcome or unwelcome.

The first event was early in the fall, just after the start of school. Joe received a letter from his sister, Anna Marie informing him that his first wife, Adele had passed away. Along with the letter there was a newspaper clipping, a copy of her death certificate as well as a copy of her and Joe's marriage certificate. When Joe silently handed the letter to Madelyn to read, she slipped to the floor in tears and sat there, legs akimbo, sobbing out loud for several minutes before Joe had the presence of mind to sit next to her and join in with the tears, minus all the noise.

"Finally!" was all he could say.

"I should be sorry she's gone, shouldn't I?" Madelyn said, beaming through her tear streaked face. "She was still very young, and your sister didn't say how she died."

Joe grabbed the newspaper clipping and read it aloud to Madelyn. It was the report of an automobile accident in which Adele had died instantly leaving behind elderly parents and a younger brother, but no other family was mentioned. "Strange, my mother was sure Adele was pregnant when she last saw her, but it looks like she never remarried," Joe said. "I guess it's a good thing that she didn't have a family to leave behind, or didn't have to suffer, or give us our freedom following a long illness or anything."

"I wish I could feel bad about her losing her life that way," Madelyn intoned dejectedly. "But somehow I can't feel anything but gratitude for her giving us our freedom."

The following day, Joe surprised Madelyn by coming home early in the afternoon. Madelyn was slightly put out at not having the opportunity to freshen up yet after doing some heavy duty leaf raking out in the yard, but Joe grabbed her by the shoulders, forcing her down onto the couch in their living room then sitting beside her. When she started to object he kissed her silent, holding her tight against him, ignoring the moist, earthy odor of her work clothes. Then, releasing his lips from hers, he said, "That's always been a good way to get you to shut up."

"Why do you…" Madelyn began, then seeing the exasperated look on Joe's face, said "Okay, get me to shut up again…just as soon as I wipe the sweat from my upper lip."

Joe quickly gave Madelyn a brief kiss. "I'm home early so I could have a chance to talk to you without having any of the kids around. There's something I've never gotten a chance to do, something I always wanted to say, and now I finally have that chance. Joe slipped off the couch and down onto one knee in front of Madelyn while reaching in his jacket pocket. He opened the ring box in his hand, holding it out to her, and with a catch in his voice and tears in his eyes, said "My darling Madelyn, my Pet, you have been the love of my life from the moment I first saw you, and you will be the love of my life, the only love, until the day I die.

Will you do me the honor of marrying me in the Church and being my lawfully wedded wife in the eyes of God for all eternity?"

Madelyn couldn't speak through the lump in her throat that was making her eyes water and her nose run. All she could do was vigorously nod her head as Joe slipped the ring on her finger.

<hr>

They were both left feeling immensely drained by the death notice and Joe's proposal, and it took them several days to summon up the energy and the courage to meet with their parish priest and divulge their long and involved story. But they managed to do it, and two weeks later, after informing both sets of relatives, they renewed their vows and had their marriage blessed in the Church. Thelma and Lionel stood up for them as witnesses, but they did not inform their children of the rite that was taking place or the reason for it. They had discussed, at length, whether or not they should tell their children, but came to the conclusion that telling them would serve no useful purpose and might actually do everyone more harm than good. But mostly, they were fearful that telling them anything would illicit questions they were unprepared to answer.

That proved to be a badly thought out decision. Gillessa was away in her first year of college so she was unaware of the change that took place with her parents. But Annette, and even little Jeannette, was aware. They had never known their mother to go up to the altar rail to receive communion, and had never known their father to attend Mass. Yet, one Sunday that all changed. Not only did their father accompany them to church, but he and their mother went together up to the altar rail to receive communion. Annette had gone ahead of them, not expecting her parents to receive the sacrament, and had returned to find Jeannette sitting alone in the pew. Then she saw her parents returning from the communion rail and gave them a questioning look, with raised eyebrows.

Nothing was said about the incident, and as they drove home after church, Jeannette began whining for her daddy to stop and get doughnuts for breakfast. "I want the big puffy kind with the sticky icing all over them," she ordered. Later, they sat around the kitchen table together, eating doughnuts with Joe and Madelyn making small talk about the work that needed to be finished on the house that was being built, until it was time for Joe to take Annette over to the model home in case anyone wanted to have a tour of it. It was on that drive over to the model home that Joe broached the subject of what had transpired at church that morning.

"I think you have something you want to ask me, don't you?"

It took a while for Annette to figure out what she wanted to say. "Well, I was surprised this morning that you came to Mass with us because I don't remember you ever going to Mass. And then I was surprised to see both you and Mom go for communion because I have never seen Mom take communion, let alone you. So I guess I'm wondering what happened, what changed everything so suddenly."

"It's complicated. But to make a long story short, I did not go to church and your mom did not receive communion before today because, years ago we eloped and were married by a judge instead of being married in the Church. But yesterday we were married in the Church, we renewed our vows, so now we can receive communion."

Annette was silent for a while, processing what Joe had told her. But then she asked "Why did you wait so long to do that?"

"That's the complicated part, and your mom and I decided we weren't ready to talk about that with you kids just yet. Okay?"

"Okay, Annette said hesitantly. "Are you going to be coming to Mass with us from now on?"

"That's what I plan on doing," Joe said firmly. "From now on!"

"Does Gillessa know about this?"

"No. Just you. And for now I'd like to keep it that way. Okay?"

"Okay," Annette replied, feeling self-important at being privy to a grown-up secret kept from her older sister. She was curious, but content with the scant knowledge for the time being.

<hr />

The second shattering event was a letter to Madelyn from her father in the middle of January with the news that her mother had suffered a severe stroke. He told her there was no reason that either she or Thelma need rush to their mother's side to comfort her since the weather was a fright and she would not know who they were anyway. She did not know who anyone was. Her father assured her that her mother was in no further danger medically according to the doctors, but her mind was gone as well as her ability to control her bodily functions or even feed herself.

Madelyn and Thelma shed many tears together and made plans to go see their mother, and especially their father and Priscilla as soon as school let out. They couldn't imagine what life could be like for anyone in St. Onge without Mama there.

<hr />

When Gillessa returned for the summer from her first year of college she presented everyone with the third life-changing event with her announcement.

"I'm not going back to college this fall," she stated decisively after dessert had been served at her coming home dinner. "Well, at least not in the way expected. I still plan on finishing college, but I will do it as a nun. I'm going to enter the convent in the fall. I've already spoken to the Reverend Mother about it, and have signed all the papers. And I have a list of the things I will need when I enter; a large trunk, a supply of a certain type of undergarments, toiletries and various other things, and I would like to go with you and Aunt Thelma, Mama, when you go back to South Dakota to see Grandma and Grandpa and Aunt Priscilla because otherwise it will be a very long time before I will be able to see them again, and…'"

Everyone stared open-mouthed at Gillessa as she prattled on non-stop, seemingly wanting to say everything she had to say before anyone tried to stop her or object in any way. "I know you will be very happy for me, Mama because I've heard you say you might have been a nun if you hadn't decided you'd rather marry Daddy and raise a family. I've never had anyone ask me for a date, and I don't see getting married and having a family as being a part of my future. So I want to be a nun and teach in a Catholic school instead. All the kids I will be teaching will be my children, and the other nuns will be my family, and of course you know who my spiritual spouse will be." Gillessa paused, looking first at her mother then her father, silently pleading for a response.

"How long have you been thinking about this?" was all Madelyn could think to say.

"Isn't this a rather hasty decision?" Joe asked. "How long *have* you been thinking about this, and why are you just now mentioning it?"

"I just got home so I didn't have a chance to mention it before now! And I've been thinking about it all this last semester."

"You've been thinking about it all this last semester, but not the first semester?" Joe queried. "What happened that made you think about it the second semester?"

Gillessa's eyes filled with tears at the question. "Just about every other girl in my class gets asked out on dates, but no one ever asks me. So I figure maybe I'm just too ugly for anyone to ever want to marry me and I may as well be a nun."

"You aren't the least bit ugly!" Madelyn said emphatically, getting up and putting her arms around her eldest daughter. "You are very pretty!"

"Then why doesn't any boy ask me out, Mama? They must think I'm ugly!"

Annette knew better than anyone why no boy ever asked her older sister out. She had seen and heard the reason for it often enough all through high school. Gillessa was painfully shy around boys. Any time a boy had looked at her or tried to talk to her she would turn away, and walk away from them. And it didn't take long for her to get the reputation of being a girl who thought she was too good for the boys at school, so the word was out…don't bother with that pretty girl, Gillessa…she thinks so high and mighty of herself that no boy has a chance of her even giving them the time of day, let alone going out on a date with them.

Annette was pondering how to tell Gillessa, boys didn't think she was ugly, they thought she was stuck-up and snooty – which was probably worse than being ugly. But she decided not to say anything at all. She thought the idea of her sister becoming a nun was very interesting. It was something different and unexpected that was happening, and it appealed to Annette's sense of adventure.

Not so for her parents, however. Her father, she noted, was especially upset by the idea. On one weekend when she was in the office at the model home she heard her father talking with uncle Lionel who had dropped by, about Gillessa wanting to become a nun, and asking 'Why would she want to do that?' and 'Where have I gone wrong?' But the most surprising thing was her mother's objection to Gillessa becoming a nun too. Like Gillessa, she would have thought her mother would be in favor of her choice. She guessed it was because of her reason for deciding to become a nun rather than having a true vocation.

By the middle of June, Gillessa had her trunk all packed with everything she would need for her entry into the convent, and she and her mother, with Jeannette in tow, drove to South Dakota for a six week visit to see as many of the family and relatives as they could fit in. Thelma stayed behind, even though she had been anxious to see her mother. She had planned on

Gillessa looking after her children while she and Madelyn went back for a visit, but thought that, under the circumstances, it was more important for her niece to say her goodbyes to everyone she wouldn't be seeing for quite some time instead.

And Annette stayed behind with her dad, Joe.

It's time for me to pop in here again. This is the summer when I was seventeen, and when I learned all the family history that you just finished reading. At times, back then, as I read and re-read all the letters my father showed me, some from him to my mother, and some from her to my father, and as I listened to him relating events, filling in the blanks between the letters, I wanted to cover my ears and block it all out. His life, recalled in highlighted anecdotes emblazoned in the corners of his mind for all posterity, recounted to me in confidence, and with the understanding that I would keep the knowledge to myself until such time as his story could be told, had a profound impact on my life. The discovery, at that young age, that my father had been involved in some despicable things, not only without a shred of remorse but with an obvious sense of disdain for his victims, was not easy for me to assimilate. Nor was the discovery of his ability to lie so adroitly, whether it was for a noble purpose or a purely self-serving one. And even though his passage through the years held many instances of generosity and respectability, in my mind they did not quite do enough to absolve him of what I thought of as an underlying deceitfulness in his character, an absolute betrayal of the trust I'd always had in him. But that was when I was seventeen and living in a more innocent time, when I still knew too little of the world and of human imperfection and struggle to know for certain that my father wasn't actually the one who made the sun rise every morning and brought out the moon and stars at night. And I still don't think I knew until I began writing my father's story so many years later and recognized it for what it is. On face value, it's a story of human struggle and finding life with a purpose; a story of growing up in hard times, getting through life the best way he knew how and

maybe making the world a little better because he was in it. But most of all it is a love story, just one of the millions played out every day all over the world. It is the story of human existence, and the absolutely miraculous wonder of it all!

Against the objections of both her parents, Gillessa entered the convent just prior to Labor Day, 1956. And the day after Labor Day, Annette began her final year of high school and little Jeannette -- who that summer had become more like just another little kid instead of the little pest she had been who considered herself to be the center of the universe --began the second grade.

Joe was kept busy overseeing the work being done on six houses, side by side on one street in Montclair. They were all three bedroom homes with the same interior layout, the only difference being that the owners could choose to have the garage on the right side or choose a plan that was the exact reversal of that. But the exteriors of the houses all had a different look; some with clapboard siding, some with stucco, and some with brick or stone. Each of the houses was still built in 60 days, a promise Joe insisted on making to clients that he wasn't willing to alter. It was that promise that often plagued Joe, causing him some stressful worry that left him reaching for the little bottle he carried in his breast pocket more often than he let on.

Then, one Monday morning in late October, when Annette left for school facing a long morning of taking the SAT exam in the school cafeteria along with her entire senior class, and Jeannette left, taking the rosary for 'show and tell' that her sister, Gillessa had given her the day before when they had all visited her at the convent, Joe drank the last of his morning coffee, kissed Madelyn as she began clearing the breakfast table, then went back to his bedroom to sit at his desk and look through some papers awaiting his signature. There was nothing unusual about the morning; nothing that anyone said or did that was out of the ordinary or seemingly out of place that could in any way alter or affect the absolute certitude of the normality of that morning. But that was about to change.

As Madelyn ran water into the kitchen sink to wash up the breakfast dishes, she thought she might have heard Joe drop something in the bedroom at the other end of the house. And as she continued on with the dishes, she became aware of a gnawing feeling that there was something not quite right about the thumping sound she had heard, and the absolute silence that followed, so she had called out "Joe? Joe?" Receiving no answer, she dried her hands on her apron as she made her way back to the bedroom, calling once again, "Joe?"

She found him lying on the floor, next to the chair he had pulled out in front of the desk. In a panic, she felt for the little bottle in the pocket of his shirt, and not finding it there realized that Joe was still in his pajamas and robe. Cursing her stupidity, she leaped up, grabbed the bottle off his bedside table, removed a pill then raced back to Joe slipping the pill in his mouth, and under his tongue. She waited a few seconds then, panic stricken by no sign of a response, began vigorously shaking his shoulder and calling his name, over and over again, louder and louder, until she felt she could not end her tear-filled screeching until it had effected his resurrection. Because he couldn't be dead! Joe being dead was impossible; unthinkable!

Madelyn somehow managed to pull herself away from Joe's side and make her way out into the hall to phone Joe's doctor, followed by a call to her sister, Thelma. Both the doctor and Thelma arrived at the same time, followed shortly by the ambulance the doctor had called for. When he pronounced Joe dead, Madelyn grasped onto her sister to keep from falling to the floor, and the doctor helped Thelma get Madelyn onto the bed where she just curled up into a fetal position, her wracking sobs echoing throughout the house.

Once Joe's body had been removed, the doctor instructed Thelma to call the schools and find someone to bring Madelyn's children home. He felt they would help to be a comfort to her, and meanwhile she should do whatever she could to comfort her as well. Thelma called the high school first and spoke with the principal. She was informed that Annette was in the middle of taking the SAT exam that would be a determining factor in college selection, and since there was nothing she could do at the moment about her father's demise, she would see to it that Annette was notified as soon as time for the exam ended – which would be approximately 45 minutes. Thelma was looking up the number for the grade school when she saw Madelyn rushing through the hall for the bathroom, and not quite making it in time, losing her breakfast in the bathroom doorway. Thelma helped Madelyn clean herself up then led her back to the bedroom, and sitting beside her, smoothed her hair back on her forehead as she told her softly it was all going to be alright. Joe was gone, but she had the memory of his undying love for her to fill her heart for the remainder of her years, and that part of Joe would always be with her.

Annette was having a problem with one of the math questions on the exam and was glancing around, as if she might find the answer floating in the air somewhere, when she became aware of the principal standing in the open doorway on the other side of the room, looking at her intently for a few seconds before directing her gaze elsewhere. Annette momentarily wondered if the rigid, exacting nun who was the head of the school suspected her of cheating or something, and quickly averted her eyes back onto the exam paper in front of her. Then she thought nothing more of the lengthy glance until the principal re-entered the cafeteria when 'time' was called for the exam and the nuns who had been monitoring the room during the exam had collected all the exam papers. It was then that the principal called Annette's name and motioned with her finger that she wanted her to come stand before her.

Annette knew that being singled out in that manner, in front of all your classmates, was never a good thing. So her adrenalin was pumping, in a fight or flight state, as she took the long walk across the room, with all eyes focused on her, toward the stern nun who had her arms folded imperiously across her chest. And though she had no idea what the inquest would be about, the question she was asked, and the ensuing information that would be given, was about the last thing she would ever have expected to hear.

"Has your father been ill?" the principal asked.

"No." was Annette's puzzled answer.

"I received word that your father passed away this morning." The principal said.

"What!" Annette exclaimed, but she got no answer to the preposterous statement that the principal had so callously made. "What!?"

Instead the principal loudly said, "Will everyone please rise and say a prayer for Annette's father who passed away this morning."

As her classmates rose and began following the principal in a recitation of the Hail Mary, Annette ran out of the cafeteria and down the hall before collapsing against a wall of lockers, bursting into tears. She was soon surrounded by several of her closest friends, along with the principal, who wrapped her arms around Annette in a warm embrace, telling her how sorry she was for her loss and that her friends would drive her home and stay with her for as long as she needed them there.

On the drive home, she rested her head against the back seat, closed her eyes, clutching the hands of friends who sat on either side of her, and thought about the impossibility of her father being dead. Just last night, after dinner, they were all still at the table talking about how he wanted to take all of them on a cruise to Europe next spring when school let out. It was going to be sort of a graduation gift for her because he had seen that summer how much she loved being on a boat in the middle of the ocean. And that brought back the memory of the two times he had taken her deep sea fishing while her mom and sisters were in South Dakota for six weeks, and how much she had loved it and could have lived out there on that boat catching albacore and those funny little sand-dabs forever! And that in turn made her think of the Lion's Club dinner he had taken her to, introducing her proudly to all his fellow Lions, while her mother was away too. They had become closer than they had ever been that summer, and it was supposed to be an adjunct of things to come, not an indication that everything would be coming to an end.

So, none of it could be real. It was all a huge mistake, and that would be made clear once she got home and saw that her father was there, safe and sound and laughing about the colossal joke that was being played on her. And sure enough, there was his car parked in the driveway when her friend pulled up near the front door. That meant he was still at home. She was met at the door by her Aunt Thelma, who thanked her friends for seeing her safely home then dismissed them. She told Annette her mother was resting and she felt that Annette should do the same. But, Annette disregarded her Aunt's advice and began searching through every room in the house for her father, and as she roamed from one room to the next, realization began to set in. Tearfully, she went to her mother's bedroom door to look in on her, and Madelyn put her arms out toward her middle daughter who ran to lie down next to her, where they held onto one another and wept together.

And when the school bus dropped Jeannette off at her front door, Thelma was there to meet her. She was the one to tell the youngest daughter she would now have a father in heaven rather than living with them – and she was the one to later make a call to the convent to relay the news to Gillessa as well.

Annette's entire class attended her father's funeral Mass. Joe's elderly mother, his sister Anna Marie and his old friend George Miller all flew in together from Massachusetts. Madelyn's father and sister, Priscilla flew in from South Dakota and Catherine and Marty arrived from Dallas. All the workmen who faithfully built the houses for him, the owners of the new homes, Howie and his family, Eve and her family, Lorraine, Lion's Club members and many other friends, neighbors, extended family members and even casual acquaintances were there to pay their respects and say their goodbyes to Joe.

All eyes were on Madelyn and her three daughters as they followed the pall-bearers carrying the casket down the long middle aisle of the church after the funeral Mass. It didn't pass anyone's attention that Madelyn and Annette clung tearfully to one another, and that they were flanked on either side by two very composed sisters, the oldest and the youngest. People remarked about that difference of effect Joe's demise had had on his daughters. It was felt that Jeannette's unemotional manner was due to her age; she was really not old enough to understand what death meant. And Gillessa's stoicism surely was due to her vocation with its calming other-worldliness that precluded a public display of emotion. But there was no accounting for Annette's seemingly inconsolable grief that was every bit as obvious as her mother's. They couldn't know about the grown up respect her father had bestowed on her that summer before he died, or the weight of the burdensome knowledge she had been given that had to remain hidden. All they could conclude is that she must have been closer to her father than her sisters had been; and in a way there was a certain truth to that.

There was a much smaller crowd at the cemetery. But there were many more tears and utterances of fond memories and lasting friendships. There were many embraces and words of condolences as well as encouragement. But, the words spoken that day that Annette would never forget, were the words of goodbye she heard being whispered by her mother, Madelyn as she watched her husband's coffin slowly being lowered into the ground.

"All my love old pal."

I thought you might want to learn what happened following my father's shockingly, unexpected death, so I'll fill you in on things. My mother never really got over her loss; she was never quite the same as she had been. The day after the funeral she began going to early morning Mass every day, a practice she continued, until a catastrophic illness made it impossible for her to do so. She became quieter in a way – more loving and accepting and forgiving, but subtly more aloof as well. She took part in family and holiday celebrations, but it felt as if she were not quite there, at least not all of her anyway. It was as if she had slipped into some sort of a refined period of waiting; just biding her time, sedately and agreeably. And that's how she remained. As for me, I kept the letters and notes my father had given me locked away in my keepsake box, as well as my heart, never breathing a hint of anything to anyone.

The following school year my mother was asked to manage the office at the Catholic high school both Gillessa and I had attended, and was still at that job for a year after Jeannette graduated from there as well. During those years I married, and when my first child was born, a girl, and my mother phoned Gillessa at the convent to tell her she had a niece, Gillessa told her she was coming home. It was a different "coming home" than our mother had expected. Gillessa had decided to leave the convent for good. She got a job and it wasn't long before she began dating a nice young man who cared enough about her to become a Catholic and marry her in the Church. I had a second daughter just a week after Gillessa's wedding, and a year later Gillessa had her first child, also a girl, followed by three boys then another girl, all little more than a year apart. Eight years following the birth of my second daughter I had a son, and six months after that my little sister, Jeannette gave birth to a daughter.

Our dear mother saw us all married with children, and all living within ten minutes or so from one another. The last three of her grandchildren, one from each daughter, were born within the same year; Gillessa's daughter first, followed by my son six months later, then Jeannette's daughter six months after that. That was a very eventful year, but for more reasons than the births of three more grandchildren. That was also the year our mother found out she had breast cancer…and that it had already spread to other organs throughout her body.

She had a mastectomy and chemotherapy, but there was no stopping the onslaught of the disease. Even though she knew she had very little time left to her, she approached her final months, then weeks, then days with a composure that belied explanation, considering her condition. She was serene and accepting of her fate, with smiles lighting up her face and her eyes every waking moment, and yes, we often even heard her throaty, infectious laugh. When she became very weak and unable to properly care for herself, she was moved into Gillessa's home. And when she required more care than Gillessa could provide, she was moved into a private room in the hospital. And the somber waiting began.

I don't recall who had the idea, but one day in early November when we three daughters were together in the hospital corridor, there was a mention of the fact that it was not likely our mother would live to see Christmas. And that brought tears to our eyes because we all remembered our mother loving everything about Christmas with an almost childlike wonder. So one of us suggested we have Christmas come early that year, and that's when we put everything in motion, with lots of help and cooperation from the hospital staff. We put a calendar up on the wall in her room at the hospital and began crossing out two or three days at a time so it looked like Christmas was getting closer. Then we put up a tree in the room, and Mama told Gillessa to get the money out of her Christmas savings account at the bank and told her what she wanted her to get for each grandchild. Every day when we would visit there would be more *presents brought and added to the growing pile under the tree. And when we saw that Mama was having fewer and fewer wakeful moments, we knew it was time for Christmas.*

The whole family filled the room. Three daughters and their husbands, nine grandchildren, three of them still babes in arms, a sister and her husband, plus a niece and two nephews. We sang Christmas carols, and tearfully witnessed Mama's joy as each child opened her gifts to them then thanked her with a hug and a kiss. But we hadn't fooled her about the amount of time that had passed. Even though the cancer had invaded her brain, she knew what we had done. And she tearfully thanked us for giving her one last Christmas with her loved ones.

Mama left us to be with her most special loved one exactly thirteen years and one month to the day following his death. Her final words were words of thanks to the doctor and nurses who had cared for her, then with a contented smile lighting up her eyes, she closed them for the last time, with the corners of her mouth still upturned as if in a show of delight at something no one else could see.

I like to think of my parents as Joe and Madelyn, together again in death the way I remember them in life. Every leisurely moment they had together was spent in one another's arms. Whether they were sitting together watching television, or standing in the garden looking at the flowers or just talking about business or anything or nothing in general, they had their arms around one another. And I saw Joe kissing Madelyn frequently – on the cheek, beneath an ear, on her forehead, whenever she was the one speaking or when neither of them said a word. Perhaps he found a freckle he had somehow missed kissing before, or maybe it was a new one, or maybe he had some other reason of his own for all the kisses. But it was wonderful to see.

And that's how I see them now, whenever I happen to think of them. They are back together once more, wrapped in one another's arms for all eternity, with Joe still trying to discover just one more freckle on the face of his beloved Madelyn that needed his attention.

And now – have you made a decision about whether or not their lives were just chance, a series of nothing more than happenstance and serendipitous coincidence? Or do you think there might have been something more at play there, something otherworldly and unknown?

And do you think that's the way it is for all the people who ever were or ever will be?

ABOUT THE BOOK AND THE AUTHOR

I AM AS OLD AS THE NARRATOR IN THIS BOOK; THAT'S BECAUSE I lived the last part of the story which is as accurate as my memory allows. The story, up until my birth in 1939, is based on the lives of my parents as related to me by my father when I was seventeen. I also have a stack of letters my parents wrote to one another that have helped me fill in some of the many blanks. But to be absolutely truthful, there may be as much as 90% of the story made up out of whole cloth…or at least I think it was. All the names have been changed, but most of the places are real. That whole background about Joe's parents and his upbringing is pure fiction. But there's a scintilla of fact about Madelyn's family and upbringing. And all of Joe's encounters with other people in his travels were also fictitious. (However, since some of those vignettes came to me so effortlessly it was all I could do at times to type fast enough to get it all in. It was almost as if the course of events was being dictated to me). And so I am left wondering; did I really make it up?

I have spent my life doing an eclectic array of very interesting things. Among those I enjoyed the most were the ones for which I was not paid;

organizing recreational activities for mentally challenged adults, theatre work with young people, helping to get a farmer's market up and running, and organizing cattle shows at county exhibitions. Paid work was nursing, working as a head-hunter in the medical field, compiling a home health care training manual and 25 + years of writing for a variety of agricultural and hospitality magazines.

I published my first novel *All Kinds of Heroes* several years ago. If you are interested in seeing what it is about you can check it out on Amazon or other online bookstores.

I have been living in Nova Scotia with my husband, one of my daughters and my son since 1978. We moved here to experience a different lifestyle and liked the difference so much we have never left. My first book takes place on the farm we have here, and the story of how we happened to move here and build our life here is the subject of a third book I'm working on. As in the book you have just read…life seems to be one coincidence after another! Or, maybe not!

If you enjoyed "All My Love Old Pal," one of the nicest things you could do for me is write a review to let me know your thoughts. You can also send me an email too, at carolkern39@gmail.com

My thanks to you, dear reader, for reading the story my father wanted me to write.

CPSIA information can be obtained
at www.ICGtesting.com
Printed in the USA
LVOW12s0556150917
548709LV00001B/1/P